THE VAMPIRE
ALMANAC
(Volume 1)

THE VAMPIRE ALMANAC
(Volume 1)

edited by
Jean-Marc & Randy Lofficier

stories by
**Matthew Baugh, Nathan Cabaniss,
Matthew Dennion, Win Scott Eckert,
Brian Gallagher, Martin Gately, Rick Lai,
David McDonald, Frank J. Morlock,
Christofer Nigro, Catherine Robert,
Dola Rosselet, Frank Schildiner,
Michel Stéphan** and **Artikel Unbekannt**

translations by
J.-M. & Randy Lofficier, Michael Shreve

cover by
Mike Hoffman

A Black Coat Press Book

Visit our website at www.blackcoatpress.com

ISBN 978-1-61227-376-1. First Printing. March 2015. Published by Black Coat Press, an imprint of Hollywood Comics.com, LLC, P.O. Box 17270, Encino, CA 91416. All rights reserved. Except for review purposes, no part of this book may be reproduced or transmitted in any form or by any means, electronic or mechanical, including photocopying, recording or by any information storage and retrieval system, without permission in writing from the publisher. The stories and characters depicted in this anthology are entirely fictional. Printed in the United States of America.

Table of Contents

Introduction

This book is an expanded outgrowth of our annual anthology series *Tales of the Shadowmen*, dedicated to the heroes and villains of popular literature, in which a number of these stories first appeared. With eleven volumes of *TOTS* published to date, it seemed appropriate to collect the vampire tales included therein, plus many new ones written especially for this volume, in a single, thematically focused, book, hence: *The Vampire Almanac*!

Throughout these pages, you will encounter some of the most famous vampires in literary history, such as Count Dracula, Carmilla, and the sinister Countess Bathory, but you will also become acquainted with less familiar names, including Captain Liatoukine, Countess Marcian Gregoryi, Alinska the Virgin Vampire, and Countess Carody. Some predate even Dracula, while others are fairly modern incarnations of the vampire myth. Our writers hail not only from the U.S., but also from Canada, England, France and Australia, bringing a diversity of points of view to this potpourri of vampiric lore and legends.

The original appeal of the myth of the Vampire is due to the fact that it deals with the resurrection of the dead, something that lies at the core of most of the world's religions. In fiction, this concept has also found its way into what we might call the "companion themes" of ghosts, revenants, and, of course, the ever-popular zombies!

Like ghosts, vampires are basically men (or women) who refuse to die, instead "living" on after a fashion—depending, of course, on how one defines "life." Maybe "existing" or "surviving" might be a more appropriate term? But, unlike ghosts, which exist in ways that range from the ineffable, ethereal and transparent to the most repulsive, ghoulish incarnations, vampires, to paraphrase Carl von Clausewitz, seek the "continuation of life by other means."

In fact, one might say that vampires are nothing more than incarnated ghosts, spirits made flesh, who are condemned to a parasitic existence, doomed to suck blood—or, sometimes, life-force or psychic energy—in order to continue their existence. Vampires are the dead who refuse to lie down and accept that they are dead, and indeed see themselves not as less-than-alive (like ghosts or zombies) but more-than-alive, even better-than-alive! As is the case with ghosts, who can inspire either love or repulsion, the vampire in fiction is a myth with two faces: one, erotic; the other, tanathologic.

Belonging to the first category of erotic vampires, to name but a few, are the byronesque Lord Ruthven, probably the first vampire seducer in popular literature, and Sheridan Le Fanu's Carmilla, whom you will find well represented in these pages. In the second category, we find the dreaded Countess Marcian Gregoryi, Bram Stoker's Dracula, and his monstrous cinematic alter-ego, Count Orlok, the Nosferatu, who are also present in this collection.

This dual nature of the vampire, stretching between love and death, creates a moral ambiguity which is omnipresent in its literary treatment, incorporating and contrasting seduction and horror, heroism and villainy. One might say that this ambiguity only reflects the very nature of life after death, and how it is perceived by its surrounding culture. Is it a desirable dream, or rather a hateful abomination? A reward or a punishment? And what price must one pay for such survival?

The stories contained in this collection incorporate all of these contradictions; in them, vampires can be both super-human and sub-human, sexual predators and impotent, romantic and passionate, and yet devoid of soul. For, ultimately, the vampire is our own face, reflecting in the mirror of our own beliefs, the incarnation of our own spiritual choices.

Jean-Marc & Randy Lofficier

LENORE

Lenore, herself, isn't truly a vampire, as we understand that term, but merely a young woman whose fiancé, William, has not returned from the Seven-Years' war (1754-63) and who curses God for it. As a result, Death comes to her and takes her to the grave of her dead fiancé, to be reunited with him in the afterlife. But she may still earn forgiveness and return to the Land of the Living. Lenore *is one of the most famous Gothic ballads of the 18th century; it was written by German author Gottfried August Bürger in 1773. Still, its influence on gothic and vampire literature has been uncontested. Scholars have claimed that* Lenore *was itself inspired by the earlier Scottish ballad of* Sweet William's Ghost *collected in* Percy's Reliques *(1765), which carries a similar theme. The name of Lenore may well have been picked up by Edgar Allan Poe for his 1843 eponymous poem which also deals with the tragic death of a cursed young woman. Ghost, revenant, spectre or vampire, Lenore still haunts our dreams, as Matthew Dennion illustrates in a story entitled...*

Matthew Dennion: *Hope for Forgiveness*

French Country Side, 1793

The area she was confined to was small, but it was worth the discomfort to escape from France. It had been an ideal country for her to live in, and feed in, without drawing attention to herself. Prior to coming to France, Lenore had been a young girl living with her family, waiting for the return of her beloved William from the war. When he had not returned, she had cursed God despite her mother's warnings that such an act would condemn her to Hell. That night, William returned and asked Lenore to accompany him for a ride. It was then that he revealed himself to be one of the Undead. He grabbed Lenore, sank his fangs into her, and turned her into one of the Undead as well. But he had also promised her that she still had a chance to receive forgiveness from God.

As a vampire, Lenore found that she required human blood to sustain herself. With this in mind, she had used whatever was left of her family's fortune to move to France, where she posed as an aristocrat. The situation was perfect. There were multitudes of peasants and no one questioned if one of them went missing or turned up dead. She was able to feed as often as needed without fear of being discovered.

That was, until the Revolution.

Until the peasants rose up and began sentencing those in power to the guillotine. They would attack as a mob, and even with her abilities, she would not be able to escape them. It seemed as if True Death had finally come for her. Then, hope arrived in the form of a letter with a flower imprinted on it. Lenore was going to be taken away from France by the mysterious Scarlet Pimpernel. He had come at night in the guise of an old farmer stricken with leprosy, and told her to climb into a hidden compartment located beneath the seat of his wagon.

The wagon was slowly rolling through the night when it suddenly came to an abrupt stop. From the driver's seat, the Pimpernel whispered:

"Be quiet and stay calm. The wagon may be searched, but rest assured they will not find you."

Lenore rolled to her side and peered through a small opening in the compartment. She beheld six *sans-culottes* standing at the top of the hill. She was not overly concerned about them until she saw an Englishman with dark blond hair and a blue and gold cloak draped around his shoulders standing nearby.

A wave of fear ran through her body when she recognized Captain Kronos, the notorious vampire hunter. The fact that he was here was no mere coincidence. Lenore knew he was specifically looking for her.

"Hold!" Kronos called out. "I am here by authority vested in me by the French Committee of Public Safety! We are to search your cart for suspected enemies of the state and of the Supreme Being!"

The Pimpernel altered his voice to sound the part of an old farmer:

"I don't know what you are talking about, friend. You are welcome to search the cart, but I must warn your men that I have leprosy. There may be remnants of the sickness on my person and my belongings."

Inside of the cart, Lenore could see the faces of the French soldiers grimace in disgust. The Pimpernel's ploy of leprosy frightened them. They would only do a cursory exam of the cart, at best. For a moment, she thought that she might remain safe until she saw the stone cold face of Kronos.

The Englishman dismounted and began walking toward the cart. He spoke in English, knowing that the Frenchmen who accompanied him would most likely speak only French.

"You and I both know that you do not have leprosy. It is a ploy on your part." Kronos gestured to the men behind him. "I do not agree with the methods these men are employing on their countrymen. I am only working with them to track down the creature that is currently hiding in your cart. I know who you are, Pimpernel, and I believe that your work is admirable. I assume that you are unaware that the woman you are transporting is a vampire. It is my sacred duty to eliminate their scourge from the face of the Earth. Surrender her now and I will assure these men that you were unaware of her presence. You may then go on with your business unmolested. However, if you refuse, I shall expose you and leave you to the sweet mercies of the Revolution."

Lenore was in shock. Kronos knew that she was in the cart and that its driver was the Scarlet Pimpernel!

The Pimpernel changed his voice to a commanding tone:

"I am sorry, sir, but I do not believe in fairy tales such as vampires. I am also sorry to say that I am disinclined to acquiesce to your demands."

"Very well," Kronos nodded. Then, he turned to the soldiers. "This man is no farmer. He is the Scarlet Pimpernel and he is unaffected by leprosy. Arrest him and I shall deal with the fugitive he is transporting."

"I shall hold them off for as long as I can while you run into the woods," the Pimpernel whispered to Lenore. "It is your only chance of surviving this encounter."

He discarded his robes, drew his sword, and leapt off of the cart. From her compartment, Lenore could see Kronos draw his sword and charge. She watched as the blades' of her greatest hope and her most dreaded fear shimmered in the moonlight and gave off sparks when they came crashing together.

Lenore was torn. She could run; with her abilities, she would be able to escape the Revolutionaries, but Kronos, she knew, was relentless. He would chase her to the ends of the Earth. Also, what of the Scarlet Pimpernel? The man who had risked his life not only for her, but for so many other innocent people as well? Was she to leave him to face the guillotine?

She remembered that her William had promised her the opportunity to obtain forgiveness from God. She thought that, surely, this must be that opportunity! If there was any life that she could save to please God, surely it was the life of the Scarlet Pimpernel!

Lenore stepped out of her hiding place. She could see that the Scarlet Pimpernel was holding his own against Captain Kronos but the *sans-culottes* were almost upon him. Moving with speed beyond the abilities of men's eyes to follow, she went from one to the other, ripping out their throats. She then went to attack Kronos, but was stopped by the crucifix around his neck.

The Pimpernel and Kronos stopped fighting and stared at Lenore. Kronos with anger; the Pimpernel with confusion.

"Choose, Captain," Lenore said to Kronos. "You can either continue to battle the Scarlet Pimpernel or you can pursue a vampire." She turned to Pimpernel. "I thank you, sir, and beg of you to continue your mission. I place my life in danger so that you may continue to save others."

With that, Lenore fled toward the woods, hoping that she had taken her first step towards forgiveness from God.

Captain Kronos did not utter a word; he simply mounted his horse and began to chase after her. And the Scarlet Pimpernel stood alone in the moonlight amongst the dead bodies, wondering at the events that had taken place that night.

LORD RUTHVEN

Lord Ruthven is the first handsome male vampire to prey on young women. Created in 1816 by John William Polidori (1795-1821), Lord Byron's personal physician, at the same time as Mary Shelley's Frankenstein, the character of this truly "Byronesque" vampire proved immensely popular. He was almost innediately borrowed by other writers, in France and Germany, who proceeded to pen various sequels and adaptations. Among the most notable are Cyprien Bérard's sequel to Polidori's story, The Vampire Lord Ruthwen *(sic) (1820)[1], several plays and vaudevilles, by Charles Nodier (also 1820), Eugène Scribe (1821)[2] and yet another sequel, by Alexandre Dumas (1851)[3]. Frank J. Morlock, who translated several of the French Lord Ruthven plays mentioned above for Black Coat Press, and also adapted an 1868 vampire play by Jules Dornay into* Lord Ruthven Begins,[4] *came up with his own origin story for the character of Ruthven and his curse.*

Frank J. Morlock: *The Confession of Mary, Queen of Scots, Regarding Lord Ruthven*

A small chapel. Mary enters and goes to her Confessor. A bell tolls in the distance.

---

[1] Available from Back Coat Press, ISBN 978-1-61227-004-3.
[2] Both included in Black Coat Press' edition of *Lord Ruthven, The Vampyre*, ISBN 978-1-932983-10-4.
[3] Available from Black Coat Press as *The Return of Lord Ruthven*, ISBN 978-1-932983-11-1.
[4] Black Coat Press, ISBN 978-1-935558-43-9.

MARY (to her Confessor): I disliked him at first sight. It wasn't so much that he wasn't good looking. I've liked men who were far less attractive, but there was something about him, the hang dog look of a constipated Puritan that revolted me. Nonetheless, I treated him politely, even affably. As a Queen, I learned long ago… Actually, I was taught that, just because one dislikes—or even detests—an individual, it is no reason to be impolite or even cold. On the contrary, such a person may be very useful as a pawn, and one experiences no regret in sacrificing them, if need be, for political reasons. And, in fact, I felt a little guilty that I disliked him for no particular reason, so I went out of my way to be gracious to him. But now, I think, I should have treated him the way I really felt towards him, and perhaps, what happened might have been avoided… *(she shrugs)* He thought I actually liked him. He became the most assiduous courtier, and did everything he could to ingratiate himself with me. That made me loathe him more, but, paradoxically, I tried even harder not to show it. Clearly, it gave him encouragement, and I believe he actually fell in love with me. He didn't dare express himself openly, because, I doubt he could admit his passion, even to himself, the sniveling wretch. But the one thing I did not conceal was that, in every respect, I favored poor Rizzio more. Later, I learned that Ruthven had gone to my husband to excite his jealousy against Rizzio. That proved to be fertile ground. Ah, why was I so naive? In any event, I blame myself for being young, inexperienced and stupid. Darnley, my husband in those days, was proving increasingly worthless. Handsome he was, intelligent he was not. But that didn't stop him from being ambitious. "Why won't you let me be king,?" he would pester me. I replied, "If you want to be king, be a man first." Of course, that was beyond him. But it wasn't beyond him to be jealous, and he soon was conspiring to murder Rizzio, while Ruthven was urging him on. A jealous husband urged on by his would-be cuckolder against a man who was only my friend, nothing more.

CONFESSOR: Pardon, my Queen, but many say that Rizzio was indeed your lover.

MARY: I have to thank Lord Ruthven for that. But Rizzio was *not* my lover; he was only my friend—and that cost him his life. Poor Rizzio. Even after all these years, I feel like crying over it. Anyway, it went on like this for some time, until that fatal night... I was dining with Rizzio alone. First, my husband came in and sat beside me, and put his arm around me. I would have shaken him off, but the door suddenly burst open and Ruthven and his gang of cutthroats came in and demanded that Rizzio step outside with them...

In a TABLEAU, we see Ruthven and several lords appear. Darnley comes forward and hugs the Queen tightly, so she cannot intervene. Rizzio hides behind her as Ruthven tries to grab him. Rizzio grabs Mary's skirt tightly. Darnley pries Rizzio's fingers loose, and Ruthven and his friends pull him away from Mary and stab him repeatedly as Mary tries to protest, but Darnley holds her back. She still remonstrates with Ruthven and her husband and is clearly vilifying them both.

MARY: They thought I was helpless, but I was soon even with them. Bothwell killed Darnley, they say, but no one can prove it. Nor that I urged him to do it. But Ruthven... What to do about Ruthven? I decided that death was too good for him...

She stops and hesitates to go on.

CONFESSOR (after a long silence): What did you do?

MARY: They say I practice witchcraft. It's not true. *(she hesitates again and finally takes the plunge)* But I know how to summon the Devil!

CONFESSOR (aghast): You summoned the Devil?

MARY (slowly): Yes, it's easy. They say in France that all you have to do is call him. He'll be there. So it was.

The Confessor steps back. In a second TABLEAU an eerie light focuses in a circle around Mary. The Devil enters. He is tall, elegantly dressed in the fashion of the day. He comes to the Queen and bows.

THE DEVIL: How may I help Your Majesty?

MARY: I demand a just punishment against an evil man.

THE DEVIL: Is not that within your power? Kill him—you have plenty who will do it for you.

MARY: That's not enough. I've dwelled on it for a long while.

THE DEVIL: And you think I can help?

MARY: Yes, I want justice for Rizzio.

THE DEVIL: Justice is not something people often associate with me. However, as for vengeance…

MARY: Vengeance, yes—but also justice of a special kind.

THE DEVIL: If you want justice, perhaps you've applied yourself to the wrong power.

He bows, and takes a step to leave.

MARY: Very well, yes, I admit, I want vengeance.

THE DEVIL: Of the cruelest kind?

MARY: Unspeakably cruel.

THE DEVIL: Then we are not wasting each other's time.

MARY: You know the one I hate?

THE DEVIL: Lord Ruthven, I presume?

MARY: Precisely.

THE DEVIL: I have a suggestion…

He whispers in Mary's ear. She listens, thinks about it, then smiles.

MARY: That's admirable.

THE DEVIL: Devilishly clever—if I do say so rather immodestly.

MARY: You will do it?

THE DEVIL: First, we must summon him here.

MARY: How can I do that?

THE DEVIL: You brought me from Hell to this frigid place; it should be a trifle easier. *(putting his hand on his forehead)* He is, I believe, having dinner at the moment. Summon his soul.

MARY: Ruthven I summon your soul to appear before me and the Devil. *(to the Devil)* Do you think that will work?

THE DEVIL: Absolutely.

A silence. Nothing happens.

MARY: It's not working.

THE DEVIL: Patience, my Queen.

Lord Ruthven appears, wearing a bib, with a fork in his hand and a drumstick in the other. He looks startled and angry.

RUTHVEN: Who wants me?

MARY: I do.

RUTHVEN: I'm not afraid of you. I say my prayers every day. I'm saved. I'm justified.

MARY: Maybe so, maybe not. But I intend that you suffer for what you did to Rizzio.

RUTHVEN (summoning up his courage): I am not afraid to die.

THE DEVIL: Oh, you'll not die at our hands, but we have a surprise for you.

MARY: You thirsted for Rizzio's blood.

RUTHVEN: Are we back to that? That's ancient history.

MARY: May you thirst for blood forever—and your progeny, too!

RUTHVEN (uneasily): What's this thirst for blood stuff mean? What kind of a curse, for it is a curse, isn't it?

MARY (smiling): Your children. You love them don't you?

RUTHVEN: You leave my children alone.

MARY: Oh, don't worry, I'm going to make them immortal.

RUTHVEN (nervously): What are you going to do to them?

MARY: They shall be vampires.

RUTHVEN: Excuse me, but what exactly is a vampire?

MARY: A vampire is an undead. It lives by sucking the blood of living persons and killing them.

RUTHVEN: Now look here!

MARY: And not only will they be vampires, but they will take special delight, as a culinary delicacy, in wallowing in the blood of their blood relatives, above all others. They will feed on your clan.

RUTHVEN (suddenly frightened): I beg you not to do this. The sin is mine, not theirs.

THE DEVIL: You've heard it before. The sin of the fathers is visited on the children.

RUTHVEN: Who the Devil are you? You mind your own business.

THE DEVIL (bowing mockingly): Devilry *is* my business.

MARY: How like you that, Lord Ruthven?

Ruthven tries to protest, but begins to choke and collapses. The lights dim as the TABLEAU ends. The Confessor returns.

MARY: They say he had a seizure over his dinner, and was sick-a bed for weeks; he was never the same again. *(with satis-*

faction) As for me, I can face my fate. I've revenged myself on my worst enemies. The Devil has let me see the future. It's not pleasant, but I have the courage to endure it. But Ruthven cannot. And he's powerless to prevent it from happening. No exorcism, no repentance, nothing will alter his fate. The Damnation of the Ruthvens is complete.

CURTAIN

Everyone is familiar with the name of Alexandre Dumas, the author of The Three Musketeers *and* The Count of Monte-Cristo. *Dumas penned a number of lesser known fantasy and horror works, such the werewolf classic* Le Meneur de Loups *(The Wolf Leader, 1857), the ghost story collection* Les Mille et Un Fantômes *(1849), and, of course,* Le Vampire, *a.k.a.* The Return of Lord Ruthven *(q.v.), a wonderful, swashbuckling epic. In it, Ruthven crosses swords with another interesting character, the witch Ziska, who will appear later in another story in this collection. Frank Morlock, who translated the play, penned this short story which brings together Dumas and his son, Dumas* fils *(known for his drama* Camille*) and characters from the popular* Rocambole *feuilleton, the charismatic villain Sir Williams and his courtesan foe, Baccarat...*

Frank J. Morlock: Entretien *with a Vampire*

Paris, 1869

"Alexander, I've come to die."

My father's words chilled me, as his giant frame stood in my doorway, but of course, I made him welcome.

His enormous body, seemingly indestructible was succumbing to a series of small strokes. The inevitable dissolution would take several months, and medicine could do nothing; the only thing was to make him as comfortable as possible.

We talked a lot: about his place in literature and the many books he had written. He finally reread *The Three Musketeers* that he had first written in 1845, and which had changed him from France's leading romantic playwright into a world famous novelist and a fabulously rich man.

"What did you think of it after rereading it?"

"I think it's pretty good."

There were many other topics of conversation, some quite painful involving our personal relationship. My father seemed perfectly lucid in every respect right up until his death. He sat in a chair and was able to watch the beach at Dieppe from my garden.

But there was one thing that made me question his sanity. He began to talk of vampires.

"Beware of vampires, *fils*."

"Of course, *père*."

"You think I'm mad or joking. I'm neither. Be especially on your guard against Lord Ruthven or whatever he's calling himself today He uses many aliases."

"Lord Ruthven–didn't you write a play about him?"

"Yes, and it cost me my fortune."

"I rather thought you went into bankruptcy because you were over-extended."

"That's what everyone thought. Poor old Dumas, he's a spendthrift; he cannot keep track of money and he went bust."

"Yes, we all thought that."

"That's what they wanted you to think. But the truth was that I was the victim of a sinister vampire plot to make it appear that way."

Now I knew my father was mad. I wanted to tell him to stop, to reason with him, but he halted my burgeoning protests with a gesture and went on.

"It's true that I had large debts *in toto*. But they were all small, and I could keep paying them off with royalties from a new book or a new play. I'd been doing it for years. In that case, what happened was that those accursed vampires went around buying them all up. Once they had enough, they demanded payment in concert, and of course, I couldn't pay them all and I had to flee to Brussels."

"Yes, but father who–why would vampires want to ruin you, the great Alexandre Dumas?"

"Because I tried to expose them."

"I don't understand."

"Vampires are everywhere, Alexandre! They feed on us and they have to live amongst us. It's the only way they can live. But the trick of the thing is to keep it quiet. If the public knew the extent of the infestation, they would demand that it be rooted out. So vampires try to 'live' as inconspicuously as possible."

"All this is–"

"Very strange, I agree. We're taught not to believe in vampires. Who do you suppose benefits from that? It's all part of the conspiracy. Once you realize that vampires are real, you look at the world differently. Things that seemed inexplicable or the result of mere chance become plain and simple–and connected. So watch out for Lord Ruthven or Sir Williams, as he calls himself, and his henchmen and friends, Rocambole and Baccarat."

"I never play Baccarat."

"Baccarat is a woman from the *demi-mondaine* as you so aptly coined the term."

"Ah, like my Camille."

"Yes, and now that you mention it, they killed her, too. Or more precisely made her one of them."

"What! Impossible!"

"I'll explain it all to you later. Right now, I feel very tired, and I need some sleep."

I was glad enough to terminate the conversation. I was certain my father had gone mad. We never spoke of Camille again and I had no desire to bring the subject up again. It brought me too much pain. I put it down to the ravings of a dying man, who was very dear to me despite all the difficulties we had had in our personal relationship over the years. My illegitimacy and his refusal to marry my mother was a recurring, indeed an endless irritant. Still we loved each other.

After the funeral, I went through his effects mechanically; and, carefully hidden, I found a meticulously wrapped manuscript. I thought it might have been a new novel he was working on as I unwrapped it. My shock was considerable when I read the title: *A True Account of My Struggle Against the Vampire Ruthven & Several of His Human Accomplices*."

Opening it, I began to read the memoirs of my father.

'Vampires are real, Alexandre,' said Victor Hugo.

'Bah!'

'The battle between humans and vampires has been going on for centuries.'

'In a figurative sense, yes, Victor.'

'No. In a literal sense, Alexandre.'

'But...'

'And in this battle, the Priory of Zion has been in the vanguard.'

'Ah, yes, your famous Priory, Victor!'

'Scoffer.'

'No. I know the Priory exists. Charles Nodier, who was a dear friend of mine, was its head, and now you. I know all that. But after all, what is it? What has it done?'

'You know that, of necessity, my lips are sealed, Alexandre,' replied Hugo.

'And you are asking me to believe, Victor?'

'I insist that you believe!'

'In the Priory?'

'Yes!'

'In an ongoing battle with vampires?'

'Centuries long.'

'And who's winning?'

'So far—a stalemate. But the battle continues and the enemy is relentless, cunning and, in a sense, immortal.'

'How can you expect anyone to believe this?'

'I'm not asking anyone, Alexandre... I am asking you, my friend and acolyte, and when I say on my word of honor—'

'Very well, Victor—I accept what you say—though my mind rebels.'

'Your mind must be engaged in the battle. I am calling on you, Alexandre Dumas, né de la Paillery, to give battle like a good Christian knight against evil!'

'Well, what precisely do you want me to do?'

'For a start. write a play about vampires. Let the world be aware!'

'I'm willing enough to do that. But it seems to me that Nodier already wrote a play 20 years ago.'

'True enough.'

'Based on Byron's story.'

'Polidori's actually...'

'In any case, why another play?'

'Nodier wrote one, it's true. But Nodier is not the dramatist you are, Alexandre. The public must never be allowed to forget that these creatures walk amongst us.'

There was a long pause.

Well, as to writing a play–willingly... Vampires, after all, might make a good subject for drama, all be it, of the sensational kind

'I agree. You shall have your play in a week.'

'You can write a play in a week?'

'Certainly. It rarely takes longer once I've got the idea in my head.'

'It takes me rather longer.'

'But you are a great poet, Victor.'

'And you?'

'I'm a vulgarizer.'

It took, in fact, a bit longer than I expected because other matters intervened, but I soon returned with the play to Victor's home, and after a very fine dinner, I read it to him.

'Well, what do you think?'

'Powerful.'

'Better than Nodier?'

'Much better–and I'm not disparaging Nodier's achievement, either. It's a great play.'

'Do you suggest any changes?'

'No–just get it before the public as soon as possible. These creatures are becoming very powerful. Soon it may be too late to expose them.'

'Well, I'll take it around to Harel. I think he'll be inter-

ested . There'll be no trouble in putting it on.'
'Don't be so sure...'

At this point, I stopped reading from my father's manuscript and reflected.

Victor Hugo, my father's friend and rival, and Charles Nodier, another old friend and mentor of my father? Battling vampires! It all seemed so absurd!

And yet, I did recall that Nodier was the head of some obscure society called The Priory of Zion indeed, and that Victor Hugo had succeeded him as the head of this shadowy organization. And then I remembered at various places in my father's works were scattered obscure references to a Priory of Zion... What did he know about this secret society? Was he a member? Was he trying to give information about it?

It was all very strange but I was looking at my father's work in an entirely new–and eerie–light.

I went back to the manuscript.

For a number of reasons that I didn't pay much attention to at the time, events kept putting off the staging of Le Vampire. *At first, Harel was interested, but then he suddenly changed his mind. Indeed, there was a pattern but I didn't recognize it. Finally, after the success of* Monte-Cristo, *I decided I was ready to stage* Le Vampire. *I let it be known I was looking for a theatre. Not long after that Joseph, my valet, announced:*

'Two gentlemen to see you, sir.'

'Their names?'

'They didn't give any.'

'Bill collectors?'

'I don't think so, sir, but I don't really like the looks of them.'

'Show them in.'

They were two tall men in black whose clothes seemed to fit them ill, like pallbearers.

'Monsieur Dumas?'

'Yes?'

'Forgive our intrusion but we understand that you've written a new play?'

'It's true.'

'About vampires?'

'Yes.'

'Lord Ruthven?'

'Yes.'

'And you intend to put it on?'

'Absolutely.'

'Where?'

'That's a good question. No producer seems interested.'

'You won't be able to put that play on in any theatre in Paris, or in France for that matter.'

'I take it you have something to do with it?'

'Yes.'

'Hum!'

'Monsieur Dumas, we realize you write for money and that, with your expenses and lavish lifestyle, you can ill-afford to forego realizing money on any work that you create. We are not unreasonable. We will pay you what you expect to make if you put this play on.'

'I don't know what I'll make.'

'What is the longest run you anticipate?'

'Not more than six months, assuming it to be a smash hit.'

'Then what do you think the box office receipts would be?'

'Your share as an author?' remarked the second man.

'Perhaps *** francs.' I named a huge sum.

'Double it.'

'Double it?'

'We'll agree to double that amount, if you'll agree not to put on that play or to publish it.'

'This is ridiculous!'

'Call us crazy if you like. You said *** francs?' And he opened a large briefcase filled with banknotes.

28

'Look, here, stop. I cannot do this. I won't accept your money.'

'You agree to stop this project for nothing?'

'No. I don't agree to anything. I wrote this play and, call it vanity if you like, I intend to see it performed.'

'That cannot be.'

'We won't allow it.'

They were very excited and speaking at almost the same time. Chirping together like angry blackbirds.

'I don't think you can stop me,' I said.

'We don't wish to make you angry. We are trying to approach you in a friendly way.'

'Why is it you do not want me to have this play performed?'

Silence.

Finally, I said: 'I am going to open my own theatre. I've been planning to do it for a long time. Now, I have sufficient funds to do it.'

'And you intend to stage the vampire play at your own theatre?'

'Yes.'

'I see that we cannot reach an amicable accord. So it comes to this: if you put that play on, we will ruin you.'

'Who is we?'

More silence.

'I think I know who we is...'

'If you do, beware. Beware, Monsieur Dumas!'

'You'll be forced into bankruptcy.'

'We'll see.'

'Dishonored, you'll have to flee to Brussels in the dead of night.'

'Worse things could happen.'

'Worse things will.'

'What do you mean?'

'In plain language, we'll be revenged on you.'

'Indeed?'

'You have friends you love. Beware for them!'

'Get out! Get out now before I throw you out!'

'We don't make idle threats, Monsieur Dumas. We came here hoping to arrange things to everyone's satisfaction. We offered you a fortune...'

'The blame rests on you,' added the second man.

They left..

'Joseph,' I told my valet. 'If those two men ever come here again, do not admit them on any pretext whatsoever.'

Well, I soon had my theater, and after producing several other plays, I was ready to stage Le Vampire. *This time, I received a visit from a beautiful woman.*

'Monsieur Dumas?'

'Ah! I cannot believe my good luck. The famous Baccarat!'

'You recognize me?'

'Yes, to what do I owe the honor?'

'I won't beat around the bush, sir. Would you like me to become your mistress?'

'I should be most honored.'

'There is only one condition...'

'I'm sure it is one I shall find delightful to fulfill.'

'You must give up all thought of producing that play...'

'What play?'

'The one about vampires.'

'You agree to be my mistress on the condition I give up staging Le Vampire?'

'That's it.'

'Who put you up to this?'

'That doesn't matter Don't you find me charming?'

'Very, but...'

'What do you care about that old play for? Men have fought duels for me, and all you have to do...'

'...Is the one thing I cannot do.'

'You won't?'

'No, I won't.'

'Then look out. And Marie Dorval, too.'

'Marie? What has Marie to do with this?'

'Nothing, except they know you love her, and–and it would be a shame if something happened to her, wouldn't it?'

'Baccarat, I don't know much about you, except by reputation, but I cannot believe you would let yourself get involved in something like this,'

Baccarat looked rather confused, mumbled some excuses and left.

Now I remembered. *Le Vampire* was produced and was a considerable success. But soon thereafter, my father's creditors became nervous, started demanding payment and there was a kind of run on the bank. An English baronet was the leader of the group. I went to Sir Williams on my father's behalf, but the Baronet was very cold and refused to accept the reasonable compromise that I was offering.

"We want all or nothing," he said. "We are not going to be put off with words or partial payments."

I told my father: "Father, they're implacable."

"So be it," he responded. "I expected they would be. They want to ruin me–money is no object to these fiends, these bloodsuckers."

I remember his words and tone at the time. I thought he was just letting off steam. But now I realize he was never using words more precisely.

"I'll go to Brussels," he added. "I have no choice. If I write something. I'll send it to you and you can publish it in your name. Just send me the profits."

"All right, father."

He left that night.

A few months earlier, Marie Dorval had died in abject poverty. The famous actress who had created so many great parts, including ones in my father's plays, had been his lover. His lack of funds made it impossible for him to help her. He had to appeal to Victor Hugo to pay for her funeral. My father was unable to hold back tears as he pronounced the eulogy.

"They killed her!"

31

"Who, father?"

"The vampires!"

"What vampires?"

"Never mind–you wouldn't understand. But they killed her to hurt me!"

I returned to my father's manuscript:

It was with great difficulty that I kept my hands off this creature that had been responsible for the death of my beloved Marie Dorval; I longed to pull him apart. But the entretien *began.*

'So, now we are alone, Sir Williams.'

'So, now we are alone, Monsieur Dumas.'

'You killed Marie Dorval.'

'Marie Dorval died in hospital of natural causes, as I've read in the papers, in destitution. Her death had nothing to do with me.'

'Nothing! You sucked her dry. You sent Baccarat to seduce her.'

'Baccarat is very alluring–it's true.'

'And poor Marie liked women as well as men.'

'A fatal weakness.'

'You killed her!'

'Have it your way.'

'And you killed Marie du Plessis.'

'Your son's famous light of love died of consumption, everyone knows that.'

'I know better. You killed them both. To hurt me.'

'Actually, the Du Plessis woman was asked to seduce your son and convince him to make you forget about vampires. But she fell in love with him.'

'You don't stop at anything.'

'You were warned.'

'I've spent my time profitably in Brussels.'

'Have you? That's good to know. Look here, you refused to cooperate and we sanctioned you for it, that's all. We're not

disposed to carry this little vendetta any further.'

'No? Well, I am.'

'What do you mean by that?'

'I mean that I've been tracking down your whole organization in Paris. I've got proof about you, Lord Ruthven.'

'My name is Sir Williams.'

'Is it? Records indicate otherwise.'

'Well, perhaps so–what of it?'

'You're a vampire So is X*** and so is Y*** and the rest of the names on this list.'

'But there's nothing you can do about it. It's not even illegal to be a vampire.'

'No, but it's illegal to commit murder and you've committed several.'

'Marie Dorval? Marie du Plessis? You'll be laughed at.'

'No, I mean the ones you committed for money together with your human accomplices.'

'Whatever for?'

'Why, for the money.'

'If I'm a vampire what need have I of money?'

'You need money because your original hoard of gold would long ago have run out, if you hadn't found means of replenishing it.'

'Join us, Dumas.'

'Join you?'

'We can make you rich again, richer than you were before. A man like you can go far–especially with our backing you–you've seen what we can do to hurt you, but we'd rather not harm you. We need people like you– people with charisma, people with go.'

'Very tempting but I don't trust you.'

'Why not? We are really easy to deal with. We are in a delicate situation. We need anonymity, and access to human blood for food. We have no desire for notoriety or personal power–we just want to live peacefully among you.'

'Peacefully, you call it? Why did you kill Marie du Plessis?'

'The girl your son loved and called Camille?'

'Yes–what was the reason for that murder?'

'Don't use such highly charged and emotional word, I beg you. Camille, or to be more correct, Marie, was one of us.'

'She was a vampire?'

'Yes, in her early stages of development. She gave great promise. We wanted her to seduce your son...'

'Why?'

'To influence you. We knew of the great love that existed between you and the boy. If he could be persuaded to dissuade you from producing the play...'

'Well, she succeeded in luring my son into her clutches. He was really mad about her.'

'The trouble was, she was mad about him, too. There's nothing as unreasonable as a vampire in love. She couldn't be trusted. We were afraid she would reveal everything to him–which would be worse–so she was terminated.'

'You killed her!'

'Not exactly. She had tuberculosis, and...'

'Bah! The girl was young and strong as a horse. She might have lived for years, possibly even survived.'

'It's true. But unfortunately, she lost a lot of blood, which weakened her and she succumbed.'

'Weakened–you weakened her, you sucked her blood!'

'Just enough so the disease would kill her. We didn't do it ourselves. We have a clean conscience on that score.'

'Conscience!'

'It's a figure of speech.'

'There can be nothing but war between us, between me and all your kind.'

Williams, Ruthven or by whatever name you choose to call the creature, suddenly snarled and flew–I mean literally flew at me.

'I'll not put up with your insolence any more, Dumas. I'll show you what you get for crossing a vampire!'

I punched him full in the face. He staggered and fell

34

down.

'You've broken my tooth, you bastard!'

'I'm no bastard.'

'Pardon, your father was—'

'Save your insults.'

Williams got to his feet holding his broken tooth in his hand.

'You know, you're awfully strong for a human.'

'My father could hold his horse between his legs and do pull-ups.'

'Really? Yes, I've heard of that.'

'Care for some more?'

'I'd like to kill you!'

'No doubt you'd like to suck my blood.'

'Oh, as to that, no. Just kill you. You're not the type whose blood we like.'

'Do vampires pick and choose?'

'We're very picky. Like mosquitoes. The best blood is that of a young virgin. In general, women are better tasting than men, young women better than old, blondes preferable to brunettes.'

He kept looking at his tooth. His own blood for once dribbled down his face.

'I really have to do something about this tooth. You'll pardon me. Rocambole!'

'A young man entered who I immediately recognized as one of the two men who several years before had come to bribe me not to produce the play.'

'Sir!'

'Get me some ice—this hurts. I'll have to see a dentist.'

'Right away, Sir Williams.'

'What do you propose to do, Dumas?'

'I told you. I'm going to expose you. And the other bloodsuckers on this list.'

'Permit me to say you cannot do that.'

'Are we going to start that again?'

'I'm merely pointing out that no one will believe you.'

'That you are vampire?'

'Yes.'

'Possibly. But I've thought of that. I have proof of the murders you committed to obtain inheritances. People may not believe you are a vampire, but they will easily believe you are a murderer.'

Rocambole returned with the ice which Sir Williams rubbed against his cheek.

A toothless vampire. People would laugh.

Suddenly, calculating his chances, he rushed at me again.

'You won't have any teeth left if you keep this up.'

'You're the only human I've ever met who was stronger than I am.'

'Too bad it didn't happen sooner. We've established that you are no match for me and that I have the power to expose you.'

'What do you want?'

'I want you to get out of France, you and all your friends, and Rocambole and Baccarat and all your human henchmen.'

'And if we don't, you'll expose us?'

'Yes.'

'You cannot kill us, you know.'

'I can put a stake through your heart and see if that works.'

'Bah! You'll be charged with murder, and one of our henchmen will come around, remove the stake, etc. Meanwhile, you'll be charged with murder.'

'I've thought of that. Which is why I'm proposing that you leave France.'

'Leave France! But it's so nice here. I really love Paris and the French countryside.'

'Go to England, go anywhere you like. I don't wish you on anyone, but you cannot stay here.'

'All right—we'll go.'

'You speak for all your brood?'

'Yes.'
'And don't ever come back.'

As I read these pages, a thought too horrible to contemplate occurred to me. If Dorval had become a vampire, and if she and my father had been off-and-on lovers over many years, might not she have...? And even I, I remember Camille–Marie always liked to nibble–what if?...

THE VIRGIN VAMPIRE

Alinska, the Virgin Vampire, is one of the most interesting female vampires. Created in 1825 by Etienne-Léon de Lamothe-Langon in La Vampire ou la Vierge de Hongrie *(The Vampire or The Hungarian Virgin)[5], she is a Hungarian girl who was fiancéd to Edouard Delmont, one of Napoleon's young officers. But after he returned to France, Edouard went back on his vows and married someone else. Several years later, Alinska (who had killed herself after being betrayed by Edouard) suddenly reappears in his life, transformed into an avenging vampire. Alinska is not only the first, implacable, female vampire (predating Carmilla by almost 50 years!) but she is also the instrument of a higher power, working for God as the tool of Divine Wrath...*

Nathan Cabaniss: *Schrodinger's Blood*

London, Today

Edward Delmont gave three knocks on the door, waited a moment, and then gave another two. He hoped that was the correct combination. His constitution was growing weaker and weaker by the day, and thus his memory was likewise affected. He wasn't even entirely sure if he had even found the right address on Cheyne Walk to begin with...

---

[5] Available from Black Coat Press as *The Virgin Vampire*, ISBN 978-1-61227-032-6.

After a solid minute with no response, Edward strained to push himself up to lean against the doorframe. He weighed barely over one-fifty pounds, and it felt like he was pushing back a brick wall. Already his breathing quickened, and spots dotted the corners of his vision. Why did he feel so damned weak?

The last doctor he saw had given him a look that could have simultaneously been read as either awe or terror, glancing up from the results of the blood tests. He bore all the symptoms of blood loss, and yet his pulse was never stronger. With each passing day, he grew weaker and more fatigued, but his heartbeat ticked along at the rate of a well-tuned clock. He was a "walking anomaly," as the doctor had put it. The physician had proceeded to send him on his way with the name and address for a man he was instructed to seek out immediately.

A man who was apparently not home. But, just as Edward had successfully lifted himself from the doorframe, the heavy oak door was opened, revealing a dark man standing within. His sharp features were accentuated by a perfectly-trimmed beard, with a turban wrapped over his hair to complete the illusion. He studied Edward like an eagle overhead might view a snake, waiting for the man to make a statement of his intent. Edward attempted to present himself, but just then, the ground disappeared from beneath his feet, and he felt himself fall forward into the dark man's doorway.

Sâr Dubnotal caught him just as the world went black.

"How are you feeling, Mr. Delmont?" the Sâr said, fitting himself into the armchair adjacent to were Edward sat nursing his cup of tea.

"A little better. Still weak."

"This condition of yours," Sâr Dubnotal continued, "how long has it persisted?"

"A little over a week," Edward said, after another sip of steaming tea. "It just came up out of nowhere…"

"You display all the symptoms of blood loss, and yet there is nothing wrong with your body itself. You're in perfect physical condition."

"That's what the doctor told me, before giving me your name. It's more than a little crazy, flying all the way from New York to London just to find you…"

"But your condition leaves you with precious few options," Sâr Dubnotal finished for him.

Edward didn't respond, merely nodded.

"Well, you've certainly managed to pique my interest," the mystic said, standing up from the chair. "Let's see what we can find…"

He approached Edward deliberately, like a surgeon readying for an operation, and Edward suddenly felt a fear creeping in at his edges. He knew next to nothing about this man. He had become so desperate for help that he was willing to accept it from anywhere, even a complete stranger whose house's interior looked like the Smithsonian of pure insanity.

The Sâr must have noticed Edward's apprehension.

"Are you frightened of me, Mr. Delmont?"

"Should I have any reason to be?"

"We will find out."

Sâr Dubnotal's hands lashed forward, wrapped themselves around Edward's scalp. The mystic's eyes rolled back into his head, leaving a filmy, off-white luster to the orbs resting uneasily in the pockets of his skull, and a low muttering escaped from his lips. All of a sudden Edward felt a coldness within his mind. Invasive, icy fingers worked their way across his memories. There was nothing he could do to stop them as they reached through his life like a clerk's hands shuffling through a filing cabinet. All of his secrets—the deepest, most uncomfortable moments of his being—were laid bare. There was one memory in particular he was desperate not to be reminded of, one he fought with all his heart to keep away from the prying hands. *The woman sobbing in the doorway, a glimpse of a blonde-haired girl peeking out from behind her…*

As suddenly as it had begun, it was over. The icy touch left Edward's mind, and Sâr Dubnotal's hands came away from his scalp. Taking a moment to catch his breath, the mystic turned once more to Edward.

"You'll forgive me, Mr. Delmont, but I have many enemies—several of which would not think twice in using you to get to me. I had to be sure you were not an unwitting accomplice."

Edward nodded in response. His hands started to shake, and although he was sitting, he felt weaker than ever. The Sâr's read of his mind had taken a good deal out of him. He only prayed he had the fortitude to hide that last memory from the mystic's all-seeing gaze...

"I don't know if I can help you," Sâr Dubnotal said, breaking Edward from his thoughts. "But I think my read of you may have given us a place to start, at the very least. Wait here."

He left the room, returned quickly with an unusual object in hand. Upon closer inspection, it looked to be a simple, glass orb.

"A crystal ball?" Edward asked. "You've got to be joking..."

"I can assure you that this is no cheap parlor bauble. It has many names across various cultures, but I prefer the more scientific nomenclature," he said, tossing the ball lightly from one hand to the other before finally holding it up to eye-level. "This is a quantum looking-glass."

"Excuse me?"

"Tell me, Mr. Delmont: are you familiar with the concept of superpositions?"

Edward paused before answering. "I can't say that I am..."

"Very simply, it is when matter or energy exists in multiple states. Consider the principle of light: we do not know for sure whether it travels in particles or waves, although it displays the properties of both..."

"I wouldn't have expected you to be a man of science," Edward said.

"And what is magic if not phenomena yet to be explained through scientific means?"

Edward shook it off. "Listen, the physics lesson is all well and good, but what does any of this have to do with me?"

"Everything," Sâr Dubnotal said. "During my probe of your mind, I first sensed it. Your body is displaying all the symptoms of blood loss, yet there is no physical evidence. You—or more precisely, the blood in your veins—currently exist in two states. It is both there... and not there."

"I don't understand," Edward said, his mind too weak to wrap itself around any of what Sâr Dubnotal was saying.

"Something is feeding off of your blood without leaving a trace. If I were to hazard a guess, I would imagine that it is reaching into your future and siphoning it off there, the after-effects of which are currently being felt by your present self..."

"You are making absolutely no sense to me," Edward said, frustrated.

"Think of it like this: everything we see in this moment—everything in the entire world—is merely one aspect of a whole. The way we move through time allows us to see only what is happening in the present, but it is not the full picture. It is merely a momentary representation. Imagine looking into a mirror, seeing your current face. You do not see the face of the infant you wore previously, or the wrinkled face of senility you have yet to wear, yet they are there all the same. All the faces exist simultaneously, but through the limits of our perceptions, we see only one at any given time."

Edward rubbed his temples, barely grasping the mystic's words. "All right, even if all that is true... Why me? And why is it after my blood?"

"There's only one thing I know of that feeds off human blood," Sâr Dubnotal said, a knowing look in his eye. "But the other part of your question--that's the real mystery..."

"Vampires?" he asked the mystic. Sâr Dubnotal nodded, nonchalantly. Edward sank back into his chair. He had come seeking the counsel of a madman. That was the *real* explanation...

Suddenly, Sâr Dubnotal stood, looking like he'd just found a set of missing keys. "Delmont... Of course!" he said, slamming his fist into the wall.

"I'm sorry?"

"Your name," the mystic said, rushing over and taking Edward by the shoulders. "It's originally French, yes?"

"I suppose. Genealogy isn't really my strong suit..."

Sâr Dubnotal broke away, began to pace the room excitedly. "Why didn't I see it before? The name alone should have been a dead giveaway..."

"I'm sorry, but... What?"

"You really know nothing about your family name, or any of your ancestors?"

Edward merely shook his head in response.

Sâr Dubnotal took a sharp breath inwards, struggling to control his excited state. "Back in the early 19th century, there was a soldier of Napoleon who fell in love with a Hungarian girl named Alinska. He promised to give his heart to no other but, upon his return to France, he chose to forget her and marry another. The Hungarian girl was so distraught that she took her own life, and was later resurrected by God Himself as a vampire—brought back to wreak divine vengeance upon the man who had wronged her. A man also named Delmont..."

"So, you're telling me, what... that a vampire from the 1800s is after me because I happen to share a name with someone who stepped out on her?"

"If you happen to be a relative of this man..."

"There must be a thousand Delmonts in the world," Edward interrupted.

"Yes, and none of them currently experiencing symptoms such as yours."

"OK, but still: why? She sought vengeance against her lover... I mean, what have I done?"

"That's just the question: what have you done?" Sâr Dubnotal asked pointedly.

"What's that supposed to mean?"

"When I read you earlier, there were thoughts you kept from me. A hidden secret…"

Edward's brow broke out in a cold sweat. "That's— That's my business. It's not your concern…"

"Mr. Delmont, I am only trying to help, which I can't do if you withhold possibly important information from me. Now, I promise you I have little in the way of moral scruples… What were you hiding from me?"

Edward closed his eyes. The simple memory of it stung, like aftershocks of pain immediately following a serious injury. It didn't matter how many years went by; the memory was still there, eating away at him a little more each day. Perhaps that nonsense Sâr Dubnotal spouted earlier was true: the past was always with us.

"I—I had this girlfriend. Really more of a friend, but— well, we were intimate. I called things off when it seemed to get serious, because I honestly just didn't feel that way about her. But then, a few years later, she comes to my door, with this little girl clutching at her ankles. She tells me its mine. There was some sob story, I don't…" Edward paused, fighting back the stinging water beneath his eyes, "I don't even remember what it was, but she needed money. A place to stay. They were both starving, she said. I figured it had to be a con—if the girl was really mine, then surely she would have told me about it earlier. But… I didn't help them. She begged and sobbed and pleaded, but I still refused to help. I could've, I don't know… I could've given her a bit of money or something. But I didn't. I just shut the door."

Edward hung his head. He thought saying it out loud after all these years of keeping it buried would help ease his guilt. It didn't.

"That's it, then," Sâr Dubnotal said, after a moment of quiet deliberation. "It would appear Alinska's vengeance was not limited to just her beloved. It must be a curse… A curse placed upon the name of your family, and all who bear it and have wronged someone who loves them."

He went over to Edward, and put a hand on his shoulder. "We move through this life so carelessly, never once stopping to consider the effect of our path. It's like that duality of travelling light: stop for a second to study it, and it all falls apart…"

Delmont could no longer hold himself back, and broke into tears.

"What happens now?" he asked, choking through his sobs.

"Alinska is reaching from the past, feeding off of the superposition that is your entire life. Right now, you exist in two states—you are like the theoretical cat trapped in the box, neither alive nor dead until it is finally opened."

"Then what can I do?"

"You can open the box and find out," the mystic said, peering deep into Edward's eyes. "We're dealing with fluctuations in time—there is no stopping Alinska from taking her vengeance on you and draining your body of blood completely, but it could take several years for this to happen. It could even conceivably take the rest of your life. However, you're currently in flux—the twin states of your being flickering in and out like mixed radio signals.

"But, if we take a moment to stop and measure you, we could right the signal. Fix your position to one state," Sâr Dubnotal said, lifting his glass bauble from earlier. "That's what this does. The quantum looking-glass stretches the perceptions of those who peer through it, revealing the totality of a thing. An entire life, from birth to death. But if we use it to measure you—to fix your position back to one state--there's no guarantee of what will happen. You could either continue on living, or drop dead right here and now."

Edward nodded, and pulled himself up from the chair. His legs began to tremble from the exhaustion of bearing his weight, but he suffered through it. It was the least he deserved.

"If all you said earlier is the case—all that about the past, present and future being a fixed point—then isn't my fate already sealed?"

"Have you not been listening to anything I have said? Fate, choice... they are nothing more than aspects of a greater whole. The only certainty of your future is that you will die; whether it happens today or fifty years from now is another matter entirely."

"Well, then," Edward said, the lump in his throat slowly diminishing, "Let's find out."

Sâr Dubnotal nodded, and lifted the glass.

THE VAMPIRE COUNTESS

The characters of the Countess Addhema, a.k.a. Marcian Gregoryi, and her lover, Count Szandor, both vampires, were created by the incomparable Paul Féval (1816-1887), the founding father (often unjustly neglected) of the detective novel. This Vampire Countess, whose modus operandi involves scalping her victims, was introduced in the classic La Vampire (1856)[6]. In the following story, Rick Lai, one of Féval's most prolific continuators, expands upon the origins of Addhema, integrating her legend into a vast vampire saga, which will reach fruition in "All Predators Great and Small" presented later in this volume.

Rick Lai: *Vampire Renaissance*

Hungary and Wallachia, 1470-1477

"Throughout Hungary and Serbia, the victims of the Undead litter the countryside. Most corpses are found solely drained of blood. Nevertheless, mutilated bodies of women have been discovered along the banks of the Sava. These unfortunates are hairless as well as bloodless. One vampire is scalping its prey."
Armand Tesla,
The Supernatural and its Manifestations (1744)

---

[6] Available from Black Coat Press as *The Vampire Countess*, ISBN 978-0-9740711-5-2

"You have such lovely black hair, my darling," observed Count Marcian Gregoryi as his right hand brandished a knife. His left held a metal goblet filled with wine. "It's a pity that you must lose it."

"You intend to cut my hair!" shouted the Countess.

"No, my dear Addhema. I've been reading Herodotus. His account of the Scythian soldiers was most illuminating. The Scythians scalped their enemies."

"I'm not your enemy! I'm your wife!"

Marcian drained his goblet before throwing it on the ground.

"Harlot! Slut! I know that you've been cheating with Janos! That's why I invited him to our castle! The fool is sleeping peacefully in the guestroom! Once I finish with you, I shall take his scalp!"

Marcian advanced menacingly towards his wife. Addhema screamed.

Suddenly, the door of the noble couple's bedchamber was thrown open. Standing in front of the couple was a tall handsome man.

"Did Addhema's wails disturb your slumbers?" asked Marcian.

"Drop your weapon!" commanded Janos Szandor.

"Only after I have taken two scalps!"

The muscular Marcian leaped at his wife's lover. Seizing Szandor's throat with his left hand, Marcian raised his knife high in the air.

"Your hair is almost as pretty as my…"

Marcian never finished because the goblet smashed brutally into the back of his head. Retrieving the metal cup from the ground, Addhema had struck her husband from behind. Relinquishing his grip on Szandor, Marcian collapsed. He sprawled face downward on the ground as his wife pounded his skull repeatedly with the goblet.

"Count Gregoryi is dead," declared Addhema. "You must throw him out the window. Everyone will believe he fell to his death in a drunken stupor."

Countess Gregoryi's prediction proved to be accurate. Born Addhema Yorga, she was the granddaughter of a nobleman who fled to Hungary from Bulgaria after the Turkish conquest of 1396. When she was only 18, Addhema had married Marcian Gregoryi. At the age of 25, she was an eligible widow. After a period of suitable mourning for her first husband, she celebrated her nuptials with Count Janos Szandor in 1470. Szandor was in favor with Matthias Corvinus, King of Hungary. The sovereign even permitted him to gain dominion over the late Count Gregoryi's vast estates along the Sava River.

Five years later, Count Szandor was summoned to an audience with Matthias Corvinus.

"What do you know of Dracula?" asked the King.

"He is also called Vlad the Impaler," replied Szandor. "Dracula is the former ruler of Wallachia. When the Turks drove him from the throne, he fled to Hungary. Your Majesty imprisoned him for a dozen years. Recently, he was granted his freedom. Your Majesty even gave permission for Dracula to wed your cousin."

"How would you explain my change of heart towards Vlad Dracula?"

"When he was incarcerated, Hungary had just negotiated an armistice with the Ottoman Empire. Dracula was punished to appease the Turks. Our relations with the Turks have changed drastically with their invasion of Bosnia. Your Majesty released Dracula to fight in a new crusade against the Turks."

"Quite correct, Count Szandor. The man is a military genius as well as a depraved hedonist. Do you know why he has been christened the Impaler?"

"Dracula takes a perverted pleasure in impaling human beings on wooden stakes. This horrible fate has been bestowed on his Turkish enemies as well as any citizen of Wallachia who has earned his displeasure. Thousands have perished by impalement on his orders."

"While he was my prisoner, his jailer told me that he amused himself by impaling mice."

"Can such a maniac be trusted, Sire?"

"It is in Dracula's self-interest to be loyal to me. As a precaution, I must appoint one of my more reliable vassals to act as his aide-de-camp. Will you take this commission, Count Szandor?"

"You honor me, Sire. I shall be your eyes and ears in Dracula's entourage."

"My only regret is that the military campaign will force a long absence from your charming wife."

"Addhema has an adventurous soul. She will insist on accompanying me."

"But surely she must remain behind to take care of your heir?"

"Our young son will be entrusted to the care of my brother-in-law, Count Yorga."

In the winter of 1475-1476, Dracula helped King Matthias recover Bosnia. During the summer, he was given command of an army to restore his rule over Wallachia. By the end of November, the forces of the Impaler were triumphant. With Count Szandor at his side, Dracula was once more invested as the reigning Voivode of Wallachia

In early December, a private dinner was held in a mansion in Bucharest, the capital of Wallachia. The host was Vlad Dracula. The guests were Count and Countess Szandor. The festivities lasted long into the night.

Seated in his chair, Szandor was slumped apparently unconscious across the banquet table.

"Your spouse does not drink wine well," pronounced Dracula.

"You must forgive my husband, my Lord," beseeched Addhema.

"I shall if you do me a small favor, Countess."

"What do you wish of me?"

"Merely to answer a question. Do you know the significance of my name?"

"Your father belonged to the Order of the Dragon, a society of nobles dedicated to crusades against the enemies of Christianity. He was known as Dracul, which means 'Dragon.' Dracula signifies the Son of the Dragon."

"My detractors often comment that my name can also be translated as Son of the Devil. My father joined the Order of the Dragon for an ironic reason. My family has a very ancient lineage."

"I know of what you speak, my Lord. The Szandors are descended from Attila the Hun. My husband told me that the great warrior was also your ancestor."

"That is true, but I refer to even more remote forebears. Come with me, Addhema. There is something that you must see."

Dracula's green eyes gazed into Addhema's. The Voivode had a commanding appearance, even though he was not a tall man. Long black hair fell on his shoulders. A bushy black mustache hung beneath an aquiline nose. While his face was gaunt, his body was stocky and strong.

The Voivode escorted Addhema out of the banquet chamber. After traversing corridors lit by torches, the duo reached a locked doorway guarded by two sentries. They were members of Dracula's bodyguard of 200 Moldavians. Fiercely loyal to the Voivode, the Moldavians cultivated their hair and mustaches in the style of their master.

Opening the door with a key, Dracula ushered Addhema inside. She saw a pillar on which rested an object covered by a black shroud. Dracula closed and secured the door. He removed the shroud.

"Behold the Draconic Adder!"

An ivory statue of a winged dragon was revealed. Its worm-like body was coiled thrice. Three horns made from rubies sprouted from its head.

"Is this some talisman of the Order of the Dragon?" asked Addhema. "It smacks of paganism rather than our Christian faith."

Dracula laughed. "The Order is composed of pious hypocrites! If they were true Christians, they would turn the other cheek to our enemies. Instead, they condone their slaughter. It amused my father to join the Order because their symbol invoked the god of our forefathers."

"I don't understand, my Lord."

"The Draconic Adder, also dubbed the Drac, roamed the Earth with the Great Old Ones before the Age of Man. His parents were Yiggurath, Father of Serpents, and Tiamit, the Dragon of Arabu. The ancient civilization of Lemuria revered the Adder under the name of Slidith. Our early ancestors were preyed upon by minions of the other Old Ones. Yiggurath had also mated with Adana the Snake Mother. Their progeny was Set, the Great Serpent. Set spawned the Serpent Men of Hyperborea. Together with the Werewolf Folk, the winged Akaana and other monsters, the Serpent Men warred on humanity. Taking pity on mankind, Slidith empowered an elite group of mortals, the Red Brotherhood, to lead a crusade against the Serpent Men and their allies. Assisting the Brotherhood were the children of Slidith, the Dragon Kings. After a brutal conflict that spanned centuries, the Serpent Alliance was defeated. However, some Serpent Men survived. Disguising themselves as humans, the Serpent Men poisoned the minds of the Lemurians against the Red Brotherhood and the Dragon Kings. The adherents of the Draconic Adder were persecuted. All worship of Slidith disappeared from our world.

"In Stygia, the civilization preceding Egypt, a scholar named Rammon unearthed records of Slidith. Recognizing the Draconic Adder as mankind's true benefactor, Rammon performed a ritual to invoke the god's assistance. Slidith rewarded the scholar by making him his Viceroy on Earth. Rammon inducted other Stygians into the religion of the Adder. His greatest convert was Princess Akivasha of the ruling dynasty. Unfortunately, human allies of the Serpent Men had also established the cult of Set in Stygia. Gaining the support of the Stygian monarch, the priests of Set murdered Rammon and entombed Akivasha alive. The adherents of Slidith were forced into hiding. The post of the Viceroy of Slidith remained vacant until the emergence of the Roman Empire. There was a certain governor of Judea during the reign of Tiberius."

"Enough of your half-truths!" interrupted Addhema. "I know the legends of the Undead! The governor was Pontius Pilate! When he died, he became a vampire!"

Dracula smiled. "You are very perceptive. Yes, Slidith is the Lord of Blood. He transformed the Red Brotherhood into immortals feasting on human blood. The Viceroy of Slidith is also called the Great Vampire."

"You talk of these vampires with admiration."

"My family has secretly venerated Slidith for centuries. We have sought to learn the details of the Ritual of the Viceroy. I studied at the Scholomance, a school of occult knowledge in the mountains over Lake Hermanstadt. There, I discovered *The Book of Simon the Mage*. The Samaritan author had extinguished the Undead existence of Pontius Pilate. The tome unmasked the method by which Pilate was elevated into the Great Vampire. Slidith requires that a candidate to be his Viceroy perform acts of extreme brutality to prove his worthiness. Pilate attempted to gain Slidith's favor by massacring scores of Jews. Eventually, it dawned on Pilate that sacrificing a single individual of great uniqueness would pacify Slidith. Pilate ordered the crucifixion of Jesus."

"Pilate became the Great Vampire by murdering the Son of God?"

"I don't know whether Jesus was truly the Messiah, but he was clearly a being of unimaginable power. Pilate then slaughtered Samaritans to further placate Slidith. This action caused Tiberius to summon Pilate to Rome. By the time Pilate reached Rome, Tiberius had died. The disgraced governor was forced to explain his conduct before the new Emperor, Caligula. Chanting the name of Slidith, Pilate swallowed poison in front of Caligula. The soul of Pilate was sent to the Pit of the

Draconic Adder. Pilate presented his petition to be resurrected as the Great Vampire. If Slidith had refused his candidacy, Pilate's fate would be eternal damnation. But his request was granted by Slidith."

"But vampires fear the cross! They are servants of Satan! Not some pagan deity!"

"There were consequences to Pilate's murder of Jesus. Vampires became vulnerable to the crucifix and other Christian symbols. Simon the Mage ended Pilate's reign as Lord of the Undead. My ultimate goal is to succeed Pilate as the Great Vampire. The impalement of countless victims has been my road to a great destiny! Unlike Pilate, there shall be no unintended results from my atrocities! Vampires are already susceptible to the dangers of the stake!"

"Fiend! Blasphemer! You mock the Christian faith that you swore to protect!"

"I'm no more a hypocrite than the self-styled Christian King of Hungary! My actions as Voivode are clearly horrid crimes, buy they have been excused because many of my victims are Moslems! You are in no position to condemn me! You're as much a dissembler as Matthias Corvinus! I have heard the rumors! You murdered your first husband to marry your lover!"

"My sins pale before yours!"

Dracula grabbed a knife that rested on the pedestal near the idol. "This blade is sacred to Slidith. A French warlock, Gilles Grenier, sold it to me. He found this weapon in the ruins of the Cathar fortress at Montségur. I have only used this knife on one other occasion. I had a mistress who claimed to be carrying my child. I carved open her belly to test her veracity."

Addhema shuddered in horror.

"Don't fret, my dear," stated Dracula in a soothing voice. "I must take insurance before I arrange my audience with Slidith. If only I could conceive one great sin to climax my career... Fortunately, Slidith is amused by pretty acts of cruelty. Raping the wife of a loyal subordinate should suffice to

54

divert the Draconic Adder. I will only use the knife if you resist me. *Ia! Draco im Bab-el! Yiggurath im Ngoth!"*

Hours later, Addhema and her slumbering husband were escorted back to their Bucharest residence by Dracula's Moldavian bodyguards. When Janos Szandor awoke in the morning, Addhema tearfully apprised him of her ordeal.

"That monster shall die by my hand!" swore Janos.

"He's married to the King's cousin," noted Addhema. "You must use guile to assassinate him."

"What do you suggest?"

"Kill him during a battle with the Turks."

"His Moldavian bodyguards would never allow me to slay him."

"You must betray Dracula and his Moldavians to the Turks."

"That would be committing treason!"

"Avenging my honor is worth any price!"

In late December, the corpses of 190 Moldavian bodyguards sprawled on the battlefield outside Bucharest. The surviving 10 bodyguards had fled on their horses from the carnage. The commander of the triumphant Turkish soldiers rode up to the Hungarian who had betrayed Dracula's battle plans.

"Where's the Impaler?" asked the Turkish leader.

Count Szandor extended a sack towards the commander. Grasping the bag, the Turk reached inside. He pulled out a human head with long hair and a mustache.

"I commend you, Szandor. You slew Dracula without our assistance."

"I had a personal score to settle. What do you want me to do with the body?"

"Throw it in a ditch!"

The Turkish commander rewarded Szandor with a chest filled with gold.

The Turks conquered Wallachia. Masking their treachery, Janos and Addhema sought refuge at the monastery of Snagov. The monastery was located on an island in a lake near Bucharest. One morning in January 1477, Janos had starling news for his wife.

"The monks found Dracula's body. They are going to give it a decent burial."

The mortal remains of the Impaler were interred in a sealed coffin. The burial occurred in the monastery's southern chapel. Three nights after the funeral, Addhema had a sudden urge.

"Come with me, Janos, to Dracula's grave. I want to spit on his headless carcass."

The Szandors surreptitiously approached the chapel in the corner of the monastery's main courtyard. Janos pushed open the heavy oak door. The couple entered a chamber with a length of 20 feet and a width of 10 feet. There was an altar at the back of the chamber. Two candles on the altar provided a dim light. At the foot of the altar was a grave. It was covered by a stone slab bearing a simple inscription: *DRACULA*.

After Janos removed the slab and the lid of the coffin beneath, Addhema peered inside. In the faint light, she could barely discern the corpse within. She bent downwards to spit on the prostrate Impaler. Suddenly, the figure in the grave rose to its full height. Its right hand seized Addhema's throat.

"Slidith has blessed my candidacy," hissed Dracula. "I am the Great Vampire now!"

The physical form of the Impaler had been altered by his transformation in the Lord of the Undead. His frame was taller and leaner. His ears were pointed. Fangs sprouted from his mouth. Hair grew from the center of his palms. Dracula was dressed in a long scarlet robe. A ring bearing an effigy of the Draconic Adder adorned each of his ten fingers.

"You were foolish to trust your husband. Months ago, he swore fidelity to me. His drunkenness was feigned on the night of the banquet. He willingly surrendered you to my carnal lust. I am indebted to you, Addhema. You provided the inspiration for my final act of earthly evil. With your husband's help, I betrayed my loyal followers to the Turks. This ultimate treachery sealed my bargain with the Draconic Adder."

Dracula released his grip on Addhema. She fell gasping to the ground.

"As I watched from a safe distance, the Turks butchered my soldiers," explained Dracula. "Beheading one of my bodyguards, Janos tricked the Turks into believing that he had murdered me. Invoking Slidith in the Ritual of the Viceroy, I consumed poison."

Dracula extended his right hand towards Janos: "Count Szandor, remove one of the rings from my fingers. It's my gift to you."

Janos complied with Dracula's command. The Hungarian placed the ring on his own finger.

"This ring shall link your thoughts to mine," said Dracula. "I shall summon my three sons. They will transport my coffin to a suitable fortress in either Wallachia or neighboring Transylvania. As I establish a base here, you shall be the first of my emissaries to the outside world. You and your future comrades shall be known as the Stepsons of the Dragon."

"Command me, Master."

"You shall return to your domain on the Sava River. King Matthias must suffer for my 12 years of imprisonment. You shall launch a rebellion against him. With the powers that I will bestow, you shall be able to resist his forces."

"My family will adopt a new motto: *In vita mors, in mors vita!*"

" 'In life, death; in death, life!' An excellent choice, Janos."

"When will you induct me into the immortal ranks of the Undead?"

"As soon as I am finished with your wife. You will need her advice in the coming insurrection."

From a sheath on his belt, Dracula removed the knife from Montségur. Holding the blade in his right hand, Dracula's left hand locked itself into the moaning Addhema's raven tresses. Yanking the Countess by the hair to her knees, Dracula placed the knife against her forehead.

"You shall be punished for your impertinence, Addhema. Janos has told me of your first husband. His idea of punishment was very original. I'm going to scalp you!"

As Dracula's blade bit into her flesh, the shrieks of Addhema resounded through the chapel.

"Poor Addhema has fainted from her pain," observed Dracula sheathing his knife. "I must console her."

Casting aside the bloody scalp, Dracula bent down towards the prone Addhema. His fangs bit into her neck. Once he had finished dining on her blood, Dracula pulled open his robe. One of the vampire's long fingernails cut into his own chest. Dracula's blood dripped slowly. Raising the head of the comatose Countess, Dracula pressed her face against his breast.

"Feast, Addhema, feast on my blood! You're the first of my Undead brides. You shall be a unique predator. You will do more than drain the blood of your victims. You will steal their hair to adorn your mutilated skull. The stolen hair will only last a few nights. You will be forced to constantly replenish it. In the centuries that follow, sweet Addhema, you and Janos shall wash Europe in blood!"

Dracula's reign as the Great Vampire had begun.

CARMILLA

Carmilla *is a novella penned by Irish writer Joseph Sheridan Le Fanu (1814-1873) in 1871. It is rightly considered a classic of 19th century English fantasy literature. Carmilla's real name is Countess Mircalla Karnstein, a vampire who, in a story recorded by Dr. Hesselius, attacks young Laura and slowly turns her into a vampire herself.* Carmilla *has been the subject of numerous film adaptations, including Carl Dreyer's* Vampyr *(1932), Roger Vadim's* Blood and Roses *(1960),* La cripta e l'incubo *in Italy in 1964 with Christopher Lee, and several productions from the famous Hammer Films:* The Vampire Lovers *(1970) with Ingrid Pitt and Peter Cushing,* Lust for a Vampire *(1971), with Yutte Stensgaard,* Twins of Evil *(1971) and finally* Captain Kronos, Vampire Hunter *(1974). Also notable are* La Novia Ensangrentada, *a 1972 Spanish adaptation by Vicente Aranda, a Polish* Carmilla *(1980), an episode of the American television series,* Nightmare Classics *(1989), starring Meg Tilly, and finally* Lesbian Vampire Killers, *a 2009 comedy starring Paul McGann and Silvia Colloca.*

Michel Stéphan: *The Three Lives of Maddalena*

Diary of Maddalena Ernestine

Strangely, more things have happened to me during these last two months of my life than at any time previously. First, it was my encounter with Carmilla Karnstein who came to stay with us, one day in September, renting our little, first-floor bedroom. Then, there was my break-up—if the word is cor-rect—with the man whom I had long considered as my brother, my sole confident and even my soul mate, Victor Franken-stein, who, the very day of his betrothal, did not even deign to look at me.

Victor and I grew up together; he is five years older than I, and comes from a wealthier family, but these differences never seemed to matter between us. He was like an older brother to me—the playmate who built a tree house for us in the woods belonging to Old Man Schluter, the student who taught me that life could sometimes be cruel, and that God could lack mercy towards some of His creatures.

I was the one on whose shoulder he cried during his first heartbreak, when he came to me, cursing all women, just be-cause a girl from the village had tired of his favors.

When Victor went to university, his visits became more infrequent, but he never missed an opportunity to see me when his schedule allowed. We then spent a few, precious hours to-gether, reminiscing about the good times we had had together, forever enshrined in our memories.

When Victor met Elizabeth, I was happy for them both. They were such a good match, and I liked to think that dear Elizabeth considered me as a true friend and not a rival. My relationship with Victor was too strong to be confined within the narrow limits of a love affair, and I think everyone under-stood then that we were truly inseparable.

When Carmilla came to live with us, Victor was already absorbed in his experiments, and it impacted his mood, but I never expected him to suddenly change so much. I always thought that Carmilla had something to do with it, but I could never bring myself to believe it completely. How could a be-ing of mere flesh and blood, even one so strange, could exer-cise that much influence over another? Victor had changed so much that he failed to even recognize me. I had become invis-ible to his eyes, a total stranger. But Carmilla had also com-pletely overturned my life. I did not believe one could experi-ence so much fascination for another woman.

She had arrived early in the fall to live as a tenant in our house, for a period of time that would coincide with her mother's return to the family castle. Baroness Karnstein had left her daughter under the guardianship of my father, with a thousand recommendations and a sum of money which, as I found out later, was more than sufficient.

Carmilla was the same age as I, but she already seemed to know so many more things. I listened, fascinated, when she joined me in my room at night and we spent quiet time lying on my bed. The more I listened to her, the more it seemed that I knew nothing about her. Her very existence remained a mystery to me. What fascinated me the most was her intense gaze, and her booming laugh, which, coming from another girl's mouth might have seemed vulgar, but which, in hers, seemed fresh and beguiling. It was like an invitation to pleasure. Carmilla was very beautiful and, sometimes, I envied her. Despite her young age, I was sure that she had caused many suitors to lose their heads. I let myself be carried away by the sweet tone of her voice and slid slowly into a state of torpor that procured me the greatest happiness. This well-being only faded in the morning when Carmilla left me alone, but satisfied.

As he had done every year, Victor's father had organized a party in the gardens of their luxurious property in Visaria, and everyone in the village was invited. This year's event would also mark the engagement of Victor to Elizabeth. It was an opportunity for me to introduce Carmilla to them. She was beginning to be well known in the village. Her magnetism and beauty were a favorite topic of conversation. The distracted way she paid attention to the world around her and her ever-distant politeness might have passed for condescension or contempt, but she was so natural about it that the entire village seemed be in love with her. I was curious to see how her charm would operate on Victor. I had to introduce them to each other. I felt oddly compelled to do so. It had never occurred to me that this might endanger his engagement to Elizabeth. Or if it had it was entirely unconscious. My only intention was to bring together the two people whom I cherished the most.

But nothing happened as I had hoped. I began by finding Victor and offering him my warmest congratulations on his engagement; then I introduced Carmilla to him. There was an exchange of polite smiles, followed by a brief handshake. And, from that moment, it was also the end of a friendship that I thought would last forever.

After that day, Victor lost complete interest in me. I did not understand immediately what had happened. I still have not understood it.

The celebrations had barely begun and already Carmilla was impatient. She intimated with her beautiful smile that she was bored and wanted to leave. Victor, meanwhile, had long ago disappeared into the arms of his fiancée.

That day, I began to feel extremely ill.

It was as if all the calamities of the Earth had befallen me at once. The following day, I was forced to stay in bed when I learned of the upcoming departure of Carmilla. Her stay had come to an end and her mother had expressed \the desire to see her daughter soon. My world had collapsed.

Today, Carmilla is gone. I no longer exist for Victor and I think I will never have an explanation for it. If there is one, I hope I learn of it soon, for I feel that my end is nigh.

The two doctors who have examined me have failed to find the cause of my illness. My father wanted to find a third, more competent physician, but I told him that it was not worth it; he should not question the wisdom of the doctors. It is strange, but I am not afraid. I know that, for me, my life is at an end, but nothing truly ever ends. Everything has new beginnings. Maybe on the threshold of death, the human mind prepares you to face the ultimate void by making you delirious or feeding you fantasies to surround your last moments with a sense of well-being, but, honestly I do not believe that is the case.

I really think, especially in the last few days, that a great adventure is waiting for me beyond the darkness, and I am not afraid.

Diary of Carmilla Karnstein

The events that I have recently experienced had, for me, the attraction of novelty, but they still did not reconcile me with mankind, as they were unfortunately far too predictable.

The time I spent in Visaria enabled me to meet a girl, Maddalena Ernestine, who was quite pleasant, and to become her friend. Indeed, I was her confidante for several weeks. She told me her life story, her joys and sorrows. I was moved by it, so I decided to give her destiny a little helping hand.

The stories humans tell about us, creatures of the night, have always terrified them, which is only to be expected, since they have always seen us through the distorting prism of their own vices. I won't ever mention their religions, which condemn us as masquerading abominations from beyond the grave. Yet do we not offer the same eternal life that these worms are unable to grasp? They imagine they can oppose us with the impotent lamentations of degenerate mendicants or shake before our eyes their grotesque crucifixes.

Maddalena Ernestine lived in her dreams, contenting herself with a passionate love stifled by too many moral principles. I had to release her from that life, and I did. Her pathetic feelings will be transcended by death and turn to true love, which she could never have known before.

When she becomes one of us, she can finally live her passion with an intensity that only afterlife can offer. She will join her lover and they will be reunited for eternity. When I think of the moments of ecstasy that they will be able to share, I understand why churches curse us, we who have the power to accomplish such miracles.

My affection for her turned to pity the day I met her beloved Victor. What a waste, how many destinies severed by petty bourgeois morality!

It was easy enough for me to look into his eyes to erase all traces of Maddalena Ernestine from the mind of the young Doctor, so that he would not see it die. Besides, Maddalena Ernestine had been moping and wishing for death a thousand times before, without knowing what awaited her on the other side of that dark mirror. Her wish will be fulfilled. Those two deserve better than a meaningless romance in the land of the living.

She will be buried in her family crypt and, as usual, the doctors will find nothing sensible to say about the reasons for her death. Then, for several months, perhaps even a year, her heart will virtually stop, beating at a rhythm so slow that it is all but imperceptible to humans, who nevertheless know it as our only weak point and would not hesitate to stab her through it.

Her body will retain the brilliance of her youth until she wakes up and finally understand what wonderful opportunity I gave her. Maddalena Ernestine may then emerge from her grave to rejoin her Victor and the two shall forever be united.

Diary of Victor Frankenstein

Dr. Pretorius finally brought me the body. That madman wants me to create a female companion for the monster. I do not know if I can twice achieve the same success.

The body is in perfect condition. It is that of a girl of 19 who seems to be sleeping peacefully. However, there appears to be something defective about her heart. It does not respond quickly enough to electrical stimulation. So I took it out of her chest and asked Karl to get me a replacement.

Pretorius and I then began to prepare the body for the main operation.

The girl was an ordinary girl, with a physique that some might have even called ungrateful. However, when I bent over her to cover her face with gauze and bandages, I was suddenly transfixed by a strange vision. I saw a tree house and lots of Sun. Much sadness too.

But I digress. Karl is coming back. He looks pleased. I promised him 1000 crowns if he were successful. I think we will soon be able to start the operation.

(English adaptation by Jean-Marc & Randy Lofficier)

Martin Gately: *The Moon Hag*

It was on the first night out of Brindisi, sailing north towards Trieste, that the trouble began. At first, Cellini, the skipper of the brigantine *Ceres,* put the whole thing down to drunkenness. Yes, the lookout had been drinking, glugging back *Stroh*, the spiced rum so beloved of Austrians, in order to keep the cold at bay. But it is only in the imaginings of teetotalers, spinsters and magazine humorists that the least whiff of alcohol causes wild hallucinations. In the end, the Captain realized that an honest man drunk is still an honest man and there is many a sober liar. It is when the habitual drunkard is denied his booze that terrible visions invade his mind. By the end of the voyage, Cellini himself was taking solace in the bottle.

So, you are wondering what the lookout saw on that first night as he looked down from the crow's nest past the great creaking sheets of the square-rigged sails to the deck. Let me first say that most sailors are terrible observers: the head of the sulphur whale, with its unusual yellow and black markings is mistaken for a sea serpent, the sea cow emerging from the depths is a mermaid, especially when the sailor concerned has not had sight of a real woman for long months. But our lookout was a professional observer, and he saw what he saw: a woman dancing on the moonwashed deck. Her long hair was black as coal and obscured her features. Her dress was white and partially removed, the bodice hanging loosely about her; she held up the skirts all the way to her upper thighs as she danced provocatively to music that apparently only she could hear.

The following afternoon, I sat in the passenger saloon with the rather handsome widow, Madame Strenkin, and we played detective, doing our level best to guess who the strange nocturnal dancer might be. Nominally, we were also playing the card game *Preferans* with Madame Strenkin's daughter making up the third and acting as dummy.

"We took aboard two gypsy girls to do the laundry at Brindisi," said Madame Strenkin. "Unfortunate girls of the lower classes may display themselves in such a way to gain the attention of men. It may not seem it, Professor Quercus, but I am a woman of the world. I know that there are streets, even in Trieste, where girls sell their virtue for pennies."

"You should not speak so in front of your daughter," I reprimanded gently.

"She must learn reality of how the world is… that is one thing that even the most expensive finishing schools seem to fail to teach," said Madame.

"I can see no purpose to a girl of ill-virtue dancing half-naked on the deck in the middle of the night when the only man who can see her is perhaps twenty meters overhead. She is a modest harlot indeed," I said.

"There are also two Slovenian woman of good birth on board ship. They do not frequent the passenger saloon and keep to themselves in their cabin," said the widow.

"Perhaps they do not care to be beaten at *Preferans,*" I said, taking the final trick of the game.

"This business is a distraction—for the sailors, at any rate. I saw one almost fall from the rigging earlier this afternoon. No doubt he was thinking of the pleasures of the flesh," said Madame Strenkin.

"The Captain has asked the First Mate to keep watch on the deck tonight. I doubt if there will be a repetition," I said.

"It is time now for our afternoon nap," she announced. "Come, Malicarla." And with that, Madame Strenkin and her striking, violet-eyed daughter, Malicarla, decamped from the saloon. With the women gone, I lit my pipe and cogitated on what had been and what might be to come in a grayish-blue fog of my own exhalations.

And so it was that the mate, Lafontaine, came to spend the night on the deck of the *Ceres*. The moon was low to the horizon when he came on watch, hugely magnified by the atmosphere, like the bloated, jaundiced faces some people are troubled by during hypnagogic sleep. It loomed, stared and leered. It bred fear. Lafontaine's every move was made under its eye. The sailor had ostentatiously buckled on his sword before he left the cabin he shared with the two other mates. Yet, somehow, it gave him no comfort, no feeling of protection. There had been murmurings among the crew that the figure seen the previous night had been a specter, or a wraith. He was not a man who subscribed to such fancies. His personal theory was that the dancing girl was a stowaway, but the ship had been searched as thoroughly as was practicable and no stowaway had been found. He had also arranged for the gypsy girls to be locked in. But the steward told him that they had been locked below decks yesterday too. However, he could have been mistaken, or one of them might have found a way to sneak on deck. It seemed to be a matter of principle to the Captain to get to the bottom of this business. This was just not the sort of ship that had cavorting women on the deck. And Lafontaine was pleased that this sensitive problem had been entrusted to him. He wondered momentarily if one of the women might be going about partially clad in her sleep, like a somnambulist. He had heard that it was dangerous to wake a sleepwalker. Possibly he would be able to guide the woman back to her cabin. But surely, even somnambulists didn't sleep walk every night. And with all the fuss that had been made today no one in their right mind would engage in such a performance again.

Looking to the west, Lafontaine could see the coast of Italy. The Captain was a cautious man. He often kept within sight of shore. But never so near that he might strike rocks or a reef. Lafontaine looked up at the moon. It seemed to be getting

67

brighter. The sallow yellow light was tainting everything. It started to feel like the moonbeams were irritating his eyes, the way the air wafted off a cornfield does at the height of summer. He rubbed at the corner of his right eye, but that only seemed to make it worse. The contagion spread to his left eye. He rubbed compulsively at both eyes, waiting for the symptoms to improve. When they did not, he engaged a modicum of willpower and forced himself to stop. He could feel that his eyes were already bloodshot, his vision muzzy. A yellow mist was rising from the deck planks now, as if the power of the moon were boiling off some residue that had long since impregnated the fabric of the ship. How long had he been on watch now? It had seemed only minutes, yet he felt utterly exhausted and fought to keep open the leaden lids of his hot and swollen eyes. He would've gone to get help, but the effort was far too much. His legs bowed under his own weight, knees sagging as if he carried heavy sacks of coal on his back. The moon was pressing down on him, forcing him down onto the planks. He lay on his back. Helpless. Did he really go to sleep then and there? It is impossible to say. He was no longer able to open his eyes. No longer able to vocalize a coherent sound.

After a few minutes, he became aware of the sweet honey-breath miasma close to his face. Warm. Pleasant. The breath of a woman. It could almost have been the presence of his mother. It reminded him of his earliest memories. Soothing. Warming. The presence embraced him without touching him. Comforted him. He reached out, sightlessly. He could not open his eyes. His hand found the unmistakable smooth globe of a woman's breast. He wished he could see. He pawed at the breast. And when he clumsily attempted to squeeze it, it drew nearer. The nipple was distended and tough. It secreted something warm and sticky onto his insistent fingers. Milk? The breast hovered over his mouth. He latched onto its stone-hard tip and sucked. Liquid jetted down his throat. The milk burned his tongue and palate. God, it tasted of filth and bitter corruption. The shock of it enabled him to open his eyes.

The face of the Moon Hag was a terror to behold. It might once have been beautiful. Now, it was little more than a skull. Yellow skin, tauter on the bone than the membrane across the top of a drum, crackled as the jaw hinged open and curved fangs slid down. Lafontaine averted his eyes from the Moon Hag's visage. He thought then that the last things he would see would be her swollen suppurating tits, heavy with pus, exuding the odor of rancid meat.

Someone was approaching, and that saved Lafontaine's life. Angered beyond measure that she had been denied her sustenance, the Moon Hag struck the sailor hard across the face with her claw-like hand. Then she was gone. The yellow mist dissipated swiftly. Lafontaine discovered that he could neither move nor speak; a strange paralysis had overtaken him.

"My dear, Captain," I began. "I am a professor of metaphysics, not medicine. But it is quite obvious to me that your First Mate has suffered some kind of stroke. See how his features droop in a highly noticeable fashion, as if he had lost all control of his muscles on one side of his face. Similarly, he scarcely seems to be able to move the limbs on his left side at all. Yet, he is young and strong. I imagine that he is likely to make a full recovery in time…"

"The crew is most alarmed," said Cellini. "Less than two steps from mutiny. They say it is witchcraft; that the *strega* stalks the deck at night. They ask for us to put in at the nearest port."

"And why not?" I asked. "Get the mate to a doctor… the proper medication may speed his recovery."

"Because, if there is a creature of evil aboard my ship, I have a responsibility not to take it to where it might find fresh victims. It must be killed," said the Captain.

"What nonsense! A man has a seizure and you start to worry about monsters… But I tell you what. Tonight, I will stand guard and kill the monster, if it even exists!" I said.

"There is a crucifix on the wall of my cabin. Perhaps you should borrow it... Though I have read that religious symbols only work if the one who wields them is a strong believer. Are you a religious man?" he asked.

"My faith lapsed for many years," I replied, "but after the death of my wife, it returned to me stronger than ever. Yes, I think that there is enough belief in the Power of God within me to cause your monster some mischief."

After this conversation with the Captain, I hurried to the passenger saloon to tell Madame Strenkin of the latest developments. The room was bereft of passengers, but the steward was there still clearing away the breakfast things. He informed me that Madame Strenkin was suffering from sea sickness and did not plan to emerge from her cabin today. The steward was pleased to see me since the Slovenian woman, Maria, had been taken ill in the night. He informed me that she was ghostly pale and he wondered if it could be anemia. These are the burdens that one must bear when one has an academic title that makes it sound as if one has an expertise in medicine. I suspect that the steward probably had more practical medical knowledge than I (I would struggle to apply a bandage successfully). Nevertheless, I undertook to look in on the young lady shortly in my capacity as the only man of science aboard the *Ceres*. But first, I would order some coffee and smoke my pipe, using up the last of my exquisite Umbrian tobacco.

It was mid-morning by the time I knocked on the Slovenian woman's cabin door. Not expecting a reply, I entered almost straightaway. I was shocked to see Madame Strenkin's daughter, Malicarla, stooping over the sick woman. I caught a glimpse of the prone woman's milk white bosom, then Malicarla hurriedly pulled up the nightdress, as if to preserve Maria's modesty. There was a suggestion of red liquid, something like the juice of a berry on Malicarla's lips. But within a split second, she had wiped it away with the back of her hand—not the action of a lady. I wondered what finishing school she had graduated from.

I attempted to rouse Maria from her sleep, but she was very lethargic and unresponsive.

"What, exactly, are you doing in here?" I asked Malicarla, with some suspicion growing in my heart.

"I'm sure that I can speak frankly to a man of esoteric learning, such as yourself," she said. "Since my time at boarding school I have realized that my appetites are not like those of other girls. They are *Sapphic* in nature."

"I am not sure that I understand," I confessed.

"In the short time that I have been aboard, Maria and I have become lovers," she said. "I know that there are some people who deny that such a love can even exist, but I assure you that it is the greatest love, the greatest passion of all."

Alternating incomprehension and suspicion, I tugged down the front of Maria's nightdress to expose her breasts. The left breast was unnaturally pale – almost blanched. The nipple was injured. There were two punctures in the areola. The nipple was also blanched; several degrees paler than the one on the right breast and dreadfully puckered, as if it had been immersed in water—or constantly in contact with saliva.

"What have you been doing to this girl?" I dared to ask.

"It is a *Sapphic* practice to suck the nipples of one's lover. Sometimes, this can result in a little bleeding—it is quite harmless, I assure you."

"I do not think that you should come in here again. This girl is not well enough to engage in the unwholesome and, if I may say so, immoral practices that you describe. You are to leave her alone, or I will tell your mother what you have been getting up to behind her back…"

"Oh, please," she begged. "Do not involve my mother in this. Our family is an old and proud one. The shock would do great injury to her health."

That I could believe.

"The family of Strenkin is an old and proud one? I did not realize that you sprang from nobility," I said.

"We are of the House of Dolingen in Styria. At present, we are traveling incognito," said Malicarla.

Far off bells rang in my memory. I had read somewhere about the nobles of Styria, and what they did whilst travelling incognito. Yet, I could not bring to mind the fact concerned. I could visualize the thick leather-bound book on Austrian nobility that lay on a dusty bookshelf of my university library hundreds of miles distant and decades in the past.

I ordered the sensual and perverse Malicarla from the cabin, bidding her not to return and I arranged with the steward for Maria to be fed raw meat, cooked liver and shredded kale, assuming anemia to be the malady. I could do little more. I realized suddenly that I could not wait to be off this ship. What had started as a silly and diverting parlor game mystery had taken on a different cast. Was something terrible stalking the deck of this ship at night or was it just some wanton woman—perhaps Malicarla herself, flaunting her young body? My imperfect memory was certainly trying to tell me something. I had a sense of awful claustrophobia and of traps closing. No, I could not properly account for it. Yet somehow, the balance had been tipped and I had lost my peace of mind. And it was all something to do with Malicarla—she had seemed so sweet and innocent when we had sat in the saloon playing *Preferans*. Now I had a sense of her slyness and cunning; satiating her lusts on a sick girl under our very noses, a she-fox who had inveigled her way into the hen coop. I would watch her as carefully as I could. I felt the strange need to procure a weapon—a firearm or some such—but why on earth was I starting to fear a teenage girl? What danger could she possibly be? She was certainly not the fairytale *strega* witch of the uneducated crew's imaginings.

The day brightened, and I was unable to settle to my usual routine of indolent inactivity: smoking, drinking (there was now no one with whom I could play cards). Instead I found myself wandering the deck and imagining what it would be like to walk there in darkness; trying to reconcile the lookout's report of a dancing girl with the sailors' ridiculous fears of a stroke-inducing witch. I rather craved the company of Madame Strenkin, but I very much feared that Malicarla would be with her and I could not stomach seeing her again—my natural inclination was to be diplomatically silent regarding her perversions, but the possibility of awkwardness and embarrassment in the cramped cabin only served to heighten my anxieties. Ultimately, I found myself on the bridge of the brigantine, with the Captain, helmsman and duty mate. It was a pleasant way to spend the early afternoon, and it wasn't long before the Captain called the Steward using the bell system installed on board and ordered for me *Kaisermelange*—coffee, milk, egg yolk and cognac. It was delicious. An injection of liquid courage, it fortified and cheered me.

At the end of his watch the Captain escorted me to his cabin, where, as he had mentioned earlier, there was an ornate crucifix on the wall. He took it down and gave it to me. I'm not sure what alloy it was made from but it was good and heavy—it had the feel of a weapon. It was conveniently sized to fit in my jacket pocket. I did not wish to be seen walking around grasping the thing like some sort of religious zealot, or an itinerant crucifix salesman showing his wares. I asked about firearms and was firmly and politely told that the two pistols and limited ammunition on board were only to be used to quell a mutiny or in other extreme contingencies. This was probably a good thing since, although I was a hunter in my youth, I had never actually shot a pistol. The cognac had improved my spirits, but it would do nothing for my accuracy. I foresaw my anxieties returning without warning when the alcohol died in my system, and then I would've had both the jitters and a loaded gun. No, let the guns remain locked in their cabinet. That was probably better all round.

So it was all arranged. That night there would be two mates and a helmsman on duty. If I ran into any sort of difficulties I was to shout as loudly as I could or go to the bridge for help. It would be fair to say that I regretted my offer to the Captain to stand guard tonight. My bravado had dwindled away. I wished for nothing more than to pass the night in my own cabin. Reading, a nightcap and then bed would've suited me well. Nevertheless, some fragment of hubris remained inside me, and I did not wish to be thought a coward.

The sun set, and I walked out of the saloon. The crates lashed to the foredeck made that area into a small scale maze. Was the hold really so full that crates had to be on the deck? They disrupted my lines of sight, and as I moved around, gave me the uncomfortable feeling that something was dodging behind them ahead of me at every turn. Something that wanted to work its way behind me. Then, the gibbous moon broke from behind the clouds and the whole ship was colored a sick yellow. The effect on the workings of my mind was highly noticeable and disorienting. A feeling like *déjà vu* invaded my thoughts. This was surely not the first time that I had walked this deck at night questing for the girl or witch who haunted it. Was this craft some *Flying Dutchman* forever cursed to sail the Adriatic—these events playing themselves out again and again like a fixed game of cards? Was something interfering with my memory? Why had I not been able to remember the historical detail about the nobles of Styria traveling incognito? Did it elude me still? No. I was getting old, that was all. It was starting to come back to me as I stood there in the sallow light of the moon. The nobles of Styria had fallen into the fashion of using anagrams of their names when they did not wish to be known. I did not need pen and paper in front of me to discern that Malicarla Strenkin was not an anagram which comprised the components of the name Dolingen. My every instinct was that Malicarla had been telling the truth, at least partly. They were Styrian nobles, although not of the House of Dolingen. Whatever might Malicarla Strenkin be an anagram of, I wondered? In the morning, I would sit down and puzzle it out.

The creature was on the deck now, its long black hair in front of its face like a veil of mourning. It swayed and trembled as if hesitating to commence its dance. The top of its black dress was pulled down and bunched around the creature's belly. I had never seen such an extraordinary pair of breasts, ripe as those of a nursing mother, and as golden as the Apple of Discord. The sight of the engorged, fleshy cylindrical nipples stirred in me desires that I had long thought dead. Urges that had disappeared since the death of my wife. I knew then that it was not Malicarla beneath that mask of hair. This was not the body of a teenage girl, it was a woman, a living archetype of womanhood, or even a goddess. There was nothing to fear. Yet I could not shrug off the nagging concern that this was a supernatural trick. That I was being lured as the fish is lured by the dance of the worm on the hook. The creature's provocative gavotte commenced. The skirts of its dress billowed with the dance and rose up higher at each pirouette. In momentary glimpses of flesh and hair I saw what was beneath the dress and I liked what I saw. Carnal lust was stoked within me and only one thing would be able to quench it.

The creature's dance increased in speed and complexity until it spun like a dervish. At the end it was just a blur, then the life seemed to go out of it and it collapsed on its back, panting, with almost a death rattle in its throat. The thing's long white legs were spread wide open. It pulled at its skirts, drawing them upwards. I loosened my belt and trousers as I saw properly for the first time the thing's slack, blood red cunt-maw. It looked dry, desiccated and dead, but the desire to penetrate it did not abate.

"No!" cried Malicarla, mockingly. "Before you ride the Moon Hag, you must first pleasure her. That is, if you wish to survive the coupling."

I looked back at Malicarla. She wore only her nightdress and there was blood on her lips. Had she been visiting Maria again? As I thought that, she smiled, as if reading my mind. Her grin displayed pin sharp teeth that were also smeared with blood.

"Get back to your cabin or I will have no choice but to seek out your mother," I said weakly.

Malicarla laughed, and it was the most terrifying sound that I have ever heard.

"The Moon Hag *is* my mother, Quercus," said the girl. "And she likes you. She always has. She has told me where she wants your tongue."

So, every myth, rumor and legend that I had ever ignored, dismissed, or pushed to the back of my mind regarding the tendency of Styrian nobles to vampirism was almost certainly true. At least I had the crucifix. It was the ace that would surely win this trick.

I crawled to the Moon Hag under the eye of Malicarla. Surreptitiously, my hand journeyed to my jacket pocket and found the reassuring shape of the metal crucifix within. I hoped that when Malicarla thought me committed to the nauseating act her undead mother desired I would be able to whip out the cross and defeat them both. I drew nearer and the decayed stench of the mother vampire enshrouded me. Yet, there was too a sickly sweetness to the decay, a kind of perfume that overrode my repulsion. What was before me, now only a few inches from my face, was not so disgusting after all. Not so different from some succulent jungle orchid. A functional arrangement of flesh petals, beautiful in its way, and not so desiccated as I had first supposed, glistening now; opening wide… something appalling emerging.

The undead baby erupted from the introitus with its mouth wide-open and milk-tooth fangs questing for my throat. I pulled my hand from my jacket pocket to protect my face, but the hand held the crucifix. A combination of disgust and terror manifested on the baby's tiny face and then it retreated back up the Moon Hag's birth canal to its uterus tomb.

"Yes, Quercus. My mother and my baby sister both wish to feed on you… do not disappoint them… throw away the crucifix… it is a barrier between yourself and the only kind of eternal life that really exists."

Perhaps I would've put the cross down… but she knocked it out of my hand before I could consider and it was sent spinning into the sea.

"Now perform your duty," she ordered. Her fingers were now impossibly long, with nails like Turkish daggers. "If you do not, I will tear your head from your neck."

I returned to the recumbent form on the deck, and I was bled by the Moon Hag and her younger daughter. And that is how I came to be a vampire in the service of the House of Karnstein, the greatest of the Styrian vampiric families. I am still the lover of Elsa Karnstein, Matriarch of that dynasty. She is subject to a "curse" greater than that of the ordinary vampire. Her daughter Carmilla—whom I first knew as Malicarla—bit her while she was with child. The infant became a vampire *in utero*—it had to be coaxed from the womb with the promise of fresh blood, and after feeding it always desired to return to its dark place of safety. When the infant hungered, it affected the mother—the child fed on the mother's own vampire blood. Eventually, the feeding cycle seemed to align with the phases of the moon; for part of the month Elsa Karnstein was her usual beautiful self, but when the infant hungered, she turned to her hag-form. By an effort of will Elsa could appear normal for short periods during the day. Yes, during the day, for the Karnsteins are unfettered archvampires; they must avoid the noon-day sun but they can go about during day quite easily with very few ill effects. Of course, they are strongest at night.

In the years that followed we developed the stratagem which I came to call "Carmilla's Game", acting out a melodrama in which Elsa took the part of a noblewoman traveling with her daughter, and when they came within the orbit of likely prey—typically a family with a beautiful virginal girlchild—I would arrive as the bearer of terrible tidings. I would say that Elsa's brother or uncle or some such was gravely ill. Elsa would then contrive to cause the prey's family to take in Carmilla as a house guest. From that point on, she could feed at will; disappearing for good when the victim died. Carmilla seemed to delight in playing out the game two or three times in the same locality, as if to highlight the parochial insularity of those from whom she leeched their lifeblood. We have fallen into such a routine now that I cannot imagine any other life, or should I say un-life. Indeed, perhaps it will continue forever. What can stop us?

Mademoiselle de Lafontaine related that her cousin, who was mate of a brigantine, having taken a nap on deck on such a night, lying on his back, with his face full in the light on the moon, had wakened, after a dream of an old woman clawing him by the cheek, with his features horribly drawn to one side; and his countenance had never quite recovered its equilibrium.

J. Sheridan Le Fanu - *Carmilla*

Dola Rosselet: *To Die For...*

Dawn rose over Vienna. It was one of those gray, pale autumns that last until evening. With the day, the shopkeepers, laborers and office workers poured into the streets of the city. They were in a hurry, clutching their coats tightly. Behind the arrogant facades of the private mansions, the Viennese aristocracy was still asleep, drunk from the theater, opera and waltzes. But in the Rammstein house an unusual commotion was stirring. The inner courtyard echoed with shouting servants, neighing horses and their clomping hooves. Standing at the window, the Countess watched her trunks being loaded. In two hours it would be time to leave. In spite of the fire crackling in the fireplace, she shivered. She huddled in her wool cape; it wrapped her like a shroud and her frail frame became lost in the folds of the heavy fabric. Her narrow neck bowed under the weight of her hair, gathered up in a bun. She was one of those women whom the years desiccate, whose full forms waste away, whose skin withers and becomes so thin that it looks almost transparent. In the twilight of their existence, one can perceive a death mask on their faces. There was a time when she was not so sensitive to the cold, but with every passing year, she suffered the chill more and more.

What madness, really, to leave Vienna and her gilded salons for the dark forests of Styria! But nothing and no one had come to deter her from her project. She wanted to spend her final days where she had grown up. Since the death of her husband, this idea obsessed her. Like a fish swimming upstream, her mind returned constantly to the past, before her life as a married woman. After her marriage, she had left her father's castle, only to return on rare occasions. Her husband was not very impressed by rustic amusements. To die of boredom, that is what he said, he who loved nothing more than the bustling city and its society parties. Her father often came to

Vienna before a fall from his horse had sent him to his grave. Since then, a steward took care of the estate. In spite of her insistent relatives, she had refused to sell it. And then, Hans had been carried to the cemetery too. With her children married, becoming parents in turn, and visiting less and less often, she felt a kind of detached affection for her descendants. She lived with her memories. Her life as a woman, her life in Vienna, vanished under a veil of fog that got thicker every day. Only her younger years lived on in her mind. Specifically the summer when she was nineteen.

Greta snapped her out of her reverie: The carriage was ready, Madame could leave. The poor girl was not looking forward to keeping her mistress company in the old castle that she imagined was as dull and boring as death. But the wages offered, and the promise of letting her go as soon as a local replacement was found, had won over her reluctance. Countess Rammstein responded with a nod, cast one last glance at this room that she had lived in for 30 years and left with no regrets.

On the ground floor, lined up in the entrance hall, the servants awaited her. She spoke to each of them and, without further ado, climbed into the carriage. Once inside, she spread a blanket over herself, put her feet on the heater and let her mind wander. She was reliving the excitement that filled her during her first trip, coming the other way. She was joining her future husband and her future home. It was high time that she marry; in a few years, no man would want her. Her father was getting on and only a marriage could assuage his worries. His daughter had lived for too long in the castle surrounded by dark woods with too many memories clinging like ivy to its gray stones. Therefore, he decided to step back into the world. They went all over Styria, to all the *Schloss*, the castles of the region. From balls to dinners, from dinners to hunting parties, their paths crossed that of Hans, Count Rammstein. Laura's tragic beauty melted the soul of this hardened bachelor and he brought her to Vienna to wed. At the time of his death, he loved her as much as the first day he had seen her.

She would rather die than admit it, but she had forgotten Hans' face. Moreover, it was terribly difficult to remember those of her children. On the other hand, she could describe Carmilla in a heartbeat. She still felt her locks of hair running through her fingers; she clearly saw the shadow of her eyelashes on her cheeks blushing with excitement. The image troubled her. She brought her hand to her heart as if she could slow its rhythm. Greta glanced at her in surprise, briefly wondering what thoughts were arousing the Countess. The mind of old people are like those of children: whimsical and baffling. Laura caressed her throat where the veins pulsed. Nothing remained of those mortal kisses, not the slightest trace. She would have liked to keep the stigmata of that forbidden embrace in her flesh. On the advice of Baron Vordenburg, the priest had burned all of Carmilla's personal effects. Only the memory of her remained. Laura, Countess Rammstein, had chosen to end her days there to be closer to her. The world no longer interested her. She felt her life leaving her and her strength abandoning her, like in the past when Carmilla had visited her, but now only the insult of time was responsible for this failing. Forty long years had passed since those ghastly events. Were they worth reliving? Nothing was less sure.

They stopped over at Mürzzuschlag and again at Leoben; the deeper the carriage penetrated into Styria, the gloomier Greta's face became. An ocean of trees covered the land, pierced here and there by a village of peasants who gaped at their passing. Fog surrounded them until late in the morning and when, by chance, the sun managed to break through, they gazed at woods as far as the eye could see. Laura, however, became more excited the closer they got, her emotion casting an odd glow into her wilted cheeks. She craned her neck to watch the countryside and constantly asked the coachman when they would arrive.

Finally, one morning, he announced that it would be their last day of traveling. Greta sighed in relief, dreaming of a warm fireplace and a comfortable bed instead of sleeping in one of the inns haunted by drafts of air and austere, peasant

81

faces. At a turn in the road, they came in view of the estate. Countess Rammstein told them to stop and she climbed out; Greta grumbled after her. The imposing castle stood out on the horizon. Its towers rose above the surrounding hills, cut out of the pale sky, as the sun struggled to break through the veil of clouds. The road wound up to the foot of the *Schloss*, skirted the moat, and then crossed a river before disappearing into the forest. The Countess sighed with joy at the sight of the familiar moat where swans used to swim and the lowered drawbridge that seemed to be waiting for her. The gothic bridge that spanned the river looked the same as in her memories and, for an instant, she even heard the tumult of a hunt in full swing. Like an echo. Again, her heart beat faster. Greta was jumping in place to warm herself; the humidity penetrated their clothes and a film of moisture lay on their coats. If they watched the ancient edifice any longer, they would be soaked. The Countess must have felt the cold infusing her old bones since she waved to the coachman to get ready to leave. By the time they got to the drawbridge, the steward was standing before the door flanked by a few servants. Greta had the distinct impression that they looked, more or less, alike, the same worn face, the same thick blood in their veins. What a dismal place!

The steward had taken great pains to make the castle welcoming: a fire burned in the fireplace, the copper and the brass handles sparkled. While the servants brought the trunks to the rooms, Countess Rammstein made a tour of the castle. With Greta at her heels, she inspected the kitchens, the annexes and the upstairs at the slow, steady pace of an old woman with aching bones. The great hall was warming, even though its hunting decorations would outrage a Viennese salon, with a view of the country through the wide windows overlooking the moat. In the long, unoccupied rooms lingered a musty smell that wrinkled Greta's nose. The Countess was supposed to stay in her father's room, but she stood a long time in the doorway of a huge room decorated with a tapestry of Cleopatra. At last, she closed the door, almost with regret, and continued her inspection.

The following days were very busy. They had to unpack the trunks, rearrange the rooms and, perhaps, think about modernizing a few things. Laura seemed to come to life in this environment. She started looking for a female companion to replace Greta, who was not hopeful. Who would want to get put away here? But the Countess was old, a little patience was needed.

The day after her arrival, she went back to Carmilla's room. Every day, she lingered a little longer in the room full of memories. Strange dreams inhabited her sleep. One night, she dreamed that she was swimming in cold, black waters, swimming without being able to stop because as far as the eye could see she was surrounded by cliffs on all sides. Her strength was failing; several times she thought she saw the grinning face of Death in the water. Suddenly a soft, warm wave engulfed her and lifted her out of the river. Carmilla's long hair, as if it had a life of its own, coiled around her hips until their bodies were touching and their breath mingled together. They floated between the sky and the water, between life and death. Carmilla cried tears of blood; Laura closed her eyes, bent over rosy cheeks and... she woke up with a metallic taste in her mouth. She was shivering under her down duvet. Was this what it meant to grow old? To feel the cold of the grave gradually infuse you, worm itself into your flesh, into your heart? Was Carmilla also feeling the terrible cold, the cold of death? Was she searching for a little heat? With this thought, her eyes filled with tears. Her sorrow lasted for days; she lost sleep and her appetite; she became numb to the world. Greta turned gloomy since the Countess stopped talking about finding a replacement, sometimes even looking at her as if she had forgotten who she was. The servants exchanged troubled whispers and anxious glances. They tried to convince her to walk a little on the grounds to admire the fall colors. She refused. Greta offered to read to her since her eyes tired quickly.

She refused this too; nothing interested her. She just showed up for meals and then disappeared upstairs, calling on them only to put more logs on the fire.

One day, while she was lying in Carmilla's room, she nodded off, lulled by the purring fire and the patter of rain against the windows. The mist of sleep enwrapped her and dragged her back through the years. It was the same room, but washed in the summer sun. Laura, not yet twenty years old, was standing with Carmilla before the window as the old Countess in her armchair watched them. The two young girls were laughing, their giggles fluttering off like butterflies. Carmilla stepped closer to Laura and touched her face or her hair. Their conversation drowned in the moving waters of the dream. Laura blushed, then her body drooped and she leaned toward her companion before catching herself and straightening up, standing properly. Carmilla was prey to an intense restlessness, as if, somewhere in the depths of her soul, a dam was threatening to burst. The two young ladies stepped away from each other and back together like two dancers repeating the same movements. Then Laura smiled one last time and left her guest's room. Once alone, Carmilla took a notebook, ink and quill from her trunk. She sat at the desk and wrote for a long time. The Countess wanted to get up so she could read over her shoulder but she was stuck in the armchair. She saw only her back and her hair, untied and brushing the floor. Then someone knocked at the door and Carmilla hurried to close the notebook and hide everything in the desk before going to open it. Her dress grazed Laura's as she passed by...

There was a knock at the door. "Madame, your tea is ready."

Greta's voice snapped her out of her reverie and brought her back to the cold, sad light of autumn. In a daze she looked around, taking a minute to pull herself together. The fire was dying in the hearth; it had stopped raining; but the heavy gray clouds were still darkening the sky. Night was coming on. She was breathing hard as if she had just come back from a long run.

84

"Madame? Is everything all right?"

"I'm coming."

At this very moment, Laura felt a loathing at the idea that Greta would enter this room. On leaving, she took care to lock the door.

That evening, buried under her blankets, she dreamed again the same dream or memory. She had never seen Carmilla write. She had also never seen that notebook. She could swear to it.

She lost herself in memory and the years vanished. The summer when she was nineteen had ended as she stood before the drawbridge with her father and Mesdemoiselles Perondon and Lafontaine. Baron Vordenburg and the priest were coming to meet them. They went upstairs in single file. The envoy of God entered Carmilla's room first, followed by the Baron while the rest of the group remained by the door. When Vordenburg opened the windows, the wind rushed in. A few dead leaves whirled around. The priest, armed with a vial of holy water and his faith, started cleansing the room of the mark of the vampire. He tore the sheets off the bed and threw them on the floor. A powdered smell of violets wafted up before being chased away by the breeze. The heady odor beset them again when he opened Carmilla's trunk. Under the usual personal effects were hidden the dresses of a courtesan, silk and lacy veils, brocade skirts and embroidered corsets, all of which joined the sheets. Then on that heap of precious clothes, they tossed her writing materials, an ivory comb with a few hairs still in it, a small perfume bottle of Bohemian garnet, a pearl necklace, satin ribbons, a mask of black velvet...

The intoxicating odor of decadence filled the room. Laura, against her will, pictured Carmilla in these clothes. The image aroused her soul and made the blood in her veins well up. Sorrow, disgust and fascination merged together and made her dizzy. Her rapid breathing alarmed her father who looked at her worriedly and took her hand. She squeezed it gratefully. Outside, the wind howled and the clouds amassed. A rumbling thunder reached their ears. The priest was using his holy water like a censer, a few sacred drops falling to the floor at every shake. The storm was closing in, swelling up and the sky darkened as if night came early. The man of God raised his voice over the din of unleashed elements. With the Baron chiming in they finished the ritual. Just as they were pronouncing the final words lightening ripped through the sky and lit up the room. With a frightening roar the clouds parted. And Laura wept with the heavens.

She remembered this scene like it was yesterday. She stood in the doorway for a long time, watching the servants carry away Carmilla's possessions to be burned. Before leaving they opened every drawer to make sure that nothing was left behind.

No trace of a notebook.

She went over it again and again when she went to bed. Ideas slipped into her mind like a sliver under the skin. This notebook existed, Laura was sure of it. It was not a dream but a reflection of the past. Morpheus took her away and sprinkled her dreams with violets and sparkling garnets. She danced with a Carmilla dressed in lace on a brocade carpeted floor. The morning found her as weary as after a night or waltzing or making love. She drifted a moment on the shores of sleep before waking up completely. A feeble ray of light escaped through the curtains, the first for a long time.

She could take a short walk outdoors, breathe in the earthy smell of the forest. Pretend, at least, to have a little interest in something else. Pull the wool over her eyes, if only for a moment. People were starting to look at her suspiciously, whispering behind her back. Not that she cared what they thought, but she feared that they would write to her children to tell them that her mental health was failing. And they might decide to take her back to Vienna. She would rather die on the spot. Therefore, she got dressed to take a walk. She choose a thick, velvet dress and Greta went with her. She lingered over every step, thinking about the notebook. What if it was some-where? How to find out? She soon felt that she was wasting her time scampering along the dirt paths. Using the overcast sky as an excuse she went back to the castle and as soon as her gloves were off she went upstairs.

She entered Carmilla's room, aroused like for a romantic rendezvous. As the fire purred in the hearth she flopped into the armchair and waited. And she waited. Nothing happened. Sleep did not come, nor Carmilla's shade, not even the scent of violets. Too nervous to doze off she became frustrated. She had been hoping with all her heart to find yesterday's en-chantment and see Carmilla again. Her thoughts were astir with impatience. Then one idea became obvious to her. She scurried down the stairs as fast as her old legs could carry her, called the servants and told them she wanted to move her room.

They did not try to discourage her but her caprice dis-turbed them. They had to rearrange some furniture to fit all her things, which took them all the next day. An eternity. The Countess spent the time walking outdoors.

When night fell, she went to bed with the eagerness of a young bride. She abandoned herself to sleep with delight. And Carmilla was there. It was evening; she heard her talking in front of the door with Laura, then the sound of a key turning the lock. Carmilla leaned against the doorframe. God, how pale she was! She was panting as if impassioned. Tears glis-tened in her eyes and rolled down her cheeks; she dried them with the back of her hand. Instead of a woman's usual prepa-rations for bed, she pulled out of her trunk a long, black dress that she laid on the bed. Laura's heart got drunk on the violet perfume. Carmilla took off her clothes; her petticoat slipped to the floor. She was nude. The flickering candles cast dancing shadows on her skin; her body quivered. She leaned over the bed, giving the Countess a view of her full breasts, her hair draping her hips and grazing the bedspread. The old woman was barely breathing. She had the fierce desire to pull her over, feel her hair's caress, bury her face against her heart. In her body, withered by the years, arose a strong vibration, the kind only extinguished by an embrace or by death. And then, an instant later, Carmilla donned her silk dress, her form turned hazy and she vanished in the shadows.

The Countess was awakened by the cold. The fire was waiting to be rekindled. The duvet was lying on the floor, along with her nightgown. The sheets were not enough to keep her warm; she was shivering. When she realized that she was nude, she blushed. The cold mottled her shriveled skin where the knotty veins pulsed and her heart was beating too fast for a woman of her age. Never had she felt so alive, as if a new lifeblood was flowing through her age-worn body. She remembered nothing except her dream and the strong desire she had felt.

Her arthritis made it difficult for her to dress. Then she rang for Greta to light the fire and asked for tea to be brought to her room. The day passed in a kind of fog. She forced herself to go outside and play her role of dowager. The walk cleared her mind a little but was tiresome. She smiled at the thought of sleeping as soon as darkness fell.

From now on, she lived only during the few hours of the night. She dove into sleep with delight and saw Carmilla again. She could not touch her but she could get intoxicated on her perfume, tremble when her hair or lace brushed by her, shiver when she heard Carmilla whisper her name. She disappeared often and came back with rosy cheeks and the hem of her silk dress muddied as if she had taken a walk outside. Sometimes, she felt her tossing and turning in bed, groaning as if under terrible torture or in excessive passion. Some nights Carmilla wept in bed. Laura listened to her heart broken by a sorrow that she could not console. The unbridgeable gulf of death and time separated them. The Countess would have given anything to travel back. She imagined slipping into Carmilla's room, despite the locks and rules, to bring her the warmth that the dead need so desperately. Oh, how she knew now that her time was coming! And once in a while, instead of disappearing into the night, Carmilla wandered through the hallways of the sleeping castle. She came back from these nocturnal strolls with a sparkling eye, unkempt hair and glistening lips.

And, of course, there was the notebook. A day did not pass without Carmilla writing. Afterward, she would carefully hide it away, out of sight of curious eyes.

The echoes of the past rose up haphazardly, in no particular order. Carmilla appeared to her thrilled, merry or in distress.

The Countess became obsessed with the notebook. She searched the room in the mad hope that it had escaped the priest's destruction. To no avail. She started over, resolved to have a carpenter come and check the woodwork. There might be a hiding place known only to Carmilla. Finding someone took a few days and the wait seemed endless, which made the disappointment even greater. Then, one night, she saw Carmilla grab a small pair of scissors, cut a lock of her hair and place it in the notebook. Her hands were shaking so much that she dropped it. She picked it up, unlocked her door and went into the hallway. She came back empty-handed, her face moistened by tears and her lips reddened by blood.

Laura's heart jumped so wildly that she woke up. A moonless night surrounded the castle. In the fireplace a few embers glowed; sunrise was still far off. Her excitement kept her from falling back to sleep. The notebook was somewhere, most probably in her old room when she was a girl. She was burning with impatience. Without a second thought, she got up, grabbed a candle and scurried down the hallway, her long, white nightgown floating around her frail form. She was like a ghost.

The place was exactly as she had left it years ago. A fine dust lay upon the draperies, the armchairs, the bedspread. She glanced around the room before closing her eyes and putting herself in Carmilla's place. She imagined her approaching the bed, her bare feet sliding across the parquet, leaning over, short of breath, the notebook clutched to her chest... The Countess' heart was like a wild horse bolting away from its loosened reins. She almost fainted, then she opened her eyes. She knew! Without hesitation she went to the bed and slipped her hand between the mattress and the frame. A cloud of dust spit out and made her cough. When her fingertips felt a thin, worn cover, tears were dripping down her cheeks.

With a trembling hand she pulled out the old, red leather notebook... Stricken with emotion she sat, almost fell, down. She brought the candle close to read. When she opened it, the scent of violets drifted out, as thin as a dying man's breath. A lock of braided hair served as a page marker. With a knot in her throat she started to read.

Carmilla's journal started thus:

"I remember that night long ago when I saw her for the first time. Her child-like features embodied a bewitching beauty. Her nature lived up to all her promises and even more. She is beautiful. A beauty to die for or to damn a saint. But I, who already lie in the grave, whose soul is already damned, what more do I have to lose?"

(English adaptation by Michael Shreve)

CAPTAIN VAMPIRE

Boris Liatoukine a.k.a. "Captain Vampire" is the hero of a novel by Marie Nizet (1859-1922) published in 1879. Born in Belgium, Nizet was educated in Paris and wrote her remarkable story at age 19, benefiting from the advice and knowledge of some Romanian friends. The mysterious Captain Liatoukine is an ageless man, pale, with feline eyes and superhuman powers. The legends claim he died and rose three times. Captain Vampire appears not to feed on the blood but the life-force of his victims. This new story, written by Matthew Baugh, taking place in the 16th century in the vast Russian plains, sees Liatoukine's path cross that of several other legendary figures of fantasy literature...

Matthew Baugh: *Quest of the Vourdalaki*

Ukraine, June 13, 1598

'Neath the light of the half-moon we rode, galloping across the steppe with reckless speed, as if pursued by the hordes of Hell itself. But we were not pursued, we were the pursuers—*we* were the riders of Hell.

I sat astride a great black courser as gaunt as death with eyes that blazed fiery red. To my left galloped Hella on a steed that matched mine, her naked body gleaming milk-white in the moonlight. To my left, Vseslav ran in the form of a great, lean wolf. Behind us came nine more mounted *vourdalaki*. It was a joyous experience for me, who had been a Cossack in life.

Riding the Steppe had been my delight, and one I had missed since joining the ranks of the undead.

Our horses were fleeter and more tireless than any mortal steeds. Yet, for all that, we could not gain on the two riders who fled before us. We had pursued them for hours, but they continued tirelessly. One of the men truly was a sorcerer, or an alchemist, or something of the sort. Vseslav himself wielded dark magics and he made a great deal of these distinctions, but they all blurred together for me.

Wrecking the sorcerer's wagon and slaughtering his servants had been child's play, but he had picked up a traveling companion, a fine gentleman with a pair of geldings that could run like the wind.

"They are slowing," Gorcha cried. "Their horses are tiring."

"Not soon enough," Hella shrieked over the sound of the wind. "Behold, they come to Father Dnieper!"

At the sight of the great river, Vseslav gave a terrible howl and pulled up. We who were his lackeys reined in also and formed a circle around him. Vseslav stood, and was in a moment a tall, fierce old man wearing a wolfskin around his shoulders. His eyes, however, remained those of the wolf.

"Why do we stop?" Gorcha asked. He was an old man with a face so stern that he must have been a horror, even in life.

"Listen!" the old wolf replied.

We did. After a moment my preternatural hearing caught the sound of human revelry, laughter, music, songs... Cossack songs.

"We are near the Zoporoghian Sich," Vseslav said. "We can follow no further."

Hella grinned and tossed back her long red hair.

"Let me go," she said. "I'm not afraid of any man, be he Cossack or the Tsar himself." She made an eerily beautiful sight standing there, her flesh smooth and perfect except for one purple scar on her neck. I certainly would have been tempted to follow her to my doom when I was a living man.

Of course, now all I could manage was a kind of nostalgic appreciation.

"No," Vseslav said. "We will not act openly."

"Then, what?" Gorcha asked.

"One of us will go into the camp, posing as a mortal."

"Who?" Hella asked.

I was wondering that too, but I kept my mouth shut. Such work was dangerous and I was too obvious a choice for comfort.

"I will go, Master," Gorcha said. "I will tear the man's throat out and bring you back his head on a pike."

That was typical of Gorcha, who was arrogant to the point of idiocy. I don't know how the old bastard had become one of us but suspected it was because he was too mean-spirited and contrary to stay in the grave like a proper corpse.

"Yvgeni," Vseslav said.

"Yes, Lord?" I replied trying to keep trepidation from my voice.

"You were a Cossack in life, were you not?"

"I *am* a Cossack, Lord."

"Anything you once were, you ceased to be when I claimed you."

"Alright then, I'm *not* a Cossack," I said.

Vseslav glared at me, then laughed.

"Well, it is my pleasure that you become one again. You have the clothes and the saber. More than that, you know their ways."

"Lord, my steed cannot cross Father Dnieper."

Vseslav nodded thoughtfully. Drawing his sword he struck the head off my horse. I rolled clear as the beast dissolved into smoke and ash. Gorcha chortled, Hella threw back her head in laughter and my Lord pointed his weapon at my unbeating heart.

"Have you any other objections?" he asked.

"None, Lord."

"I have another minion in the camp," he said. "His name is Liatoukine. When you are there, make yourself known to him. The two of you shall stay close to the foreigner."

"You wish him dead, Master?"

"It is less important that he die than that he be prevented from reaching Lysa Hora by St. John's Eve," he said. "If you can kill him, of course, that is always to be preferred."

I nodded and set out at a run. Behind me I heard the laughter of my kith and kin. Vampires are not good comrades, I have found, and are petty in the extreme. I had preferred the company of my steed—foul-tempered demon that he had been—to any of them. Vseslav should not have treated him so. A Cossack would never have treated any horse like that; not even a Hell-horse.

The river flowed strongly and was deeper than a man is tall, but that was no obstacle to me. Some of the undead cannot cross running water, but my kind knows no such limitation. I doffed my boots and strode through, gripping the rocks with my toes.

The Sich was located on an island in the midst of the river. Cossacks have no fortifications so they secure themselves against attack by Tatar or Pole by making the river their moat and changing the location of their base secretly and often. I was sitting on the bank, wringing out my clothes when a sentry came upon me.

The man—a veritable giant, more than six and a half feet tall and easily three hundred pounds—glared down at me and leaned on his musket.

"You did not cross on the ferry," he said.

"What way is that for a Cossack to cross a river?" I said. "I swam."

"A brave boast, if true," he replied.

"True enough, as you can see," I said, squeezing several cups of water from my sleeve."

"You say you are a Cossack?"

I nodded.

"I have not seen your face in the Sich before."

"I am a Cossack of the Don," I said, "come from Muskovy to visit my southern cousins."

The giant grunted, amused.

"Still," he said, "I must be certain. Is there anyone here who can vouch for you?"

"Liatoukine," I said.

The big man, whose name was Ayub, took me through the center of the camp. Everywhere I looked, men gathered around the campfires to sing and dance, to wrestle, to gamble and to drink. The corn brandy and vodka flowed freely and I felt both sad and nostalgic that I no longer had a taste for any drink that was not red and warm.

After a time, we came to a knot of men who were amusing themselves in a novel way. They had taken a Jew and stood him against a tree with his sidelocks pinned out to the sides with daggers. While the man stood trembling, the Cossacks took turns throwing axes at him to try and sever his locks. The officer supervising this was a slender, pale and elegant man who lounged off to one side, occasionally offering words of encouragement to his men. I knew him for a vampire at a glance.

"Hey, brother knights," Ayub shouted, "I have something for you."

"A foundling?" the vampire asked, rising and striding toward us.

"One 'Yvgeni' by name," Ayub replied. "He claims to be a Cossack of the Don and says that you will vouch for him."

"Yes," he said looking me over.

"In that case, I leave him to you." Without waiting for a reply the giant turned and strode away.

"He doesn't like you, that one," I said.

Liatoukine sniffed. He glanced at his men who had resumed their axe-throwing game.

"What do I care? He is a lout and a peasant."

"He is a Cossack," I said. We are all brothers and nobles to each other."

"You bristle," he said, his tone ironic. "Why? Human associations mean nothing to us."

"We have a mission," I said. "Two men came into the Sich earlier tonight. They were fleeing from our master."

"I know the men," Liatoukine said. "The Koshovoi Ataman ordered them placed in the stocks. Come, I will show you."

He strode off and, after a last glance at his men and their game, I followed.

"You don't approve?" Liatoukine asked when I caught up. His voice told me he was amused.

"What did the Jew do?"

"He's a Jew; what other reason do Cossacks need?"

I shrugged; for what he said was true. There were usually quite a few Jewish merchants who made camp near the Sich to sell food or corn brandy, or clothing, or any of a hundred other useful things. This worked to everyone's advantage; the Cossacks got the supplies and the Jews were paid handsomely, for Cossacks cultivate a healthy disregard for money and usually pay with whatever they have in their pockets, even if that far exceeded the asked-for price. The problem came when a Cossack wanted strong drink, but had lost all his money gambling or spending freely. At that point, the Jew became—in his eyes—a devious, dishonest thief.

I had never cared for this. The Jews I have known seemed fair-minded, harmless folk. Most Cossacks despise them for not being warlike, but it always seemed to me their only real sin was being foolish enough to do business with such a dangerous and drunken lot. I say "drunken," for finding a sober Cossack in the Sich is as rare as finding a goat eating a wolf.

I was caught up enough in my thoughts that I didn't pay much attention to the merry antics of the brothers as we passed to the stocks, which stood a little away from the camp. I saw that the Koshovoi Ataman had given them the same penalty that is given to a Cossack who steals. Not only were they bound in the stocks, but a heavy cudgel hung from a tree near-by. Any Cossack passing by was welcome to strike them with the weapon. If they were still alive in the morning, they would be released.

"Your course is clear," Liatoukine said, gesturing to the cudgel. It seemed to amuse him to pass the duty to me rather than take it on himself. That made him the kind of officer who I had never cared for in life. In fairness, I have to say they are more like vampires than Cossacks. The riders of the steppes are brutal, but they are seldom so petty.

I picked up the knout and moved to the stocks to face the two. They were an interesting pair, finely dressed in some foreign fashion. The first was a bearded fellow, tall and thick with muscle and fat. The other was also tall, but as lean as his companion was heavy. He had a clean shaven face and mismatched eyes, one brown and the other green.

"I suppose you've come to kill us," the bearded man said. He had a deep voice and sounded more weary than frightened.

"Close your eyes and I will make it quick as I can," I replied.

"I don't suppose it would make a difference if I told you that I came here seeking help to end a great evil, would it?" He studied my face for a moment, then sighed. "No, I suppose it wouldn't. You Cossacks aren't at all like I'd heard. You're more interested in your pleasure than in honor won in combat."

"Oh, you think so?" I said. My tone was a little heated, for his words stung the pride I still felt for this place.

"Do you tell me different?" he asked in earnest surprise, "then put down your club and listen to me."

His voice was made for giving speeches and intrigued me. I lowered the weapon and waited for him to say more. Liatoukine was less interested. He strode up to me and, with a growl of contempt, snatched the club from my hand and raised it.

"Ho, brother knight," a quiet voice said. Liatoukine and I both spun in surprise for it is seldom that one of the living comes upon our kind unheard.

The man we saw was tall and gaunt with age, with a gray mustache whose ends hung to his chest. He glowered at us from under shaggy brows with an expression both fierce and amused.

"What are their lives to you, Khlit?" Liatoukine demanded.

"Nothing," the old man replied, pulling out a corn-cob pipe and packing it with tobacco. "If you are bold enough to defy the Koshovoi Ataman, that is your affair."

"What do you say? He is the one who pronounced sentence on them."

"Aye," Khlit replied. "But that was before I spoke to them and heard their story. I think our leader will want to hear these words before they die. I have sent my foster son, Menelitza, to fetch him. But if you would see him disappointed when he comes..."

From the expression on Liatoukine's face, I could see that there was no love lost between him and the old Cossack. Khlit's face, by contrast, gave away nothing. His fierce expression was more a thing of habit than any emotion Liatoukine inspired. He lighted his pipe and stood there smoking.

"Very well," Liatoukine said, slimming back into his superior smile. "We shall see, Khlit *bogatyr*."

I peered closer at the old man. Was he truly a great hero, as the vampire named him? I had been away from the Sich for longer than I had realized, not to know the name of a *bogatyr*.

He was a striking figure in his boots of red Moroccan leather and pants of Nankin silk, spattered with pitch to show his contempt for appearances. His astrakhan hat was perched on the side of his head, revealing that his head was shaved, except for a long, gray topknot. It was his curved saber that captured my attention most. It was not the nearly straight and guardless *shasqua* favored by most Cossacks, nor the heavy

Polish saber with its knuckle-guard, but a scimitar of the Turkish pattern, beautifully made and—unless I missed my guess—of Damascus steel.

"It seems we have an interlocutor," the man with the mismatched eyes said. From the humor in his voice, it seemed to me that he considered the stocks to be only an inconvenience. His fat companion only grunted in reply.

After several moments, a handsome, dark-skinned youth appeared, leading a man in the regalia of the Koshovoi Ataman and a large group of Cossacks. The youth moved to stand at Khlit's side and the Ataman glanced first at them and then at me and Liatoukine.

"Poor timing for your sport, Boris Liatoukine," he said. "The *bogatyr* tells me these strangers bear listening to."

"I do not agree," Liatoukine said. "A sorcerer like this has the Devil's own tongue to seduce the ears of the innocent."

"A good thing that no one in this camp is innocent, hey?" Khlit asked, eliciting general laughter.

"I appreciate the opportunity to he heard, noble Cossacks," the heavy man interjected. "I would appreciate it more if I was free to stand and face you eye to eye."

"Well said," the Koshovoi Ataman said. "Sabalinka, cut them loose!"

A big man with yellow topknot and mustache stepped forward and drew the sword he kept slung across his back. This was a massive, two-handed weapon, straight and double edged. It seemed more a sword for a knight of old than the agile weapon of a Cossack and was clearly the source for the name "Sabalinka," which means "little sword." The muscular man hefted the weapon as if it weighed no more than a *shasqua* and swung it at the lynchpin. Wood split and shattered and the stocks came open, releasing the foreigners, who straightened, rubbing their necks.

"I thank you, noble Cossack," the bearded stranger said, raising his powerful voice.

"Tell us your story," the Koshovoi Ataman replied. "Then we will decide whether to help you or whether to give you to Ataman Liatoukine for his men to sport with."

The man nodded and looked out among the gathering. He had impressive charisma and seemed to catch and hold the gaze of every man there for an instant.

"Noble Cossacks," he said, "I am Quentin Moretus Cassave, of the Flemish lands many thousands of *versts* from your steppe. I am no sorcerer, as your esteemed Liatoukine has claimed, but merely a scholar."

That prompted rough chuckles and a few grumbles from some of the men. Scholars are not well thought of in the Sich. It's all well and good for the *batkos* in their monasteries to study the Holy Scriptures, but no Cossack would ever indulge in such effeminate practices. Scholarship was considered a particularly Polish sort of vice and was highly suspect. Cassave seemed to understand this and dropped his voice dramatically. Though he still made himself heard, every man there strained to catch his every word.

"I am no fighting man," he said. "I'm sure many of you have thought I would rather be in my comfortable home, poring over my books, and you're right. But in my studies I have become aware of a dark prophecy." He paused for a moment and looked across the silent assembly. This man might not claim to be a sorcerer, but with a few words he had captured the Cossacks with the magic of his speech.

"There is a mountain outside Kiev, so I have read," he continued. "It is a barren place, so unholy that not even trees or shrubs will grow there. It is said that the witches gather there each St. John's Eve to try to raise their dark master, Satan himself, known in pagan times as Chernabog!"

A murmur went through the crowd, and I saw more than a few of the men cross themselves.

"*Lysa Hora!*" one man said. "I grew up near that bald mountain and what he says is true."

"You see?" Cassave thundered. "On St. John's Eve, when all Christian folk are home abed, the witches and sorcerers gather to practice their unspeakable rituals and pray their abominable prayers. On that night, the spirits of the dead rise up to share an unspeakable orgy with all the fiends of Hell."

"This man is playing on your superstitions," Liatoukine cried. There was a touch of anxiety in his voice, for he and I both knew that the stranger was uncomfortably close to the truth. His story was inaccurate, but only in the details and those he was probably shading for dramatic effect.

"Superstitions?" Cassave boomed. "Is the werewolf that runs the steppe at night a superstition? What about the vampire with her seductive song who slips behind the rider on his horse and sucks the blood from the back of his neck? No, noble Cossacks, these things are not superstitions... and neither is the prophecy."

"What is the prophecy?" a big voice demanded and I saw the speaker was the giant Ayub.

"What is the prophecy?" Cassave repeated. "Only that this year—Anno Mundi 7065[7]—the ritual will succeed. The witches will raise Chernabog from Hell to shroud the land with perpetual night and to sit enthroned on the Bald Mountain, from whence he would rule the world."

"Preposterous!" Liatoukine protested. "Brothers, what this man says is superstitious nonsense! Even if it weren't, why come to the Sich? Would not a foreigner go to the Tsar and his court in Muscovy where there are other scholars to listen to him?"

"I did," Cassave said, his voice quiet again. "I went to the Muscovites and told them my story. Alas, they said the same thing that the noble Liatoukine says, that there are no vampires and werewolves, that the sorcerers do not gather on the Bald Mountain on St. John's Eve and that only superstitious fools would believe such a tale."

---

[7] Cassave is figuring this by the Byzantine Calendar which started counting years at the supposed date of Creation. It was used in Imperial Russia until the 19th century reforms of Peter the Great.

There was another murmur through the crowd, for Cassave's words hit home. The Muscovite court has always seemed far off and foreign here in the Ukraine, and these days even more since the nobles had given up speaking Russian in favor of French. To hear that they dismissed the beliefs of the steppe-dwellers as foolishness was no surprise.

"I came to the Zoporoghian Cossacks for two reasons," Cassave continued. "First, because I knew that you would understand that these things are a real and present danger. Second, because I had been told that no one but the Cossacks of the Steppe would have the courage to take up sword and ride against the forces of darkness."

He paused and glared around. For all that he was a scholar, his expression was as fierce as that of Vseslav himself.

"Was I told true?" he demanded.

There was more murmuring. Cossacks are not cowards. And had the challenge been to ride into battle or even to certain death they would not have balked. The supernatural is quite another matter, though.

"My godfather will lead and my sword is with him!" young Menelitza said. He strode to stand at Cassave's side, Khlit following a little more slowly.

Cockcrow saw a little band of ten Cossacks and two foreigners heading north, a modest increase to the group Khlit, Menelitza and Ayub had started. Ivan Sabalinka had joined us, as had Zaroff, an aristocratic Cossack who preferred a Tatar warbow to the set of pistols most of us carried. He was attended by man as huge as Ayub whose name was Ivanushka. Liatoukine and I had joined the expedition, of course, as had two of his men, the stout Taras and his older brother, Doroscha. With Cassave and his companion, whom he called "Magister," we were twelve strong.

"Like the Holy Apostles," Ayub said. "It is a good omen."

I was not so optimistic. A group of Holy Apostles ought not have *two* Iscariots.

We rode hard that day for we had 500 *versts* to travel and only nine days to do it. I was surprised to see how well the two foreigners kept up. The Magister rode like a Cossack and never seemed to tire. Cassave, while not a natural horseman, bore up uncomplaining, apparently through sheer force of will. I rode close to them, remembering my master's instructions.

That night, we huddled around our little campfire, sharing a simple dinner and the small daily ration of corn brandy.

"Why such a small fire?" Cassave asked. His tone was not complaining but curious.

"A big fire would give away our position," Zaroff said.

"The undead don't need a fire to know where we are," Ayub said with a shiver.

"More light might be a good idea," Cassave said. "These creatures thrive in darkness."

"The fire is small so the Tatars do not see us," Menelitza said. "If they do, we'll have more than vampires to worry about."

"I must say, I admire the ways of the Cossacks," Cassave said. "They are very different from the ways of my homeland, though. For example, in France, a soldiers' camp is a place of discipline and drilling. Your Sich is so much livelier."

"There is time enough for swinging swords when there are heads to split," Ayub said and several of the others chuckled in assent.

"Very true," Cassave said, seriously. "I am certainly impressed with how quickly you go from revelry to a disciplined advance.

"It is the way of the Cossacks," Ayub said. "In times of war, our whole life is the campaign. In times of peace, we celebrate being alive."

"Your celebration is also different than I am used to," Cassave said.

"How so?" Menelitza asked. "Don't French soldiers gamble, drink and dance?"

"Certainly," the scholar replied. "But in France, they tend to do those things in the company of pretty girls."

"Women have no place in the Sich," Khlit said, taking his pipe from his mouth.

"True!" Taras cried, springing to his feet. "Home and hearth are death to a Cossack, and a pretty girl's arms are damnation. Too much time with women steals a man's strength. What a man needs are a fast horse, a good sword, the company of his brothers, and plenty of Polish throats to cut!"

This brought cries of approval from the assemblage, though Sabalinka remained silent and Menelitza blushed. I noticed Khlit's stern eyes on his godson as well and wondered what the old wolf was thinking.

My thoughts were interrupted by a woman's voice raised in song. It was an old ballad, lonely and beautiful, and the singer had a voice to break a man's heart. The Cossacks were held silent, staring into the darkness.

"*Vourdalak*," Ayub finally said, crossing himself. "No living woman could sing such a song."

He was right, of course. I recognized the voice as Hella's and I saw lust blossom on the other faces in the firelight. They were thinking of slender arms entwining them, of red lips to kiss and milky skin to caress.

It is an effective technique, though not one I particularly approve of. I am enough of a Cossack still to prefer the honest shedding of blood in open combat to lying promises of love. And they are all lies, of course. No vampire I have ever known desires a lover, and certainly not a human one. For us, the only true passion is the hunt and the kill.

Khlit rose and kicked dirt on the fire.

"Doroscha, take the first watch. Ayub will relieve you at midnight."

The Cossacks slept—except for Liatoukine and myself, who pretended to sleep—until midnight, when Ayub roused the camp.

"Doroscha is gone!"

"Gone?" Taras yelled. "How can he be gone?"

"The vampires have taken him," Ayub said, making the sign of the cross.

"Bah!" Liatoukine said. "He was frightened of these children's stories and fled home with his tail between his legs."

"Have a care," Taras said, his hand on the hilt of his saber. "My brother is no coward and any man who calls him that will face my steel."

Liatoukine looked at him with an air of regal disdain. He did not touch his sword, but I knew that he could move with the speed of the undead. He could draw and strike Taras' head from his shoulders in less than the space of a heartbeat.

"Perhaps I spoke too soon," Liatoukine said. "Perhaps he went to take a piss and got lost. Perhaps he will be back any minute.

Taras' knuckles whitened on his sword haft and the fight seemed inevitable, then Khlit stepped between them fixing his wolf's gaze on first one then the other.

"There is no time to fight amongst ourselves," he said calmly. "Taras, at first light we shall find your brother. If he has been killed by an enemy, then Boris Liatoukine shall beg your pardon. If he has fled, you shall beg his."

"We should search for him now!" Taras said.

"No," Khlit said in a quiet but fierce voice. "If there are enemies abroad, human or devil, I do not want to meet them while we are scattered and stumbling in the dark."

"You sound more like an old woman than a Cossack!" Taras said. He moved to the place his horse was saddled and sprang on its back.

"Cossacks, we search for Doroscha!"

Several men started toward the horses but hesitated when Khlit drew his curved sword.

"Taras!" he shouted, pointing the blade at the mounted man. "Go and search, but no man from this camp goes with you; and whether you find your brother or not, do not come back."

Without a word, Taras wheeled his horse and rode into the night.

"Ayub and Menelitza, finish the watch," Khlit said. "From now on, no man watches alone. Beware of vampires coming in the form of our former comrades."

"What if Taras or his brother return, and they are still human?" Menelitza asked, gathering his weapons.

"Kill them," Khlit said. "Vampires and deserters deserve the same fate."

I sat up with them for the watch, as did Cassave.

"Your companion seems remarkable untroubled by all this," I said. "He never even stirred."

"The Magister is not bothered by much," he replied. "I only wish I had his calm."

"Feh!" Ayub said, and spit into the campfire. "A Cossack is calm in the face of death, but only a fool sleeps so soundly when the hordes of Hell are abroad."

"The Magister is no fool," Cassave replied with a soft chuckle. "He had taught me many secrets of the seen and unseen worlds, and I have only begun to touch the surface of his wisdom. If he sleeps, we can rest assured that there is no danger... at least, not to him."

"A strange man," I said. "How do you know you can trust him?"

"We have a bargain, he and I," Cassave said. "Besides, he is the one who gave me the means to our victory over Chernabog."

"A holy weapon?" Ayub asked.

Cassave's eyes twinkled with humor as he produced a slender silver urn from his robes. The bright metal was covered with mysterious glyphs that I could not read. In honesty, though, having never learned to read even my mother tongue, all letters are mysterious to me. I could only say for certain that it was not Russian writing.

"I will catch him in this," Cassave said.

I shook my head and Ayub laughed.

"Surely, the Prince of Darkness is too big to fit in such a little vessel?"

"Have you heard of the Jinn?" Cassave asked.

"I have," young Menelitza said. "The Turks and the Tatars speak of them. They are evil spirits made of smokeless fire who wander the Earth doing mischief. Their king is Satan, whom the Muslims call Iblis."

"We have another scholar among us," Cassave said in an appreciative tone. Menelitza bowed his head shyly and glanced at me and Ayub, no doubt worried that we would deem his knowledge effeminate.

"Tell me, mighty Cossack," Cassave continued, "is the campfire bigger than you or smaller?"

Ayub's forehead puckered in thought, something I suspect his brain was unaccustomed.

"Smaller," he said.

"And if we were to pile a dozen stout branches on the campfire... would it still be smaller?"

Ayub shook his head slowly with an expression that mingled suspicion and awe.

"No," Cassave said in an even tone with no hint of mockery. "It would be the same fire, but grown greater than any man. And if the fire should dwindle for lack of fuel?"

"It would become small," Ayub said, feeling his way through the question.

"And?" Cassave prompted.

"Small enough for your little pot..."

"Excellent!" Cassave said clapping the giant's shoulder heartily. Ayub beamed proudly and I could see that the foreigner had won him over.

"As it is with fire, so with the jinn," Cassave said.

"But how would you compel the Devil?" Menelitza asked. "Would that not be an act of dark sorcery?"

"One would think so," the scholar replied, "but that is not so. Do not the Tatars and the Turks tell how the wise King Solomon captured the jinn and bound them to lamps and rings and many other vessels?"

The youth nodded, a little uncertainly.

"It is not sorcery that will help us, but the holy wisdom of this man of God," Cassave said.

My companions were clearly impressed by the foreigner's words, but I was more suspicious than ever. For all his words flowed like honey, Cassave was no holy man.

We lost two more the next night. All the men slept soundly except for Zaroff and his servant, Ivanushka, who were on watch, and myself and Liatoukine, who feigned sleep.

Around midnight, Hella's sweet song was heard and the handsome Cossack picked up his bow and slipped away from the camp, forbidding his servant to follow. A short time later the singing stopped and Zaroff screamed in terror.

The camp roused in an instant. Khlit called for order but this did not stop Ivanushka from drawing his saber and racing into the dark to go to his master's air.

"Torches!" the old wolf shouted. "We follow but we stay together."

Each man lighted a brand and mounted his steed. It took us less than a quarter of an hour to find Ivanushka. The giant lay amid a jumble of rocks, his spine twisted so badly it was clear his back was broken.

"Where is your master?" Khlit demanded. "Why did he leave the camp?"

"It... it was the song..." Ivanushka said between gasps. "When I followed I saw him... with beautiful woman... skin as pale as the Moon..."

"Where?" Khlit repeated, but the giant fell silent and his eyes glazed over.

We searched for Zaroff but found only his Tatar warbow and quiver of arrows abandoned on the steppe.

"We should take these back to the Sich," Ivan Sabalinka said. "He would want his son to have them when he comes of age."

"I will carry them," I said. For the life of me (or whatever passes for life in my case) I couldn't say why I did that.

The next day we made good progress, but I could see that the days of hard riding and nights of fitful sleep were making the men haggard. I could see that this pleased Liatoukine, but my unbeating heart felt a touch of something—not sympathy perhaps, but nostalgia. These were brave men and riding with them made me think of my former life. I took no joy in the fact that they would all soon be dead.

In the early afternoon, Khlit called a halt.

"The Magister tells me that we will find something there that will help us." He pointed to a low mound in the distance.

"The *kurgan*?" Ayub asked. "Do we look to magic and ghosts to help us?"

In response, the old wolf spurred his horse and the rest of us followed. We were a little apprehensive for, while these ancient burial mounds are common on the steppe, there is something ominous about them. I told myself that nothing the *kurgan* could hold should frighten a creature of the night, but even a vampire can be superstitious, I suppose.

Someone had dug into the side of the mound, forming a chink in the rocks that led within. Khlit had no interest in entering the mound, however. He was much more interested in the massive hive than a colony of bees.

"There is your magic," Cassave said, laughing. "The same magic that Odysseus used against the sirens."

The men gathered bundles of tall grass and set the ends asmolder to lull the bees to sleep. Despite this, all were stung as they gathered handfuls of wax. I alone managed to avoid this on the pretext of taking the horses a safe distance away, and this proved most fortunate.

Cassave tended to the men afterwards, using the tip of a dagger to pluck out the stingers. Ivan Sabalinka's face twitched, more with annoyance than pain, as the scholar performed his ministrations. Menelitza took his turn with the exaggerated stoicism of a youth determined to prove his courage to his elders. Ayub's skin had turned bright red around the stings and his breathing was labored. Cassave showed concern over this, but the giant only laughed.

"All that I need is a healthy dose of corn brandy," he said.

Cassave took a small vial of some blue liquid from his robe and offered it to Ayub.

"It is not corn brandy, but I think you will like it."

Ayub sniffed the potion suspiciously, then drained it. He made a face as it went down, but that expression turned to one of wonder as the red blotches faded and his breathing returned to normal.

"By the Father and the Son," the big man said.

Cassave turned to Liatoukine only to be dismissed with a gesture of contempt.

"I am no weakling to fear the stings of insects," Liatoukine said.

"Bee venom is not to be scoffed at," the scholar said. "If I had not given Ayub my alchemic treatment, his throat would have closed and he could not have breathed."

The Cossack drew back his sleeve and held out an arm. I could see no less than half a dozen tiny stings embedded there, some still quivering.

"As you see, Boris Liatoukine is made of sterner stuff," he said.

"No redness... no swelling." Cassave said, half to himself. "I wonder..."

He brought the dagger to Liatoukine's arm as if to flick out the stings but instead plunged the tip deep into his flesh.

"Madman!" the Cossack shouted, leaping away and drawing his saber.

"Look!" Cassave held out the weapon for us to see. "There is no blood on the blade and none on Liatoukine's wound. I wondered why the beestings did not affect him and now I know. Boris Liatoukine is no living man!"

With a snarl of rage, Liatoukine stepped toward him but Khlit interposed himself with his own curved blade drawn.

"This man—this *foreigner*—lies!" Liatoukine shouted.

110

"He speaks truth." The Magister, silent until now, spoke in a calm voice. There was something unnaturally compelling about his words. I knew that I should leap to Liatoukine's defense but was so fascinated that I made no move.

"You should confess it," the Magister said. "It was a brilliant stroke... Who better than a Cossack to infiltrate a band of Cossacks? And you have none of the weaknesses that would betray so many of your kind. You walk in daylight... you bear the cross on your sword... you can even enter a church and receive the blessing of the *batkos*..."

"How do you know these things?" Liatoukine demanded. His outburst—and the truth it betrayed—startled me. I could see that Liatoukine also was shocked at his own words. How had this foreigner compelled him to say this?

"I remember now," Khlit said. "When I was a lad of sixteen, just come to the Sich, there was a Cossack who had murdered another. We gave him the traditional punishment by placing him under his victim's coffin and burying him alive in the same grave. I see that some men are too evil to remain in the ground."

"Fools!" Liatoukine snarled. "You simper on about good and evil, holy and unholy, but there are no such things. There are only the strong and the weak, and I am strong!"

He lunged at Khlit with a speed beyond human, yet the old wolf brought his blade up with such skill that he parried the blow. Menelitza sprang to his godfather's defense but Liatoukine leapt away with such speed that, to mortal eyes, he seemed to vanish.

I seized my sword hilt. I didn't want to help Liatoukine kill my brother Cossacks, but my duty was clear. Before I could draw, the Magister laid a hand on my wrist and I felt my resolve melt away.

Liatoukine slashed at Menelitza and the lad fell, badly wounded. Khlit sprang forward but even his skill was nothing to the vampire's speed. He disarmed the gray-haired warrior and sent him stumbling to the ground. But as Liatoukine raised his blade for the final blow, a shot rang out.

111

Boris Liatoukine staggered forward a pace, a look of astonishment on his face. Behind him I saw Ivan Sabalinka bolding a smoking pistol. Then Ayub leapt at him with a mighty roar, striking his head from his shoulders with a sweep of his saber.

We spent much of the afternoon gathering wood for a pyre which we built on top of the kurgan while Cassave tended to Menelitza's wounds and Khlit hovered nearby. The old wolf puffed his pipe stoically, but I could see he was stricken to the heart with worry for his godson.

"Who are you?" I asked the Magister when our tasks had taken us out of earshot of the others.

"Can't you guess?" he asked with a sly smile. "I'm certain you know my name."

That sent a feeling of cold through my blood. I chose not to voice my thoughts, preferring not to have my suspicion confirmed.

"What do you want?" I asked.

"I want nothing," the Magister replied. "My only joy is in helping others gain what they want. Take Cassave, for instance. He wanted knowledge and I gave it to him. From that grew his new desire to capture the gods of antiquity and keep them in vessels."

"Why does he want such a thing?"

"If you ask Cassave, he will tell you that man created the gods and not vice versa."

"Surely that is blasphemy," I said.

"How touching that a vampire should be concerned with that. I'm certain the theologians would agree with you and consign our good scholar to the flames. I am rather fond of theologians and their wisdom. In any case, Cassave says that the gods weaken and die when men cease to believe in them. But those who are not completely forgotten still possess power, and the man who catches them will have that power to use as he will."

"What does he want with such power?" I asked.

"I did not ask him."

"What Cassave says cannot be true," I said. "Man cannot create gods—certainly not the Almighty!"

"So you believe. Cassave believes otherwise."

"What do you believe?"

The Magister smiled.

"Cassave is a great scholar. I am very fond of scholars and their wisdom."

When we completed the pile of branches, we laid Liatoukine's head and body on it and set it ablaze. Having seen to that, we carried Menelitza to the yurt of a Tatar herdsmen only a few versts from the kurgan. Khlit gave the man gold coins and the promise of more when we returned. His grey eyes offered a different promise if Menelitza were to die.

We rode hard the rest of the day, hoping to make up the time we had lost.

We continued the rest of the way without incident and I began to wonder if we would make it. Vseslav's orders had been to stop Cassave from reaching Lysa Hora at any cost, but I wondered why he did not send help to me. Perhaps after seeing Liatoukine's fate, I was not eager to take these warriors on by myself, and the Magister now terrified me beyond measure. Hella sang to us every night but, with beeswax plugging their ears, the Cossacks slept soundly through her call.

When no attack came I wondered if my master expected me to slay the Cossacks myself. I doubted myself up to the task, and the thought of fighting the Magister filled me with dread. After our conversation, I feared the strange man as much as Vseslav himself.

At midday on the ninth day out of the Sich—the Eve of St. John's day—we caught our first sight of Lysa Hora. Normally it is not much as mountains go; a gently sloping dome bare of trees but green with grass and scrub brush. On this day, the clouds had gathered, thick and turgid, hiding the Sun and making noon feel like twilight. That low hanging sky was the deep green-purple of a bruise. No moisture fell from the clouds—if something as clean as rain could come from such a diseased sky—instead, they were lit from with by the dull red and fiery orange of unseen lightning.

Lysa Hora seemed almost to touch the lowest of the clouds and in that light seemed a blackened knob of bare stone.

Khlit called our little group to a halt and we gazed at the bald mountain. Finally, he turned to Cassave.

"Well, sorcerer? Where on this mountain would you have us go?"

"The top," Cassave said, pointing. "That is where Chernabog's followers will light their fires and dance. That is where the gate to Hell will open to let the dark god and his minions through."

"They have the high ground," the old wolf muttered. "That means we must charge them up the slope on spent horses."

"There is a better way," Cassave said. "I will tell them that I am a fellow acolyte of darkness, come to witness the advent of Chernabog."

Khlit stroked his moustache in thought then nodded.

"Close enough to the truth to be a good lie," he said.

"As we draw near the ceremony, you must steel your hearts," Cassave said looking at each of us in turn. "You will see things—witches and demons and all manner of fiends. Sky and earth will split asunder and fire shall rain upon you. You must keep courage and faith if you are to win your way through."

"Courage and faith?" Khlit said, raising his voice in a tone of disdain. "When has a Cossack ever needed to be reminded of these things? We live our lives in the hope of glorious death fighting the Poles and Tatars and other enemies of Christ. Do you think we will flinch at fighting his greatest foe?"

"I like that!" Ivan Sabalinka said. "We'll tweak his nose just like old St. Dunstan, by Harry!"

I thought it a peculiar oath, no doubt born of his distant homeland, but Ivan's words stirred my soul—or whatever passes for one in the undead.

We dismounted and Khlit rationed out the last loaf of black bread and the last bottle of corn brandy. Ayub took a great mouthful of the first and washed it down with a lengthy swallow from the latter before passing them to Sabalinka.

"Noble Cossacks," Cassave said. "Have a care. This fine liquor is good for celebrating, but it does not lead to sound judgment."

"Sound Judgment?" Ayub roared with laughter. "Scholar, we are storming the gates of Hell. What use have we for sound judgment?"

All of us ate and drank until the bread was gone and the bottle empty; all save the Magister who stood apart from the group and stared at the mountain. This puzzled me and I went to him with a cup of the corn brandy but he shook his head."

"You will not drink with men who ride to their deaths with you?" I asked, a little angrily.

"*You* ask me that, Yvgeni?" he asked with his sly smile. "I wonder where your allegiances lie. Do you know any more?"

Having no answer for that, I glared at him, then drained the liquor from the cup.

"Your friend, Liatoukine can touch the cross and you cannot," he said.

"He is not my friend."

"Do you know how he does this?"

"He does not believe that anything is holy or unholy," the Magister said. "For him, there is only what he wants. The one who cannot see a difference between good and evil is dangerous. I prefer to be honest about my nature. It is... cleaner."

It was dark when we reached the slopes of Lysa Hora, and so dark that the humans could barely see one another—could see nothing at all save for the bonfire on the summit where the witches held their Sabbat. I, on the other, hand could see everything. Around us a great invisible procession of ghosts and infernal spirits rose and drifted past us. Another flicker of heat lightning illuminated the mountain. The phantoms remained invisible to my companions but the light illuminated the revelers around the fire. Vampires and humans, dwarfish creatures and misshapen giants, hags and their familiars, mingled with werewolves, satyrs and animated corpses—some reduced to skeleton—in perverse revelry.

Khlit drew pistol and saber and the rest of us followed suit.

"Steady, Cossacks," Cassave's voice was soft but carried to all of us. "Do not let yourselves be provoked by anything you see."

Indeed, as we neared the fire, the worshippers seemed too consumed by their orgiastic frenzy to pay any heed to us. I saw Hella—nude, as usual—dancing in the throng and stern Gorcha as well (nudity did not suit him.) Mighty Vseslav stood in the center of the throng, almost in the fire as he read words I could not understand from an ancient-looking book.

Then the fire blazed up a hundred feet into the air, framing an impenetrable column of black smoke. I forgot everything else as I watched the flame-wreathed smoke swell and grow denser.

"Chernabog," I heard Cassave whisper in the sudden silence.

"Yes, mortal, the Black God is risen!"

All our eyes turned to the speaker, whom I saw was Vseslav, wrapped in wolf skins. Hella stood at his right in all her pale beauty and to his left, Boris Liatoukine. Our former comrade was dressed in a long robe, having abandoned his Cossack finery. I saw no sign of the injuries the Cossacks had given him.

Vseslav pointed at us and spoke.

"My children," he said, "these humans have come to desecrate our Lord and to thwart our plan to shroud the world in eternal night. In the name of Chernabog, kill them!"

I started to protest that I was not human—that I was one of them—but my brethren never gave me a chance. A werewolf sprang at me and I shot him in the face. A creature as much serpent as human tried to bite me and I cut him into two writing pieces.

"Cossacks, protect me!" Cassave shouted, pulling the silver urn from his robes.

The Cossacks needed no instructions from him and had already begun fighting. Khlit shot Liatoukine through the heart and threw away the empty pistol to draw another. Ivan had drawn his massive two-handed sword and whirled it so fiercely that none dared to close with him. Ayub lopped the head from a skeleton with his saber, then split the skull of a satyr with another stroke.

I noticed several things: first, our blades and bullets worked against the hellish army better than they should have. I wondered if this was a blessing from god, or something the Magister had done. Each shot dropped one of our foes, each sword stroke cut deep, and the wounds did not instantly heal.

Second, I noticed that the Magister had vanished. I didn't know when this had happened, but was too hard pressed to wonder.

Finally, I discovered that I liked fighting alongside my fellow Cossacks. I suppose I should have shown my loyalty by turning and striking the Cossacks down, but that would leave my back open and I had no doubt Vseslav's undead would tear me to pieces.

From the corner of my eye, I saw Gorcha spring on Ayub from behind, one gaunt arm-locked around his massive body, while the other tangled in his hair, drawing his head back and baring his throat. Ayub struggled, but even he could not match the gaunt vampire's great strength. Without an instant's hesitation, I drew my second pistol and fired the ball into Gorcha's face. It was treason, but I despised Gorcha and had grown fond of Ayub.

Above us, the column of smoke unfolded itself like a bat spreading its wings. Now it had the shape of a colossal horned man with glowing eyes and skin as dark as the space between the stars on a cloudless night. The colossus stretched in triumph, then a look of disbelief came over his face.

Cassave stood nearby holding the urn over his head and chanting. Chernabog tried to struggle but was drawn inexorably into the vessel as pipe smoke is drawn into a man's lungs. It took only seconds before the colossus was entirely captured in the tiny urn and the sorcerer clapped the lid shut.

"Do you see?" He raised the vessel over his head and the mob of fiends shrunk back in fear and awe.

"Where is your god now?" Cassave taunted. "Perhaps I should be your god!"

As he spoke, I looked for the Cossacks. Ivan Sabalinka was down, his sword broken and blood pumping from a terrible wound on his neck. Khlit had fallen and Ayub, who alone seemed unharmed, hurried to his friend's side.

"By the power I have taken this day, I—Quentin Moretus Cassave—have become your new master. Do homage to me."

My mind rebelled against that idea; a human with the power of a god, a man who controlled the forces of darkness. I had long ago resigned myself to being Vseslav's creature, but I would not be the slave of Cassave.

My pistols were spent, but I still had Zaroff's Tatar warbow slung on my shoulder. I unlimbered the weapon, fitted an arrow and let fly.

The missile struck the urn, punching through the thin metal and lodging there. Darkness seeped from the hole around it, then exploded, drinking up all the light on the mountain. I heard the scream of a titan in anguish and the Magister's voice, laughing.

I woke, not remembering when I had lost consciousness. The Sun had not yet risen but the clouds were gone and the early light of dawn painted the eastern sky.

"You are finally awake," a woman said.

Sitting up, I spied Hella sitting on a rock nearby. She was still naked but there was nothing seductive about her pose. In the soft light, she looked almost innocent.

A glanced around and saw bodies strewn on the ground, including Khlit, Cassave and Ayub. I rose and went to them and was surprised when I felt a surge of relief that they were all breathing. Sabalinka, alas, was not. The other bodies, a mere dozen, all human and all bearing the mark of pistol or saber, lay scattered across the slope. Of the vampires and their demonic allies, I could see no sign.

"What has happened?" I asked.

Hella stood and stretched.

"When you released Chernabog, his minions scattered like chickens in the rain. They will not try this again. My Master is pleased."

"Your master... Vseslav?"

"Vseslav has fled also," she said. "When you find him, he will forgive you all because of the final blow you struck against Cassave."

I looked down on the Cassave's unconscious form.

"He is a dangerous man. Perhaps I should kill him?"

"No," Hella replied. "My master is interested in Cassave. There are still things for him to accomplish."

"You speak as though Vseslav is not your master," I said.

Hella laughed; a delicate bell-like sound.

"He only thought he was. I have always served the one you call the Magister. He is pleased by your actions. You put an end to a foolish plan and helped to humble a presumptuous rival."

"Who is the Magister?" I asked. I still dreaded the answer to my question but decided I needed to know.

"Cassave was wrong in claiming that Chernabog was Satan himself," she said with a sly smile. "Vseslav and the witches mistakenly put their faith in a lesser power, but the true Devil is not mocked."

"I see," I said. "What does he want of me, now?"

"Go and rejoin Vseslav," Hella said.

I nodded and, catching one of the horses, I turned and headed down the slope. I only looked back once, just as the dun broke the horizon. Hella was gone and the three men were beginning to stir. I looked away, knowing that I had no place in the world of men.

But it had been nice to be a Cossack again for a while.

THE VAMPIRE CITY

*Paul Féval is back with another of his fabulous creations: Se-
lene, the Sepulchre, Scholomance, the Vampire City, introduced in the eponymous 1867 novel [8] whose heroine is none
other than writer Ann Radcliffe Anticipating the concept of a
merry band of vampire hunters, Radcliffe, eager to save a
friend from the dreaded vampire lord Otto Goetzi, gathers at
her side a small group comprised of Merry Bones the Irishman, Jack Gray, her faithful servant, Dr. Magnus Szegeli and
the intrepid Polly Bird. With their help, she launches an attack
against Selene, a city invisible to human eyes, but for one hour
a day... Here, British writer Brian Gallagher offers another
take on Selene and its internal rivalries, pitting Captain Vampire against some of his fiercest rivals in the two stories that
follow, which herald the threat of the encroaching modern
world of science and technology...*

Brian Gallagher: *City of the Nosferatu*

Transylvania, 1830

The journey from Vienna to Transylvania had been
straightforward, pleasant even, Boris Liatoukine thought. This
diversion to see the Count was a minor delay, but a necessary
one. Count Dracula was not a figure to be ignored in a matter
as delicate as that which was to be discussed.

---

[8] Available from Black Coat Press, ISBN 978-0-9740711-6-9.

They were high up in Dracula's castle, overlooking the Borgo pass, sitting opposite each other over a table. It was night, Dracula's preferred time. Liatoukine knew that the Count could exist in the day—just as he himself could. However, Dracula's powers were far greater at night. Far more than his own, in fact—which was perhaps the point of making him wait until darkness fell to see him.

The Count decided to sum up their conversation thus far.

"The Habsburg Emperor Francis in Vienna believes that vampires are infiltrating his Austrian empire? And your Tsar Nicholas as well?"

"Quite so," replied Liatoukine. "It's based on a number of incidents, usually involving a vampire being caught. More often than not, they seem to be influential members of society."

Dracula did not seem impressed by this.

"This is hardly new," he said. "I myself wield some authority here. And you too carry some small influence at the Imperial Court in St. Petersburg—despite being a mere Captain in the Russian Army." The unkind comment regarding Liatoukine's rank was delivered with a little smile.

Liatoukine knew it was best to ignore the remark; Dracula was not one to annoy or be trifled with. "It is the scale of incidents that concerns then; they are all too frequent," he replied. "Of course, some of us are captured and destroyed on occasion but…"

"*Us?*" inquired Dracula.

Liatoukine decided to choose his next words very carefully. It would not be wise to imply that the Count was just another vampire who might be destroyed by mere humans. His history was substantial for any one, human or vampire. Had he not studied at the Scholomance, where he'd learned the secrets of the Evil One himself?

"Forgive me, Count. I meant the vampires of the Sepulchre. They have long had their people in positions within human society. Their being caught from time to time does have the benefit of ensuring a certain degree of fear amongst the

122

populace. There have never been enough incidents to provoke the authorities into action. Some even harbor doubts as to the existence of those like us."

"What, then, has changed? Why are the great powers starting to take the existence of vampires seriously?" asked the Count.

"Because the frequency of such incidents has recently multiplied. We know that the Sepulchre always have had their people hidden amongst the humans. So far, so good. But now, the Emperors seem to think that they are under threat. Their police have captured some minor vampires who were, frankly, just too careless. The large recruitment the Sepulchre appears to be indulging in is not providing the best quality of converts. From interrogation, scraps of information have emerged. The Sepulchre is being mentioned regularly. This only matches the rumors that the humans already knew—although they call the Vampire City, Selene. The Emperors are communicating with each other via their Royal families—this helps avoid any political issues. Action is underway in several countries: the Austrian Empire, Russia, the Ottoman Empire, France... even England."

"England?" said the Count. "I have an interest in that country"

"The Sepulchre has placed one or two of their people there in the past. A few years back, an expedition led by an Englishwoman to Selene led to chaos and the death of Otto Goetzi," said Liatoukine.

"I am aware of that incident. The Radcliffe woman was a remarkable individual. I am intrigued by a nation which can produce such a woman. Goetzi was a fool—how could he permit her and her associates to cross Europe to destroy him in his very lair? What she did in invading the Sepulchre was another factor that brought her country to my attention. The British are now of great interest to me, especially their science and their ambitions. They do not limit themselves to Europe. They fascinate me, because they are the future. Here," he gestured at the window to the country outside, "we are still backward and mired in superstition."

Liatoukine thought that perhaps the local superstition was not so backward, given who was residing in this very castle, but he kept the thought to himself.

The Count pondered, stroking his large moustache.

"I have little time for the Sepulchre's foolish games. I have my own dreams of the future in England. I do not wish to see them disrupting that country, or Central Europe, for that matter. Do they wish a full-blown war with the humans? Fools! What will they do when the Imperial armies stand outside Selene with their cannons? Yes, I know that the Sepulchre only exists in our reality for an hour every day, but do they think that no damage can be caused in that hour? Every day?"

Liatoukine nodded his agreement. The Count considered him, gazing at him with his red eyes.

"Pray, tell me... (they both smiled at the use of "pray") What precisely is your involvement in all this?"

It was time for Liatoukine to expose his own interests.

"The Tsar has been in touch with the other Monarchs in this matter. There have been certain incidents in St. Petersburg. Indeed, I myself had to swiftly execute a nobleman. There are many who fear me there. Some are even aware that I am not what I seem. This works to my advantage. A more mistrustful, ever fearful, atmosphere, however, could achieve the opposite and destroy all my efforts."

"For myself, I most certainly find fear to be useful," Dracula said.

Liatoukine ignored his remark and continued:

"Fortunately, the Tsar feels he can still rely on me in certain matters. I have been of use to him in the past, especially in the recent successful war we waged against your ancient enemies, the Turks. So he suggested that I should look into the matter, and see what should be done. I was dispatched to Vienna to discuss the 'vampire problem' with the Habsburg Emperor himself. The Austrians have a prisoner in their Croatian city of Zagreb, whom they are not even certain how to kill. I

124

would speak with him, and then destroy him myself. Our position is especially perilous in the Austrian Empire, as such prisoners only increase the humans' knowledge of us."

"Even here, in Transylvania, I have become aware of the growth of these inferior vampires within the Austrian Empire," interrupted Dracula. "Lawyers, petty officials, and so on. Wisely, they have avoided all contacts with me, presumably believing that I am still unaware of their presence. However, they have not been widely detected by the humans. I assume this recent increase is due to the infiltration strategy by the Sepulchre that you mentioned earlier?"

"Yes, I suspect so," said Liatoukine. "The infiltration has been most intense in areas where our kind has traditionally been the strongest, such as the Magyar lands. My concern is that, if the humans are pushed, they will retaliate. We are powerful, but there are millions of them, and we are but thousands, if that. Hidden as we are, lurking in the shadows, our very existence denied by men of science—some in our employ—we thrive. The lower orders of life fear us as spectres of the night. But if we were to take over, resistance would quickly replace fear; we would be right in front of them—an open target. Using selected humans as our servants would no longer work; some of them are already being exposed. And as you said, human weapons could smash even our strongest holdouts."

Dracula rose and strode to the window, gazing out. He placed his hand on the stone wall, as if to reassure himself of his castle's strength. Tall, thin and pale, like many of his kind, he also had pointed ears and red eyes. Perhaps it was just as well that he was rarely seen outside his castle nowadays, thought Liatoukine.

"Yes, yes… this is so," said the Count at last. "Vienna thinks it rules here. They would no doubt muster their troops against me if they felt my existence was a threat to them. I would prevail. Nonetheless, it would be extremely inconvenient. However, I sense that you are not simply here for discussing the problem, Boris Liatoukine. You have other intentions in mind, don't you?"

"Indeed I have, my Lord Count," replied the Russian. "A name has occasionally been mentioned when the Austrians have interrogated the vampires they captured, prior to their destruction: Orlok. I believe I have heard the name before, always in relation to this region…"

"So you think I may be connected to all this?" asked Dracula.

"No, my Lord, not in the least. Your independence—as well as mine—from the Sepulchre is well known."

"Quite." Here Dracula started to almost look amused, "However, the name Orlok is indeed familiar to me, and it explains much. You may, in fact, be able to resolve matters far more easily than you might have thought…"

On horseback, Liatoukine approached Zagreb. What Dracula had told him was most useful indeed. He came to a military building in the center of town, where he knew he was expected. He was immediately taken to a commander named Sponsz. The soldier couldn't help but wonder about his visitor. How was it that this mysterious, tall, gaunt Russian with his strange burning eyes had been granted such liberties? He had been ordered to extend every courtesy to him, and tell him whatever he wanted to know. In his career, Sponsz had come across many strange things, but always kept quiet. His masters knew that he could be trusted.

"Tell me how your prisoner came to be in that cell?" inquired Liatoukine.

"Yes, sir," Sponsz began. He was unsure on how to address a Russian army nobleman and officer, but "Sir" seemed to evoke no rebuke, so he continued: "Baron Grando was captured at the home of one of the mayor's most trusted advisers, alone in his office. Horrifying cries and screams were heard. Some of the servants burst in to see the Baron drinking the adviser's blood from his wrist whilst holding him down by his neck.

"Given that the Baron is seventy, this was a considerable feat. In fact, it took ten men to overwhelm him. Six others were killed in the process. A lamp was knocked over, causing a fire. We made use of this to tell the public that there had been an accident and that the deceased were burned to death. The survivors, who had helped subdue the Baron, were only too glad to keep quiet."

Liatoukine nodded. He rather suspected that the fire was started later on, rather than being the result of a genuine accident, but kept silent.

"I understand that the Baron was injured?" he asked instead.

"Indeed, sir. A number of men tried to kill him. It is best that you see for yourself"

They headed downstairs, to a long corridor, along which there were doors leading to what clearly were cells. A number of these seemed to be made out of the same stone than the building. Clearly, no ordinary prisoners were kept here. They stopped at one such cell, which had its own guard standing outside. The guard opened a spyhole and checked on the prisoner. He confirmed that all was well. Sponsz, however, took a second look to make sure. With a little difficulty, the young guard opened the heavy stone door.

"You may wait outside," Liatoukine told Sponsz.

"I regret, sir, but I can't. The regulations say that if a dangerous prisoner is to be visited, there must be a soldier present."

Liatoukine did not know if this was true, but Vienna clearly wanted their man to report back on what would be said. *Very well*, he thought, *they have sealed their servant's fate.*

Liatoukine strode in, followed by Sponsz. The guard closed the door behind them. The cell was bare, without any natural light. There was what appeared to be a block of stone with a figure sitting on it. It was tied down to the stone by chains. On a table nearby, a lamp flickered. Sponsz went over to it and turned it up. The increased light provided more details of the figure. Thin and pale, the creature smiled at his visitors. To anyone else other than Liatoukine and Sponsz, this might have come as a surprise—if they had recovered from the shock of seeing a stake sticking from the man's chest, where his heart should be.

Liatoukine pointed to the stake.

"The men who overwhelmed the Baron attempted to destroy him by traditional means," explained Sponsz. "As you can see, it failed, but I thought it best to leave things the way they were."

Liatoukine also noticed several holes in the Baron's shirt that looked like bullet holes. Clearly, other methods of destruction had been tried, which had also proved unsuccessful. Not all vampires could be killed in the same way, although the stake was the most common method. The Russian was surprised they had not tried decapitation. Perhaps orders had already come through that the prisoner needed to be interrogated first.

"Come to see what cannot be killed?" sneered the Baron. "Another servant of that useless Emperor in Vienna?"

Liatoukine looked at him more closely. Grando seemed to shrink back. From that look, he had not only understood that the Russian Captain was a vampire, but also a powerful one. The Baron did not know how he knew. He just did.

"Are you here to free me, my lord?" he asked.

The sneering tone had gone. Sponsz picked up on this and shifted uneasily. Clearly, this Russian was of some significance.

Liatoukine ignored the question. He looked at the floor. There was a layer of ash on it. He crouched down, touched it, and sensed the remnants of departed vampire spirits.

"My Lord," said the Baron, "what you feel is what's left our kind—the ones killed over many years by the Austrians. They leave their ashes here to intimidate those of us they capture."

Clearly, the Austrians and their Croat subjects knew more about vampires than they'd let on, thought Liatoukine. Something to be remembered.

"*Our kind*? Does he mean, noblemen?" asked Sponsz, although his real suspicion was painted on his face.

Liatoukine turned to him. He grabbed him by the throat so he could not scream. He didn't bother answering the question. He stared deep into Sponsz's eyes. The Commander felt waves of terror flood through him. He could no longer move. He realized what was strange about the Russian's eyes: the pupils had turned into vertical slits, like a cat's!

Then, he could no longer think of anything. His heart had given out.

Liatoukine dropped him to the floor.

"That is how I dispose of people," he said.

Grando looked awestruck. "What of his blood?" he asked.

"His life-force is what I take. I do dislike having blood on my uniform." He went over to Grando and removed the stake. The hole started regenerating. "We must move fast to leave here..." He went to the chains and pulled at them. "This will take a few moments..." He grappled with the chains behind the Baron.

Grando was clearly pleased with these developments.

"Of course, you are obliged to help me. Vampire is loyal to vampire, vampire does not kill vampire! Not like the humans, who slaughter each other for no reason. They would have killed me if they could, but they couldn't find the right method..."

Liatoukine ignored his talk.

"Tell me," he said whilst seeming to grapple with the chains, "it is clear to me that you have only recently become one of us. I sense a familiarity about you, although we have not met before. Perhaps I am aware of the one who created you. Who is he?"

"It was Orlok, my lord, *Graf* Orlok."

Was the emphasis on the title of "Graf" supposed to impress him? Liatoukine thought? "Orlok!" he exclaimed. "A dear friend of mine. I have not seen him in many decades. I hear he has some new plans?"

"Yes, yes, my lord! He has plans to extend our influence into the Empire. He is selecting many of the more influential of us for his purpose. We will soon control the Empire and will not have to hide anymore. He has promised me that I will be a young man again."

And Orlok is doing all of this himself? From the Sepulchre?"

"Yes. From time to time, he visits certain cities, changes select people such as I, and then we carry on with his work in our areas. He intends Selene to become the capital of the new Empire. He has great ambitions for Russia, too, which is perhaps why you've heard of his plans?"

Liatoukine had heard enough; this confirmed what he already knew. Best to get onto the other reason why he was here. He noted that the hole in the Baron's chest had already healed. Good.

Liatoukine pulled a knife from inside his tunic and plunged it into the Baron's chest. There was a gasp from the uncomprehending nobleman. Then, the Russian Captain proceeded to cut out the Baron's heart.

"What are you doing?" cried the Baron.

Liatoukine ignored him. He never felt the need to explain himself to fools. Besides, time was a factor. The last thing he needed was for the guard outside to wonder what was going on, although he could hear nothing through the heavy door.

Once finished, he placed the heart in the small box he had brought in with him. Inside was a bottle of oil, which he poured over the heart. Lighting a small splinter, he set it alight. It burned with extreme intensely—the oil had special properties that made it so. Nothing was happening to Grando; sometimes the burning of the heart would destroy his kind of vampire. *No matter*, thought Liatoukine.

He placed the stake back into the Baron's body, where it had been previously, even though the hole was now rather larger. The utterly confused Baron piped up again.

"My lord, I am uncertain as to the meaning of all this. Why are you burning my heart?"

Was Grando really so ignorant? The oil had almost done its work. Since he had some time, he might as well enlighten this idiot, he thought.

"You are the kind of vampire whose heart, when burnt, provides a fine ash with certain properties—properties that are not present if you are ordinarily destroyed and reduced to ash"

"Properties, my Lord? I do not understand?"

Liatoukine looked inside the metal box. The oil had done its work. Carefully, he closed the airtight box. Then, with one swift blow, he decapitated Grando with his sword. The head spun in the air. Liatoukine caught it with one hand. The head pulled away from his hand and rested back on the body, re-attaching itself. No doubt, the Croats had attempted this method before then.

The Russian Captain had no particular idea on how this vampire could be killed, and no time to find out. His own powers would have to do. He took a gold coin from his pocket and smashed it into the Baron's skull. Half of it stuck out.

"My Lord, I must protest... this is no way to treat a fellow vampire! Graf Orlok will not be pleased! Vampire is loyal to vampire!"

Liatoukine just stared into the Baron's eyes, using the same power he had used on Sponsz earlier. The Baron was going to say something, but suddenly, his head started to decay. It turned into a skull. Liatoukine let it fall to the floor, with the gold coin still lodged into it. The body had similarly rotted away. He went over the chains that still restrained the body and now broke them effortlessly. Liatoukine kicked the Baron's skeleton, which further disintegrated into ashes, with the stake still in the middle of what was left of the ribcage.

Taking his sword off his belt, Liatoukine went to the heavy metal slot on the door and banged on it with the handle of his sword. The slot opened. Liatoukine shouted through it:

"Quickly, man! Open!"

With some effort, the door was duly opened and the guard from outside rushed in and looked in horror at the scene.

Liatoukine pointed at what was left of Grando with his sword. "You fools! The chains were not strong enough! The creature got free and attacked me. I could have been killed." He gestured towards Sponsz's body. "This one died in terror—his heart must have given out."

"How were you able to kill it?" the stunned guard asked.

Liatoukine pointed to the gold coin sticking out of the skull. "Gold, man, gold. To be pressed into the skull only. Are you people here not aware that some vampires can only be killed in this way?"

The guard shook his head. The humans needed an explanation for Baron Grando's death, and that gold nonsense was as good as any other. Orlok would no doubt sense the death of his minion, and may even suspect who was responsible, but he would not know for certain—let alone be able to prove it.

The Russian Captain left the cell, affecting to be in need of wine. He was, of course, full of energy, as always when he drained another vampire. What drivel had Orlok fed Grando? "Vampire is loyal to vampire, vampire does not kill vampire?" Indeed!

If the local Croat authorities doubted Liatoukine's story, they did not show it. In fact, the Russian Captain made great play of how he had been put at risk, and so on. He used his powers of influence just to make sure to be believed. He was further assisted in his task by the attitude of some officials who were only too glad that the Baron had been destroyed, and displayed their thanks in a most embarrassing manner. Liatoukine pretended to be mollified and instructed that the Emperor in Vienna should be told that this unfortunate outbreak of the "vampire plague" would be swiftly dealt with by Liatoukine himself.

The Austrians provided him with a military escort of four cavalrymen, led by a lieutenant, to the border between their empire and Serbia. They rode out of Zagreb and through the fertile lands of Slavonia. They stopped at a small town for a few hours of rest. Liatoukine made himself popular with his escort by treating them to free ale at a local inn. Whilst his escort was busy drinking, he saw to some business with a local smith, a task that he had not wished to have done in Zagreb, in order to avoid spying eyes. He needed some work done in order to help him make a certain point with the rulers of the Sepulchre, when he got there.

After a night's sleep, they arrived at Zemun, known as Semlin in German. It was the last stop before crossing the border, and then onward to the Sepulchre. Liatoukine had given some thought to simply going around the town in order to maintain the element of surprise when he would arrive at Selene's gates. However, if Orlok got wind of his coming, due to his spies—incompetent as they seemed to be—it would be best for Liatoukine to suggest that he was in no way afraid of the other vampire.

Zemun contained a number of discreet spies who had been working for the Sepulchre for many years due to its proximity to the Vampire City. These spies would soon report his arrival. Liatoukine considered that this news might, in fact, unsettle Orlok and, more importantly, other powers in the Sepulchre.

To make sure that his presence was known, the Russian Captain met with the mayor—calling it a courtesy call, as the Austrian cavalrymen were escorting a Russian officer on a diplomatic mission. A surprise early morning call for the mayor, pleasantries exchanged in his office, nothing more.

Liatoukine could not help but notice the occasional green tint on the window in the mayor's office. The Russian Captain knew well that this was a sign of vampiric infiltration—not surprising for a place with such strong connections with the

Sepulchre. It confirmed that, beyond using human informers, there were also vampires here. Perhaps the mayor himself was one? This was reckless indeed. Human settlements around the Sepulchre had traditionally been left largely alone in order to prevent any unwanted attention. The humans certainly feared Selene, but such fears did not turn into any aggressive intent. If this had changed, Orlok's influence was indeed proving to be baleful.

Liatoukine also noticed that the cavalry lieutenant had glanced occasionally at the window. Further, he had noticed the use of languages amongst the men who comprised escort. German, of course, but they also spoke in Croatian, and the officer had betrayed his knowledge of Latin. Educated men... No doubt some among them might even know French, and perhaps Russian too? Clearly, these men were more than mere cavalry men in the service of the Emperor... Perhaps, they suspected his true nature? No matter. Today, they were allies, after a fashion. Nevertheless, it would be wise to remember this in the future.

They concluded their business and headed to the Serbian border. Soon, they reached it and came to a halt.

"This is where we must leave you, sir," said the lieutenant.

"Of course. I should be able to get to Belgrade to continue my mission without any difficulties," replied Liatoukine.

More to the point, he thought it was important that the secret of the Sepulchre be kept from these humans. He had, in fact, no intention of going to Belgrade, although he had arranged for Vienna to be told that he was.

After his escort had gone, Liatoukine moved across the border and rode towards Selene, eventually reaching its outskirts. The Vampire City, of course, was neither visible, nor tangible. Where it stood, all that could be seen was barren land, with dead trees and no life of any kind. It gave off a feeling of death and corruption. This was how humans were deterred from approaching it. The city somehow co-existed in the same space as that barren marsh, but on another plane of reality. As a vampire himself, he could enter either space, but he waited an hour or so until 11 a.m. for, at that time, Selene became visible for an hour to all.

It duly appeared on schedule, materializing slowly. A city of dark shapes, buildings at strange angles, and any such movements that could be seen inside were fleeing and disturbing to human eyes.

Liatoukine looked at the Vampire City. Some thought this was God's way of signaling its existence to the humans. For centuries, the locals had barely spoken of it, simply keeping well away from its dark walls. However, there were many legends. With the humans' rapid scientific and military development, Liatoukine wondered not only if the secrecy would last, but if confrontation would not become someday inevitable—a confrontation that vampires couldn't hope to win. Perhaps that was God's plan as well? Perhaps that was also why Orlok was behaving as he was—trying to control the humans before they became a threat?

Whenever that confrontation were to take place—and the later, the better—Liatoukine had every intention of being far away. And preferably, on the winning side.

Liatoukine now entered the Vampire City. He tethered his horse to a tall, dark pole made of some unknown substance, with no apparent purpose. The beast was clearly afraid, but the Russian Captain simply placed his hand on its neck and it became utterly docile. He did not leave all his weapons with the horse. Instead, he took his sword and two pistols. He then proceeded on foot.

He walked through the dark streets, encountering strange figures as he walked. They let him pass, looking at him strangely. Vampires tended not to enter the city when it was visible to humans. Liatoukine had done so deliberately, in order to unnerve. Further, he could have proceeded to where the middle of the city was and let it materialize around him, but he wished to take in the current atmosphere of the Sepulchre. He had not been here for a while. It was as unappealing as ever.

He knew some of the figures he passed by reputation. A number used the city as their base. Others had fled here from lands were they had been exposed. Some had "retired." He was unimpressed by the city and its inhabitants. He did not share his kind's love of the extreme macabre. Humans were weak. However, they provided much in the way of entertainment, pleasure, and a refined society in which to partake and, occasionally, dominate. He considered that much more preferable than skulking around in some invisible mausoleum.

Soon, he came to the central plaza of the Sepulchre. Here was a temple, an imposing chapel of sorts. Its columns were interspersed with statues of tigers ripping the hearts out of young women, frozen in fear. He went up the steps, past the statues. These were actually real women, who, in death, had been transformed into statues by their vampire killers for the express purpose of being displayed here. Liatoukine was responsible for much death, but could not see the point of this spectacle. Vampire art was never his thing.

He was greeted—if that's the word—by what appeared to be little more than a skeleton dressed in a Russian military uniform. The skull had vampire fangs. Presumably this was Orlok's own effort to unsettle him. The skeleton wordlessly gestured to follow him, and led Liatoukine into the hall. At the end was a raised platform, on top of which were five stone stands, with figures behind them. This was the Vampire Council, those who currently governed the Sepulchre. They were bathed in a dull green light.

Liatoukine recognized them. There was Count Szandor, Baron Iskariot and Baroness Phryne. He noted one, wearing garments that were fashionable in Europe a few years back. This was the second Otto Goetzi; the first being infamous for letting humans intrude into the city and almost getting himself destroyed in the process. There was, however, no mistaking the one in the center: tall, bald, large ears, with rat like teeth, wearing a long coat... They had not previously met, but this was Graf Orlok, no doubt about that.

Littered around the hall were a number of vampires of all kinds. This was unusual; the Council tended to meet and hold its audiences in secrecy. Presumably Orlok was expecting trouble and had gathered his lackeys?

Orlok stared at Liatoukine.

"Welcome, Boris Liatoukine. I am Graf Orlok. We have heard of your journey here. What brings you home?"

This was certainly was not home for Liatoukine; but Orlok was clearly playing to the notion held by the other Council members that the Sepulchre was the home of all vampires—and thus, that it had power over all of their kind.

Liatoukine got the pleasantries out of the way. "Greetings, Orlok, fellow council members..." Then, he decided to get straight to it as it seemed they knew full well why he was here. "Vampires have always infiltrated human society in the past. We need to, if only in order to protect ourselves—and of course to gain enrichment and nourishment. However, it seems that we are increasing such operations far more aggressively than in the past. It appears as if we are trying to take them over completely." Liatoukine used the 'we' simply to imply brotherhood. He didn't mean it, of course.

"Quite so," said Orlok. "It is long past time we took control. Our city appears every day for an hour. Currently, only fear and our influence keep its existence at the level of rumors. But this will not last. As the humans develop their sciences and communications, too many will come to know of the Sepulchre. News of its existence will spread. The human empires are large and powerful. One or more may decide to move against us. This may prove perilous for us. I trust, then, that you do not disagree with our new strategy?"

"As it happens, I do disagree. It is *your* strategy, Graf, is it not?" Something that passed for a smile appeared on Orlok's withered face, and he slowly nodded his head. The other Council members said nothing. Liatoukine noted this. Perhaps they were not too enthusiastic about the new strategy, and happy for Orlok to take the blame if anything went wrong?

Liatoukine pressed on. "You are pushing too hard. The humans are becoming far more aware of us, at every level of their society. I can assure you of this. In my own Russia, officials have destroyed many of your agents. The Emperors themselves have been secretly conferring about us, notwithstanding their political rivalries in other, more mundane areas."

"I know of this," responded Orlok, "but it does not matter. Control will pass to us, overtly or with the humans acting as our marionettes."

"No, it will not," Liatoukine stated. "Even if you manage to enslave all the royal families of Europe, and all their ministers, it is foolish to think that you could control millions of humans. Do you think the God-fearing masses will put up with vampire control? Operating in the shadows, having us dismissed as mere superstition is one thing, but this aggressive push towards mastery of Europe will bring us into open conflict. We cannot fight millions of them. What will you do when they surround the Sepulchre and bombard you with their cannons every day for an hour?"

Some of the council looked unsettled. Liatoukine pushed his advantage.

"They are already destroying your agents. I come from Zagreb; there, they held one of you infiltrators prisoner; they interrogated him, then destroyed him. It is clear to me that the Austrian Empire has far greater knowledge of us than we thought. They have prison cells made especially for us. I suspect they may even be aware that the Sepulchre is real, and not just some local peasant's tale. There can be no doubt that a confrontation is coming. Rather than put it off for decades— time during which we can perhaps find a solution—it will be upon us within a few years, maybe even a few months."

"And you, of course, are completely loyal to us?" responded Orlok. "Perhaps you can explain your greater loyalty to the Russian Empire? Your fighting for them? Even now, you are on a mission for them. You think I did not know? Is it really the case that you are here for our benefit? Or for those of your masters in St. Petersburg?"

Liatoukine's loyalty was to himself above all. However, he certainly preferred St. Petersburg to the Sepulchre. And he had much sympathy for the Russian Empire. The assimilation of other lands into the Empire, the crushing of the lesser kinds, especially the peasants, yes, that was real power! Perhaps, one day, they would take control of the Sepulchre itself—under his guidance of course. However, there was the more immediate problem of Orlok's activities. It was time to go further on the offensive.

"My loyalty to my kind is not in doubt," said the Russian Captain. "Your spies seem to know that I am on mission to look into the so-called 'vampire plague' on behalf of my Tsar, working in tandem with the Habsburgs. But it is only the ideal cover to protect our own interests, which is why I am here. At least, I have not been uncovered, unlike so many of your servants." He paused. "Aside from your competence, perhaps it is your own motivation that we should question?"

This was an open challenge. Orlok hissed back in anger, but Liatoukine did not let up.

"How did you become a vampire, Graf Orlok? Does the rest of the Council know?"

They clearly did not. Orlok was known to have mysterious origins and that it was best not to inquire about them. They gave no answer, and Orlok was certainly not going to enlighten them. His hands were now outstretched, his long fingers with their razor sharp fingers moving as if digging into Liatoukine's neck. The Russian Captain pressed ahead. There was no going back now.

"Most of us became what we are by having been converted by another vampire's bite. Some of us have the power to absorb humans into themselves and to then release them, changed into whatever their masters want them to be. Their physical form can be changed, to be made grotesque, to even destroy the memories of who they once were…"

Otto Goetzi intervened. "We know this, Liatoukine. I myself was converted by a Great One in such a manner. I have taken his name to match his appearance, the very form in which he shaped me. Get to your point."

Liatoukine knew this; in fact this second Goetzi assisted the accursed Radcliffe's human incursion many years before. Somehow, he had been forgiven by the Council after the first Goetzi's death. Liatoukine did not know—or care—about how that had been accomplished. The first Goetzi was, in fact, not that well regarded, despite what his successor said. He was known for his sadism; this version of Goetzi had been a young village woman once known as Polly Bird and Goetzi turned her into a copy of himself.

"Of course," responded Liatoukine. "But first, I wish to be clear about who Orlok is—or was. There was once, some time ago, a young Transylvanian nobleman..." The atmosphere in the room changed a little. An element of fear and foreboding could now be felt from the Council. More hissing from Orlok. "I do not need to bore you with the details, but Graf Orlok, then a handsome young man, thought that he could displace the power and influence of Count Dracula himself."

There were stunned gasps from the Council. All knew Dracula. All knew that he was the most powerful vampire of all.

"Orlok of course, had no idea that Dracula was a vampire. He had scoffed at the local peasantry's fear of him, dismissing it as mere superstition. Hearing of his attitude, Dracula invited him to his castle. Orlok was not much seen after that. His family all seemed to die mysteriously, disappeared, or became seen only at odd hours. Orlok himself was also rarely seen. And soon, the locals started to fear Orlok, with good reason.

"For Count Dracula had not merely killed him, of course. He had absorbed him. He then allowed him to reemerge but only as a copy, a doppelganger of Dracula himself. Orlok would carry out business on his behalf, the things the Count considered to be lesser tasks. And when these tasks were carried out well, Dracula would let Orlok out of himself not just in the form of a copy, but in the misshapen shape we see today, in which he would terrorize the locals."

"Are you saying that Orlok is a servant of Dracula?" interjected Goetzi. "That he is here serving him now?"

"Far from it," replied Liatoukine. "A few years ago, Dracula dismissed Orlok from his service. No reasons were given. Perhaps we can infer a degree of incompetence on Orlok's part? After all, Dracula left him in his current, charming form… Orlok became resentful at having been cast out. He left his land and came here. Where he seems to have done quite well."

"What do you know of these matters?" Orlok finally said. "You're but a barbaric vampire from the East?"

Barbaric? Orlok would pay for that, swore the Russian Captain, who resumed addressing the rest of the Council.

"Forgive me, my lords. Orlok has already questioned my loyalties, and now he mocks my very knowledge of him. Please be assured that my information comes straight from Count Dracula himself. Indeed, he has authorized me, if it came to that, to present you with this letter…"

He handed the letter not to Orlok, but to Goetzi. The latter noted the seal, and opened it. The note, no more than a few words, was handed round the Council. Was that a trembling of their hands Liatoukine thought he saw?

"As you can see," he resumed, "Dracula himself has authorized me to speak on his behalf in this matter. He and I share the same concerns over the current strategy. I trust that settles any doubt over my knowledge, or indeed my loyalty to our kind. Unless, you doubt the word of Dracula?"

The Council said nothing.

The note had been passed to Orlok. He shook it at Liatoukine with his outstretched hand.

"Dracula does not rule here!" he screeched. "He rarely leaves his castle! His days of power are long gone!"

But Liatoukine was not intimidated.

"Do you intend to test him on that? He remains part of you, Orlok. Dracula is both fascinated and intrigued with the British Empire. He thinks in terms of the decades ahead, and some here know that he wishes to have... interests in the heart of the British Empire. You, yourself, know this, Orlok. You think you can do better than him. Be faster than him. Thus, your policy of recent years."

Orlok crushed Dracula's note and shredded it with one hand before casting it aside.

"I offer power and security to our kind. Dracula offers nothing. Nothing!" he said.

Liatoukine ignored this and continued:

"You appear to have focused mostly on the Habsburg Empire. Perhaps you have an ulterior motive for this? You hate and fear Dracula. You resent him, but cannot destroy him. He is, after all, your creator. His lands, at least nominally, come under Austrian governance. Perhaps you seek control of the Habsburgs not for our kind's benefit, but to control their armies which you plan to use to attack Dracula's castle? They would do something you are too fearful and weak to do yourself?"

This accusation moved Orlok to sheer rage.

"You dare question me? How dare you!"

He gestured to one of his larger minions standing in the hall, who then moved towards Liatoukine. The vampire in question looked like a peasant, probably converted by Orlok himself. *Perfect*, Liatoukine thought. Time to make the point for which he had prepared with the smith he had visited earlier.

He drew his pistol. The peasant vampire sneered. After all, everyone knew that bullets were harmless to a vampire. Liatoukine fired. The peasant exploded in a fireball. All present were shocked.

Liatoukine was most satisfied. Had this not worked, his powers would still have been sufficient to deal with the attack, but he was inordinately pleased with his success. He swiftly made his point:

"Clearly, I was merely defending myself. Please notice, however, that I destroyed that upstart using bullets containing the ashes of a vampire's heart. Such ashes are a known weakness for many of us. Imagine the humans with their pistols—their bombs even—containing such ashes. They would be many casualties on our side. These weapons the humans are capable of devising are beyond our imagination. Let us not provoke them into using them against us now by stirring a foolish campaign they are already aware of."

The argument was clearly running away from Orlok. All could sense the mood, in the way that only vampires can, amongst themselves.

Liatoukine pushed harder.

"What is Orlok? He is nothing but a copy of Count Dracula. Trying to outdo him. He is a counterfeit, not the real thing at all. His very ideas are derived from his creator!"

The taunt hit home. Orlok screeched again. His one chance to retrieve the situation was to demonstrate his power and impose his will by killing Liatoukine. He started moving towards his intended victim.

Liatoukine was prepared. He swiftly used his other pistol and fired. The bullet smashed into Orlok, sending him flying backwards, but did not destroy him as it had his minion was. Liatoukine could see why: his foe's coat had been reinforced in some way. *Very well*, he thought. He would simply use his own powers. Or decapitate him. Or both.

He issued one final taunt: "I see. You protected yourself with your coat, but did not provide such protection to your minion, for all your talk of our kind."

Orlok levitated forward, ready for the final confrontation, but Goetzi intervened. "Enough! There must be no more disunity here! Orlok—it is over. We can no longer afford the risks of your strategy. It could bring destruction upon us all. It must end." He seemed to speak for the Council, for they certainly did not disagree.

Orlok hung in mid-air. He floated down. His coat was damaged where the bullet had hit him. He waved his hand across it and what was left of the bullet fell to the floor harmlessly. The coat itself seemed to regenerate. He turned to the Council, slowly looking at each of them in turn as he spoke.

"I will not stay to witness your destruction. All of you will die at the hands of the humans some day, but not I. I shall leave the Sepulchre tonight. I will not return." With that, he walked out of the hall.

Liatoukine wondered about Goetzi. Why had he taken his side? His taunting of Orlok as a mere copy could have been applied to Goetzi too. It must have struck a nerve. Then, again, perhaps Goetzi intervened out of kinship, to save Orlok's existence?

"Where will he go?" wondered Goetzi.

"I care not," answered Liatoukine. "His time is, I suspect, limited. He can never be free of his old master's subconscious. He will forever be influenced by it, and try to outdo him in some way. And he will no doubt fail. Dracula plans decades ahead. Orlok attempts to rush things, as we have seen. I will leave the winding down of his strategy in your hands and will take my leave. Unlike Orlok, daylight does not affect me"

Liatoukine rode away from the Sepulchre. He had a long journey back to St. Petersburg. On the way, he would send word to Dracula of his success.

He had served many interests well that day: the Empires, Dracula, his fellow vampires, but, above all, his own. His stature and influence with the Sepulchre and Dracula, on the one side, and the Royal Courts—in particular, St. Petersburg—on the other, would both benefit. And he had enjoyed himself, too. The defeat of Orlok had not been guaranteed. He was a powerful foe. Liatoukine had enjoyed the danger, the thrill of it.

However, Orlok was not entirely wrong. At some point, the humans would cease to ignore the Sepulchre out of fear and disbelief. Something would have to be done. Exactly what, Liatoukine did not know. Even in Russia, some suspected him. They would soon call him "Captain Vampire," if he was not careful. But for now, however, he was secure and able to use his influence to ensure that his not aging never became an issue. Lone vampires such as himself and Dracula could remain safe, but would an entire city?

My studies of the Undead, and of my late adversary, Count Dracula, have revealed the existence of a Graf Orlok who lived some years previously in Transylvania. He, too, had a fearsome reputation, although not as great as Dracula's. It would appear that, after a period of absence, he returned to his home in 1830, but a few years later, left to come here to Wisborg.

Following his trail here, I have been taken aback by subsequent events that occurred in 1838. From the documents I have found, it appears that Orlok had similar intentions to that of Dracula, although here in Germany and not in England. Even his adversaries were people similar to those of us who fought Dracula. And his strategy was the same. This Orlok even had the same desires as Dracula—taking an unholy interest in Ellen Hutter, the wife of Thomas Hutter. However, things did not end well for her as they did for our own Mina Harker. Ellen gave her life to trick Orlok into consuming her blood until dawn. The rays of the Sun then destroyed him without trace. Not a weakness that Dracula had, and a very different conclusion to our adventure. She did not survive.

However, the coincidences are too much to be ignored. Furthermore, in the records I have found here, Orlok mentions something called the Sepulchre—a city of his kind. I have heard other rumors of such a city, whispered amongst communities in Central and Eastern Europe plagued by vampires. It is sometimes referred to as "Selene."

There have been too many references for me to ignore, and this Orlok affair of years past has unsettled me. There must be some connection to Dracula. I have not, in the past, been inclined to try to convince the world of the existence of such creatures as vampires. But I may have to reassess matters. The existence of Selene, or the Sepulchre—whatever it may be called—is a matter too great to be ignored. I must research it further.

There can be no graver a threat to humanity than a City of the Nosferatu.

COUNT DRACULA

And now it is the turn of the Lord of Vampires himself, the most famous undead in the history of horror literature—Count Dracula! There is no need to explain who Vlad III Dracula, Prince of Wallachia, nicknamed The Impaler (1431-1476) was, nor the fictional construct invented in 1897 by Bram Stoker (1847-1912)—another Irishman! Our readers have already become acquainted with Rick Lai's bold and complex web of vampiric intrigue in "The Vampire Renaissance." Rick, who is a fan of Mexican vampire movies, now integrates them into his canvas, which also connects Dracula to Louis Feuillade's Vampires, who, despite their name, are not "real" vampires but a merciless gang of thieves...

Rick Lai: *All Predators Great and Small*

Mexico and England, 1892-95

Excerpt from L'Essence du Dragon *by Charles Maurice Loridan (1866)*

The popular misconception is that vampires are servants of Satan. The Cult of the Undead really owes its allegiance to Slidith, the Dragon Lord from the Pit of Ngoth. Among the secret acolytes of Slidith was the Roman prefect of Judaea, Pontius Pilate. By deliberately sentencing Jesus of Nazareth to crucifixion, Pilate stained his soul with a monstrous sin. After committing this unspeakable crime, Pilate performed a ritual of metamorphosis to become the Great Vampire, Slidith's surrogate on Earth. As a consequence of Pilate's action, vampires

147

became vulnerable to the sign of the cross. Pilate's bloody reign ended when his heart was transfixed by the blade of a Samaritan seer. The mantle of Great Vampire remained unclaimed until Vlad Dracula became the ruler of Wallachia in the fifteenth century.

Slidith will only accept a mortal of pure degeneracy as his supreme satrap. Sometimes the quality of a single blood-thirsty act is enough to win the Dragon Lord's favor. Pilate demonstrated this through a simple judicial murder. Known as Vlad the Impaler, Dracula proved that Slidith can be equally impressed by quantity as well as quality.

Vlad Dracula's brutality sparked his transformation into the Great Vampire. His impaling of thousands in Wallachia encumbered his soul with sins against humanity. The historical accounts of Dracula's death are false. He wasn't killed by the Turks. Dracula was the vassal of King Mathias of Hungary. Repelled by Dracula's barbarity, Mathias imprisoned him for 12 years. Mathias had a change of heart once the Ottoman Empire threatened his borders. The Hungarian monarch released Dracula to lead an army on a crusade against the Islamic invaders. Resentful of his mistreatment by Mathias, the Impaler secretly betrayed the army to the Turks at the battle of Bucharest. The Turks masked Dracula's treachery by unveiling the severed head of a double in Istanbul. Following this crowning deed of duplicity, Dracula committed ritual suicide with poison. The atrocities attached to the Impaler's soul assured his reincarnation as the Undead sovereign.

Dracula's self-indulgence is limitless. He narcissistically pines for a Soul-Mate, a woman forged in his own image.

Claude Gabriel Dupont-Verdier's Journal, October 31, 1892
I invaded the Mexican tomb with Aguilar and his brigands. We read the inscription: "Here lie Count and Countess Frankenhausen–and Frau Hildegarde, their faithful servant who would not abandon them even when they journeyed into the Great Beyond–1885." My quest for the ultimate romance nears its completion.

José Alejandro Balsamo's Diary, November 3, 1892

In 1875, I learned that Count Frankenhausen, the last Great Vampire, was spreading terror throughout Mexico. For 10 years, my agents pursued him. Finally, Frankenhausen was destroyed by one of my vampire hunters at the Haunted Hacienda. I foolishly believed the horror of Frankenhausen had ended.

The crypt of the Frankenhausens has been looted. All three corpses were stolen. The Cult of the Undead must be the responsible. The culprits have to be attempting the Count's resurrection.

The Count's powers validated Grost's theory that "there are as many species of vampire as there are beasts of prey." All victims of Frankenhausen's bite became mindless vampires. Anyone bitten by them was similarly transfigured. These blood-drinking creatures were more akin to the zombies of Haiti than the Nosferatu of Eastern Europe. These lumbering creatures blindly obeyed the Count's commands.

The remains of the Countess and Frau Hildegarde are inconsequential. The Count devoured the blood of Eugenia, a human woman whom he had married. The resulting Undead Countess had the mentality of an idiot. Hildegarde, the Count's daytime protector, didn't even mature into a vampire. After a spear pierced Frankenhausen's heart, she leapt from the second floor of the Haunted Hacienda. The fall didn't kill her. Without a master, the moronic vampires went on a rampage. The injured Hildegarde became a banquet for the Count's former slaves.

Once the vampires returned to their coffins at the onset of dawn, proper steps were taken. I had extracted an acidic liquid from the roots of the black mandrake plant. This substance was fatal to vampires. Hildegarde's Undead resurgence was thwarted by my anti-vampire serum. The same fluid slew Eugenia and the other vampires in their graves. Even the Count's corpse was inoculated. The mandrake vaccine is not infallible. Its prevalence inside the bodies can be defeated with necromancy.

Count Cagliostro, my grandfather, deduced the Frankenhausen family's dominance of the Cult. Vampires of the Frankenhausen bloodline sired human offspring. Upon reaching adulthood, the firstborn of each generation evolved into the reigning Great Vampire. The Curse of the Frankenhausens was exorcised when my mandrake extract cured the Count's daughter. She is now happily married.

My son-in-law has a far-fetched theory. Supposedly, the Frankenhausens acted as figureheads for Vlad the Impaler, a secret Great Vampire hiding in the Carpathians. Ricardo's speculations are ludicrous. The Turks decapitated the despot in 1476. No headless husk could be afflicted with the Undead pestilence.

I pray for the safety of my daughter Anna and her children. Extra steps will be taken to protect them in our estate. A reanimated Count Frankenhausen would seek vengeance against my descendants. Even though I disowned Anna's sister decades ago, my fears extend to her. There were recent rumors of a Countess Cagliostro in Panama. Was this my Joséphine, or did she have a daughter?

Claude Gabriel Dupont-Verdier's Journal, September 14, 1893

The Great Vampire is in England. The horrible massacre of the *Demeter*'s crew confirmed his presence. He must have guided that derelict ship to land at Whitby. My own *Jarvee* had earlier made a far less dramatic voyage to these shores. The cargo of three Mexican coffins never disturbed Captain Thompson and his sailors. The choice to store the relics here in London rather than Paris was fortuitous.

Count Frankenhausen's remains were cremated in the cellar of my Georgian mansion. My knife slashed the throat of the young prostitute from Mrs. Blake's bordello. Her blood dripped into the ashes as I recited the incantation from Prinn's *Les Mystères du Ver*:

In the fane of Yiggurath, the Source of All Malice,
*   And his progeny Slidith, Lord of the Blood Chalice,*
I summon forth the Great Vampyre
*   By his minion's charnel pyre.*

A wave of mist erupted upward from Frankenhausen's ashes. The haze assumed the semblance of a gaunt man. His dark hair and beard were tinged with grey. I was granted an audience with Dracula.

Dr. Caber's Letter to Joséphine Balsamo, September 15, 1893
Dear Joséphine,

A vial of Medjora diphtheria was missing from the storeroom. An investigation established your sister as the culprit. I challenged Sabine about the theft. She ranted incoherently about suicide. Her offense wasn't reported to my uncle and his associates. Please hurry to London. Sabine needs you desperately.
Your friend,

Urania

Claude Gabriel Dupont-Verdier's Journal, *September 15, 1893*

Dracula returned to my cellar after dusk. I handed him the mystical ruby, Akivasha's Tear. He sliced his palm with the scimitar sacred to the Old Ones. The jewel grew brighter as the Great Vampire poured his blood on it. His lips chanted the Aklo hymn to Yiggurath, Father of Serpents.

The two stone coffins no longer contained decaying carcasses. The occupants displayed the fullness of life. Hildegarde Einem climbed out of her coffin. She wore the stern clothes of a housekeeper. Her face exhibited the ravages of age. Her blonde hair was widely streaked with grey.

"Master," she murmured, "you didn't forsake me."

"Look closely, Hildegarde," decreed Dracula. "Who am I?"

"You're Count Franken– No; you're the nobleman whose castle the Count visited before his departure for Mexico."

"I am Dracula, the true Great Vampire. Siegfried Von Frankenhausen merely masqueraded in that role. He and his ancestors belonged to the Stepsons of the Dragon, my inner circle in the Cult of the Undead. Each Stepson owns a ring identical to mine. Every Frankenhausen firstborn inherited my ring until one of José Balsamo's agents intervened."

Dracula showed his ring to Hildegarde. She recognized the thrice-coiled effigy of a winged dragon with three ruby horns. It was Slidith, the Draconic Adder first worshipped in Lemuria and Valusia.

"I don't understand," declared Hildegarde. "Why do you have Stepsons?"

"They act as my eyes and ears. While I rest in my native soil, my Stepsons are awake in diverse parts of the world. They mentally communicate their experiences to me through our rings. The Stepsons transmit glorious visions of carnage and seduction. At the very least, they relieved the oblivion of my dormancy. Vampires normally don't dream."

"Master... I'm thirsty."

"My servant Gabriel has anticipated your hunger. You may dine after I leave. Restrain any designs on Gabriel's blood. He's too valuable as a mortal to me."

Dracula pointed towards the other vampire. "Eugenia, rise from your coffin! I command it!"

A lady in a white nightgown vacated the second casket. Dark curly hair draped her shoulders. There was no intelligence in her eyes. She motioned aimlessly toward my Master. Akivasha's Tear had mutated the Frankenhausen vampire virus into the more common Transylvanian version. Eugenia now had radically different abilities than in Mexico, but her mental faculties were still damaged. Hildegarde's wits were intact because her initial Undead rebirth miscarried.

"Walk with me in the moonlight, Eugenia," ordained Dracula. "The tribe of Cagliostro disrupted my supreme ambition. You shall be the instrument of my revenge." Eugenia exited with him up the stairs.

I opened a locked door with a key. "Your nightly meal," I heralded. The room harbored four female adolescents. Hildegarde immediately attacked them. Within minutes, the captives were all drained of blood. They would never be vampires. In contrast to its Mexican offshoots, the Transylvanian disease only spreads with the victim's additional drinking of the Undead's blood. Jillian Blake has been paid handsomely to deliver these maidens. The girls will not be missed by their procurer. Mrs. Blake falsely believed that her protégés were en route to Madame Delhomme's prosperous brothel in northern France.

Hildegarde advanced toward a wall mirror. "I have no reflection," she lamented.

"There is a special mirror upstairs. Permit me to escort you."

"What does the Great Vampire intend to do with Eugenia?"

"She's the subject of an audacious experiment. Who was destined to succeed Count Frankenhausen as Dracula's Stepson?"

"Frankenhausen's daughter, Brunhilde. She would have been a Stepdaughter."

"More of a Soul-Mate. For centuries, Dracula has schemed to infuse a woman with his own personality. The Soul-Mate requires superior breeding. He ordered Frankenhausen to wed Eugenia Guzman de La Selva because her maternal grandfather was the renowned soldier, Baron Kralitz. Furthermore, Kralitz's mother was a Durward and his wife was a Szandor. The Durwards were the preeminent duelists of England. Eugenia's pedigree extends directly back to Count Szandor and his Bulgarian bride, fierce rebels against King Mathias of Hungary in the 1480's. With her additional Frankenhausen heritage, Brunhilde would have been the perfect Soul-Mate. Unfortunately, she was vaccinated with José Balsamo's purifying acid. Brunhilde is totally immune to vampirism. Denied the daughter, Dracula will settle for the mother."

We finally reached the room where my "mirror" was stored. At our entry, Hildegarde was startled by a painting hanging over the mantelpiece. It was Joseph Bridau's *Hecate Reborn*. "Is this some sort of joke? I posed for that picture in 1840!" She contemplated the portrait with regret. "I was so beautiful."

"Examine your hands! They're young and firm! Blood has restored your youth!"

Hildegarde ripped off her clothes. Seeing her naked skin, she relished in her rejuvenation.

"Those garments were unsuitable, Hildegarde. These are more appropriate."

Hildegarde put on an exact copy of the white Grecian-style gown modeled for Bridau. Although her elegant legs were entirely covered, the dress closely clung to her superbly proportioned physique. A long sleeve sheathed her right arm, but her left shoulder and limb remained bare.

"It's regrettable, Gabriel, that you don't have a copy of the bracelet in the painting."

"But I have a substitute." I slipped the golden Valusian armlet on her left wrist.

"My portrait was commissioned by the Gabriel family while I was their governess in Austria. Gabriel must be your surname."

"It's my middle name. My mother was one of your charges. I've desired you since beholding Bridau's master-piece as a boy. My adoration drove me to research your sub-sequent history. You left my mother's family to become young Siegfried Von Frankenhausen's tutor. Accompanying the adult Count to Mexico, you ran afoul of Balsamo's vam-pire hunters during a decade-long battle.

"The death of my French father left me a fortune. I near-ly exhausted it to bring you back to life. The *Jarvee*, my pri-vate vessel, scoured the globe in an occult crusade. In Boneport, Louisiana, I found the sole surviving edition of

Loridan's *L'Essence du Dragon*. All other copies had been incinerated with the author in a warehouse fire. Besides Dracula's plans for a Soul-Mate, the book documented the rites capable of resuscitating any vampire. The Great Vampire's blood must envelop the ruby called Akivasha's Tear. It took me years to exhume the gem in an Egyptian tomb. Aided by Mexican outlaws, I violated the Frankenhausen Mausoleum. Locating Dracula in London, I offered him a singular trade. As payment for Eugenia, he would grant me my ideal woman...You."

"A fool's bargain, Gabriel. I only seduce with the lamia's kiss. Dracula forbids me to taste your blood."

"Your bracelet overcomes that restriction, Hildegarde. I wear its mate. Both bear the likeness of Slidith, son of Yiggurath and half-brother of Set. The magic of this Great Old One bonds the intellects of the bracelets' bearers. My mind will penetrate yours. The Master conceded the vampire's inability to dream. I can fill your daytime slumber with carnal delights. Let me be your incubus."

"You tempt me. Gabriel is too angelic a name for a tempter. Our nuptials will be sealed with a baptism. I christen you *Satanas*."

Sabine Balsamo's Diary, September 20, 1893

Dr. Caber related that my sister is coming to London. When she uncovers the truth about the poison, her rage will be monstrous. Death's merciful embrace attracts me. The Grim Reaper haunts my sleep, but his form isn't a hooded skeleton. He's a man with a pointed beard.

The apparition of my delirium beckons me to a spectacular realm. He says it is a glorious world where the dead can savor endless evenings of narcotic bliss. The dark messenger offers me this paradise if I welcome him into my house. So far, I have refused.

Claude Gabriel Dupont-Verdier's Journal, September 21-22, 1893

My days were filled with wanton ecstasy. Lust consumed Hildegarde. Vampires generally arise briskly at dusk. Enthralled by our erotic fusion, my concubine reluctantly left her coffin hours after sunset. I teased Hildegarde by proclaiming her the first vampire to chronically oversleep. Purchases from Mrs. Blake satiated Hildegarde's diet. After moving Eugenia's coffin elsewhere, Dracula ignored us for days. I erred in forgetting his existence.

Soon after nightfall, our sensual refuge in the Dreamlands was interrupted by a husky female voice. "Hildegarde, you lazy slut! Attend me! I command it!"

"I obey only the Great Vampire!" replied my lover.

"Enough of your insolence! Feel my wrath!"

In the world of dreams, my darling disappeared. Waking suddenly in my bed, I rushed downstairs to the cellar. "Satanas....save me!" wailed Hildegarde. She was out of her coffin. Blood splattered her white dress. Holding her stomach, she knelt before a macabre interloper.

I beheld a woman in a black ensemble consisting of a sleeveless tunic, pants and boots. Leather bracelets adorned her wrists and her upper arms. The back of her jet hair was tied in a plaited bun. Two long braids of hair fell to her waist. She wore a dark fur cape. A gold chain clasped the cloak around her neck. A ring with Dracula's dragon crest was on the fifth finger of her left hand. The intruder's long sharp nails were stained with Hildegarde's blood.

"How appallingly domestic!" noted the cloaked brunette. "You've given Gabriel a pet name. Do not seek succor from his quarter. Your Satanas hasn't the courage to defy me."

"Countess Frankenhausen," moaned Hildegarde, "please...no more..."

"Don't address me by that name. Eugenia is dead. My progenitor, Count Szandor, was the first Stepson of the Dragon. I celebrate my lineage as Szandra, Countess Dracula."

"Forgive me, Countess Dracula."

"Effete gods grant forgiveness. I impose penance. My boots are tarnished. Clean them."

"I'll fetch a cloth, Mistress."

"No, Hildegarde. Lick off the dust with your tongue."

My dearest complied with this demand. Szandra put her fingers in her mouth. She sucked the blood off her nails as Hildegarde debased herself. The Great Vampire had altered Eugenia's appearance through sorcery. Only faint traces of Frankenhausen's wife endured. The Soul-Mate of Dracula is leaner with red eyes instead of blue. Eugenia's brain had been a blank slate. It now housed the cunning of a maniacal warrior. This female surrogate of the Great Vampire gloated over our humiliation.

"My handmaiden has been tardy due to her trysts, Satanas. I suspected a potential pregnancy. The only recourse was to dissect her belly. My suspicions were incorrect. Hildegarde, you may stop. Your odious condition merits a bath. I don't require your services any further tonight."

Countess Dracula vanished as a cloud of mist.

Vampires do not wash in water. Running water is fatal to them. They bathe in blood. I bought more specimens from Mrs. Blake to supply the cleansing fluid. Hildegarde's sanguinary immersion healed her injuries. She put on a duplicate of the torn Grecian raiment in silence. A rift developed between us. Not only had I witnessed her degradation, but I had done nothing to circumvent it.

The next day, Hildegarde's performance was... uninspired. She dismissed me from the Dreamlands long before dusk. I cursed Szandra for ruining my lecherous utopia.

Immediately upon dusk, Hildegarde emerged from her coffin. She stood patiently for hours awaiting the coming of Szandra. Finally, a swirl of smoke transmuted into Countess Dracula.

"You have learned from your mistakes, Hildegarde."

"Yes, Mistress."

"Your improvement deserves a reward. Like my consort, I mandate three Sisters of the Night to be my acolytes." Countess Dracula fondled Hildegarde's yellow locks. "As the most senior of my Sisterhood, you shall conscript another devotee of my choosing."

"Who shall be the next Sister, Mistress?"

"My consort has the ability to sense souls in torment. Do you understand this peculiar skill?"

"The Master can feel the thoughts of a person troubled by visions of death and madness. Is the candidate an asylum inmate?"

"No, merely a contemplator of suicide. Her induction into the Sisterhood shall punish the inventor of the most formidable weapon ever employed against our Cult."

"José Balsamo! Have you chosen Señora Anna Peisser, Don José's daughter?"

"No, our quarry is Anna's niece."

"I would have preferred a daughter. Anna infiltrated the Frankenhausen household posing as a servant 18 years ago. I hunger to repay that strumpet."

"My consort researched the Balsamo family. Anna and her husband Ricardo have five children. The youngest is an eight-year old girl. She's the fourth Joséphine descended from Count Cagliostro. Unlike her predecessors, this Joséphine has black hair."

"We could journey to Mexico and make Anna's daughter the third Sister."

"An excellent idea, Hildegarde. Her niece has a reprieve tonight because a proper invitation is lacking. Would you care to scrounge the streets for a midnight repast?"

"We can partake indoors. Thanks to Mrs. Blake, our food larder is well-stocked."

Joséphine Balsamo's Letter to José Alejandro Balsamo, October 6, 1893
Dear Grandfather,

We have never met. I am the child of your prodigal daughter. Her name was the same as your mother's. It is mine as well.

I discovered your whereabouts three years ago during a visit to Panama. You may distrust the validity of this letter. Permit me to prove its veracity with information available only to our family. Joseph Balsamo, Count Cagliostro, had two wives. The tragic passing of the first, Lorenza, was publicized by the novelist Dumas. She needn't concern us. Shortly after the Affair of the Queen's Necklace in 1785, our forebear wedded Sharita, an Indian priestess. Cagliostro investigated the terrifying depredations of Kurt Von Frankenhausen throughout Germany. This alleged Great Vampire retaliated by converting Sharita into a deranged lamia. The Bavarian Inquisition apprehended Sharita and burned her at the stake.

A grief-stricken Cagliostro had an assignation with Joséphine de Beauharnais in Fontainebleau during 1787. Their daughter was born a year later. She was the first of our line to be dubbed Joséphine Balsamo. After her natural mother became Napoleon's Empress, my namesake posed as the goddaughter of the illustrious beauty. In the wake of Waterloo, the original Joséphine Balsamo was wooed by the enigmatic Henri de Belcamp. Her lover revealed his real identity as Prince Serge Dolgorouki of Russia. Belcamp was merely his alias in Paris. Dolgorouki transported Joséphine to the court of Czar Alexander II. There she adopted the title of Countess Cagliostro. Deserted by Dolgorouki in 1816, she bore his son—you, my grandfather. Born Joseph Alexander Balsamo, you utilize the Spanish variant of your name in Mexico.

The Cult of the Undead still terrorized our family. In 1818, your mother received an urgent plea from her older half-sister, Sara Balsamo. Sharita's daughter was pursued in Moldavia by Gorcha the Vourdalak and his bloodthirsty brethren. My namesake gallantly rescued her sibling by slaughtering Gorcha's band of vampires. Great-grandmother trained you to continue the war against the Undead. Your labors are devoted to combating this abomination. News of vampire outbreaks in Mexico prompted your resettlement there in the 1860's.

You married Felina de Valgeneuse in 1844. My mother's birth in 1845 was followed by that of her sister Anna two

159

years later. In 1867, a serious schism developed between you and my mother. She rebelled against your decision to move the family from Europe to Mexico. The clandestine cabal known as the Black Coats recruited her. She envisioned them as no different from the Masonic societies that your grandfather used to spread liberty, equality and fraternity. You argued that the Black Coats only promote treason, revenge and extortion. All your objections were accurate. Unfortunately, I am also entangled in the intrigues of the Black Coats. It's too late for me to escape my hateful servitude. By writing you, I risk my life. It's an offense punishable by death to disclose our organization's activities to outsiders. This rule is so stringent that no member is permitted to keep a diary.

My mother's affair with a munitions dealer led to my birth in 1868. My sister Sabine was born two years later. While I resemble our mother and great-grandmother, Sabine is slim with black hair.

My father wrongly assumed Sabine to be his child. My mother confessed Sabine's true parentage to me and Leonard, our loyal retainer. Sabine was never intended to learn her real origins.

Your daughter Joséphine perished in 1880. She was lured into a fatal ambush by an ex-suitor. As my mother lay dying from her wounds, she asked me to take two oaths. The first was to protect Sabine always. The second was to destroy the family of the contemptible betrayer. Leonard buried your daughter in a purple robe befitting an Empress. Her ring bearing the golden ram insignia was bequeathed to me. Despite my current ownership, I always imagine my mother wearing this ring.

There was another legacy. You had two sliver brooches fashioned as five-pointed stars. They were presents for your daughters. My mother wanted Anna also to join the Black Coats, but my aunt sided with you. Anna's rejection infuriated my mother. She enticed a burglar to steal Anna's pentagram. My mother later regretted this sisterly feud. She cautioned me and Sabine never to repeat it. Our mother divided the brooches between us.

After the funeral, Leonard persuaded my father to provide for our upbringing. Sabine and I were sent to a wonderful Parisian school staffed by nuns. My fiery nature made me a disciplinary problem. Reports of constant infractions compelled my father to separate me from Sabine. Exiled to a strict boarding school in Provence, I took my pentagram with me. Upon graduation, I gave it as a gift to a fellow student.

I then was initiated into the Black Coats. They served as the means to fulfill my mother's dying wishes. An alliance with the Back Coats allowed me to ruthlessly avenge her. It also permitted me to provide for my sister. Sabine's enrolled at St. Swithin's Medical School in London. To avoid the onus of the Balsamo name, she was registered under the anagram of Absalom. The Black Coats agreed to pay for Sabine's education in exchange for her induction into their medical research center. The director of this group is named Urania. Although her family is a notorious criminal dynasty, she surprisingly has a trustworthy nature. Many denigrate her as scientifically brilliant but impractical. I deem her to be a real rarity: a true friend. Urania acted as a mentor to my sister. During a visit to the laboratory of the Black Coats, Sabine stole some poison. Urania immediately wrote me after covering up my sister's crime.

I own a London abode where my sister resides under the Absalom alias. Arriving there from France on September 22, I interrogated her.

"Urania is convinced you're suicidal. Why are you depressed?"

"There's no use pretending anymore, Josine. You hate me."

"How could I? We're sisters."

"No, we're only half-sisters. My father was the man who betrayed Mama."

Stunned by her words, I sought to console my sister. "You're still my flesh and blood. Mama never wanted you to know. Did Leonard say something?"

"I won't tell you."

"Then don't. The only important thing is that I love you." My voice choked with emotion. "I don't care how you learned Mama's secret. We shall always be sisters."

Sabine hugged me and wept. She still shielded her informant after our reconciliation. It must be Leonard. He has known about Sabine's true lineage since the moment of her birth. Because of Leonard's past fidelity, I haven't acted on my suspicions.

The next morning, my sister was much better. I expected to stay with her. An early morning edict from my superior in the Black Coats interfered. She dispatched me with a proposal for an architect in Bristol. Any flunky could have performed the task, but this heartless tyrant regularly saddles me with unnecessary duties. I departed by train before noon. My return was scheduled the next afternoon.

In my absence, Sabine faced pure horror.

Sabine Balsamo's Diary, September 23, 1893

My endless turmoil is over. All doubts about Josine's affection for me have been eliminated. Why did Madame Koluchy send her to Bristol? I miss my sister's radiant smile.

The day was beautiful and sunny. I decided to stroll down Piccadilly Circus at noon. I met a charming woman by happenstance. She accidentally stepped on my foot. Ashamed of her *faux pas*, she insisted on treating me at the local tea shop.

My acquaintance is Countess Alucard, a fascinating aristocrat with braided raven hair. She recently arrived from Hungary with her husband and maid. The lady seemed very wealthy. She was wearing a stylish black dress and veil. A gold bracelet was on her left wrist.

The Countess was extremely loquacious in her thick Hungarian accent. Labeling tea inferior to coffee, she barely touched her cup. Amused by her ramblings, I invited the Countess to visit my home. She knows me only by my pseudonym of Absalom. The Countess asked if her maid, Fraulein Einem, could come. Of course, I assented. Countess Alucard has the most stilted way of speaking. I remember her awkward question: "Do we have permission to cross your threshold?"

As we were leaving, she noticed her husband in the crowd. He's a bearded man strangely resembling the spectre of my nightmares. I am still

(*Editor's Note*: Sabine's diary terminates abruptly. There are no further entries.)

Claude Gabriel Dupont-Verdier's Journal, September 23, 1893

Hildegarde blocked my entry into her mind for several hours. Finally my paramour opened the door to her thoughts. I created the illusory boudoir where we always rendezvoused. Hildegarde's psychic simulacrum appeared. My astral double embraced her, but she remained cold and unresponsive. Our conversation took curious detours.

"Satanas, does Alucard signify anything?"

"It's the Master's name backwards. Some of his Stepsons use it as a *nom de guerre*."

"How can Dracula live in the daytime? Sunlight should be fatal to our kind."

"Years ago, the Great Vampire conducted a ritual sacred to Slidith. It was supposed to grant Dracula full immunity in daylight, but the ceremony was only a partial success. He can survive the sun, but all his powers are rendered dormant by it. And he still needs to rest periodically to renew his strength."

"The Master imparted this ability to his Soul-Mate. She braved the daylight today."

"You're in the Dreamlands, Hildegarde. How could you possibly know?"

"Because I told her," announced Countess Dracula. I was startled by Szandra's intrusion. Her astral self wore the same barbaric garb flaunted nightly. One of her wristbands had been superseded by a Valusian bracelet. This accessory must decorate Szandra's arm in the waking world. Her clairvoyant communiqués had beguiled Hildegarde. My lover had degenerated into Sandra's daytime voyeur.

"Did you enjoy my chat with Anna's niece?"

"I did not. She's an insipid creature, Mistress."

"I detect a tone of jealousy. Don't fret; you'll always be my favorite. Sabine will merely be a thrall whose eternal suffering will amuse us."

"Thank you, Mistress. Shouldn't Satanas go elsewhere?"

"Let him stay. Some men wish to watch…such things."

I won't describe what happened next in the Dreamlands. Saturated with disgust, I fled the imaginary region to the actuality of my quarters. I went downstairs and brooded over Hildegarde's coffin. With the setting of the sun, she rose from her resting place. Icy indifference emanated from her.

"I have no time for you, Satanas. My Mistress craves my attentions."

"Don't forsake me. I yearn for your company."

"You can easily satisfy your request. Your bracelet will enable you to observe as I gratify the whims of Countess Dracula. You may even learn *something*."

"Such as?"

"How to make love to a woman." She changed into a bat and fluttered away. Regardless of her taunts, my longing overwhelmed me. Merging with Hildegarde's mind, I perceived the outside as her.

I spied a house from a high distance in the sky. Szandra abided outside the building, I took my natural form. The Countess smiled at me with fondness. "My precious Hildegarde," she intoned.

We glimpsed a light on the second floor of the edifice. Becoming mist, we passed through the cracks of the windowsill. We materialized in a bedroom. Sabine Balsamo was seated at a desk. She was busy writing in a notebook. A diary? I will peruse it later. Finally the chronicler noticed us.

164

"Countess Alucard! How did you get in? Why are you wearing those clothes?"

Szandra stared into Sabine's eyes. She was plucking memories from this pathetic female. Through our bracelets, my Mistress transferred these remembrances. I projected the silhouette of a blonde in a green dress into the sight of our initiate. In her imagination, I became this other woman.

"Josine!" exclaimed Sabine. "Please tell me what is happening!"

"Countess Alucard is a gifted medium," I explained. "She can contact our mother."

"Mama…"

"Please sit down, my sister. Close your eyes and think of Mama." Sabine foolishly complied. "Remember," I resumed, "when we last saw her alive."

"Mama was on her bed. Her shoulder was mutilated from the stab wounds. She died screaming vengeance against her enemies. I can't continue, Josine."

"Open your eyes, my sister!" I dissolved the illusion and bared my fangs. "Sabine Balsamo, die like your mother!"

My scrawny prey leaped from the chair in panic. "Nosferatu!" yelled Sabine. Grabbing a star-like object from her desk, she waved it in front of me.

"A pentagram is no match for a vampire," I boasted. My right hand snatched the talisman from her and tossed it behind me. I ripped open the left side of the puny girl's blouse. My teeth sank into her shoulder. I feasted heartily.

"Don't be too greedy," Szandra whispered into my ear. "Our novice must not truly die."

I reluctantly ceased. Szandra yanked Sabine's head upward by seizing the top of her hair "Now you know, daughter of the Cagliostros, how your mother felt as life slipped away. She cried for their blood of her tormentors. Do you?"

"Blood…" muttered Sabine groggily. "Give me the blood of the woman who did this to me."

"I'm very generous with the spilling of blood" volunteered Szandra. I extended my left arm. The Mistress cut my wrist with her fingernail. She pressed my bleeding flesh over the mouth of our victim.

"Drink, Sabine," purred Szandra.

Joséphine Balsamo's Letter to José Alejandro Balsamo (continued)

My train arrived in London late in the afternoon of September 24. Urania was gracious enough to meet me at the station with a carriage. Hearing of my unnecessary trip, Urania sought to expedite my reunion with Sabine. At my domicile, we made a horrendous discovery.

My sister was lying unconscious on her bedroom floor. Blood flowed profusely from two gashes in her left shoulder. Luckily, Urania always carried her medical bag. After bandaging Sabine's shoulder, Urania arranged an emergency transfusion with me as the donor. If not for Urania'a ministrations, Sabine would have bled to death.

As she slept in her bed, Sabine mumbled, "Josine... Protect me... Vampires..." I knew all about the Undead from the family stories. My sister had clearly been targeted by the cultists. I didn't expound my beliefs to Urania. As a scientific rationalist, she would be unwilling to accept the reality of these supernatural predators. Presuming Sabine the victim of a demented assailant, Urania left to gather some Black Coat bodyguards.

After my friend's exit, I realized that the sun had already set. "Great-grandmother, grant me strength," I prayed. Vampires are vulnerable to crucifixes. None were in the house. I improvised by retrieving two pokers from the downstairs fireplace. As I wandered back through the passageway to Sabine's chambers, I heard feminine giggling. My sister's persecutors had returned. Crossing the pokers, I entered the room. Two women were near my sister's bed. They had torn open the bandages on Sabine's shoulder. One was a brunette in a black leather outfit with a fur cape. Her companion was a blonde attired in the manner of a Greek goddess. The duo slowly retreated before my impromptu cross.

"You call that makeshift atrocity a crucifix," mocked the brunette.

"Our adversary's religiosity is deficient, Mistress," ridiculed the blonde.

"Of course, Hildegarde. We saw this libertine in Sabine's mind. Joséphine Balsamo, Countess Cagliostro, you're merely counterfeit nobility. I am a true Countess, the Soul-Mate of the Great Vampire."

"You must be the wife of the current Count Frankenhausen."

"The Frankenhausens were merely pawns. The real Great Vampire is Dracula!"

Legends depict vampires cowering in terror at the cross. This pair merely froze as if coerced with a pistol. Are the stories false? Or was my cross diminished by its haphazard structure?

"The cross is only as potent as the purity of its holder," jeered Countess Dracula.

"It's strong enough to hold you here until dawn," I attested.

"The sun will not destroy me," warned the Countess.

"But what about me?" pleaded Hildegarde.

"Do not despair. Our antagonist is flawed. I can read her soul."

The scarlet eyes of the Countess probed deeply into mine. The figure of Hildegarde blurred. She was replaced by a woman in a purple robe. Her face mirrored mine.

I gasped "Mama!"

"Please lower your cross, daughter. I must kiss you."

"You can't be Mama!"

"You always deny those who love you the most," said another speaker. There was a girl next to my mother. She was wearing a pentagram brooch. I dare not write her name. She was slender with dark hair just like Sabine. I was confronted by my former classmate from Provence.

"You were always attracted to me, Josine, but you couldn't admit your true passions."

"That's not true. I only pretended to care for you."

"Remember when the headmistress sent all the students to bed. We didn't fall asleep. You were the prefect with the keys to the residence. We crept out into the night to watch the stars together. I told you my aspirations to be an artist."

Tears filled my eyes as I recalled these excursions.

"Frequently, Josine, we went to an unused portion of the school. There I sketched you in secret. I knew every line of your face...every facet of your body."

"Please stop," I begged.

"You must relinquish the pokers, Josine. I can't come to you unless they're surrendered. Only then will you feel the caress of my lips."

Uncrossing the pokers, I gave one to my mother. She flung it on the ground. I glanced at her hands. She had the ring with the golden ram. That same circlet was on my finger. The contradiction dragged me back to reality. The mirage dissipated. My mother reverted to Hildegarde.

I plunged the remaining poker into Hildegarde's chest. As the writhing vampire fell, my classmate devolved into Countess Dracula. She gripped my throat. My hands tugged on the chain of her cape. The Countess hurled me across the room into a wall. Dazed from the impact, I collapsed.

"Mistress..." wheezed the fallen Hildegarde. "She only scraped the edge of my heart...help me..."

The Countess plucked the poker out of her lackey's torso. Hildegarde rose to her full height.

"You damaged my clasp, Cagliostro," snarled the Countess as the cloak dropped off her back. "Your sister will pay for this sacrilege."

"And so will the younger Joséphine," added Hildegarde.

"All in good time," predicted the Countess. "Both Sabine and Anna's little child shall be yours. First, beat this upstart to a pulp." The Countess handed the poker to Hildegarde. The blonde raised the rod with her right hand. I chanced upon my sister's pentagram on the floor. The brooch is silver, a metal sometimes anathema to vampires. I threw the star at

Hildegarde. She blocked the flying object with her left hand. The brooch's pin pierced her palm. She issued a sharp whimper. Tucking the poker under her arm, Hildegarde struggled with her right hand to remove the imbedded pentagram. The star rubbed a gold bracelet on her left wrist. She screamed "My arm is burning!" A blue flame engulfed Hildegarde. It disintegrated her and the poker. The brooch fell to the ground.

"You destroyed my servant! Now I will destroy you!" screeched Countess Dracula advancing towards my prostrate body. Her claw-like fingers slowly inched toward my stomach. "You have maternal instincts, Cagliostro. Maybe you're pregnant. Let's see!"

"Leave my sister alone!" shouted Sabine standing behind our nemesis. The lacerations on my sister's shoulder had vanished. The slaying of Hildegarde had revoked the mark of the vampire

Countess Dracula howled in agony. The tip of a metal stake burst from the front of her tunic.

Sabine had driven the other poker through the lamia's back impaling her merciless heart. The vampire dropped to her knees in front of me. I exulted over the shock and disbelief in her eyes.

"Before you roast in Hell, Dracula, learn this lesson. Never underestimate the Cagliostros."

I laughed triumphantly. Countess Dracula then smiled cryptically. Her face was filled with rapture. Then her eyelids closed as she fell back lifeless. The Countess wore a bracelet akin to Hildegarde's. I picked up the pentagram and dropped it on the gilded ornament. Blue fire blanketed the cadaver. The slain vampire faded from existence. The pentagram was unscathed.

No vampire can infest a home without being invited. My sister divulged how the Countess engineered an invitation during a contrived meeting in the street. The Countess had been with a man professing to be her husband. He must be Count Dracula. Urania arrived later with several men. I gave them Dracula's description: a tall thin man with a dark beard. The

Black Coats were slowly mobilizing against the Great Vampire.

Claude Gabriel Dupont-Verdier's Journal, September 25, 1893

I drew Hildegarde's soul into my bracelet when her corporeality was lost. That pentagram must have been consecrated as an Elder Sign, a charm hostile to the symbols of Slidith and the Old Ones. Her right hand had held the star earlier without consequence, but the striking of the Elder Sign against the Valusian artifact on her left wrist ignited a devastating combustion.

Hildegarde's entrapped essence does not receive my thoughts. I can only hear her cries of despair and loneliness. Her mistreatment of me has not dampened my lust. I pleaded with Dracula to reconstitute her flesh with Akivasha's Tear. He would only vow to resurrect Hildegarde along with Szandra. The Great Vampire had witnessed the demise of his Soul-Mate through their enchanted rings.

As a precaution, the Master had linked Szandra's spirit to her cloak. If the mantle was extant, Szandra could live again. To ferret out the cape, Dracula embarked on a bold strategy. He directed me to infiltrate the Black Coats. Hildegarde stole Sabine's diary. It contained valuable data about the criminal organization. The diary cited names of important members—Moriarty, Caber, Koluchy, Dorrington, Saladin and Nikola. This infamous roster included London's purveyor of vice, Jillian Blake.

Excerpt from Confessions of a Black Coat *by Larry Parker (Unpublished Manuscript)*

The biggest dunce in the Black Coats was Urania Caber. In the autumn of 1893, she instructed me to burn a fur cape as a favor for Countess Cagliostro. Of course, I did no such thing. Being grossly underpaid, I sold the item to Jacob Dix the pawnbroker.

Claude Gabriel Dupont-Verdier's Journal, *October 3, 1893*

Contacting the Black Coats under the auspices of Mrs. Blake, I stumbled upon a startling fact. They're searching for Dracula. When I apprised the Master, he instituted counter-measures. Already pursued by Van Helsing, he can't afford to fight the Black Coats. A retreat to Transylvania is warranted.

The Great Vampire is not content with defensive maneuvers. Dracula bids me to orchestrate new aggression. The *Jarvee* will be arriving in Mexico with a message for Aguilar. Once his desperados secure a certain prize, the ship will haul the merchandise across the Atlantic. Captain Thompson was reluctant to lug such freight. I overcame his qualms by promising him ownership of the *Jarvee* for this final service.

Joséphine Balsamo's Letter to José Alejandro Balsamo (concluded)

I'm perplexed by Countess Dracula's dying grin. My sister thinks that our opponent was at peace after her release from the vampire curse. I don't share this opinion. Her smile implied a new conspiracy against our family. The instigator of this offensive must be the Great Vampire. According to our inquiries, Count Dracula fled England by a ship bound for the Black Sea.

Hildegarde mentioned Anna's daughter. Anxiety over her welfare motivates my letter. Dracula's disciples may still seek to turn her into a vampire. Did Anna name her child after my mother? Or was Anna thinking of your mother, the slayer of demons? Two Joséphines have already disgraced the name of your esteemed parent, grandfather. My mother and I were corrupted. The youngest holder of our ancestor's name must be spared an equally cruel destiny.

As a member of the Black Coats, I am little better than a vampire. Like the Undead, the Black Coats prey on humanity. The leaders of my organization are sadistic autocrats. I never informed them about Dracula's true nature. They merely view him as a lunatic stalking my sister. My motives for this subterfuge are simple. I dread that the Black Coats might seek a partnership with the Great Vampire.

My mother during her lifetime kept a picture of Anna. I always admired my aunt's wonderful ebony curls. Is her daughter also a brunette? Does Anna call her daughter Joséphine or the Spanish counterpart, Josefina?

Ever since my experience with Countess Dracula, I've been plagued by a recurring nightmare. I see a child with dark hair abused by fiends. Her persecutors are not vampires but men in black coats. Please cherish and protect Anna's daughter.

Your granddaughter,

Joséphine

José Alejandro Balsamo's Diary, May 6, 1894

Masked bandits raided our hacienda. They kidnapped Josefina. Ricardo and the servants are out searching for her. I implore God to let no harm befall my innocent grandchild.

The Eulogy of Satanas to his Beloved, April 30, 1895

Darling Hildegarde, you cannot read my words. Your disembodied purgatory persists on Walpurgis Night. One prerequisite is absent for your liberation. I require the blood of the Great Vampire, but he is no more. Van Helsing's followers exterminated him in Transylvania.

Your enemies, the heirs of Count Cagliostro, shall not flourish. I plot to avenge you by manipulating the Black Coats. Sabine Balsamo disregarded a cardinal prohibition. She kept a diary with references to the syndicate's hierarchy. Thanks to you, that book is mine. If my criminal peers study her notations, Sabine's life would be in jeopardy. At the proper time, I'll strike at Joséphine's beloved sister.

You always loathed Anna Peisser. Her only daughter is enslaved. Again you're responsible, my sweet, for this development. You proposed Josefina Peisser as a Sister of the Night. Dracula dictated her abduction. Captain Thompson hired Aguilar and his pistoleros to capture the girl. The *Jarvee* smuggled her into Europe. Dracula hoped to personally turn Josefina into a vampire. His destruction caused a modification to this act of retribution. Josefina has been hidden in France. I've sold her to Madame Delhomme's brothel in Chartres. The child will be taught to be a voluptuary rivaling Szandra in depravity. The Balsamo clan rejoices in anagrams like Absalom. I mimic our foes with an anagram of "vampire." Anna's daughter has been renamed *Irma Vep*.

I excuse your flirtation with Szandra. You were attracted to the avatar of the Great Vampire within her. Szandra will no longer be a barrier to our union. I've abandoned my hunt for her cloak. There is no reason to reconstruct her anymore. The essence of the Great Vampire will never separate us. It will dwell inside my breast

Loridan has shown me the way. He described the methods that Vlad the Impaler used to become the Great Vampire. The modern equivalent of Vlad's excesses shall be my pathway to immortality. It may take decades, but I will control my own cadre in the Black Coats. My underlings will commit countless crimes of butchery to befoul my soul. The inevitable outcome will be my arrest by the police. When that calamity arrives, poison will extinguish my life. The Old Ones will reconstitute me as the Great Vampire, the successor to Dracula. My own blood will fuel Akivasha's Tear. You shall feel the fleshly pleasures as my Soul-Mate. We shall walk the Earth for all eternity.

Frank J. Morlock: *The Adventure of the Benefi-cent Vampire*

I regret to say that when Holmes was idle for long peri-ods of time he could become rather disagreeable.

"Look at it, Watson. Fog as thick as soup, fog you could cut with a knife, perfect weather for the most baffling mystery, and nothing, not even a purse snatching. The lack of imagina-tion amongst the criminal classes in England is truly appal-ling."

He went on like this for some time, increasingly restless.

"Well, here's something, Holmes. Several books have been stolen from the British Museum."

"Probably just misplaced."

"No, the book thief left a note of apology, but saying that his need for the manuscripts involved a matter of life and death."

"Now, that is peculiar. What sort of books were stolen, Watson?"

"French plays, Holmes."

"Bah! Why would anyone steal French plays?"

His mood was improving by the moment.

"Here, read the item for yourself."

Holmes was just about to engross himself in this minor mystery when Mrs. Hudson arrived with the mail.

"A package for you, Doctor Watson."

I opened the package and found it contained a smaller package with a notation: "*Dear Doctor Watson, please remit the contents of this package to your friend Mr. Sherlock Holmes. It is a matter of great urgency.*"

"Actually, this seems to be for you, Holmes."

Holmes pulled his nose out of the account of the theft and opened the package.

"This is some kind of joke."

"What is it?"

"These appear to be the missing French plays."

"Why on Earth–?"

"Why, indeed, would anyone go to the trouble of stealing French plays from the British Museum to send them to me?"

"What kind of plays are they, Holmes?"

"Vampire plays."

"Really?"

"One by Charles Nodier published in 1820. The other by Alexandre Dumas in 1851."

"Dumas? The fellow who wrote *The Three Musketeers*?"

"Yes."

"I didn't know he wrote plays. I used to love reading his works. But what an odd thing to steal."

"Even odder to send them to me."

Holmes began to glance through the manuscripts.

"It was a thumping good story, Holmes."

"What was?"

"*The Three Musketeers*. Any idea why they sent it to you. Any letter?"

"No. But whoever did, had a very peculiar handwriting. He apparently uses an Eastern European script. I would guess it to be Rumanian, from the Carpathian region, and at least 500 years old. Not very common today."

"How can you know that?"

"A detective must be aware of different handwriting styles."

"So whoever wrote on this package has been dead for 400 years, eh?"

"Exactly."

"Sometimes, Holmes, your deductions amaze me..."

"Ah, you don't believe it, eh?"

"I find it difficult at the moment."

But at this moment Mrs. Hudson appeared again, and seemed rather upset..

"It's that little papist priest who came here to see you some time ago."

"Father Brown!"

"That's him. He's back. This is a respectable house, Mr. Holmes. I've put up with many strange characters appearing here, I consider your line of work, but if papists are to be regular visitors–"

"But just because Father Brown is a Catholic priest doesn't mean he's a bad person, Mrs. Hudson," I exclaimed.

She sniffed as if she doubted it. "He's not trying to convert you, is he?"

"I have no idea what the purpose of his visit is, Mrs. Hudson. And the only way to find out is to show him in."

Father Brown entered, in his self-effacing way. He removed his coat and placed his umbrella in the stand.

"Ah, it's you, Father Brown. How are things in your parish?"

"Rather unsettling, I'm afraid."

"No more witches, I trust."

"Oh, no. They're gone–forever, I hope."

"But what brings you–"

"An abomination of a different sort."

"Indeed?"

"This time it's vampires."

"What a coincidence, Holmes."

Holmes shushed me.

"Please explain, Father Brown."

"I can't explain directly. I learned something in confession. I can't reveal it. But let us say I have reason to believe that strange and disgusting things–are taking place, and–well, I have to go back a little to explain. My duties have expanded to acting as Chaplain at a resident school in my parish. It's known as the Rivven School for Girls. It was founded in the

1850s by an English Lord named Rivven, for young girls. It is more or less a convent. But admission is free to young girls of all classes and religious persuasion. Lord Rivven died some years ago and was succeeded by his son, the present Lord Rivven, who runs the school. Everything is paid for from Lord Rivven's immense fortune. While the girls do not live in luxury, they have all they could need. Lord Rivven set the school up on his estate, and the school actually adjoins Rivven Castle. The result is that Lord Rivven frequently visits the premises to make sure that everything is done properly. He not only insures that the girls are well educated, he takes particular care that they receive good food and proper exercise."

"That is singular. In most schools the cuisine is usually detestable at worst, unpalatable at best."

"Not at Rivven School. Lord Rivven is particularly attentive to that."

"And how do vampires figure in to this scholastic idyll you've been describing?"

"Several of the older girls whose confessions I have heard have–indicated–that–"

Here, Father Brown hesitated, pondering how much he could say, then he plunged forward.

"–That they are being visited at night by a mysterious man–who–well, I shan't–I cannot go into details. The young women thought it was simply a sinful dream. But you see, they are all having the same dream. So much so that I am convinced there's a reality to it."

"And this visitor?"

"Is a vampire!"

"Bah!"

"I am not superstitious. I discounted it at first, but– then there are the bite marks–"

"Bite marks!"

"Faint, but visible on the necks of each of these young girls. And they look pale, as if they have lost considerable amounts of blood. They are lethargic."

"Do you suspect anyone?"

"A European gentleman bought an old mansion near the Rivven School, several months ago. He gives his name as Count Valberg and claims to be a political refugee from I don't know what regime. Possibly Russia."

"And you think he's the vampire?"

"Yes."

"Why?"

"All these incidents began shortly after he arrived–and besides that–"

"Besides that?"

"He answers the description the girls give of their nocturnal visitor."

"You've seen this Valberg?"

"I made it a point to visit him."

"Did you question him?"

"I asked him if he'd ever been to the school, and he denied it. Valberg is a man of striking appearance. If you once look at his evil face, you'll never forget him."

"Evil?"

"Yes, I'm sure of it."

"But how does he gain access to the girls?"

"Ah, that is the question. I don't know. The girls rarely leave the school and only with a chaperone. And no man would be admitted, especially at night. Valberg has never attempted to visit the school according to the matrons. So, it's another mystery. But vampires have means–"

"Let's exhaust other possibilities first, before looking to the attributes of vampires. What does Valberg do for a living?"

"Nothing. He seems to be very wealthy. He bought a large mansion near the school, but he rarely goes out, never entertains and stays to himself."

"And he comes from Eastern Europe."

"The Balkans. Transylvania, I believe."

"Transylvania? Hmm..."

"Will you help me, Mr. Holmes. If this continues, I fear for the lives–for the souls of these young girls."

178

"Yes, certainly. Something is amiss. Have you informed Lord Rivven of your suspicions?"

"Just yesterday. Before that, he's been visiting his family estate in Staffa, on business."

"Staffa. That's odd, " Holmes mumbled.

After more discussion, we agreed to accompany Father Brown to his parish. On our arrival, we discussed the way to proceed.

"Shall I talk to the girls?"

"It's a delicate matter. I cannot reveal what they told me, but I've informed them, Emily Warren, Dorothy Phelps and Lisa Waters, that I proposed to ask a detective to investigate the situation, and they all agreed without any hesitation to talk to you."

"I'll want to speak to them separately."

When we entered the school, we found everyone in consternation. We were met by the headmistress, Mrs. Palmer. She was a handsome, no-nonsense woman in her early forties. She came immediately to Father Brown.

"Oh, Father Brown, you cannot imagine, the most terrible thing has happened. Lisa Waters has disappeared. And no one knows what has happened to her."

Father Brown was greatly concerned. He introduced Holmes and myself to Mrs. Palmer and explained who Holmes was.

"Thank goodness you've returned and brought Mr. Holmes with you. I don't have a man around here to help me who's worth a damn. Pardon, my French, Father Brown. Would you believe it, when I told Lord Rivven what had happened, he became ghastly ill and has taken to his bed. What I need is a real man."

"Mrs. Palmer, did Lisa Waters take her clothes with her or leave any note?" asked Holmes.

"Not a word. She has simply vanished. No one saw her leave. Her bed was unmade. She apparently slept in it, got up in the night–and simply left."

"But surely the doors are locked?"

"Yes, and there's no sign they were tampered with. Besides, they're noisy. Someone would have heard them if they were opened at night."

"Then, perhaps, she's still in the school somewhere."

"We've looked high and low, Mr. Holmes. Not a sign, not a trace. The girls are terrified. And what's worse, they all loved Lisa."

"May I see her room?"

Mrs. Palmer led us upstairs to the dormitory. To my surprise, each girl had a private room, neatly furnished with simple but well-made furniture and curtains on the widows. A desk, a bed and an armchair. A small window looked out over the garden.

"Isn't it unusual for girls to have so much luxury in a school of this sort?"

"Lord Rivven is very good. He makes sure that the needs of every girl are attended to."

After looking around, Holmes announced, "There's no evidence that anyone was here–no sign of a struggle."

Mrs. Palmer went to the closet and looked in.

"I can't be absolutely certain but none of Lisa's dresses appears missing. All the hangers are in use."

"Most observant, Mrs. Palmer."

"Thank you, Mr. Holmes, I pride myself on being meticulous."

"And none of the other girls saw or heard anything?"

"I heard her get up," said a young girl who had poked her head in the doorway.

"This is Emily Warren, Mr. Holmes," said Mrs. Palmer.

"Around what time?"

"I think it was around midnight, a little after perhaps."

"And that was all?"

"Yes. She didn't make a lot of noise. I thought perhaps she was studying, or restless. I didn't hear much more."

At Father Brown's request, Emily agreed to speak to Holmes privately. But Holmes insisted that Father Brown be present.

180

The interview was still taking place when Mrs. Palmer came in, visibly upset.

"I must see Mr. Holmes immediately."

"He's interviewing Miss Warren, and even I–"

"Well, I can." And she proceeded to rap harshly on the door. Holmes opened it and she spoke rapidly; I had the feeling that she was controlling herself bravely, but that she was on the verge of hysteria.

"We've found Lisa, Mr. Holmes, you must come immediately." And she whispered something in his ear. Holmes, Father Brown and I followed Mrs. Palmer to the end of the garden at the rear of the school. There in a thicket near the fence lay the blood-soaked body of Lisa Waters. She was in her nightgown. I examined the body.

"Her throat was torn out. It looks as if it was done by an animal."

"An animal?"

"See–claw marks–and how raggedly the flesh is torn."

"What kind of animal would do something like this?" exclaimed Mrs. Palmer. "The body has not been eaten."

"A rather large one, judging by the size of the wound. The paws would have to be of human dimensions."

"A bear, perhaps?"

"We've had no bears in this neighborhood that I've ever heard of."

"Well, there are no bite marks," I said to Father Brown, with an attempt at gallows humor. "So it's clearly not a vampire."

"Vampires have claws as well as teeth, I'm told. And they would be about the right size to do a thing like this."

"The thing is, the girl was not killed here. There's no sign of a struggle in this wet ground, no footprints, or paw prints. The body has been dumped here."

"But why?"

"It seems to me it's some sort of a warning." The voice came from behind us. We all turned.

"Ah. Lord Rivven. I'm so glad you've recovered."

181

Lord Rivven was an exceedingly handsome man of average height. He had beautiful curly hair, and his pallor reminded me of a picture I'd seen of Lord Byron.

"I'm not entirely well, Mrs. Palmer, but I had to come see what had happened to poor Lisa."

He looked at the young girl's body.

"What a shame. What kind of person would do such a thing? And such a sweet girl, too."

"You said you thought it was a warning," interjected Holmes. "What did you mean?"

"Did I say that? I was thinking it, but I didn't realize I'd given voice to my thoughts. I don't know precisely what I meant. I'm a bit feverish still. You mustn't pay too much attention to what I say. I'm not myself– and this horrible act–has upset me dreadfully."

"Lord Rivven, I am a doctor, and if you will allow me to examine you, perhaps–"

"No, no–I have a delicate constitution, that's all. I'm extremely nervous. I thank you, Doctor, I'll be all right."

I reached to touch his forehead but it was cold, with no sign of fever. Lord Rivven, after offering us his full cooperation, and offering to pay a huge reward for information helpful to the case, begged to be excused.

"What a strange man, Holmes."

"Very strange. But I must look at Lisa Waters' room one more time. Are you coming, Father Brown?"

"No, I have to perform the last rites for this poor girl, and I–"

"Well, we shall see you soon then."

Holmes and I returned to Lisa's room. Holmes began by carefully going through her desk again.

"Ah, this is singular."

"What is it, Holmes?"

"Lisa appears to have been reading Doctor Polidori's story, *The Vampire*."

Holmes began to read it. Holmes read rapidly. "The Vampire's name is Lord Ruthven, as in the plays by Dumas and Nodier. Nothing surprising in that, but–"

"Another coincidence, Holmes!"

"It's no coincidence, and now I recollect Ruthven is pronounced Rivven."

"Someone is trying to make it appear that Lord Rivven is responsible for Lisa's death," said Brown as he entered the room.

"What makes you believe that, Father Brown?"

"My intuition. I think if Lord Rivven had anything to do with it, the body would not have been found here..."

"But why would anyone want to make Lord Rivven appear guilty of a crime like this?"

"Perhaps, the real vampire," I ventured.

"Perhaps, the other vampire," said Holmes.

"The *other* vampire?"

"Lord Rivven is clearly one of the undead. But this is not his work."

"The other vampire must be extremely ruthless and extremely cunning."

"I believe it is Count Valberg."

"But how did he get in?"

"Do vampires need doors? An open window, a keyhole suffices for them."

"Did you learn anything from speaking to the young girls, Mr. Holmes?" interjected Father Brown.

"Only that they think Lord Rivven is the most beautiful man they've ever seen and that they fantasize about marrying him."

"Nothing else?"

"They admit to having had 'very improper dreams' about being visited at night by a tall, dark, handsome man, with huge eyes. They're not sure exactly what he did to them, but they are very sure it aroused them in a strange way, gave them longings, and that he bit them on the neck before leaving them."

"And Lord Ruthven was the visitor?"

"No, it wasn't Lord Ruthven. The description they gave

me fits Valberg's. I think we should interview this 'gentle-man' immediately."

When we knocked on Valberg's door, we were met by a small, rather odd-looking servant.

"You want to see Count Valberg?"

"Yes."

"But does he want to see you? Ha?"

"Would you tell him I'm here," said Father Brown.

"He knows already, but I'll tell him. Wait here."

After a few moments, the servant returned with an aris-tocratic-looking man of extremely gaunt and pale appearance.

"That will be all, Renfield."

"Yes, master."

"What can I do for you, gentlemen?"

Father Brown explained that we were coming to seek his assistance in the disappearance of a young girl from the Rivven School, and introduced Holmes and myself, to Count Valberg, who bowed politely.

"I'm not sure I can help you, although I should gladly do so, if I can. I'll answer any questions you may have."

"Did you send me the play scripts of two vampire plays taken from the British Museum?" asked Holmes.

Valberg looked rather surprised, and he seemed to be playing for time.

"Plays, you say?"

"French plays about vampires."

"What makes you think I would do that?"

"I think you did it–for reasons I do not yet fully compre-hend–to make me aware of Lord Rivven."

"You mean, that spindly little dandy who pretends to be a benefactor of orphan girls?"

"I wouldn't describe him in quite that way, but yes, he's the person I have in mind."

"I don't even know the gentleman. We've never met."

"Yet, you describe him accurately, if derisively."

"Did I? Yes, so I did. But I have a sardonic sense of hu-

184

mor, Mr. Holmes, nothing more."

"You describe yourself as Count Valberg, no doubt humorously since your real name is–"

"*Dracula*!" said a voice behind us.

"Who said that?"

"I did, Mr. Holmes."

We all turned to see Lord Rivven standing calmly in the doorway.

"How did you get in here, you little runt?" asked Valberg–or more precisely Dracula. "Weren't you taught to knock?"

"I entered here the same way you entered Lucy Waters' bedroom and ensnared her into going with you into the garden of the Rivven School where you butchered her."

"Nonsense. What proof have you of that?"

"Cards on the table, Count. You came here to ruin me."

"Why should I do that?"

"Because you are jealous. You're old and ugly, I'm young and attractive to women. You cannot abide to see me happy."

"I don't even know you. Nor care to."

"But you know of me. Well–you've succeeded. All that I've worked for since coming to England from France nearly half-a-century ago is in ruins, thanks to you. So you can congratulate yourself on that."

"What do I care about your plans or your projects?"

"You are uncivilized. This is England, not Transylvania, my dear Count."

"The same rules apply. There are no rules."

"You butchered Lisa Waters to discredit me."

"Well, yes, I did. I resent having to go hunting for sustenance every day while you feed off these poor unsuspecting young girls like a leech."

"Stop being maudlin! You have no right to attack those under my protection."

"You don't have a game preserve."

"Those girls are mine by right. I brought them here, I

nurtured them, I saw to it they had the best, most wholesome food."

"What kind of vampire are you, anyway? A vampire who sits at home like a dairy farmer extracting blood from these young human females the way a farmer patiently milks heifers. Have you no shame?"

"Shame? Why is it shameful? I've devised a way to live without doing the human race any great harm–I appeal to you gentlemen, if my methods are not better."

"Yes, but are you a vampire? Vampires are hunters, born to terrify humans, hunt them, kill them, feast on them, and give them nightmares–not just to suck a few drops of blood from their necks and leave them with nothing worse than a hickey!"

Lord Ruthven stamped his foot in fury.

Dracula continued scornfully: "A miserable excuse for a vampire you are." Then emphasizing each word separately he said: "You couldn't frighten a silly old woman! Vampire, where are your fangs?"

Ruthven was hopping with rage.

"We'll see about that! I hold you responsible for murdering–butchering Lisa Waters. I loved that girl. I spent so much time making sure she ate the most delicious foods–her blood was–so pure–so delicious...:" The thought seemed to mesmerize him and momentarily still his rage. "You can't imagine."

"I do imagine. I imagine you were going to bottle it and sell it all the other vampires in Europe."

Ruthven looked at Dracula with a "how did you guess that?" expression on his face, but then resumed. "You have a twisted imagination."

"Perhaps, but her blood really *was* delicious. I commend you on fattening her up so nicely. I had trouble not licking it up like a dog."

"Licking it? You are not a gentleman, sir."

"That's insufferable coming from you. Blood farmer!"

"No–I'm simply a gourmet. Like anything else it all depends on diet. I employ a wonderful cook, see to it they eat the

186

most nutritious, the most wholesome, the freshest food. You just cannot imagine how important diet is to the flavor of blood."

"Ah, you're a gourmet," Dracula sneered.

"And you're a gourmand. You must learn to sip your pleasures."

"Sip. I was a soldier. I eat heartily, with a good appetite."

"Yes, I suppose nothing much can be expected of a petty noble from Transylvania."

"Petty nobility! My pedigree is older than yours. I was a Prince."

"I don't think your patent of nobility is older than mine, but even if it were, you are merely a Transylvanian princeling. I'm English. So even if you were a king in the little pond you come from, you are still nothing compared to me–or any other Englishman for that matter."

"Insufferable puppy!"

Dracula rushed at Ruthven. But as he did so, Ruthven seemed to grow taller, wings sprouted from his back. The struggle was ferocious, ugly and long. But finally Ruthven succeeded in pinioning Dracula.

"What do you think you are doing?" screamed the Transylvanian.

Ruthven's wings began to flutter, preparatory to taking off, like a vulture clasping carrion.

"I'm taking you to a place where you can no longer hurt anyone I love."

"You cannot kill me."

"No but I can put you in a place from which you cannot escape, and I can give you the beating you deserve. And I am going to do just that!"

Again Ruthven's wings beat ominously, and clasping Dracula helpless in his arms, he flew straight toward the large bay window. At that moment, a lightning bolt struck shattering the window. Ruthven flew through the broken glass with Dracula firmly in his grasp.

Renfield, the servant, rushed in, screaming, "Master,

master!"

Father Brown emerged, as we all did, from the paralysis that had gripped us from the moment Ruthven had entered the room. He held up a crucifix to Renfield, who, upon seeing it, collapsed with a scream.

As we came to ourselves, we realized that a violent electrical storm had broken out. We could see that lightning also seemed to have struck the Rivven School.

"We must hurry to rescue those innocent girls! Hurry up, Watson!" shouted Holmes.

We rushed to the school, where Mrs. Palmer was leading a fire brigade.

Holmes, Father Brown and I, together with several firemen, rushed into the school and succeeded in rescuing all the girls. That seemed to be all we could do. We could hardly explain what had happened, and indeed no one knew.

Later, both Count Valberg and Lord Rivven were reported missing and, although there was a smattering of rumors, the general consensus was that they had somehow perished in the storm without leaving a trace.

Back in London, in the comfort of our flat in Baker Street, we tried to assess what had happened.

"You'll never be able to publish this adventure, Watson."

"Why not?"

"No one will believe it. And worse still, no one will believe the truth of those cases of mine that you have already published. They'll be treated as fiction, too."

Father Brown, who was with us, said:

"The power of jealousy is amazing. It affects even the undead."

"It was like two bull males fighting over a harem. It has been observed in nature," I put in.

At that moment, we all felt a sudden chill in the room.

"Good God, Holmes, why is it so cold?"

Before Holmes could answer, Dracula seemed to appear out of nowhere and said:

"No need to look for a draft. My presence has that effect

sometimes."

"Dracula!"

"Forgive the intrusion, gentlemen, but I wanted to set the record straight and I flattered myself that you might want to hear the conclusion of this interesting story."

"You escaped?"

"Easily. I told you I was a soldier. Not so little Lord Ruthven. It was easy to overpower him, and I doubt you will hear anything of him again. I'll be much surprised if he ever gets out of the situation in which I left him. I should like to have impaled him, but that is a method that doesn't necessarily work with a vampire. We'll let that go. Do you know what has happened to the girls at the Rivven School?"

"We managed to save them all from the fire."

"They're all vampires now."

"What?"

"And they're spreading vampirism all over England."

"But, Ruthven said..." I protested helplessly.

"Ruthven lied. Before appearing in my home, so unceremoniously, he turned all the girls into vampires. Now, instead of bottling their blood, as he planned to do –his trip to Scotland was to acquire a bottling plant–he has released all these charming little vampires on England. Soon, the entire island will be in their precious little clutches."

"This is fiendish!"

"Did you expect a fairy tale?" Dracula strode to the window and opened it widely. "Would you like to see them? Shall I call them?"

Without waiting for answer, he began to make a strange mewing sound. "Come to me, my lovelies!"

Suddenly, there was a whir of wings, and a swarm of bats came through the window and began circling around. I want to stress that none of us felt any horror at the time. They buzzed about gently, then suddenly all the girls from the school, with the notable exception of Lisa Waters, appeared and the bats had vanished.

The girls huddled together shyly, giggling like the school

girls they were or joking innocently on a kind of lark, as you would expect girls to do on an outing.

"Aren't they adorable Mr. Holmes?" said Dracula. "Who would imagine–can you show Mr. Holmes and Doctor Watson, and Father Brown, too? Can you show these nice gentlemen your fangs, my dears?"

And again, there were titterings and shy laughter as each girl rather coyly presented her burgeoning canines.

"They're shy–but the day will come. They'll make perfect wives and hostesses. I never would have thought of the idea myself–and much as I despise that sniveling Lord *Rivven*, (he gave Ruthven its proper Scottish pronunciation, and spat, after doing so) I have to admire him. He was a genius. Now, girls, you are on your best behavior!"

Dracula admonished a couple of girls who were prowling around Holmes' pipes and looking for his tobacco. "Myrna, here is a morsel fit for a king," Dracula cooed, stroking the hair of one of the prettiest and most adventurous of the–dare I still call them "girls?"

"And a king is a morsel fit for me," she purred and smiled slyly.

"Most vampire girls," continued Dracula, "especially young ones, simply marry and live off their husbands much as their human contemporaries–impossible to distinguish them. But Myrna is a little wild. Time will tame her, I think. Oh, I shall have influence, Mr. Holmes. My charmers shall not marry just anybody. They will marry ministers, preachers, generals, civil servants, captains of industry. And I shall rule the world by proxy."

"Holmes, we've got to do something to stop him."

"Impossible, I'm afraid, Watson, this a phenomenon beyond my humble abilities."

"Ah, Doctor Watson, I want to tell you that I love your stories–and I so admire Sherlock Homes. When I have dined, and there's nothing more to do for the day, I can think of no greater pleasure than settling down by the fire and reading one of your delightful stories." Turning to Holmes, the vampire continued: "I am such a sincere admirer of yours, Mr. Holmes. I am hoping that, someday, you and Doctor Watson will allow me to assist you on one of your investigations. I don't have much experience, it's true, but I'm very strong, and I can, if need be, have wings and penetrate the most inaccessible places. I should be proud to be your assistant at some future time–and yours too, Father Brown, for I predict a great future for you in matters of detection. But for now, I must leave you all... Time to go, my darlings!"

And the girls, as suddenly as they had appeared, vanished and a swarm of bats began flying out the open window in droves.

Frank Schildiner imagines a meeting between the Dracula of The Legend of the 7 Golden Vampires *(1974) and Gouroull, the Monster of Frankenstein, as reinterpreted in the writings of renowned film writer Jean-Claude Carrière (writing under the pseudonym of Benedict Becker) in a series of French horror novels from the 1950s...*

Frank Schildiner: *The Blood of Frankenstein*

China, 1925

Gouroull knew he was in the location the coolies had mentioned—the land where the dead walked and ruled humanity. It was an engrossing tale, though he gave no hint of interest as they babbled on, frightened as all humanity were by the very sight of him—Victor Frankenstein's most terrifying creation. Gouroull cared neither about their fear or their gratitude; he merely wished their information.

It all began with the little man. That was how Gouroull thought of Dr. Herbert West, a small man with an agile mind. He'd been unafraid and fascinated by Frankenstein's most lethal creation, interested enough to speak to him and listen to why Gouroull was haunting the blood-spattered grounds of the trenches of France.

"You wish a mate, one like yourself. It can be done, there is a process I read about recently. I discovered the notes of a nobleman named de Musard. We will need the blood of a vampire lord," West explained, growing more excited as he spoke to the giant undead creature before his eyes.

"Dracula in Transylvania, Karnstein in Styria," Gouroull rasped and turned to leave.

"No!" West cried, "I was not finished. It must be a vampire who used an ancient process to create a copy of themselves. Only the oldest and most powerful can attempt this feat. It requires both ancient vampiric blood and certain alchemical processes that are unknown to all but their small fraternity."

"Where then?" Gouroull asked, studying the little man. Impressive in his own way, for a human, Herbert West was only moved by the creation of life from the dead. This was useful for Gouroull's plans for the future. Where Victor had once refused to create a mate for him, West would succeed—and his plans could then move forward at an even faster rate.

"I have information on Dracula, though what I have is sketchy at best. He is said to have created many of these copies. I have heard of ones in Mexico, the American Southwest, Africa, China..." West stopped speaking, seeing a reaction from Gouroull.

"China," Gouroull rasped, having visited the country in the past. He'd traveled to Tibet, having heard of monks that could raise the dead through the use of magic rather than science. That intrigued him enough to travel the distance, only to find their art was like that of the ancient alchemists—making clay golems, which was of no use to his plans. He'd left a short time later to investigate, finally finding of Ping Kwei and the connection to Dracula, Lord of the Vampires.

The journey was great, but the scent of death slowly grew stronger with each mile. The province of Szechwan was at the furthest end of the Earth compared to his more familiar grounds in Europe, but fatigue didn't affect him in the slightest. Though he resembled humanity, he never suffered from any of the human miseries that would have made such a long journey nearly impossible.

And this village, Ping Kwei, was remote, even for such a forsaken country. It was surrounded by barren hills and small deep caves. The scent of blood and death, a corrupt, horrific stench, amused Gouroull as he headed closer to its source. According to the coolies, the village was of no interest; the temple in the hills overlooking it was, supposedly, where the dead walked and feasted upon the living.

The tale told to Gouroull was of seven immortals made of gold, creatures called *Jiangshi*, who were stronger and faster than any man, and had returned from the dead time and time again. He grinned at the thought, his huge sharp teeth glinting in the darkness. That would be the test, whether they could return again after he had tested their mettle.

The temple was a many-storied building, a near ruin filled with many corpses. The coolies had been incorrect in one detail: instead of seven creatures of power, there were eight!

Gouroull soon realized that the eighth was by far the most powerful. The others were lesser beings, less important, and he would brush them aside if they got in his way when he dealt with their master.

Gouroull was about to step forward, but stopped when he spotted the torches approaching the temple. Seven humans were coming, their strides intent and war-like. This simplified his plan. Gouroull's interest in the lesser beings was minimal; he would deal with their master and test his power after the humans had disposed of the others.

"Sifu Lee, they are coming!" Chien Fu exclaimed, jumping about energetically.

He was a man of medium height, dark hair and a wide infectious grin that hid his true mastery at unique forms of fighting. His dark clothes were neglectfully tied and all knew he would remove his jacket the moment the battle began.

"Calm yourself," Sifu Lee intoned, his voice as relaxed as his tautly muscular form.

His every motion was precise, no action wasted in his every move. Everyone looked to him as the leader, sensing he could defeat any foe in the end.

"Bring them on! My fists will destroy them all!" Lo the Muscular roared.

He was a tall man with long hair held back in a topknot ponytail and a powerfully muscular physique that made him look taller than everyone present. He was even rasher than Chien Fu, but his kung fu was very dangerous.

"Men!" Lady Swallow said, rolling her eyes as she drew her golden sword.

She was a beautiful woman with hair in the same style as Lo's, but dressed in a loose brown jacket and pants. She was not quite beautiful, but she was striking and more than one of those present glanced at her delicate curves with interest.

"Sifu Lee is correct. Calm and control will be our way to victory," Sifu Wong stated, his umbrella swinging slowly as he walked with the others, looking more like a man out for a daytime stroll than one going into battle.

A tiny man with an intense face and a long queue that he occasionally tossed over his shoulder, there was an electrical air of power around him, one that belied his size and relaxed demeanor.

"They advance, prepare yourself," One-Armed Fang said, his voice just above a whisper. He held a shortened sword in his one hand and seemed to possess an air of melancholy that hung about his person like armor.

The final member of the team was a thin muscular bald man in the bright yellow robes of a Buddhist monk. His name was Liu and he possessed a mischievous air about him, as if he knew you were about to fall down and he intended to laugh as he stepped over fallen form with a gentle giggle.

"Buddha bless us. And remember to hit them, Chien Fu."

Chien Fun was about to answer when the seven vampires stepped into the torchlight. They were all tall, with green rotting skin, sharp incisors and faces hidden beneath their golden masks. They all wore large golden medallions in the shapes of bats around their necks and in their hands were huge Jian-styled swords.

The lead vampire, a twisted creature dressed in white robes, screamed a warbling unintelligible word and charged Sifu Lee. Lee stepped aside and tossed the vampire with a simple quick sweep. The vampire snarled and Lee adopted a deep fighting stance, his face impassive.

"Did that monster say 'destroy them,' or 'please wash my auntie'?" Chien Fu asked, tripping and causing the vampire's sword to miss him by mere inches. His fighting style was acrobatic and made him look as if he was perpetually falling down and causing nearby objects to hit his opponent.

"Pay attention to your opponent," Sifu Wong replied as he blocked the vampire's sword by knocking the attacker's arm aside with his umbrella. Just as before, he never appeared to waste his movements, moving in an off-handed manner.

"No opponent can defeat me!" Lo the Muscular screamed, just as a vampire stabbed him in the chest. He yelled loudly and waved his arms about before crashing to the ground and laying still.

"He was incorrect," Liu stated leapt over the vampire attacking him, landing on his feet, his hand before him in a pose of prayer. He tapped the vampire on the shoulder and ducked as it swung, kicking it aside and watching as the creature stumbled to the ground.

One-Armed Fang and Lady Swallow did not reply as they engaged their enemies, sword to sword. Their styles were vastly different, but fascinating to watch.

Fang's attacks were lightning strikes, his shortened sword moving too fast for the eye to see. Meanwhile, Lady Swallow sword snaked out like the tongue of a serpent, causing the vampire to leap about and block far more than it was able to attack.

Gouroull stood in the doorway of the main chamber of the temple, watching as the leader reentered the main chamber. The room was large, round and possessed multiple altars with chained dead women lying on the slabs. They were completely drained of blood and a large cauldron filled with blood rested nearby. The room stank of blood, rot and death, all perfectly incarnated by the tall, bald Chinese man who strode about, muttering curses.

Moving into the light, the man turned and stared at Gouroull. He seemed surprised but not too surprised to see the giant creature that was Frankenstein's masterpiece, a towering being with alabaster skin, a flat squared head and inhuman yellow yes. For a heartbeat, neither moved, their eyes locked and studying each other completely.

"I have met your kind before," the Vampire Lord stated in clear, lilting English. "You are one of the creatures of the accursed Frankenstein. Serve me and I shall reward you well."

Gouroull smiled, his sharp teeth glinting as he stepped closer.

"Who are you?" he rasped.

The vampire smiled and straightened, "I am Kah, High Priest of the..."

Gouroull snarled and shook his huge head: "You lie!"

The vampire's eyes widened, but he too smiled and nodded.

"So it is true! You are not a foolish wretch like your brothers. I am Count Dracula, Lord of the Undead! Again, I say: Serve me and I will reward you!"

Gouroull did not reply. Instead, he suddenly charged Dracula with a speed that belied his size. Grabbing the undead creature, he threw him across the room towards one of the altars. The stone shattered under the shock, and the dead girl who'd been lying on it flopped to the floor. But, in less than a second, Dracula rose and charged. Crashing to the floor, the Vampire Lord pinned Gouroull's arms to the ground and bit down, hard, with his stiletto-like incisors.

Gouroull's flesh was hard, stone-like, and completely alien, yet Dracula's powerful vampiric strength pierced the skin and he began to drink the monster's dark blood.

"Aaaahhhh!" Dracula shrieked as he reared back in agony.

Gouroull's blood was no blood! It was an ichor that resembled nothing human or animal; it was something so alien that it burned his lips and throat of Dracula like acid!

Gouroull pulled free of the Vampire Lord's grasp, grabbed the creature's neck and, in turn, bit down hard, ripping out most of his throat. Frankenstein's terrifying creation

197

seemed to mimic the vampire's action, drinking deeply of the undead creature's blood. He shoved Dracula aside and pulled out a metal vial, spitting the lifeblood of his enemy into the container.

Sealing the vial, Gouroull rose and began to leave the temple, his goal accomplished.

"Hold," Dracula coughed, his body transforming into a large man dressed in black. He was coughing blood and aging, turning into dust as Gouroull turned to watch. "Know this, miserable unfinished thing... You have earned the eternal enmity of Dracula! I shall hunt you down and we shall meet again!"

Gouroull nodded once, smiled again and replied, "Good."

And he left.

After Sherlock Holmes and Frankenstein, Dracula is now pitted against Judex, the avenging crime-fighter who wears a slouched hat and a dark cloak, created by Arthur Bernède and Louis Feuillade in a 1916 serial...

Christofer Nigro: *The Ultimate Prize*

Actress Gabrielle Deslys found herself surprisingly calm when she entered the hotel room of the Grand Hotel, despite being in the company of a man she had just met hours earlier at the after-show party. Nevertheless, she found herself quite charmed by the Count, and his striking, almost hypnotic, eyes had truly captivated her. Despite his suave demeanor, there was a sense of power about him that she could scarcely describe. She felt this attribute was well befitting of a man of his position in his native Carpathians, however, and she found herself thoroughly flattered that he had traveled all the way from that part of Europe to see her perform on stage. She was still initially surprised that he had been given entry to the after-show party on such short notice, but she had since come to realize that a man like the Count doubtless had ways of convincing even the most stubborn members of her Marseilles entourage who acted as door sentries to give him a free pass.

As Gabrielle looked about the elegant décor of the suite, the Count offered her a glass of wine.

"May I offer such a beautiful young woman a glass of this city's finest wine?" he asked her as he uncorked the bottle. "It has reached a fine age. You may have as much as you wish, for I do not drink…wine."

"Are you trying to get me in a state of inebriation, Count?" the 38-year-old actress asked her regal escort with a wry tone.

The Count laughed lightly. "It is only my desire to see to your pleasure, Madame. For your pleasure equals mine."

"Very generous of you, my dear Count. But I must say, in all seriousness, you flatter me by calling me 'young.' And I cannot help but wonder if your remark about something older—like the wine—always amounting to better is accurate. When an actress reaches my age, these things are no longer the truth. That is why I find myself all the more flattered that you still find me worthy of this type of admiration."

"You have no cause to doubt the extent of that admiration, Mademoiselle! Your loveliness is as profound as it ever was, I can assure you of that."

"But even if I retain a great degree of that which was instrumental in the success of my career, this will not be true for much longer. Aging is the bane of humanity, and even more so to those who belong to a vocation where the beauty of youth and the continued limberness of the body are so essential. And please remember that I'm a dancer as well as an actress. How long will I be palatable to either of these professions? How long will it be before all that I have built vanishes, and gentlemen like you no longer seek my company?"

The Count grinned upon hearing those words, exuding the mien of a schemer. It made Gabrielle quite uncomfortable, but it was also clear his thoughts would lead to words that would actually suggest a viable solution.

"What you have said about humanity and the curse of aging are quite astute, my dear lady. And what's worse, the brevity of youth and how little can be accomplished under such a short span of time makes its passing all the more tragic. But it need not be that way for everyone."

"How can you say that, Count? No human being is spared the physical deterioration that comes with age. It is a universal curse among our species."

"*Your* species, perhaps, beautiful Gabrielle, but not all who look and walk like men belong to that inferior race. And those of us who do not need not fear the passage of time and the grief it brings."

A look of profound shock befell Gabrielle's lovely visage, as the Count's tone was in no way flippant. But her inclination to be terrified was soon overwhelmed by her curiosity.

"What exactly, do you mean by that, Count?"

"What I mean, my dear Gabrielle, is that despite the alias that I used to gain entrance to your party, my real identity is that of Dracula, Son of the Dragon."

To prove his boast, the Count opened his mouth and extended the two large fangs that he and others of his kind used to puncture the throats of mortals to procure their required sustenance. His glaring eyes took on a bright reddish hue, almost glowing despite the illumination of the suite's electric lights.

Forcing herself to speak despite being near-paralyzed with shock, Gabrielle managed to utter:

"Dear God, you're…you're actually…"

"If you're trying to acknowledge the whispered rumors of more than two decades, then you are quite correct, my dear lady."

"But this… this is impossible…"

"While a mouth can lie, the eyes cannot, Gabrielle. And I would like to think my offer to you is quite clear. I have long admired you and your illustrious career, and have hoped you could share some of that life with me. May I grant you the ultimate prize, so you will need never again fear the ravages of time?"

Gabrielle choked out a response. "You want to make me into a vampire? But then, I could no longer walk about in daylight. And I would have to… feed upon other people to survive. Count, I am not an evil woman! I have never harmed others! I cannot live like that…"

"Yes, elevating yourself to one of the Undead does come with certain… inconveniences and requirements which may seem unpleasant, even vile, to the standards by which mortals are typically raised. But consider…

"For one thing, I soon learned after my ascension that the ability to walk in daylight is vastly overrated. The more interesting facets of existence tend to occur at night—including all of your performances. And for another, mortals are quite the hypocrites. They boast of concepts such as justice and peace to put their conscience at ease, yet they annihilate large numbers of themselves over trivialities such as money and land. The Great War that just ended was wrought by *your* species, not mine. Note how those amongst the mortals with the most wealth consider themselves higher forms of life, above the majority who lack such privileges. Look at how they exploit their 'lessers,' treating them as lapdogs, using them to increase their own power. Do they not create horrific weapons to wreak destruction upon each other? I did the same when I ruled Wallachia during my years as a mortal, and I have done so in Transylvania since my ascension; but never have I apologized because of silly notions of morality. Vampires do not do to each other what humans regularly inflict upon their own kind."

Gabrielle turned her gaze from Dracula. "But it's not like that. I would be killing other humans for their blood, making me no different than…"

"Do you mean, just as humans kill lesser animals for their meat and hides? You wouldn't be doing it to acquire anything as puerile and meaningless as money. You would be doing it to survive—and you would kill far fewer humans over the course of an indefinite lifespan than the multitudes of humans typically killed by their own kind over a mere week by the weapons they create. Or even those peasants who kill each other while committing petty crimes.

"Moreover, dear Gabrielle, once I help you ascend, you would be human no longer. You would be as above the mortal rabble as they are above the pig or the goat. You would be taking nothing more from them to survive than they routinely take from scores of animals for the same reasons every year since time immemorial."

A look of abject turmoil continued to mar Gabrielle's exquisite features. "Dear Lord, I just want to continue to practice my craft, and to retain a life of quality while doing so. I don't want to become a predator for countless years. Why did you place this choice before me, God? *Why*?"

"I assure you that the God you worship has nothing to do with this, Gabrielle. The choice is offered by me and *me alone*. You worry about becoming a predator, yet you ignore the predatory nature of those who oversee the very vocation you value so highly. You know how quickly they will cast you aside once your beauty and nimbleness have passed. And you know how soon those days are coming. You are aware how equally pernicious are those who control this fledgling moving picture industry, in which you have managed to make some inroads; you can readily guess how much more so they will become should its popularity expand in the future.

"You saw how the appearance of those elderly mortal women who stood amongst us at the party. You see how decrepit you will become in just a few years. Just imagine slowly dying of a wasting illness, like cancer or tuberculosis, while being unable to control your own bodily emissions in a hospital bed, forced to suffer the indignity of having to be cleaned by others. Imagine senility overcoming you, taking away your mental faculties, the last thing of value you would have during that period of decline..."

"Please, Count, stop talking about these things!"

"Even if I were to stop, you would be unable to cease *thinking* of them, lovely Gabrielle. The seed has been planted, the die has been cast, and a decision must now be made."

"No! I will not..."

"*Think*, my dear lady. Think of what you could accomplish in your chosen vocation with an endless number of years at your disposal. You would be able to helm masterpieces that surpass those currently playing in the picture theaters! You could do what I have often done: change identities after enough time has passed, and operate under the guise of a younger relative to whom you would have bequeathed your fortune. This ruse could forever keep the secret of your true nature from the unbelieving masses. Granted, there are troublesome fools, like the Van Helsings to contend with, but they can be evaded or dealt with, especially with one such as me at your side.

"Further, you could have many lovers amongst both male and female mortals in addition to myself, to love for eternity. You will be the one discarding them when they are no longer needed, rather than the reverse, as you now have reason to fear."

Gabrielle shed tears, covering her face in anxiety over the thoughts flashing through her psyche like the fast-moving images on the picture screens.

"No... no..."

"Make your decision at once, Gabrielle! You have but seconds! After that, shall leave this place and walk out of your life forever, and you can slowly deteriorate as do all mortals!"

"Very well, damn you! I won't let that happen to me! Do it, Dracula. Do it *now!*"

As tears continued to roll down her face, she tilted her head and bore the fair skin of her neck to the nefarious Count. Smiling in triumph and anticipation, Dracula opened his mouth and greedily sunk his fangs into Gabrielle's jugular. She first winced in pain at the twin lacerations, but, within moments, the physical pain was replaced by a strangely euphoric sensation that reminded her of an intense orgasm.

Her look of pain and tumult was slowly replaced by a hesitant smile as Dracula drank her life's blood and simultaneously injected her with physiology-altering enzymes...

A few months later, Jacques de Trémeuse sat on a large comfortable *canapé* in his headquarters deep below Château-Rouge. His old friend Prosper Cocantin was there. A beam of delight crossed the detective's beak-nosed visage as a cup of the herbal tea he loved so much was handed to him. He eagerly took a few sips.

"Is it to your liking, my friend?" Jacques asked his guest.

"*Pas mal*, as always!" Cocantin replied with a great look of satisfaction. "The English truly have nothing on you when it comes to tea."

"I'm glad you are pleased. But now onto business… How are things in Paris?"

"I'm afraid the business at hand is most serious."

"Have you found a pattern to the disappearances?"

"Some of the finest minds are looking into the matter, including Inspector Maigret, but whoever is involved appears to be quite crafty. All the reports indicate that each disappearance—mostly men—have been individuals amongst the entertainment vocation. Among their number have been a well-known playwright and the respected owner of a theater."

"That sounds like a worthy lead. Whoever is behind these disappearances, it must be someone of high profile who walks in those circles."

"I agree, otherwise the culprit would not be trusted by these people of influence."

"Have there been any ransom demands? Or signs of a struggle at any of the last places the victims were known to frequent?"

"Nothing of the sort. This makes me believe that none of them detected an imminent danger, because they allowed the perpetrator to remain alone with them. He or she must not appear menacing. Everyone who has investigated the matter agrees that these are not simple cases of moguls taking impromptu vacations without telling their staff. Some of the victims had important engagements, and it's totally out of character for them to evade such responsibilities. I am telling you, my friend, there is foul play at hand here."

"I concur. However, I've read in the press that in one case, a suicide note was found, and in another, the pay stub of a one-way cruise to the Greek Islands."

"*C'est vrai.* But in both cases, that was still utterly uncharacteristic of the victims' normal behavior. Their reputations preclude such abrupt, irresponsible actions. Besides, for so many incidents to have occurred in rapid succession over only three months…"

"Indeed. I suspect that the perpetrator created bogus excuses to cover the fact that his victims will never be seen again. Much care was taken to hide the bodies so that the cause of death will never be known. And yet, no ransom notes… That is strange…"

"It led me to think that the presumed murders—let's call them that—are part of a calculated revenge spree. People of great power in the entertainment world are known for leaving many disgruntled thespians, writers and others behind due to their whims and rapacious business decisions."

"No doubt. Let's conjecture that the perpetrator is among those who work for the elite, but not actually one of them. Someone who has means as well as inroads into the private world of these individuals, but not the clout, financial or otherwise, to effect retribution via a boardroom or a bank. Hence, they had to use means outside the system to dispense their reckoning."

"That, my friend, is surely something you can relate to, *non*?"

"You slight me by making such a comparison, Cocantin. You know that I dispense justice to the guilty whom the system fails to punish. My actions are never based on petty selfishness."

"No need to take what I said the wrong way, Jacques. But let us be honest about a certain similarity between what you do and…"

The large-nosed detective's spiel was cut off by a much younger voice emanating from behind them on the threshold.

"Aw, please not another fight over this again," said the Licorice Kid, a youthful informant of Judex, and now Cocantin's ward. "Let's clobber the bad guys, and not each other, *d'accord*?"

"What are you doing here, my lad?" his surrogate father asked him.

"Got bored at home, and jus' wanted to help out like I always do," the adolescent boy replied as he adjusted his distinctive hat and overly large suspenders. "Do ya got any more of that tea or maybe a cigar or somethin', Uncle Jacques?"

"Ask Uncle Roger," Jacques replied, rather brusquely. "Right now, we're in the midst of studying the patterns surrounding the disappearances of…"

"Oh, do ya mean those rich theater people?" the Kid queried. "I been followin' that whole story in both the paper and on the streets. I'm a tradesman by nature, and gettin' and givin' info is what I do, ya know? I was hangin' 'round the theater after sneakin' in to see the late special showin' of *Bouclette* an' after that, I saw the star walk out with the producer who dis'peared. Wow, was she ever a looker!"

"No one reported seeing that, my boy," Cocantin retorted.

"Yeah, well, that's 'cause they don't know 'bout the secret back door of the theater that the stars use sometimes to sneak out so no one knows if someone is leavin' wit' someone else that they don't want everyone to know 'bout. But I know 'bout it 'cause I'm no dummy and I always use that door to sneak in. Ha!"

Cocantin's face suddenly turned red. "You mean to tell me, you've been sneaking into the theater all this time without purchasing a ticket, young man!"

"Don't be too harsh on him, my friend," Jacques said. "His illicit entries may have given us the important clue that will enable us to solve these crimes. Justice will be dispensed, and as always, I shall be its conduit!"

Sequestered in her hotel room at the Grand Hotel shortly after her latest feeding, Gabrielle looked into a mirror in anguish over her inability to see her reflection.

"Damn it all!" she shouted. "This suite would have to be fitted with one of those mirrors backed with a silver coating that cancel out a vampire's reflection! How can I enjoy my eternal beauty if I cannot admire it in the great majority of available mirrors!"

Gabrielle's impassioned fit was interrupted when the lock on the door was suddenly forced open. Entering the room was a different tall, dark-clad man with a flowing black cape—but this one had a slouch hat atop his head, partially obscuring his features. In each hand he held two high-caliber revolvers of a design she did not recognize.

"*Qui diable êtes-vous?*" she yelled.

"*Bonjour*, Mademoiselle Deslys," Judex said in his icy voice. "Would you care to explain your motives for taking the lives of those people you murdered before I mete out justice for your actions?"

Gabrielle grinned at the sight of the imposing vigilante before her, making no attempt to conceal her extended fangs.

"So, you are the infamous vigilante Judex, *non*?"

"*Oui,* Mademoiselle. And I see by your oral characteristics and curious lack of fear at the sight of me that you can no longer be categorized as human. I believe that may explain everything."

"See fit to judge me if it pleases you, vigilante. I did what I had to do to secure my career, and to avoid the curse that degrades and eventually claims all human beings. You would have made the same choice if offered the ultimate prize—as I was."

"So you took this state of being of your own volition? That means that you are especially deserving of justice. Though I sympathize with your fear, taking a gift that requires the continual sacrifice of innocent lives is ignoble and unforgivable, despite the power of that fear. A truly good person— as you always purported to be with your expressed sympathy for the underprivileged—would have faced such an unpleasant fate over bringing harm to innocents."

"There are no true innocents in this world, vigilante. You of all mortals should know that. Everyone makes choices at some point for self benefit that are to the detriment of others. The entire system under which we live is predicated upon such actions."

"Even if there were ten billion people in this world, all committed to such actions on a daily basis, it wouldn't make them *right*. It wouldn't justify not trying to find another way to acquire such benefits, even if it took much more work and much longer to achieve. You deliberately chose to become a predator of humans for personal gain, and for that, justice will be carried out. But first, who did you obtain this pernicious 'gift' from?"

"From me, you insipid fool," came a voice with a noticeable accent from the other side of the room.

As incredibly swift as Judex was when he turned to face the source of the voice, the arm that suddenly extended and grabbed his throat in a crushing grip was faster still.

The powerful arm then hurled the vigilante against the wall on the far side of the room as if his 225 pound frame weighed no more than ten. Regaining his senses with impressive speed, Judex turned to look at the individual many feet distant who had had the temerity and power to hurl him so effortlessly.

Standing before him, appearing to fully materialize within a cloud of mist, was a man of equal height to his own, also dressed in a black garment and cape, but with hellish red eyes and protruding fangs.

"Welcome to your doom, Judex," the stranger told him. "For never before have you faced a foe like Dracula."

My God, so the rumors are true, the vigilante thought. *This is going to be incredibly difficult; but for the sake of justice, I must prevail.*

Expertly somersaulting across the floor, and retrieving his revolvers from where they lay on the rug, Judex opened fire on the Vampire Lord. Dracula simply stood there impassively as the lead bullets seared through his body with negligible effect.

"I see you have failed to come prepared," the Prince of Darkness observed. "You're a poor excuse for a creature of the night, and you know that my opinion in that regard is quite well informed."

"You have escaped justice for too long, Dracula," Judex said with no emotion save for a hint of anger. "Prepare to pay your debt to Her at long last!"

Dracula simply laughed. "Let us see you attempt to collect that debt, dark one. I wager the power you fight for will be sorely disappointed this night."

"We shall see."

Realizing that his revolvers would be next to useless against a vampire, Judex swiftly holstered them and seized a long, razor-sharp blade from a slot in his boot. He had read enough reports and folklore accounts to know that vampires could be slain if their head was severed; he would make a strong attempt to decapitate the Lord of Vampires, or die trying.

Rushing at Dracula with impressive speed, Judex slashed the knife towards his opponent's neck with a powerful stroke, hoping to at least halfway severe it with this initial swipe. But Dracula's preternatural speed proved superior, and the Vampire Lord caught the dark avenger's wrist on the downswing.

Determined to escape the vice-like grip and carry out his gruesome intent, Judex initiated a palm heel strike to Dracula's chin, hoping to stun him into releasing his hold. Though startled by the unexpected force of the blow, the Prince of Darkness barely lessened the strength of his grip, and his quickly executed backhand blow would have shattered the vigilante's jaw if not for Judex's skill at rolling with such cracks.

Nevertheless, the dark-clad crusader was knocked senseless by Dracula's strike. The vampire then effortlessly lifted Judex off the ground and smashed him into the wall. Though badly stunned, Judex's tolerance for pain and will to overcome were formidable, and he managed to deliver two strong reverse punches to Dracula's face, followed by a brutal forward kick to the vampire's solar plexus.

The unexpected nature of these blows succeeded in knocking the Vampire Lord back a few feet, and Judex successfully pulled out of his grip.

The caped crime fighter then leaped to the ground to recover his blade, only to have Dracula crunch his arm under his the heel of his shoe before he could grab the weapon. Judex forced himself not to shout in pain as his deltoid bone cracked. Before he could carry out his plan to pull Dracula's leg out from under him, the Vampire Lord again lifted him with minimal effort and tossed him several meters across the room. This time, the vigilante struck the dresser holding the mirror, shattering the glass to pieces and landing on the ground, broken and stunned nearly to unconsciousness.

"I grow weary of this foolishness," Dracula said with annoyance. "You have proved an irritant, and your attempt to take what I have given to my new paramour angers me. I shall end this now. I believe that you would make a grand lackey of mine were I to change you into a *true* creature of the night...."

"He doesn't understand!" Gabrielle shouted from her vantage point across the room, wondering if she should assist her benefactor and lover. "Make him into one of us, so that he understands! He will be grateful, as I am, and only by ascending will he come to know the delight of eternal youth!"

"That is my intent, dear Gabrielle," Dracula assured his lady love as he approached the fallen hero.

With a sudden heave, Dracula hoisted Judex to his feet, pushed him against the wall, and twisted his head back with the intention of sinking his fangs into the vigilante's jugular. The adventurer struggled with all his might, but his lesser level of strength and the extent of his injuries made his valiant efforts seemingly futile.

"You will... not escape... justice... no matter what you do to me... vampire," Judex choked as loudly and defiantly as he oould.

"Justice isn't a major factor in this world, my soon-to-be-soldier-of-the-night," Dracula told the struggling hero in his grip. "Only *power* matters, as you shall soon see."

Just as Dracula was about to make an attempt to sink his fangs into Judex's flesh, his keen hearing picked up slight footsteps behind him.

He turned to see the diminutive figure of the Licorice Kid, holding a small, metallic squirt pistol.

"*Bonjour*, Monsieur Dracula," the boy said as he pointed the pistol at him. "I snuck in the church before comin' here, an' guess what I filled this up with?"

The boy then squirted a thin stream of holy water at the Count's eyes, burning them severely.

The Vampire Lord bellowed in agony and fell back against the wall, releasing Judex from his grip in the process.

"Hurry an' get 'im, Monsieur Judex!" the boy shouted. "My squirter gets only one shot!"

"You're a fool to admit that, little boy!" Gabrielle exclaimed. "Now I will spank you until you bleed!"

As she moved towards him, the Licorice Kid astounded her by pulling a small cross attached to a string of rosary beads out of his pocket.

"Oh, yeah? Well, look what else I took from the church. I'm no dummy, ya know!"

Gabrielle hissed violently at the sight of the hated icon, and then recoiled from it, helpless to proceed with her attack.

This gave Judex enough time to get back to his feet, despite how unsteady he was.

"Kid, I told you to stay behind!"

"Yeah, I know. Aint'cha glad I didn't listen?"

Dracula suddenly turned back towards Judex, the flesh around his eyes terribly scarred, but already partially healed. Once again moving almost faster than the eye could follow, the Vampire Lord seized the vigilante by the throat, holding him against the wall and choking him with monstrous strength.

"Uh-oh…" the Licorice Kid said aloud.

"I'll rip your throat out for this!" the Vampire Lord howled with extreme fury.

"Not if I rip yours out first," Judex replied, quickly grabbing a large shard of silver-coated glass from the shattered mirror that lay on the dresser and slashing Dracula across his throat.

Remembering that silver is a major weakness for some vampires, Judex managed to inflict a grievous injury upon his opponent. The Vampire Lord again released his grip and backed against the wall as smoldering blood streamed from the horrific gash torn across his larynx.

Acting without delay, Judex grabbed another, larger shard of the silver-coated glass and shoved it into the left side of Dracula's chest, skewering his heart. The vampire attempted to wrest it from his torso, but only succeeded in painfully slicing up his fingers from further exposure to the sharpened silver.

"There… will be… another time…" Dracula managed to sputter as he fell to the ground, his flesh bubbling from his bones and leaving nothing but a bare skeleton behind.

"Wow, major case of heartburn!" the Licorice Kid yelled with a triumphant thrust of his fist.

Not reacting to the comment, Judex turned towards Gabrielle, now holding another large shard of the glass in his hand.

"Are you ready to receive justice, like your inhuman lover just did?" he asked her.

A look of anguish overtook her features, as if her mind was torn in contemplative indecision.

"No!" she finally hollered in a tormented voice. "Please don't make me give up the ultimate prize! I'm not evil, I just don't want to lose it all!"

"You already lost it all the moment you took Dracula's offer," the hero said. "You sacrificed others for your own benefit. If any spark of goodness remains within you, Madame Deslys, then do the right thing. Submit to justice, and meet your fate with some honor."

"No…" was her only, barely audible response while she stood shuddering, as if something within her were struggling against her strong desire to take bat form and escape through the open window.

Determined to make certain that one of the two equally potent urges didn't lose to the other, Judex hurled the shard of silver-coated glass with expert aim at Gabrielle's chest. It penetrated enough for the silver to cause her debilitating agony.

He then rushed forward, pulled out the shard as she dropped to the floor, and brought it down on her throat with all of his might, severing her head and ending her undead existence.

Judex then turned to the Licorice Kid as he forced himself to remain on his feet despite the injuries he received.

"Thank you for the assistance, Kid. How did you know I was going up against vampires when I wasn't aware of it before breaking into this room?"

"Well, I saw Madame Deslys walkin' out that back door at the theater with Dracula once or twice, and I kinda thought he dressed a lot like the actor who pretended to be him in that play I used to sneak into the theater every other night to see. And when I heard you connected the disappeared people to her, then, well, I just kinda figured the guy I saw her with might be the *real* Dracula. An' so I stopped at the church while I followed ya here, and ya know the rest. Like I always say, I'm no dummy!"

Judex couldn't help but smile that time, something he very rarely did while in vigilante mode. He never ceased to be impressed with this young man whose resourcefulness and bravery had so often been an asset to him.

Looking at the bloody scene before him, the streetwise Licorice lamented, "I kinda can't help but feel sorry for the lady a bit. She only wanted to stop gettin' older, and…"

"I feel sorry for her too," Judex interrupted. "But not too much. She made a bad choice with horrid consequences for both other people and her own soul. Justice had to prevail."

Upon hearing that the late Gabrielle Deslys' final will and testament, which she penned before becoming a vampire, had left her ample estate and entire sizable earnings to the poor of Marseilles, Judex's sympathy for her increased. He began wondering if, perhaps, he should have trusted her enough to give her the opportunity to make the right decision at the last moment, rather than taking it out of her hands.

In the end, however, he believed that the triumph of justice was more important than the possible victory of her soul.

Hence, he would live with himself for his decision, whether it was made in haste or not.

Nevertheless, seeing that she was a good and generous soul at heart, and had simply been led down the dark path due to desperation—a very human foible he could well relate to—he used his resources as Jacques de Trémeuse to collaborate with her own agent and publicist to feed a plausible but false story to the press to explain her death in a non-sinister fashion.

It read that she developed a severe throat infection due to a case of influenza, and that, despite several surgeries in an attempt to cure her, she refused to let the surgeons do all that was required out of fear of leaving large, permanent scars on her neck. He felt the irony of the bogus story for the press regarding wounds to her throat was a form of poetic justice considering the far less believable truth.

And justice in all its myriad forms were of great interest to the man called Judex.

Finally, this story transports us several years into the future, in Berlin, during the fall of the Nazi regime, when Leo Saint-Clair, the French superhero known as The Nyctalope, invented by Jean de La Hire in 1911, confronts the Lord of the Vampires...

Christofer Nigro: *Requiem for a Regime*

Berlin, Early April 1945

Leo Saint-Clair walked purposefully down a secluded side street sequestered within a city that he knew was soon to be under siege.

He was well aware that the Soviet forces were rapidly approaching the heart of the Nazi government, and he doubted that Hitler's remaining forces, which were gathering to defend its municipal borders, would be sufficient to halt the forward progress of Stalin's Red Army. Because of this, it was of crucial importance that he should succeed in a mission that was both essential to the Vichy government, and of a highly personal nature before the Russian ground assault reached the area and turned it into a battlefield: the rescue of the great archeologist Aristide Clairembart.

Clairembart's good friend, the already legendary aviator Commandant Robert Morane, was busy fighting under the auspices of General de Gaulle in the FFAL, and would have had a considerably more difficult time getting into Berlin than an agent of the Vichy government like Saint-Clair did, which is why he had asked the Nyctalope, using back channels, to rescue the archeologist.

Unlike Morane, Saint-Clair couldn't bring himself to fight against the French government alongside the "Free French" that de Gaulle was leading, despite its growing popularity amongst the population of his beloved but occupied nation. These days, Saint-Clair had little respect for Maréchal Petain, the once triumphant winner of Verdun, and even less for the Nazis, whose ideology made him cringe in disgust, but he did understand the notion of pragmatism.

He still believed that the best interests of his beloved France didn't need the kind of civil war that the policies of de Gaulle might foster, especially not at such a precarious point in history. He respected and supported what the Allies were doing, but at the same time, his homeland and its interests had to come first. He didn't like the collaboration between the Vichy government and the Nazi regime, but he felt that working with the latter for the preservation of the former had been a necessary evil. In any event, the Nyctalope was aware that the end was nigh, for his gathered intelligence made it clear that the next few months would determine the final fate of Nazi Germany, as well as the French regime that had supported it.

As he walked down a street littered with the debris of buildings and vehicles, blown to bits by the recent shelling, that cool spring evening just as the setting sun cast portentous shadows upon the wreckage, he knew that he had to get Professor Clairembart out of this hellhole before the arrival of the Red Army.

The Nyctalope looked rather nondescript dressed in an ordinary business suit, approaching a mostly undamaged building. He had taken special precautions to look as inconspicuous as possible since he didn't want it to be known that a Vichy agent was working in Berlin against Nazi interests on the "liberation" of Clairembart. Of course, the archeologist had a knack for getting himself into trouble due to his immoderate enthusiasm for cracking any archeological mystery of extraordinary merit. And what he had been brought here to identify certainly fit that particular bill, if it turned out to be authentic.

Within the fourth floor of the abandoned building, the Professor sat at a heavy table glaring at a black and white photograph that had been handed to him by one of three irate *Wehrmacht* officers. The one that seemed to be in charge, who identified himself as Heinrich Müller, bade the Professor to identify an object he saw in the photo.

"Now, Herr Professor," Müller said sternly, "if you truly wish to leave this place and get back to that comfortable hotel we have provided for you, then you will tell me if the artifact you see in this photo is truly the Spear of Destiny, *Verstehen Sie mich?*"

It would seem that being one of the world's renowned experts in my field doesn't always work to my advantage, the Professor thought as he solemnly glared at the photo. He was well aware that if he identified it as *the* genuine Spear of Destiny, he would never be allowed to leave Berlin alive. He needed to play this carefully, and hope that Bob Morane was aware of his predicament. *Damned Nazis, I hope I live long enough to see Bob—or anyone else!—arrive to put a bullet into their skulls...*

"Rest assured that I am considering this very carefully, Herr Müller," the Professor replied in his best "poker" voice. "But due to the poor quality of the film, I must be certain before I render a professional opinion..."

Müller slapped the archeologist on his shoulder, causing him to wince in pain.

"No more dawdling, Professor. You and I both know that the photo was taken by the best camera German technology has yet to invent. You are privileged to be the man whose expertise has been sought to identify this remarkable find."

"There have been rumors circulating around about a recent German expedition to the Arctic," the Professor hastily responded, trying to keep up his verbal delaying tactics as long as he could, "so perhaps if I knew more about the circumstances surrounding this discovery..."

Müller proceeded to grab the archeologist by the back of the neck and slammed his head on the table with great force, then promptly pulled his face back up so that he could view the photo again.

"You try my patience at your peril, Professor!" the Gestapo officer shouted. "You are in no position to be asking

218

questions instead of answering them, so you had best carry out your task without further banter, or by the hand of Woden, I shall…"

Müller's words were abruptly cut off as a bullet hole suddenly appeared in the middle of his forehead. The Nazi frowned and let out a loud sigh before falling to the ground in a pool of blood.

About damn time, the Professor thought as he wiped blood and bits of brain matter off of his face.

Acting with impressive reflexes, the other two German soldiers quickly raised their firearms and each released a fusillade in the direction of the open doorway from which the shot that had killed Müller had come. But all they could see was darkness accompanied by an eerie silence.

"*Gott im Himmel!*" shouted one of the soldiers. "We must have hit whoever it was!"

"It's too dark to tell for certain," the other replied.

"You Nazis do not consider the dark your ally, as I do," a smooth male voice speaking German with barely a hint of a French accent responded. Then, a second bullet hit the belly of another soldier, who gasped in horror and agony as he collapsed onto the floor.

"*Mein Gott!*" the remaining soldier bellowed, shooting another salvo of bullets into the dark as panic overtook him.

"I don't know who you are, *schweinhund*, but if you don't surrender immediately, I will kill the scientist!"

However, upon turning towards the Professor, the bemused soldier discovered that Clairembart had time to surreptitiously take possession of Müller's own Luger. Before the hapless Nazi could adjust to this state of affairs, the Professor shot him through the head.

Leo's tall, well-dressed form then stepped out of the darkness and into the light of the room, his firearm still pointed in the event of another attack.

"Bonjour, Professor," Leo said, "and good shooting. Bob Morane sent me. My name is Leo Saint-Clair."

Wiping off the dust from his jacket, Clairembart replied:

"The Nyctalope in person? I am impressed. But I knew Bob wouldn't let me down, and if he couldn't come himself, he would send another in his stead. And for what it's worth, I have always known that your true sympathies lie with France, not the bunch of traitors that you serve, or that vermin..." he added, pointing at the dead Nazis on the floor.

"You are correct, Professor," Leo replied, "but we must get you out of here quickly. I'm going to take you to a location where a convoy is waiting for you, which will spirit you out of Europe altogether, until the carnage is over."

"But I must tell you why they brought me here," the Professor stated. "It is of the utmost importance. You have heard of the Spear of Destiny, I suppose?"

"Of course," Leo replied. "It is the fabled weapon said to have pierced the side of Jesus Christ himself during the Crucifixion. It's reputed to have been imbued with limitless divine power as a result."

"Indeed!" the Professor responded. "And should anyone gain possession of it and master the prerequisite degree of will and occult knowledge necessary to access its cosmic energies..."

"...Then that individual shall gain power enough to challenge the gods themselves..." said a new arrival, speaking with a strong, guttural Middle-European accent.

Startled, Leo and the Professor turned to discover a tall, elegantly dressed man with dark hair, dark attire, pallid skin, and a flowing cloak standing in the doorway, with wafts of mist twirling about him. His eyes were like blazing hot coals, and they sent tremors up the spine of even one as ostensibly fearless as Leo Saint-Clair. It was not often that anyone approached him without being detected, so he considered this new player a major cause for concern.

"May I presume that this gentleman is not with you, Commandant?" asked the Professor warily.

"You are safe in making such a presumption," Leo replied, turning towards the chilling intruder. "Who are you, and what do you want?"

The stranger laughed.

"Come now, do you think only the Nazis would learn that the Spear of Destiny has at last been found? I am in Berlin for the same reason as Herr Müller. It is my intention to learn the truth from our esteemed archeologist. As for who I am, you may address me as Count Dracula."

I had heard reports claiming that Dracula was not just a character from Stoker's novel, thought Leo, *but I suppose that after all I've seen, the reality of such a being should not come as too much of a surprise...*

Quickly pushing the Professor aside, the Nyctalope drew his gun and fired off several rounds at the Vampire Lord. However, each slug passed through the dark figure without causing him any discernible harm.

Dracula laughed again.

"It would seem that you do not take folklore seriously, do you, my friend?" Bearing his fangs like an animal ready to attack, the Vampire Lord began approaching the Nyctalope.

Throwing his useless firearm aside, Leo leapt at the Count, pounding him several times with his fists, hoping to stun him long enough to allow the Professor to escape.

However, Dracula withstood the flurry of blows and, equally adept at hand-to-hand combat and far superior in strength to Leo, he grabbed the Nyctalope and hurled him 20 feet across the room and into the wall at the far end.

Leo coughed up some blood and quickly forced himself back to his feet, ready to continue the battle.

"You impress me, mortal," Dracula confessed as he faced his defiant opponent. "You would make a formidable member of my Undead, and would have a place of honor in the new order I plan to create—if you agree to serve me."

"How does one say 'up yours' in vampire tongue, Count?" was Leo's only response.

Dracula gritted his teeth, his face exuding boiling mist as his eyes flared. "You will regret both this decision and your insolence."

"I highly doubt it."

Upon that declaration, Leo resumed his assault on Dracula by launching a brutal but well coordinated barrage of punches and kicks, providing an awesome display of his martial arts prowess in the process. However, Dracula, renowned for his warrior skills, blocked and countered every single one of Leo's blows. Still, the Vampire Lord found himself taken aback when the Nyctalope managed to land a shattering round kick to his jaw. Attempting to follow that kick with a reverse punch, Leo suddenly found his fist caught in Dracula's hand. The Frenchman gritted his teeth in agony as the Vampire Lord exerted a crushing grip upon the bones and muscles of the Nyctalope's hand.

Drooling a thin stream of blood as a consequence of the Nyctalope's blow, Dracula glared down at Leo, who was trembling in pain. "Few mortals have ever been able to strike me so," the vampire snarled. "And fewer yet have managed to cause me pain. But it matters not, because I will have you swear fealty to me and serve in my personal guard. Look into my eyes and acknowledge me as your master, the only true master of all those who call the darkness their home..."

Leo could feel the power of Dracula's mesmeric gaze pouring into his consciousness like a psychic tsunami, but he had studied the Mystic Arts at the feet of some of Tibet's most powerful mages. The Nyctalope's teeth gnashed together as he summoned every iota of his own superhuman will to avoid becoming the thrall of the Prince of Darkness.

"Embrace your inevitable destiny, my formidable friend," Dracula said, redoubling his efforts. "Swear fealty to me, I command you!"

Vacillating like a branch caught in a gale, tears running from his eyes, struggling like never before in his life, Leo proved the proverbial immovable object to Dracula's irresistible force.

"I... will... never yield... to the... likes of you... demon! Never!"

"We shall see, miscreant!" Dracula exclaimed as he continued to redouble his efforts to capture his prize.

But just then, his concentration was suddenly shattered when one of the heavy chairs in the room smashed into his back. Buckling under the impact, but remaining on his feet, the Vampire Lord turned to face the one who had dared to strike him from behind: Professor Clairembart.

Abruptly released, Leo fell to the ground, gasping profusely in both relief and fatigue.

"Ah, I see you are still here, Professor," Dracula said. "You should have made your escape when you still could."

"I'm not about to leave my friend alone with you when he risked so much to save me, monster," the Professor replied. "I may not be a hero, but I don't abandon those who would risk their life for me."

"I approve, Professor," Dracula replied. "Your show of courage will only work to my advantage. Perhaps I shall turn you into one of the Undead, so you can become my personal advisor—after you tell me everything you know about the Spear, that is. Look into my gaze…"

The Professor found himself unable to turn his eyes from Dracula's hypnotic glare as waves of psychic force invaded his mind.

"Tell me, Professor," the Vampire Lord said with great authority. "Did that photo show the real Spear of Destiny? Is it here, in Berlin?"

"I… It looked… I don't…"

"Tell me, you foolish mortal!"

Suddenly, the Nyctalope pounced on Dracula from behind, taking advantage of his knowledge of *chi* and human anatomy to attempt to lock the Vampire Lord in a hold designed to inflict debilitating agony. Dracula found his control over the Professor slipping as he experienced a prodigious jolt of pain. However, the Vampire Lord was more than mortal, and his ability to withstand pain had been considerable, even before he had become the mightiest of all vampires.

"You shall die for this!" Dracula screamed as he tore Leo from his person with supernatural strength, and slammed the

223

Frenchman's body against the ground, knocking the wind from his lungs.

Raising his arm in the air, the Prince of Darkness prepared to sink his hand into Leo's chest and tear out his synthetic heart.

"Let us see how well you recover from *this*, fool!"

But before Dracula's powerful hand could tear through Leo's rib cage to extricate the delicate artificial organ within, a wooden shaft skewered his shoulder from behind.

Howling in pain, his wound sizzling as if it were in contact with a torch, Dracula leapt to his feet and tore the offending weapon from his shoulder blade.

Another combatant had entered the fray: a man of average height but athletic build with longish silvery hair and bright hazel eyes that seemed almost white. The newcomer reloaded another wooden bolt in the crossbow gun he carried and fired it, aiming for Dracula's heart. But the Vampire Lord's uncanny speed enabled him to pluck the lethal shaft out of the air before it could puncture him.

"Ah, Mr. Harker," the Prince of Darkness said. "I should have known you would show up here. Word has been out that you have been trailing me since my revival. Don't you ever learn?"

The man identified as Harker kept his weapon pointed at the Count.

"You're the one who never learns, Dracula. I will never rest until you're permanently laid to rest."

"You and your relatives continue to treat me as prey, when in essence you're only saving me the need to hunt you all down like the vermin you are!" the Vampire Lord exclaimed as mist continued to emit from his pores.

Meanwhile, the Nyctalope was back on his feet and stood beside Harker.

"Shall we take him together, Mr. Harker?"

"By all means," the vampire hunter replied.

The two men charged Dracula simultaneously, only to have him swiftly decorporealize into a cloud of mist. They passed through him harmlessly, and Leo's attempted flying side kick smashed into the wall directly behind the intangible Lord of Darkness.

The swirl of iridescent mist wafted towards the doorway, but before cutting his losses and exiting, Dracula's hollow-sounding and disembodied voice uttered forth the following:

"I no longer have time for this inanity. There will soon be a reckoning for both of you, and I have all eternity to carry it out."

After that ominous declaration, the mist floated outside and quickly metamorphosed into a large bat, which promptly flew out the nearest window and disappeared into the night skies.

The Nyctalope and Harker now looked at each other.

"Thank you for your assistance, Mr. Harker," Leo said sincerely. "I recognized your name, of course, but I thought you were only..."

"Fiction?" the other man replied, smiling. "I'm afraid not. My family has committed its life to destroy that fiend. I have been hunting Dracula for months now. But I believe you have the best of me..."

"My apologies," said the Nyctalope, with the hint of a military salute. "I'm Commandant Leo Saint-Clair."

The expression on Harker's visage suddenly turned hostile.

"You're the Nyctalope! A man I once greatly admired, whose exploits inspired me when I was younger. But I've heard you've become a *collaborateur*... You now work for the Vichy!"

"That is true," Leo said sadly. "I have no love for the Nazis, but I had to do what I did to safeguard the best interests of my country in very trying times, and not jeopardize the safety of its citizens. Did you know that we lost over 100,000 civilians to the Luftwaffe during the Exodus? What would you have done in my place, especially if your Edward had remained King and ordered you to put down your weapons, Mr. Harker?"

"Not bloody well put politics over principles, that's for certain," the Englishman replied hotly.

"That's easy for you to say, but politics do rule the world, there's no getting around that fact. In order to serve the greater good, it is sometimes necessary to compromise."

"There is a fine line between compromise and being *compromised*, Commandant. And I think you crossed it when you agreed to work for those murdering bastards."

"Ah, but I do not work for the Germans! I never have and never will. I work for France."

Professor Clairembart knew that tempers were being frayed and promptly stepped between the two warriors.

"Gentlemen, can we please dispense with the posturing and agree that it's bad form to discuss politics in civilized company?"

Looking at each other with expressions of gloom, the two fighters understood that they could have been allies, but the chasm between them was now far too wide to be bridged.

"I need to ensure that Dracula doesn't get his hands on the Spear," Harker said. "As for you, Saint-Clair, just get the Professor out of here before the Reds come in."

"It will be done," Leo replied in a calm tone.

He put his hand on the archeologist's shoulder and escorted him out of the building. As they exited, Clairembart said:

"Don't take Mr. Harker's words too much to heart, my friend. We both know that during wartime, people are forced to make choices. Things are not always black or white. Such times often bring out both the best and the worst in humanity, as the condition of this city makes abundantly clear."

"Thank you, Professor," the Nyctalope somberly replied, "but Mr. Harker's words were not unjustified. I have always sought to do what was right for my country, but I have realized that I am not infallible, no matter how brilliant I'm supposed to be. I fought in trenches, you know? I was wounded at Ypres. It was unthinkable for me not to support Maréchal Petain, when he begged for my help. But did I do the right thing? Did I, as Mr. Harker accused me, put politics over principles?"

As the two men disappeared into the Berlin night, Leo Saint-Clair hoped that history would ultimately judge him less harshly than the vampire hunter who may have become his friend had they met at a different time and place...

KOSCHEI THE DEATHLESS

In Russian fairy tales, Koschei (also known as Kashchey, Kashchey or Kościej in Polish) is a villain whose sole reason for existence seems to be to kidnap princesses! He is not a vampire, properly speaking, but is described as "immortal" or, more precisely "Deahless", because his death is external to him, often hidden somewhere, inside an egg, etc. Koschei has often appeared in Russian literature, operas, films, etc., and is confronted here by the same hero, the Nyctalope, whom we saw in the previous story...

David McDonald: *The Girl from Odessa*

Odessa, 1919

Leo Saint-Clair stepped from the train, shuddering as the cold winter wind cut through him. He pulled his fur-lined jacket tighter around his shoulders, and looked around for the attaché who was meant to waiting for him. He cursed under his breath as he noticed the sign leaning crookedly against one of the station walls, *Saint-Clair*, printed in what Leo imagined were the crooked letters of a man used to writing not only in a different language, but a different alphabet. Before he could work up a real head of steam, and get into some of the more esoteric profanities he has picked up in his travels, his attention was pulled away by a commotion further down the platform.

He walked towards the sounds of yelling, taking in a rather odd scene. A shabby-looking porter was cowering in the

228

shadow of an impeccably dressed English gentleman. An oaken cane with what looked like a solid silver head was clutched in his raised hand, the wrist of which was held firmly by a massive figure dressed in a faded but precisely creased set of fatigues.

"Damn it, Ballantine!" The man's face was red beneath his luxurious whiskers, moustache and sideburns bristling. "Let go of me! I'm going to flog this cur from one end of the platform to the other and teach him that an Englishman won't stand for this sort of insolence."

"Now, calm down, sir. I am sure he didn't lose your bags on purpose." The big man's voice was calm and even, and had a soft Highland burr. "Now, laddie, away with you before Mr. Flashman does something both of you will regret."

The porter didn't need to be told twice, and scurried away, throwing a sullen glance over his shoulder before darting into the station master's house. Ballantine released his companion's arm and stepped back.

"Well, sir, let's try and organize some accommodation for you. Hopefully your bags will turn up in the meantime."

They began to walk away, only to halt, startled as Leo yelled after them.

"Mr. Flashman, sir! Wait a moment, if you please."

Leo hurried towards them, only to come to a sudden halt as both men whirled to face him, Flashman's cane gripped tightly in whitened knuckles and the big man's fists clenched.

"And who the deuces are you, man?" For a moment, Leo thought he saw fear on the Englishman's face, but if had been there, it was quickly replaced by anger. "I warn you, I have had enough of botheration today and my patience is almost exhausted."

Leo was too excited to be upset by the harsh words. The man before him matched his father's stories perfectly. He looked a touch younger than Leo would have expected, with only the smallest touch of grey in his thick hair and moustache, still strong and vital looking. But the name and his companion banished any doubt from Leo's mind.

229

"Forgive me, Mr. Flashman, I have the advantage of you," Leo said, extending his hand. "I am Leo Saint-Clair. I believe you knew my father?"

Flashman looked at him blankly for a moment, then a wide smile spread across his face and he seized Leo's hand, pumping it vigorously.

"You are Jean's son? By Jove, your father and I had more than our share of adventures together!" The smile died slightly. "It's a wonder I survived them, frankly."

Leo was a little surprised by his reaction. "Come now, Mr. Flashman, my father told me many tales of your daring adventures! He told me you thrived on danger and were never happier than when risking certain death."

Flashman choked slightly. "Oh, yes, of course. Faint heart never won fair maiden and all that."

"And, I heard you did well for yourself in the war too?"

"I did my duty, that's all." Flashman seemed uncomfortable with the line of questioning, which confused Leo.

Ballantine broke in, indignation. "Mr. Flashman is being too modest! He won the Victoria Cross and all."

Leo whistled softly. "It seems my father did not exaggerate your bravery, sir."

Before he could ask any questions, Flashman interrupted him.

"Oh, how remiss of me." He gestured to the bigger man. "Monsieur Saint Clair, this is Sergeant Major Ballantine."

Leo shook hands with the sergeant, conscious of the exaggerated gentleness with which Ballantine folded Leo's hand in his. The Frenchman had seen this before, in extremely strong men conscious of not hurting anyone by mistake. He knew that the big man must be formidable and resolved to keep him on his side.

"Pleasure, sir."

Leo turned back to Flashman. "Where are you staying? Shall we take dinner together? I am always happy to hear stories of my father."

Flashman cleared his throat uncomfortably. "That might be a problem, Leo—may I call you Leo?"

"Of course, Mr. Flashman!"

"Harry." He went on. "You see, the damnable thing is that my bags have been misplaced somewhere, along with all my money. I fear that we will have to avail ourselves of the hospitality, limited as it is, of His Majesty's embassy."

Leo was already shaking his head. "Nonsense, Harry! I will not hear of it. I can advance you some funds and when your bags are recovered you can reimburse me."

"Oh, I would hate to impose."

Leo smiled. "My father told me how many times you saved his life. It is the least I can do."

"...So I threw the last grenade into the machine gun nest, and no sooner had it exploded that I leapt in, bayonet in hand, and gave the Boche what for!"

Whatever reluctance Harry had shown when it came to discussing his wartime exploits had long since dissipated, washed away by the copious amounts of champagne he had drunk since they had made their way to Leo's hotel. He reclined on a luxurious velvet couch, holding court amidst an admiring group of simpering young ladies and awe-struck young men.

The Londonskaya was something of an Odessa landmark, one of the last vestiges of Tsarist Russia. Opulent and expensive, it had always been a favored stopping place for wealthy foreigners, and even though the Revolution had swept away the old empire, it had maintained its exclusive air and continued to operate to the same high standards, left alone by a government happy to take its cut of foreign currency.

It had been a very long day for Leo, and he had been happy to sit back and listen. Harry was a natural-born storyteller with a flair for the dramatic, so it was no chore, especially when he was telling tales of his adventures with Leo's father. He had just finished one set in the hills of Afghanistan when Leo felt a gentle tug on his sleeve.

"Begging your pardon, sir, but I just wanted to thank you," Ballantine said. "It's a hard thing, being alone in a strange city with no money and no friends. I am getting a little old for sleeping in the streets."

"My pleasure, sergeant. I am sure Harry would have done the same for me." Ignoring the sergeant's strange, muffled snort, Leo hesitated a moment and went on. "Please forgive my rudeness, but may I ask you a personal question?"

Ballantine nodded.

"According to both Harry's and my father's stories, you were both in your forties when he first met you. That was almost thirty years ago, and you look no more than fifty, and a young fifty at that!"

There was a touch of bitterness in the Scotsman's smile. "Well, sir, being the good soldier that I am, I volunteered for certain extra duties in my younger days. In their wisdom, my superiors used me as a subject for certain experimental procedures. Amongst other things, it seems to have slowed down my aging."

"There are many men and women who would pay a great deal for such a thing!" Leo exclaimed.

"Some things are not worth the price, laddie. Trust me on that." The big man looked away, eyes on some far off place. "They changed me, in so many ways, not just what they did to my body, but the tasks they set me. When you've changed that much... Well, it's hard to ever go back to where you came from."

Leo thought about the way his own life had been changed forever, and the secrets he hid within, and reached out, placing a hand on the sergeant's shoulder.

"You must trust me on this, Ballantine, I, too, know what it is like to be changed like that." Suddenly uncomfortable, he took his hand away and sought to change the subject. "So these stories of Harry's, how much of them are true? No disrespect intended, but they seem quite incredible!"

"Every word, as far as I know. Mister Flashman has a knack for finding himself in dangerous spots." Ballantine's smile was completely free of the earlier bitterness. "Fortunately, he has an even greater knack for getting us out of them alive!"

Both men laughed, and turned back to listen to the next tale of daring, only to find that a deathly hush had fallen across the room, and that Harry had halted mid-sentence, staring ashen faced at the doorway.

Framed in the entrance was an elderly man, dressed in an immaculate black military uniform. His shadowed eyes and flowing white hair and beard gave the impression of great age, but as he walked towards them, his shoulders were square and his back ramrod straight. The crowd gathered around Harry scattered, people hurrying from the room without even a goodbye. The old man stopped in front of them, his lip curling in disdain as he raked them with a withering glance.

"So, it seems we have some illustrious guests." His voice sent a chill through Leo; it was cold and dry and empty and made him think of a freshly turned grave. "I am Commissariat Koschei, head of the Security Services of the People's City of Odessa. I am here to discuss your business in my city."

The way he said "my" reminded Leo of a particularly depraved old lecher saying the name of an innocent young woman who had wandered into his clutches. Its obscene possessiveness made Leo's skin crawl. From the way the Englishman was squirming in his seat, he could see that Koschei's voice and tone had discomfited Harry as well.

"We are merely tourists enjoying a trip to your fair city." Harry's voice had lost any trace of drunkenness, and Leo couldn't help but admire its steadiness considering the baleful gaze of the old man. "A pleasure to meet a distinguished gentleman as yourself, I am…"

Koschei cut him off mid-sentence, his voice cracking like a whip.

"Do not waste my time with your dissembling. I know exactly who you are. You are Harry Flashman, war hero and adventurer, but more importantly, sometime agent of His Majesty's Government. And your companion is Leo Saint Clair, who fulfills a similar role for the French Government." The voice softened, becoming oily in its solicitousness. "But let us not speak harshly. Odessa is something of an open city. We are far enough from Moscow that we do what we please, and it pleases us to allow foreigners to come and go because it makes Odessa the gateway to the Rus. Controlling that gateway gives us a great deal of power. But be warned, this is my city, and if your business in anyway threatens my interests, I will not hesitate to crush you."

Koschei raised a claw-like hand and clenched it into a bony fist. The lights dimmed and the air was filled with the sound of shattering glass as every bottle along the top shelf of the bar exploded at once. Without another word, the old man turned on his heel and strode from the room, leaving the three foreigners staring at one another in shock. When the silence was broken, it was Harry who spoke.

"What a waste of good booze!"

The mood in the hotel bar was much more somber than the night before. There was no crowd of admiring listeners hanging off Harry's every word. In fact, aside from the sullen bartender, who was apparently still sulking from the clean-up job, they were alone. None of them were able to muster much in the way of enthusiasm. Koschei's presence still lingered, casting a chill over them and sucking the very vitality from the room. Harry hadn't even bothered to start telling any of his stories, and was taking a desultory sip of his champagne when the door opened. His eyes widened as he choked on his mouthful. Leo whipped around, heart in mouth, expecting to see the old man,

The young woman walking across the thick, lush carpet could not have been a greater contrast to their unwelcome visitor of the day before. It was not merely her youth—Leo guessed she could not be more than seventeen—but the way she lit up her surroundings, outshining the glittering chandelier that had been grudgingly lit by the hotel manager when night had fallen. Long blonde hair flowed down her back, breaking like golden waves over the shoulders of her black evening gown. Full red lips pursed in slight consternation as vividly green eyes took in the three men, then she took a deep breath and said:

"It is dark outside and the Moon has not risen." Her voice matched her appearance, melodious and with a rich timbre.

"But the light within can be taken wherever you go." Harry and Leo looked at each other in amazement as they finished the response in the same breath.

"What the deuces, Leo?" Harry exclaimed. "How did you know the answer to the code?"

"I could ask you the same thing!"

Ballantine's voice cut through their conversation. "Begging your pardon, sirs, but it seems pretty plain to me. You've both been sent here on the same mission and to meet the same person." He smiled gently at the young woman. "Isn't that right, ma'am?"

The young woman drew herself up to her full height, and tried her hardest to look down her nose at the sergeant.

"The correct term of address is 'Your Illustriousness,' not ma'am. I am Countess Anastasiya Belinskya. I demand an explanation! Only one of you was meant to staying here, the other was meant to be at the Hotel Otrada!" Her voice rose in pitch and volume with each word until she was shouting.

Harry had leapt to his feet and now stepped forward, bowing low from the waist and taking her hand, kissing it gently.

"Colonel Harold Flashman VC at your service, Your Illustriousness. I do apologize for the change in plans, but an unfortunate mix-up at the station precluded me from staying at the Otrada. I thought I still had a day before our meeting to arrange things." He gave her a hopeful smile. "May I offer you a glass of champagne and a more private conversation?"

The Countess disentangled her hand from Harry's. "Never mind that, I am here now and in no mood for pleasantries."

Harry frowned. "Whatever you wish, Your Illustriousness. Let us discuss getting you to Great Britain as quickly as possible. My superiors are very interested in the documents you carry."

"Hold on, Harry." Leo hurried over. "*Enchanté*, Countess, I am Leo Saint Clair and my superiors are also, shall we say, interested in your documents. I was under the impression that an arrangement had already been made for your travel to Paris?"

"Nothing has been decided yet, gentlemen. I want to hear what exactly your respective governments are offering in exchange." There was a faint flush to her cheeks. "You may consider me mercenary and grasping, but these documents are all I have left to my name. Our family's manor was burned to the ground; it was only I who survived. I need to ensure that I am provided for. After all, these documents contain much information of value, and cost much to obtain."

Before either man could reply, a deep voice issued from the shadows by the bar.

"There is no time for bargaining now. If you do not get the Countess out of Odessa tonight, then neither of your governments will get the documents. Koschei knows we are here, and he will not be far away."

"Gentlemen, this is Father Grigor. He has been our family's priest since before I was born, and it was he who saved me from the flames," Anastasiya said.

Leo was disgusted that they had allowed themselves to be distracted by the Countess, and had not noticed her companion. No matter how beautiful she was, a man that big should have stood out in any surrounding. He was as at least as tall as Ballantine, but almost twice as broad across the shoulders. Dressed in simple monk's robes, bound at the waist with a length of rope, his chest was covered with a ferocious black beard streaked with grey. Leo could see Ballantine sizing the priest up, and he wondered whether the sergeant was thinking the same thing that was on Leo's mind and wondering whether he could take Grigor down if needed. Leo thought such a fight would be a sight to see indeed.

"We need to get out of here now," the priest said.

"Too late." Harry gestured towards the street entrance. The door was ajar and, through it, they could hear the sounds of marching feet—a few score of men at least if Leo was any judge.

"I think Koschei has arrived."

The soldiers stood unmoving in the square, unnatural and menacing. The pale light of the Moon glinted from eyes that did not blink and gleamed on teeth revealed by the rictus grins of death. They had no guns, instead carrying the slightly curved swords that had become a familiar sight to Leo as he traveled through the region. His original guess had been off by a considerable margin—there were at least a hundred men, if not more.

"They are corpses!" Leo said.

"You don't say," Harry snapped. "Anything else you want to point out?"

"Go easy, Mr. Flashman. I think we're all a bit rattled." Ballantine didn't sound rattled. He had been the first to move, manhandling a huge cabinet in front of the doors, lifting it as if weighed nothing at all.

Harry stepped back from the windows. "I saw rifles in the manager's office, Leo. Bring back as many as you can carry and ammunition."

Leo didn't argue, happy enough to follow orders that made sense. He knew Flashman had commanded men before, and there was no time for ego. When he returned, Harry and the Countess were arguing nose to nose.

"Dammit, woman, do as you're told!" Harry turned to the priest. "Father, can you reason with her? Take her upstairs. This is no place for a woman."

Quick as a cat, Anastasiya whirled and snatched one of the rifles from Leo. In one fluid motion, she brought it up to her shoulder, sighted and fired through the glass. One of the corpse soldiers staggered, his left eye now a dripping, gory mess.

"I do not need to coddled," she snapped. "I know how to use a rifle and I will not sit idly waiting for Koschei to come for me."

Harry blinked. "Fair enough, have it your way. I am not sure what good rifles are going to do though."

"What do you mean?" Leo asked.

Harry pointed. "Look"

The soldier that the Countess had shot had gotten back to his feet and rejoined the formation, oblivious to the blood running down his face.

"What do you think they are waiting for, sir?" Ballantine asked.

"That." The priest's deep voice was somber.

The soldiers began to move, forming a clear passage through the center of their ranks. A dark shape strode through it, resolving into the terrifying figure of Koschei. He stopped and looked up at them.

"Gentlemen, there is no need for bloodshed tonight. Simply hand over the girl and you can leave unmolested. I do not want to provoke your governments into a rash act." Koschei smiled, a ghastly expression on that withered face. "Send her down and go."

"I'll be damned if I do!" Harry shouted. "Chivalry aside, I'd be barred from my club for life if I folded to a Russkie scoundrel like you."

Leo laughed. "How can I act a coward in front my father's renowned friend?"

Ballantine's reply was simpler, obscene and to the point.

Koschei scowled, his face darkening. "So be it!"

"Thank you." The Countess voice was quiet, stripped of its earlier haughtiness.

"Don't thank us yet, Your Illustriousness," Harry said. "Wait until we are on our way to Mother England."

"Or France!" Leo said.

Their joking was interrupted by Koschei's chants, words spoken in some tongue that was never meant to be heard by men. It rose to a crescendo as he pointed at them, and the dead began to march. A ragged volley of shots rang out as the defenders began to fire into the oncoming corpses. The soldiers staggered, but still kept coming on inexorably.

"Go for the knees!" The Countess didn't wait to see if they were obeying her, but put her words into action.

Each shot found its target, leaving a corpse convulsing on the cobblestones. They did not seem to be in pain, but denied the use of their legs, they were only able to claw their way forward an inch at a time.

"Oh, clever girl!" Leo shouted, receiving a shining smile in return.

His elation was short-lived. There were still scores of soldiers on their feet, and the chanting had started again. As Leo watched, Koschei held his palms about a foot apart, cradling a rapidly growing globe of pitch black darkness. Just before it touched his skin, he flung his hands open and away from himself, sending the globe arcing towards them.

Diving away from the windows, Leo only had time to shout, "Down!" before the world exploded and everything went dark.

Leo could only have been unconscious for a few seconds, but when he came to the entire shape of the room had changed. The windows were gone, and wood and rubble formed a ramp leading down into the square. There was a huge gash running down the center of the room, a gaping crevice that revealed the vast cellars below.

"Is everyone alright?" Leo looked around, and breathed a sigh of relief as his companions each answered.

"We may be in a spot of bother though, old chap," Harry said.

Leo could only agree. The corpses were beginning to move towards the ramp, and it would only be a matter of minutes before they began swarming into the room.

"Countess, grab some rifles, get behind the bar and try and keep them off us as long as you can," Harry snapped over his shoulder. "No arguing, just do it."

"I'm not stupid, I can see what needs to be done," she said. Grabbing the rifles, she vaulted over the bar gracefully, and began to lay out the rifles and rounds of ammunition, looking like she was ready to hold out forever.

The four men stood in loose formation, waiting for the dead. Ballantine and Leo had grabbed lengths of wood, and Leo felt slightly comforted by the sturdy weight in his hands. Flashman had slid a long blade from his cane, and its edges glimmered strangely, unlike any steel Leo had seen.

Harry caught him looking and grinned. "Silver. Remarkably effective in these sort of situations."

"What about you, Father, do you need a weapon?" Leo asked.

The priest held up massive fists. "These are the only weapons I need."

His face began to twist, his features coarsening and thick fur sprouting from his skin. There was the sound of ripping fabric as his muscles started to swell, his shoulders and arms thickening. Fangs protruded from his mouth and claws grew from his fingertips. As the other men watched, he continued to grow until, finally, a huge figure towered over them. Eight feet tall and unmistakably bear-like in appearance, it lifted its head and roared its defiance at the oncoming figures.

"If I'd known priests could do that, I wouldn't have dared draw naughty pictures in the margins of the *Songs of Solomon*," Harry said.

No one replied, as the first dead were climbing through the shattered window frames. As their feet hit the floor, Anastasiya began to fire, coolly picking her targets, kneecaps shattering as she found her mark. But for every corpse she crippled, two more took its place and, soon, the dead were upon them.

Leo swung his piece of timber in a steady rhythm, crushing skulls and shattering bones. To either side of him loomed

Ballantine and Grigor. The priest lashed out with massive arms, talons raking through flesh as he sent corpses flying to all corners of the room. The bodies would lie still for a few moments then drag themselves to their feet and stumble back into the fray. Ballantine was almost as impressive as the priest, far stronger than any normal man should be. Lifting one of the enemy above his head, he sent it hurtling into a group coming towards him, sending them in all directions like a boy playing skittles.

Flashman darted in and out of the pack, his sword weaving in intricate patterns, clashing against the curved swords of his opponents. When his blade bit into dead flesh, it seemed to do a more lasting damage than the wounds inflicted by the other men. Where the soldiers ignored staved-in chests from Leo's weapon or ragged gashes from the priest's claws, he saw one go down with Harry's blade through its heart, and stay down!

"To Flashman!" Leo yelled.

Instinctively, the other men began to herd the dead into Flashman's shining circle of silver and steel, protecting him from being overwhelmed and allowing him to deliver the *coup de grace* time after time. Anastasiya saw what they were doing and added her covering fire to their strategy. The pile of unmoving corpses began to grow, slowly but surely. Leo was just beginning to allow himself to hope when there was a flicker behind him, and the sound of chanting began to fill the air.

Leo whirled to see Koschei behind them, standing at the edge of the gash running through the floor. His chanting was reaching a crescendo, and horror clenched in Leo's chest at the sight of another of the black globes forming between the old man's hands. A wild shout on his lips, Leo sprinted towards the old man and leapt at him, hand outstretched, his only thought being to protect his companions from another of those devastating blasts.

Just before he hit him, he saw a look of surprise and terror on Koschei's face. Then, they were falling into the cellars below, the precariously balanced rubble of timber and stone tumbling into the void with them.

The cellar was not simply dark, it was pitch black. A normal man would not have seen his own hand held in front of his eyes. But that did not bother Leo, the Nyctalope, who looked around in wonder. The cellar was massive, far bigger than he would have thought necessary for even a hotel, even one as luxurious as the Londonskaya.

The roof was vaulted and curved, and he could clearly see the gash they had fallen through, now filled with debris. Ladders ran up the walls to hatches, and strange block and tackles and ropes and pulleys dangled from the ceiling. Directly below one of them, he found the answer to his question. Stacked neatly were barrels of what must be gunpowder, while nearby, in another pile, cannon balls stood in a neat pyramid. All around him were stores of ammunition and weapons. Leo realized that this must be a cache put aside for a time of need.

There was a crash behind him and muffled cursing. Leo turned to see Koschei staggering around, arms outstretched.

"Where are you, Frenchman?" The old man's voice was a shriek. "I will tear out your kidneys and eat them in front of you!"

Leo began to carefully move in a circular pattern around the old man.

"What's the matter, old man? Can't see in the dark?" He moved a bit further around, then spoke again. "How do you plan on catching me?"

Koschei's head moved from side to side as if trying to get a fix on Leo.

"I don't need to see you. I can hear the thumping of your heart." His grin was unpleasant and knowing. "I can hear the way it beats; I can hear your fear."

The old man began to move towards Leo, hands feeling in front of him.

"I'm coming, Frenchman."

Leo concentrated on the beating of his heart, feeling the way that the delicate mechanism pumped the blood through his body. As always, he marveled at its technological artistry as he, gradually, began to slow its beat, until it stopped. A wave of dizziness reminded him that he only had a few moments before the lack of blood flow would render him unconscious and helpless. He picked up a lump of timber and padded noiselessly towards the old man.

"Where are you? Where have you gone?" There was a note of panic in the Koschei's voice that made Leo smile. "You can't hide forever, I will..."

There was a sickening crunch as Leo wrung the timber, catching the old man across his shoulders. With a grunt, the Nyctalope hit again and again, driving Koschei to his knees. But the old man was not finished. With terrifying speed, he lurched up and crashed his fist into Leo's chin, sending him reeling backwards, dazed and hurt. His back slammed into something hard and round, and he heard an ominous shifting noise as something metallic moved behind him. The cannon balls!

"Where are you?" The old man was howling with a mad rage that chilled Leo's blood. "I am going crack your bones and suck out the marrow while you weep for mercy."

Groaning with pain, Leo fought to bring his will to bear on his still silent heart. Finally, he felt the first beat, then another, as it sprang back to life.

Koschei shrieked in triumph. "I hear you! I am coming!"

He launched himself, sprinting towards Leo, arms outstretched and claw-like hands ready to rend and tear.

At the last second, Leo leapt to his right, letting the old man's momentum carry him into the cannon balls. With a terrific crash, the pile collapsed, burying Koschei beneath hundreds of pounds of lead.

Leo walked over and looked down at the monster. His limbs were bent at unnatural angles and blood pooled at the corner of his mouth, bubbling as he breathed laboriously. His eyes snapped open, and glared up at Leo and then, incredibly, he began to laugh.

"Do you think you have defeated me?" Koschei's voice was little more than a wheeze, but it was full of a terrible mirth. "They do not call me Koschei the Undying for naught. You could cut me into a thousand pieces and they would draw themselves together even if it took a thousand years! I may be trapped, but when I am free, I will hunt you down."

"A thousand years, you say? If I blew you into a million pieces, it might take even longer, *non*?"

"What?" Some of the mirth had left the old man's voice. "What are you doing?"

Leo began to whistle a jaunty little tune as he began to gather barrels of gunpowder and fuses, dragging them back to where the old man writhed helplessly.

This was going to be fun.

The fight with the corpse soldiers was over by the time that Leo dragged himself up one of the ladders and through the trapdoor. His companions were sitting exhausted in whatever chairs they had been able to find, surrounded by piles of cadavers.

Grigor had reverted to his human form; wrapped in his tattered robes, he was chatting with Ballantine, while Flashman was drinking a glass of champagne and trying to flirt with Anastasiya, who seemed rather uninterested. As Leo approached, they all leapt to their feet, gathering around him and smiling in relief.

"Leo, old chap, am I glad to see you!" Harry said. "I was getting a bit worried there for a moment."

Leo felt a light touch on his arm and looked down into the viridian eyes of the Countess.

"That was very brave, leaping on Koschei like that." Her smile was enough to take away some of the sting of his cuts and bruises.

"Yes, well done, laddie!" Leo staggered as Ballantine clapped him on the shoulder. "Koschei wasn't expecting that now, was he?"

"But, where is Koschei?" Grigor asked, worry evident in his deep voice. "I had heard that he could not be killed."

"Koschei is shortly going to find out what happens when you get too close to one hundred pounds of explosive. It may not kill him, but it will be a while before he bothers us again." He looked around at his companions. "But, I'd suggest we get as far away as we can get in about..." he looked at his watch, "...three minutes."

"Sounds like a good plan, Leo." Harry gestured extravagantly towards the front of the hotel. "After you, Your Illustriousness."

As they walked away, as casually as if they were going for a stroll rather than trying to avoid being blown up, Leo could make out snatches of conversation.

"..England is lovely this time of year..."

"...oh, I know all the right people..."

"...with shooting like that, you must come hunting with me..."

Leo swore and hurried after them. He had a feeling that his biggest challenge was still ahead of him.

NOSFERATU

Count Orlok, better known under the name of the film of which he is the anti-hero, Nosferatu (1922), is a repulsive version of Dracula, designed to replace the original character whose rights could not (or would not) be purchased by German filmmaker Friedrich Wilhelm Murnau (1888-1931) and his partner, writer Henrik Galeen (1881-1949). If Dracula has received very different interpretations, Count Orlok will be forever represented in our memories by the formidable silhouette of actor Maximilian Schreck (1879-1936), wearing a wonderful makeup designed by the film's artistic director, Aubin Grau...

Catherine Robert: *A Game of Death*

Journal of Johan Volkov

July 5

The trip to the castle was longer and harder than I had thought it would be. The paths of my childhood have, for the most part, disappeared and we got lost several times. If my friend were not urging me on, I would have turned back. Sightseeing and exploring the area held no interest for me. But André loved it. I felt like the only reason he came with me on my vacation was for this visit. The obsession of a young geek, an amateur of horror stories, whom I unfortunately encouraged. My friend had unconsciously taken advantage of my goodwill on my arrival in France.

Thus, when he begged me to take him to visit the sinister abode, I could not refuse. I had made the mistake of telling him about my home and maybe a lack of self-confidence made me reveal that not far from my village was a castle that had become legendary. A mistake I regret now because even if I put no faith at all in the beliefs of the past, my own are still sensitive. Nobody would have told the truth about the huge building that towers over the countryside. People turn mute when it comes to the count or they lie with a conviction rooted in decades of wariness. Nobody wants to bring in tourists, cheap thrill seekers, the curious and those who just have to hear some lewd detail. They point north or south or east or west as their fancy dictates. All the little villages do the same and they have guarded the secret for more than a century and a half.

As soon as I talked, I saw my blunder, but it was too late, my friend would not stop hassling me. And here we are now, settling in where, supposedly, Orlok lived.

As I said before, our path was not easy. The vegetation had done its work and I had to find other trails, almost invisible, to make our way. We had left early in the morning but we arrived late in the afternoon. And the problems did not stop because we had to get inside a place that was completely walled in by the peasants at the time, filled with those ancestral fears that drive me crazy. The wall surrounding the estate, to my great astonishment, stood before us in perfect condition as if it were maintained daily.

Deep down I wanted to get out of there, so using the wall as an excuse I tried to convince my companion. But the guy had thought of everything and pulled grappling hooks and ropes out of his bag, assuring me that it would take no time at all to get into the castle.

Since I was already there, why not, right? I followed him. We scaled the stones, came down the other side and then entered pretty easily.

I am not scared, of course, but I am looking forward to going back down into the valley tomorrow and seeing my old bunică, my grandmother. All of this seems really childish to me, even if me have to admit that the place couldn't be gloomier. The years have done a lot of damage and the roof now has a bunch of holes. Some of walls have collapsed. The humidity has done its work; the furniture is rotted, some even broken; the drapery is torn, falling to pieces. There's not an inch where dust hasn't settled in thick layers. All the rooms we have had time to explore this evening are in the same state of decay. I found it dreadful and depressing. André loves it. He feels like a kid with Christmas presents. So, I pretended to appreciate the outing as much as he while we were eating some of the food he had brought. I wonder now how he could have carried all this stuff without getting exhausted. He is not very big but his bag, I realize, must be heavy. Adrenaline from the excitement, I guess.

July 6

To my amazement I let him convince me to stay one more night. André is sleeping right now but I'm not sleepy. I'm taking the opportunity to write. I have to start at the beginning, from when we woke up. The night was pretty calm, although I woke up twice thinking I heard voices in the dark. You'd think the atmosphere was getting to me in spite of my convictions. My friend, on the other hand, slept the night through. On waking, however, he behaved a little strangely, not seeming to recognize me at first. Then he burst out laughing and I found the same guy full of zest for life and curiosity. He spent the day searching everywhere, obsessed by a craving for discovery that I didn't have the courage to share with him. I sat in one of the less ruined rooms, sparsely furnished with a windowless anteroom. The only window in the room itself looked over the forest below and it was so high up that for a moment I felt dizzy. Another door opened onto a salon that was, I'm happy to say, little affected by the ravages of time. Books lay about that were tattered but readable and that was what I did while waiting for André.

It took him several hours to show up. He sat down on the sofa, which kicked up a cloud of dust that made me cough, then opened a bottle of wine. I asked him where he had dug it up and he said he simply took it from the stock. After pouring two glasses, which he had washed with care, he toasted to a new life. A weird toast that I didn't dwell on, worrying more about the quality of the wine. But since my friend showed no aversion to swallowing his, I did the same and we ended up fishing the bottle. It was after this that we had the conversation that I will try to transcribe accurately.

"It's been so many years since I've savored the sweet taste of such a drink!"

"Right. Since we left my parents' house."

"Of course, my friend, of course, but this is special to me. Have you never dreamed of certain things, dreamed so strongly that when they happen you find yourself in a state of almost total ecstasy?"

Thinking that he was talking about his mania to visit the castle I answered that everyone hopes for impossible things. He looked at me with a strange smile on his face and I had the unpleasant feeling that we were not talking about the same thing.

"What would you say about playing a little game? A very simple game really that will help pass the time. You play the role of guest and I'll be the count. And we'll just improvise."

I smiled, seeing the puerile pleasures of my old friend. And if this was all it took to please him, it was certainly no sweat off my back. He started his role right away.

"Do you know, my friend, that in a weird way you remind me of someone? A man whom I once knew and who caused me great trouble. I was careless enough to let him live. Like him you are full of youthful charm and I feel his same strength in your muscles and your heart."

I didn't know what to say, so I kept silent and he went on. I had the feeling that he didn't really want me to participate in his rambling; he just wanted me to be a good audience.

"Do you know my story?"

As I nodded he continued.

"Astonishing isn't it? How is it possible?"

I finally entered the game, explaining to him that a whole legend was built up around him. He frowned but said nothing except, "Tell me what they say."

"André! This is getting old. You know I'm no expert on these things even if I grew up around here. Maybe exactly because I grew up around here. You didn't grow up with the weird rituals that were supposed to protect us from god knows what danger. You didn't grow up being forbidden to go out after dark. I have no desire to dive back into past beliefs."

My old bunică would have scolded me if she could hear this but she wasn't here and she wasn't faced with a crazy guy in the throes of absurd delusion.

"So, you don't believe in vampires and all that gossip. Do you believe in anything?"

"Nothing and you know it!"

I had no desire to play this stupid game and I let him know. He pouted but didn't press me. I let him know in no uncertain terms that we would leave tomorrow.

Now I'm going to try to sleep. Today tired me out more than I thought. I can't wait for tomorrow to get back and write to Sophie. She'll probably get worried if she doesn't hear from me soon.

July 8

I spent two more nights at the castle. To my utter disappointment it was impossible for me to convince André yesterday and I can't just leave him here alone. It's morning and I hope that this time I'll manage to drag him away from here. This place is a bad influence on him. Since he started role-playing the other day he's stayed with it. He acts like the count and is having fun annoying me with his weird speech.

Several times he asked me if I knew how he got back here. Once again I didn't know what to say. I've never been a fan of the vampire craze and I realize now that even though my family and village constantly warned me, they didn't tell me much about it. The subject seems to be plaguing André. He told me that he remembered very clearly what happened in

Wisborg, that night with Ellen, how she retained him and those lowly people managed to get the better of him. And the sun finished him off.

"Then I woke up here. Between the moment when I burned in the sunlight and this awakening, I haven't the slightest memory. Do you believe they could have brought me back?"

Another weird question. And even weirder behavior. My good friend is slowly starting to scare me. I'm afraid for his sanity. Physically, on the other hand, he's never been in better shape. He looks more muscular, his skin more firm, and his eyes sparkle with vitality.

Just the opposite of me. I'm not sleeping much and when I doze off I'm troubled by dreams. Dreams or nightmares. Several times a night I wake up seized by a nameless terror. Someone touches me; I feel light caresses on my cheeks and my body responds by offering itself to a desire that disgusts me. I just want to see Sophie again. This desire is all the more bewildering in that I can't recall any kind of face or form, just the feeling of a seductive presence. I didn't tell André about it because of my natural modesty and the certainty that it would only aggravate his condition.

Now I have to find a way to convince him before I'm too weak to make the trip back. Since along with my lack of sleep I can now add a lack of food. Our provisions are gone and except for the cherry trees and some wild carrots found in the old vegetable plot, we have nothing else to eat.

Evening

I haven't had any results. And I was badly shocked to find the climbing gear had disappeared. Right now I'm in dire straits, truly dangerous if it continues. André assured me he had nothing to do with the grapples and ropes disappearing. I know he's lying but I won't say anything. I just have to find where he hid them but the castle is so big and I'm so weak.

Nevertheless, I can wait for him to fall asleep—because he sleeps very well—to start my search.

I hope I can find something. I regret not exploring the place with my friend since I'd have a better idea where to start looking.

July 11 (I think)

The days are a little mixed up in my head. I'm having a harder and harder time thinking logically. I'm a prisoner in an empty castle and I don't understand anything that's happening.

Something frightening is going on. I don't what or why but I feel it. André is like himself. I laugh as I write this because, no, really, he's not at all the same. If I'm physically being held prisoner by these walls, he seems to have his reason imprisoned by god knows what—a dementia that must have been dormant and I helped awaken it in spite of myself.

In the grip of a man sinking into madness and with nights peopled by more and more disturbing hallucinations I fear for my own sanity. I'm remembering scraps of history that my old bunică told me about the lord of the night, which I listened to distractedly. I would love for her to be here with me. Not that I believe in these legends even for a second, but it might soothe my tortured mind.

The nocturnal apparitions terrorize me the most. I'm trying to stop sleeping but this is no longer enough. They are here even when I'm awake. Invisible but tangible, just as much as they are intangible. They search me out, brush by me, touch me, whisper strange things and I can do nothing, I can't resist them and my body responds to their approach, to their diabolical caresses. Oh yes, it responds! I think I can feel the weight of their bodies—there are two of them, I think, no more—as my hands touch empty space and my lips, to my great shame, savor their voluptuous mouths that I can't see. Their breasts squeeze against my chest and I pant like a savage beast.

I dare not say more. Who knows if one day Sophie will find this notebook. She'd be upset and yet my love for her is true. Just thinking about her helps me deal with this situation as the phantoms harass me. There, I've said it! Phantoms, spirits, ghosts, specters or I don't know what demonic being. But they're here, I'm sure of it. Now that I've said it, I can accept the reality of it.

What to do about it?

July 17 (approximately)

I'm going to try to transcribe my last conversation with André. But my memory is a little foggy. I'll do my best. Keeping a journal helps me, like having a grip on a world that's slipping away from me. As long as I can, I'll write, so as not to go completely crazy.

"So, Johan, how are you doing?"

"Leave me alone."

I had no desire to talk to him. He was scaring me. I don't know what madness he'll end up in but I know I have to be on my guard. I've started fearing for my life. If I ever upset him how would he react? The question gnaws at me. To think that my best friend might be a mortal danger to me makes me sad and lonelier. But he wanted to talk, as happens to him sometimes.

"Come now, what's wrong? Aren't you enjoying yourself as my guest any longer? I believe I understand. You miss your girlfriend, which is natural. Sophie, I think. Did I tell you I find her charming?"

All of a sudden I became aware that if we get out of here the danger is not just threatening me but also everyone I love and everyone who crosses paths with my friend. André is mad. Here I understood that it's my responsibility to fix the problem. I focused all my attention on his words, as strange as they seemed to me. Maybe I could find a crack to get through.

"Don't worry, you will see her again soon. We won't be staying here much longer. I'm almost ready. And you'll be coming with me, of course."

This was not a question and I had nothing to say.

He continued, "You know, I've thought a great deal about what happened in Wisborg. After my demise, of course, before anything I remember. I've come to the conclusion that they must have taken my coffin into the vault. I found it there. Maybe a gesture of mercy from Hutter and his friends."

At the mention of his supposed enemies he snarled and his eyes gleamed with a cruelty that I'd never seen before while he tightened the grip on his glass and ended up breaking it. His eyes flamed up even more on seeing the blood, which he lapped up greedily on bringing his hand to his lips. I shivered. He really thought he was the count and if I'd ever had any doubt, at that moment, watching him, it disappeared.

"What a pity that so much time passed since the day of my death, me the undead. I could have punished those wretches. Alas, it's too late for that but not too late for me. You're puzzled, aren't you, my friend? You're trying to understand but you can't. I needed time too but unlike you I was never hindered by disbelief."

While speaking he drank another glass of wine. He served me one also but I had decided not to touch it in spite of the temptation to lose myself in oblivion. I had to keep my mind sharp.

"I was lord of the night, more than alive, and suddenly I was in my castle wandering around. It was empty, as usual, and it did not take long for the peasants to wall in the estate. A pointless protections, you agree, against the undead who can change shape."

I remembered that Dracula could change into animals like the werewolf or hyena. I'd had to suffer André's fascination for the genre and the films reeling off behind my back when I worked. A few details came back to me. I decided to try an experiment to bring my friend back to his senses.

"So, you can transform yourself. Why not give me a demonstration?"

With a scornful gesture he waved off my challenge like that of a five-year old child.

"Are you an idiot, Johan? Do you think I need to prove anything at all? Soon you will have all the proofs you need. But it will be too late. It's already too late."

254

What was he talking about? I had absolutely no idea. But he was so convinced that I almost believed him. That everything was lost and it was useless to struggle. I pictured my sweet and tender Sophie. For her I could not give up. André knew her, knew her address. She trusted him and he was dangerous, the most dangerous being I had ever met. I had to protect the woman I loved.

"Why is it too late?" I had nothing else to say. I felt a little stupid but I had to keep up the conversation.

"I can't answer you today. Tomorrow I think it will be time. Let's go to sleep now."

And he left me in my room. My room! A surprising admission. Was I accepting the idea that maybe this was going to be my end? However, I'm supposed to go with him when we leave. He told me so and it didn't sound like he was lying. But can I be sure? Everything seems to have several possibilities now and the facts don't have the same weight as before. I want tomorrow to come. To leave this night and its horrors behind me but also to know what he intends. I am tortured by the thought of what he plans to do. My imagination runs wild in so many potential scenarios that I'm lost.

I'm going to try to sleep. I need to regain a little strength, hoping that my visitors forget about me for a few hours, which I have no faith in.

July 18 (maybe)

The sun is already high in the sky and I still haven't seen André after we woke up. I think he's waiting in another room but I don't know what he's preparing. Me, I'm waiting for him to come. I'm armed with a huge knife that I found in the kitchen. I'm determined to use it if I have to. For me, for Sophie, for the others. Our last conversation, this morning, left be perplexed. And although I have a hard time believing his fantasies, nevertheless I've started asking myself about the truth of certain things. Basically, I really am the victim of ghosts. Why would such a claim be impossible? Here's what he told me.

255

"As you learned yesterday, we'll be leaving today. When I say 'we' it's not far from the truth but not exactly the whole truth. I see that you're dubious, so let me explain. Since you've been expecting an explanation I owe it to you and it will give me great pleasure.

"As you know, I was the victim of an attack, which we've talked about, and my dusty remains were brought here. When I awoke, I was happy to find my castle but I was quickly disenchanted. Something had changed; my being, my body was different. My powers had vanished. No more transformations, no more control over the elements. But there were more surprises to come. I soon realized that I was no longer a material being. I could pass through objects without feeling them, without being able to touch them. Quite simply, I had become a ghost. Was this a punishment? I didn't care, I only wanted to leave here. By the time I got used to this new state, my castle was sealed up on all sides and no one living could enter. Therefore, I wandered within these walls for two centuries, waiting. Alone. Or almost because I know that other spirits haunt this place, maybe my victims who could find no rest. But even if I knew they were here I couldn't and still can't contact them. But I who was the prince of the undead, a more than alive, I became a more than dead. My powers are much greater than your normal phantom. They could never take possession of a body. Me, I figured out how to do it very quickly."

Here he stopped his story and smiled at me. I knew where he was going with this, even if I couldn't accept the possibility. But this is no longer the case, the more I write.

Thus, it should really be Orlok in my best friend's body. At the time I found nothing to say, so he continued:

"But your friend doesn't suit me. He looks healthy but he's not. I feel the first signs of sickness in his flesh. I need a young receptacle in good health. You fit the description perfectly. But I'll give you a little time to digest the news. You and I are soon going to be closer than close."

And he was gone, leaving me alone with my questions and my doubts. Little by little I came to believe him. That's why I took this knife. I hope I have the strength to use it before he puts his last plan to work.

If I fail, maybe they'll find this notebook. I'm going to hide it so it's easy to find. André or Orlok—I don't know what to call him—doesn't know about it, so there's little chance that he'll stumble across it. But I also know that the chances that a visitor will find it are even slimmer. But I have to try.

If I fail, I want to tell Sophie how much I love her and ask forgiveness from my friends and relatives.

Journal of Sophie Maillen

July 26

Johan finally got back last night. I was very worried. He gave me no sign of life during his vacation at his parents. It hurt me and I was ready to make a scene but he didn't give me time. His explanation calmed me down.

Poor André. I hope he'll recover. How unfortunate that he got sick over there and has to stay until he gets better.

But I'm happy. The man I love is back. I think he's going to ask me to marry him soon. I'll say yes, of course. And we'll have a good old-fashioned wedding.

Today he told me that he can see me only at night. I can't wait. I love him so much.

July 30

Johan is strange. It's like he disappears completely during the day and he's not like he was before. Harder, colder. The worst is at night when he sees me. Everything happens like in a dream. I want him so bad but being with him seems unreal, almost unnatural. I don't know what he's doing to me, I just have the feeling that something's not right. This morning I felt very weak, maybe anemia. I'll go see a doctor if it continues.

(English adaptation by Michael Shreve)

VAMPIRES VS NAZIS

The notion of pitting a Vampire against the Nazis was not entirely invented by F. Paul Wilson, but his novel The Keep *(1981), adapted for the screen by Michael Mann in 1983, is one of its best illustrations ever. In this story, Australian writer David McDonald was also inspired by Slavic vampires such as the infamous* Vij *of Nicolas Gogol (1835)...*

David McDonald: *The Lesser of Two Evils*

Poland, September 1942

Normally it would have savored the taste of their fear, it would have been the perfect seasoning for their flesh. But something was not right. Normally the humans would only venture into its woods when the hateful sun was high in the sky or, in times of great need, with flaming brands easy to hand. They would certainly not stay any longer than they needed to; as soon as they had found wood for their guttering fires or meat for their empty stomachs, they would scurry back to their hovels, throwing furtive glances over their shoulder all the way. The ones it didn't take for its meal, of course.

But, these humans—these humans were different. It had been following them for days and nights for it was old and cunning and wary of traps, and it had sensed something not quite right about them from the start. They were a ragtag group, old men and women, a few mothers and some sickly children, not an able bodied man amongst them. The old men wore their sideburns long and curled, and the women covered their hair with scarves. They seemed unaccustomed to the woods, each night they struggled to start a fire and often were reduced to huddling together for warmth in the dark.

It could have easily slaughtered them all, or taken them one at a time. But, it had lived so long that curiosity and a desire for novelty outweighed its hunger. Each night, it would creep close and listen to their conversation, trying to puzzle out the enigma of their presence in its forest. Sometimes, it would climb into the treetops and perch in overhanging branches, mere feet from the unsuspecting humans below. It was difficult to make out their conversation; they used a dialect that was far removed from the one it had spoken when it had walked beneath the Sun, long ago. But there was one thing that transcended any language barrier, and that was the sheer terror beneath which they constantly labored.

It began to pick out words that occurred with increasing frequency as they moved deeper into the forest. The first time it heard them say "*Leśny Dziadek*" it grinned, revealing snaggled yellow teeth with evil points. It was not without vanity, and it took pleasure in knowing that it was still remembered even by those who did not live on its doorstep. But, while they spoke its name with a vague dread, like the way a child speaks of the creature it only half believes lives beneath its bed, they saved their real fear for another word, a word which peppered their discussion: *Nazi.*

It puzzled over the word, turning it over in its convoluted mind. What could it mean? What could inspire such fear? What could inspire more fear than *it* did? There was only one way to answer its questions and it resolved to retrace the humans' trail and discover what it was they were fleeing from. It knew that it would easily find them again, for it knew this forest intimately.

It leapt from tree to tree, viciously clawed hands on the end of long, gnarled arms grasping at branches, digging into the wood and launching it to the next with a convulsive bunching of ropy muscle. Its yellowed eyes gleamed over a sharp pointed nose poking out from a stringy beard that was long enough to tuck into a plain black leather belt. Tattered grey robes flapped around its hunched and wizened body. It laughed an old man's cackle as it bounded from perch to perch; it hadn't had this much fun in decades! Every so often, it would drop to the ground and sniff the dirt, just to make sure it was still on their trail, but the stench of fear was better than a paved road. Finally, it came to the edge of its domain, and looked out over the local village.

The last time it had come close, after a smelling a particularly toothsome child, the village had been a sleepy little hamlet, a few horses and chickens the most traffic the one main street could boast. Now, it was a kicked hornet's nest of activity. Bright beams of light stabbed into the night sky, while columns of men tramped past. They were obviously soldiers; they were clad in identical grey uniforms and wore steel helmets. It didn't recognize the weapons they wore over their shoulders, but it could sense their latent menace. Massive wagons that needed no horse to draw them growled their way through the churned up mud, glowing eyes lighting their way.

Voices rang out through the still night air, and it snarled as it recognized their language: "*Niemiaszek!*"

It spat. For centuries, they had swarmed over the motherland, looting and plundering. They were powerful warriors, and preying on them had often brought great risk to the creature, despite the advantages it possessed over mere humans. And while it would take what meat it could, it preferred the young, and the warriors' raids would often drive the villagers away from its woods, leaving it only the tough, gamy meat of men in their prime. Oh, it had lots of reasons to hate the foreign invaders, even if it didn't... No! It would not think about the life it once had before it became what it now was, remembering was something that would cause it great pain.

It watched the soldiers come and go for the rest of the night, puzzling over their strange behavior. Over the years, it had seen enough armies to be able work out ranks and hierarchies, and this group was no different; in fact, they were strict when it came to formalities. However, no matter what the rank of the normal soldiers, there was one group that they all deferred to: these soldiers dressed in black, with silver lightning badges at their throats; they swaggered down the street as if they expected all to make way before them. They were not disappointed, the grey-clad soldiers avoided them whenever possible, and were appropriately submissive when it was not. Intrigued, it decided that it would follow the lightning soldiers and see what it was that made an object of fear. Maybe this was what the word *Nazi* referred to? No matter, it was confident that no mere man could rival its powers and offer it harm.

The next day, it carefully trailed a large group of the black-clad soldiers, almost a hundred of them. While it hated the daytime, and would only venture out under the greatest necessity, it could bear the Sun's light and the discomfort it brought. It flitted from shadow to shadow, so silently that not even the most alert of the men ahead of it had the slightest idea that something was stalking them. They marched for almost two hours before coming to another village, this one substantially bigger than the one at the edge of the forest. The risk of discovery meant that it could not follow them into the town, so it curled up in the fork of a tree and slept fitfully.

It was awoken by a commotion that grew rapidly louder and closer. The soldiers were back, and they had company. Using their fists and the butts of their weapons to keep order, they were herding a formation of villagers before them. The villagers had a similar look to those it had seen in the forest, from their clothes and facial hair to their expressions of fear. It wondered what the connection was, and whether this was what the others had been fleeing from. There were at least three or four hundred villagers all told, and the chaos that came with such a mass of confusion made it easy to follow them undetected.

They marched for another two hours, making substantially less progress despite the soldiers' best efforts to hurry the pace. Finally, they halted, and the soldiers divided the villag-

ers, separating out the able-bodied men. It saw numerous
blows dished out to protesting families, but the arguing came
to an abrupt halt when one of the black-clad soldiers pulled
out a small weapon and pointed it at a particularly belligerent
villager. There was a sharp crack, and the villager collapsed to
the ground. After that, there was no more debate; the villagers
simply went where they were told, shoulders slumped in sullen resignation.

Once the healthy men had been separated, the soldiers
took what looked like small folding shovels from their back-
packs and distributed them to the men. There were some
barked commands, and they began digging. The shadows
lengthened as the day wore on, and it wondered what the point
of their labors was, and whether it could be bothered waiting
around to find out. Before its patience was tested any further,
there was another series of orders; the men stopped digging
and began to stack their tools in a jumbled pile. Once they
were done, the soldiers poked and prodded them with the
strange weapons he had seen slung over their shoulder until
they lined up along the edge of the trench that they had dug,
their backs to the soldiers.

The soldiers pointed their weapons at the villagers, and
with a terse command, a wave of smoke and thunder erupted.
The men fell like wheat under the scythe, toppling into the
trench, and, in a matter of seconds, not a single one was left
alive. There was a chorus of wails and moans from the villagers in the other group, but the soldiers on guard walked
amongst them, using fists and boots to quieten any that got
overexcited. They also began another winnowing, and it could
see that those being culled from the herd were without exception young and lithesome women. A detachment of shoulders
marched them off back towards the village, and once they
were out of sight, the others were forced towards the trench.
Already in a state of shock from the horror of what they had
just witnessed, they put up little resistance.

The creature was still reeling itself, but not from any fin-
er feelings or sympathies. It was trying to fathom what magic

these soldiers possessed that they could slay without touching, and whether they might actually be a threat. Or, was it merely a newer type of crossbow? Another rippling wall of sound hit it as the remaining villagers were eliminated; those who didn't topple into the trench were rolled in unceremoniously by the laughing and joking soldiers. After a few minutes, the soldiers turned and began to march back to the village, leaving the creature to its thoughts.

It stood at the edge of the gouge in the earth, looking down on the piled corpses. There was little sentiment still burning in that withered chest, but, for the creature, death had always been something personal, something intimate. It killed to feed its hunger, both for flesh and for the chase, but it was never anything less than a sacred experience. This carnage was something else, seemingly indiscriminate and, above all, wasteful. It began to feel a strange emotion, one that had not stirred for centuries, that it eventually identified as anger. How dare these foreigners come into Holy Mother Poland and take what belonged to it? The anger opened other doors too, revealing memories pushed down and forgotten for so long they were only recalled in flashing images. It tore its long claw-like fingernails through the turf as images hammered into its eyes...

He felt the warm glow of pride fill him as the smiling woman held the baby up to him. He cradled it in strong, muscled arms, savoring the weight of his son. His son. Leaning forward, he brushed the damp hair from the child's forehead with a gentleness that belied his size, then kissed his wife softly on the lips.

"I love you, Zofia. Thank you for giving this farmer a strong son."

"I love you too, Ka..."

Her voice cut off and the smile fled her face as mailed fists hammered on the door. As he reached for the axe hanging above the lintel, there was the sound of splintering wood. Four men in chain mail, their surcoats emblazoned with Maltese crosses, burst through the door and rushed across the room, their battle cry echoing from the low ceiling.

"*Gott Mit Uns!*"

As if responding in prayer, the first man fell to his knees, held up from the ground only by the axe blade buried deep in his skull. Before the new father could wrench it free one of the other assailants swung a viciously beaked mace, sending it crashing into the axeman's head. There was a flare of light and then only darkness.

He awoke to agony. His legs burned with a pain he would not have thought possible, and when he tried to move his head felt as if it had taken that blow of the axe. He gathered himself, and rose shakily, gasping as he saw the wreckage of his legs. The skin had melted and bubbled, cloth burnt away and charred into the flesh, as blackened and burnt as the ruins of the cottage that lay before him. Such was the devastation that it took a moment for the sight to register, and for him to recognize it as his own.

"Zofia!" His voice was hoarse, his throat raw with smoke. "Zofia!"

There was no answer, and he moved closer to the burning wreckage, shielding his eyes from the heat that still roiled from the coals. A strange scent wafted through the air, reminding him of the rare times they had pork on the table. Despite his pain, saliva filled his mouth and he swallowed nervously. He took another step forward and then froze. There in the heart of the flames were two shriveled, blackened figures, only barely human. One was much smaller than the other, cradled in the larger figure's arms.

"No! Zofia!"

He tried to move closer but, despite his best efforts, the heat would not allow him to approach. Sinking to his knees, his chest heaved as he was wracked with sobs, the outpouring of grief consuming him. How long he stayed that way, he could not have said but when he opened his eyes the red glow of the flames had died down, and had been replaced by an ee-rie green glow.

"You poor, poor man."

The farmer staggered to his feet, almost falling as he whirled around to face the direction from whence the voice had come.

"Be at peace, *mon ami*. I mean you no harm."

The man's Polish was fluent, but more like that of the *szlachta*, the nobles, than that of the villages. Still, the farmer could understand most of it, except for the strange foreign words. The accent, too, was like nothing he had ever heard. But all those oddities paled in comparison to the baleful green glow that shone from the stranger's eyes, washing across the clearing. As the farmer watched, it guttered out, leaving only the flickering flames to illuminate the stranger's nondescript features. The farmer crossed himself, but was too weak to run. All he could do was square his shoulders and pretend to be unafraid.

"Who are you? *What* are you?"

The stranger smiled, revealing sharp teeth that glimmered wickedly in the moonlight.

"You may call me Monsieur Goetzi. As to what I am?" The green light flickered again in his eyes. "I am merely someone like you, someone who has had what is his taken away from him by those who are more powerful than he."

"You are nothing like me!"

"You mean these strange qualities I possess?" Goetzi laughed. "They are nothing for you to be scared of, *mon ami*."

The famer spun to his right. The second sentence had been echoed by another voice, and its source was an exact duplicate of the stranger, green fire boiling from its eyes. As the farmer watched, it strode towards the original, and reached out its hand to meet Goetzi's outstretched hand. As they met, there was a flash of green light and the duplicate disappeared, absorbed into Goetzi's body.

"Demon!"

The farmer turned to run, but before he could take a step Goetzi was on him. Hands like iron pincers gripped him and bent him backwards, his spine screaming protest. The farmer struggled, muscles tempered by a lifetime of back breaking toil hewing wood and tilling the soil bunching as he pushed against the monster's grip, but for all his efforts, he might as well been a child in its parents arms. Fingers wrapped in his hair, yanking his head back and baring the soft, vulnerable flesh of his throat.

There was a moment of pain as the creature's fangs pierced the skin, and then a blissful numbness spreading through his limbs. Strange visions filled his mind, a moonlit city, greater than all the tales the villagers had heard of Warszawa combined. The tall buildings were constructed from a striped, glistening stone that he would later learn was known as jasper, and their peaks capped by onion shaped domes. Vast amphitheaters were packed with baying crowds while strange beasts fought the death on ivory sands, and marble avenues shone under never ending twilight. Somehow he knew that the sun was a stranger here, and that the Moon, the silver queen of the night, ruled supreme.

"Ah, Selene," Goetzi whispered, his breath hot in the farmer's ear. "The Vampire City. One day, she will rule the world, and I will rule her."

The farmer whimpered as he felt the inexorable draining of his lifeblood ease slightly.

"You do not need to die, *mon ami*. Before I can take the throne of blessed Selene, I must build my own kingdom. Those fools who call themselves our Elders will never allow one they consider beneath them on the Council, and it is only from there that I can ascend to my rightful place. I must return as a conquering hero, or all my plans are as dust."

The peasant tried to speak, but all that he could muster was a low groan.

"Ah, so you wonder what this could possibly mean to you? I am but one man, and so I need loyal servants to do my will. From Dalmatia to Paris I am seeking out men, of—how

266

shall we say?—suitable qualities to be my agents. While I put my plans into place, they will wait, their powers growing, until the day that I am ready and only then shall they rise up. Through them, all Europe shall be mine and the Council will not be able to deny me my rightful place."

Goetzi stroked the other man's face, almost tenderly.

"I can feel the anger burning within you. It permeates every drop of your blood. I can taste your rage, and I know that you would do anything for revenge. We are alike, you and me; I know what it is like to have what is yours taken away by those who are stronger. But I can give you the power to protect what is yours, and make you the one that other men fear. All you need to do is swear fealty to me."

The farmer thought of what he could have done with the stranger's strength, with his unearthly power. In his mind, the invaders fell beneath his blows, and his wife and son lived. No! They were gone, and nothing he could do would bring them back. But he could have revenge, if not on the men who had taken his family, then on the world that allowed such things to happen. Filled with a dark resolve, he nodded his assent.

"I thought as much." Goetzi drew a ragged thumbnail across his own throat, sending thick, black blood washing across the farmer's face. "Drink of my blood that I have given you, and call me Lord."

The villager fought his gorge as he lapped at the foul liquid, feeling it burn all the way down his throat, veins of fire spreading through his body. For a moment there was agony, then only darkness.

When he awoke the stranger was gone, and his wounds were healed. A burning thirst consumed him, a thirst that only grew as the days passed and could not be sated by any amount of water. In the end, he gave in to its demands, weeping as he drank the living blood from the throat of a poor washerwoman who made the mistake of straying from the safety of her village. Each kill was easier, until he began to glory in the hunt, savoring his strength and speed and the taste of blood and flesh beneath his fangs. Invaders came and went, his motherland groaning under the weight of their feet, but those who ventured into the woods he called home were never seen again.

Centuries passed and his powers grew, but Goetzi never called upon him. The dark magic of the woods filled him, changed him, and he became a legend. Whatever spark of humanity that remained flickered and died in the long lonely nights, but if it noticed it cared little. The woods, and everything within belonged to him, and no one would take them away from him. No one.

It screamed rage at the sky, feeding its anger in desperate desire to drown out the pain of the memories, letting its fury bring forgetfulness. It focused on what it had seen and resolved that it would keep its vow that no one would ever take what was rightfully its again. These strange soldiers might have weapons beyond anything it had ever seen, perhaps even magical ones, but it knew this land like the back of its twisted hand and how to make it a living hell for any invader. He would find out what the purpose of these soldiers was, and make sure they were thwarted. It chuckled deep in its throat, it was a long time it had thought beyond its next meal and it quite enjoyed the sensation.

Despite their head start, it arrived at the village well before the black-clad soldiers and settled into watch and wait. The first detachment arrived with their human treasures, and loaded the majority of them into trucks, which left immediately. The few who remained were escorted to a long low building, and swallowed up by its forbidding aspect. It dozed fitfully for a few hours, woken by the return of the remaining soldiers. This occasioned a mini-conference between a few men who carried themselves as if they were used to giving orders. Finally, there were more barked commands, and a group of about thirty men broke off from the mass and headed in the direction of the forest. It stiffened, and a green glow entered its eyes. They were obviously going after the group who had fled into the forest, and it was determined that they would not find the hunt to their liking.

The black-clad soldier walked as if there was nothing for him to fear in the forest. He had his strange weapon at the ready, and he was obviously well trained by the way he was constantly scanning his surroundings, and his bearing was of a man confident he could deal with any threat that presented itself. He was bringing up the rear of the column, and he was yanked up into the overhanging branches so quickly and neatly that none of his companions noticed.

It held the soldier at arm's length in front of, talons wrapped so tightly around the man's throat that he could not utter a sound, the air having no egress. It leered at him, enjoying the terror in his eyes, and the way its victim's fists hammered against its forearms in desperation. He may as well have been trying to strike an iron bar, and the soldier's face changed shades as he slowly suffocated. With a final twitch, and the reek of excrement as his bowels let go, it was over and it began to feed.

It fed well the next few nights. The soldiers were all seasoned men, but this forest had been its home for centuries, and it knew each twist in the path where it could lurk and snatch a man into the brambles, or the ravines where the only crossings were fallen logs where it could easily cling to the underside like some bloated spider, reaching up to clutch an ankle and send a man screaming into the jagged rocks below. There the victim would wait, dead or alive, for it to descend to consume the delicious flesh.

As the days wore on, it could see the well-oiled discipline that had distinguished these soldiers from others it had seen breaking down. The strain and tension was taking its toll, they began to talk back to their leader, and one man even tried to strike him. The haggard faced officer did not waste any time reasoning with the offender, but simply pulled out his smaller weapon and sent him crashing to the ground. He was a particularly tasty morsel, his meat well flavored with madness and with fear.

On the fifth day, it took the officer right from the center of the line, leaves shredding around it as their weapons popped and banged. They came after it, but they could not find it and its prey, despite the fact it teased them with the officer's screams, killing him slowly and savoring his torment. It ate his eyeballs first, scooping them out of the sockets while he still lived. Once it had stripped the most delectable morsels away from the corpse, it dropped the body into their hasty camp. As it had planned, this was the final blow to their discipline and, to a man, they turned and fled for the village, and for safety.

As they crashed through the undergrowth, it shadowed them in the branches above. In their panic, they were easy prey, far too simple to bring it any huge pleasure. There were too many of them for it to be able to taste them all; some it simply killed, snapping a neck with a twist of its powerful arms like a farmer's wife killing a chicken for the pot, or ripping out a throat with its claws like it was tearing off a hunk of the coarse bread the peasants lived on. Finally, there was only one soldier, sobbing with terror as he approached the edge of the forest. It could follow his progress easily by his labored breathing and the rank smell of terror sweat and it was waiting in the very last tree as the soldier ran beneath.

Its prehensile toes gripping a branch, it swung down and shrieked at the soldier, who back pedaled furiously trying to stop. He fell on his backside with a scream of his own, a dark stain spreading at his crotch, and waited for his end, but it was already gone. It wanted word of its hunt to spread through the soldier's camp as a warning not to trespass on its territory again, and to leave its property alone.

It was watching over its herd with a feeling of proprietary satisfaction when it sensed the intruders. It had been following the fugitives for about a week, leaving the odd deer in their path, or clusters of berries. It had not needed to feed on them, its larder was stocked with the slowly rotting bodies of the unfortunate soldiers, and for now it was simply happy to gloat over its victory. Their entire demeanor had changed, there was laughter and the occasional song as they wandered the forest, it seemed the oppressive shadow of fear had lifted from them. It was so in tune with the forest that it knew how many men had just entered its boundaries, and it felt no fear, only a malevolent joy, at the thought of slaughtering the half dozen men who even now were approaching.

Five of the soldiers were of the same kind as the ones it had feasted upon, but the sixth was somehow different. He, too, was in a black uniform, but of a more ornate style, with padded shoulders and a double breasted tunic. Even from where concealed itself, it could sense the power that burned in him. He was decked with amulets that prickled the air with their enchantments, and he was steeped in the stink of dark magic. The other soldiers treated him with the same mix of terror and subservience the grey-clad soldiers had afforded them. There was obviously no love lost; whenever they felt he was not watching, the other soldiers would discuss him in low voices, casting furtive glances in his direction. Even if they could not, it could see that he was aware of their speculation but the only sign he gave was the contemptuous half smile that seemed his constant companion.

Not for the first time, it cursed its ignorance of their barbarian tongue. It would have liked to have been able to discover more about its new foe, a man named Eckhart, who the soldiers constantly referred to as something called a *Thule*, but it would have to simply trust its powers and skills. It flexed its arms, listening to its knuckles crack and scratched its claws down the trunk, watching the sap bleed from the deep gouges. The creature grinned; no mere human would be able to challenge it, Monsieur Goetzi's gifts would see to that.

It found its harrying tactics a little more difficult this time around, as the soldiers made a point of keeping bunched together, except for Eckhart who strode arrogantly ahead of them. But when dark fell, it was easily able to creep in close to where the five normal soldiers slept and, without waking a single one before it was ready, dispose of them. It killed each one the same way, a calloused palm over their mouth pressing them into the ground, and a sharp nail drawn across their throat, leaving them to choke in their own blood. Once it had finished watching the light fade from the last man's eyes, it turned to take care of Eckhart, but froze. The Thule was gone! It scanned the ground for tracks, growled deep in its throat at the realization it had been tricked; the soldiers had been a diversion and Eckhart was headed straight for its herd.

It raced though the treetops, bounding from limb to limb. Thin lips were pulled back from a grimace that would have terrified any witness, such was its desperation to beat Eckhart. Why it felt such need, it didn't know, or wouldn't admit to itself that it might be born of any concern for its herd; instead, it tried to put it down to not allowing any one to take away what belonged to it. That would not happen, not this time. It knew to get to them, the Thule would have to cross a ravine; if it could just get there first, then it would have a considerable advantage. After all, this was its forest.

It stood just before the moss-covered log that bridged the ravine, panting with exertion that tested even its limits. Where was Eckhart? Something, perhaps one of the amulets or charms the Thule carried, was masking his exact location, but it knew that it had passed him on its way to ravine. Now all it could do was wait. There was no other way to get to the herd, unless the Thule spent days circling the edge of the woods. It sensed that Eckhart was not the sort of man to go around something if he could go through it. It turned to walk out on the log, where it could hide underneath and wait... Then, what felt like a boulder crashed into the side of its head and, after a flash of white light, everything went black.

When it awoke, Eckhart was casually leaning back against a tree staring at it. He realized it was awake and smirked at it, before addressing it in heavily accented Polish, with the occasional German word mixed in.

272

"So, you weren't just a devil made up by these Slav *untermensch* to frighten us, *ja*?" He spat on the ground. "*Gott in Himmel*, you are ugly."

It didn't reply, but merely stared back malevolently.

"It doesn't matter what you look like, anyway. You are going to earn me a promotion when I get you back to Germany." The Thule laughed; while it had little mirth, there was a cruel undercurrent. "The scientists will have a lot of fun finding out what you are. They are sick of working on filthy *Juden*; they will spend hours taking you apart piece by piece."

It rose unsteadily to its feet, still woozy from the blow. It hadn't felt anything like that since it had changed, and it didn't enjoy the sensation at all. It grinned and tilted its head from side to side, hearing the crack of bones settling back into place. It was going to enjoy ripping the flesh from this *Niemiaszek's* bones.

It came in low and fast, talons extended, aiming straight for his entrails. For a moment, it thought it had missed and run into the tree trunk behind the Thule, but, as it flew back, spitting blood, it realized the only thing it had run into was Eckhart's fist. Faster than even it could track, the *Niemiaszek* was upon it, fingers that felt like iron tongs wrapped around its throat. The Thule pivoted and hurled the creature, and, this time, it did hit a tree, sliding down and landing in a tangle of limbs.

How could this human be so strong and so fast? It shook its head trying to clear the cobwebs, and to fight down the rising fear. It was time for a different strategy.

This time when it came at the Thule, it waited until the last minute and feinted right before darting to the left. As it raked its claws across the human's upper thigh, it felt the wind of Eckhart's blow whistling over its head. It shuddered at the strength behind the Thule's limb; now that would have done some damage! As it was, its talons tingled with a dull ache where they had cut into the Thule's flesh, and, instead of the bright jets of arterial blood from a severed femoral artery, there was only a slow welling. His charms were potent indeed, but the wound was obviously hurting him; the human was now favoring the leg as he circled it, and there was a new caution in his eyes.

"I will take you back to the Fuhrer," Eckhart said. "Dead or alive, it is up to you, *ja*?"

It was too sore to bandy words with a human, even had it understood what he was referring to.

Eckhart continued, trying to distract it: "So, how long have you been skulking in this forest? The Slavs I tortured claimed you have been here for centuries." He paused, and spat. "Normally, I would just put that down to superstitious ignorance, but now that I have seen you for myself, I guess I owe them an apology. Not that it would do them much good right now."

It attempted to use the Thule's amusement against him, this time trying to go high and shred his throat to ribbons. Instead, the Thule's arm caught it across its chest, as solid as an iron bar, crashing it to the ground.

"The Fuhrer has commanded us to create a Reich that will last a thousand years. We will give him a master race that will live that long, and regain our rightful place in his favor." He smiled. "You look puzzled. We at the Thule Society use modern science to sift the truth from barbarian superstitions, unlike those credulous fools at the *Ahnenerbe*! We will discover what it is that gives you your powers and use it as it should be used, for the betterment of the Aryan race."

It knew the soldier was baiting him, trying to provoke it into another futile attack, and it resolved to bide its time, and wait for an opening. But what the Thule said next drove all thoughts of restraint from its mind:

"And as for the filthy *Juden* you are harboring in your woods, they will be my next order of business. They are trying to link up with the partisan bands to the east, but I think they would better serve as test subjects in my laboratory." His grin was as hungry as a wolf's. "At least, that way you will get to see them again!

It snarled, and flung itself at him as if trying to grapple with him, but, at the last moment, it rolled to the side and grabbed a fist-sized rock. Before the Thule could react, it threw it as hard as its unnatural muscles allowed and struck him in the face. His mouth exploded into spray of blood and pieces of teeth, and he reared back in agony. The soldier tried to say something, but all that emerged was a terrible guttural moaning, and then it was upon him. Its hands locked around his throat, and its jagged fangs latched onto Eckhart's face, and it began to chew, cartilage and skin and bone being no match for its fury. The Thule beat at the sides of its head with clenched fists, but the shock was telling on his strength, and it was able to shrug them off.

Trying to scream, the Thule staggered backwards until he felt the heels of his boots come down on the very edge of the ravine. His arms windmilled as he tried to regain his balance, dirt and rocks falling to the depths below. It shrieked its triumph as the warm salty blood gushed down its throat, clinging on even as they fell.

The last thought that went through its mind was that, this time, it had won, and that what belonged to it would not be taken away ever again.

The sounds of bird song cut off and the rustle of small animals stilled, as the forest fell silent. Nothing moved, as if the world held its breath in anticipation. A crooked hand rose above the edge of the ravine, before digging its claws into the soft, moist earth. The other appeared, and slowly, with pained and deliberate movements, it began to pull itself up and forward. It sobbed softly, wracked by the kind of pain it had forgotten was possible, yet propelled on by a compulsion that burned deep within.

As it staggered to its feet, it felt torn muscles sobbing in protest and broken bones grinding together. Its battle with the Thule, and the terrible fall, had left it battered and bloody and bruised, but it could feel Monsieur Goetzi's magic beginning to work through its body, repairing the damage. The healing

275

was not gentle or soothing, merely concerned with restoring its body, and it shrieked as tendons writhed and bones popped back into position.

It held up its hand before its face and watched, mesmerized, as broken fingers straightened and cuts healed over. It could feel itself growing stronger and a terrible hunger rose up from within, its body crying out with the need to replace the energy expended on its restoration.

A feral green light shone from its eyes, and its nostrils flared as it caught the scent of more of the invaders entering the forest. The herd needed its protection still, and now it knew that until they were safe, the magic would not let it rest.

It threw back its head and shrieked exultantly, a terrible sound in the stillness. It was time to hunt once more.

COUNTESS BATHORY

Like Bluebeard and Dracula, Elizabeth Bathory is a historical character, a Hungarian countess born in 1560 who died in 1614, and who became famous in the annals of History for having tortured and murdered over 600 young girls. Subsequently, his sinister legend gave birth to the rumor (likely unfounded) that she was bathing in her victims' blood to remain young. The history of this Bloody Countess has inspired many adaptations, including Countess Dracula *by Peter Sasdy (1970) with Ingrid Pitt, and* Les Lèvres Rouges *by Harry Kumel (1971) with Delphine Seyrig. Win Scott Eckert, author of several books on Philip José Farmer, was inspired by the latter when he wrote this story...*

Win Scott Eckert: *Les Lèvres Rouges*

Paris, 1946

Ilona Harczy hung naked in the damp dungeon, her arms spread and chained at the wrist to the stone wall. She was unconscious. Her wrists and fingers were scabbed over with dozens of small cuts. A brown and withered vine snaked under her dangling feet.

When Ilona next awoke, the blonde woman was there.

Somehow, even in the darkness, the woman glowed, an icy bluish light emanating from a jewel hung at her throat. Her skin was pale, almost translucent, showing blue veins beneath. In a flowing white gown, she floated ethereally above the cobblestone floor. Her lips were painted bright red.

The woman gently took Ilona's wrist and made another small cut. Ilona moaned as blood welled. The pale woman kissed and licked Ilona's wrist. Only a few stray drops of blood escaped her lips, falling upon the floor and the almost-dead plant.

The blonde woman continued to kiss Ilona's wrist, and the bleeding stopped. Then she cupped Ilona's breast in her hand, and softly kissed Ilona's neck and short dark hair.

"Now my love, it is complete," she whispered. "You do love me, don't you? You must, you know."

The blonde woman moved away into a shadowy corner. Two humanoid forms were illuminated as the woman approached them, the light from the jewel glowing brighter and brighter. The woman embraced each in turn, pulling thick necks to her waiting mouth. She intoned nonsense words that Ilona didn't understand.

"*Iä-R'lyeh! Cthulhu fhtagn! Méne! Iä! Iä!*"

The jewel shone even brighter, its soft bluish light filling the room.

Then the three were gone, and Ilona lapsed once more into oblivion.

Nestor Burma looked up at the statuesque figure silhouetted in the doorway of the *Fiat Lux* Detective Agency's inner office. "How may I help you, Mademoiselle…?"

"D'Andrésy. Monique d'Andrésy." She stood in front of him, raven hair spilling over the shoulders of the London Fog raincoat belted at the waist with a loose knot. "You are working on a case with an American doctor? Francis Ardan?"

Burma leaned back in his creaky office chair and put his feet on the desk. The room's only light was a feeble cone emanating from a small desk lamp. He puffed at his bull's head pipe, red light from the coals illuminating his tired face.

"Mademoiselle d'Andrésy, I may be an anarchist, but I wouldn't last long as a private detective if I made a habit of breaking my clients' confidentiality."

"But, Monsieur," she breathed, "my need is great."

She slowly walked around to the client chair beside Burma's desk. Instead of sitting, she stepped one leg up on the chair and propped an elbow on her upper thigh, leaning her chin on her hand. Long nails were done in a perfect French manicure. Facing him, took a drag of her cigarette.

"Perhaps we could come to an… understanding?"

Burma's eyes followed the curve of her leg from the four-inch pump to the lacy black top of a gartered silk stocking–and further. The folds of her raincoat fell away, the belt hanging loosely. Apart from the stockings and garters, she wore nothing else, intimate or otherwise.

"I am sorry, truly, but I don't think such an understanding will be possible."

Monique d'Andrésy bent farther over him, providing a clear view of her rather ample charms. She was splendid, in every way.

"Mademoiselle, please…"

"What is it Burma, are you *une pédale*?"

"No, Mademoiselle, in fact you present quite a persuasive argument. But as tempted as I am, it is quite impossible." He puffed at his pipe again. "I believe incest is illegal in France. Now, perhaps I can help you with your coat? It appears you're catching a chill."

"What–?"

Two hands thrust out from darkness behind and gripped her upper arms. The hands were large and bronzed, tendons and muscles stretching across them like small cables. It was no use trying to struggle free.

She sighed.

"Doctor Ardan, I presume?"

"Adélaïde Lupin," Ardan replied.

She glared at Burma. "So Arsène Lupin is your father as well?"

"Not the man who raised me as his own son," Burma said. "But yes, I am Lupin's child from one of his many affairs."

"Clearly blood is not thicker than water." Adélaïde glanced meaningfully at the strong hands holding her solidly in place.

"Please, Mademoiselle d'Andrésy–er–Lupin, I am not the one who slunk in here attempting a licentious seduction."

"Perhaps, but you obviously helped set me up. You knew we're siblings–"

"Half-siblings," Burma said.

"*Oui.* You could have said so earlier."

He shrugged. "We've never met before. I don't owe you anything. Besides, I wanted to see what angle you'd take. Quite inventive."

Another voice came from a dark corner as a third man stepped forward. "Your family reunion is very touching, but we have business."

"Yes, time is of the essence," a fourth added in a slight Germanic accent.

Adélaïde sighed. "Gentlemen, on the one hand, I'm not so immodest that I think you need reminding of my current state of *deshabillé*. On the other hand, as Burma said, it is somewhat chilly in here. Is this some bizarre burlesque, or might I be permitted to cover myself?"

Ardan freed one slender arm, and she awkwardly cinched up her coat. He applied gentle but firm pressure to her shoulders, forcing her to sit. She crossed her legs, one elegant and distracting thigh still exposed at the fold of her coat, and lit a fresh *Red Apple*.

"So, Francis, I said we'd see each other again, and here we are. I can think of better circumstances, though. Something along the lines of a snowbound cabin, roaring fire, a bearskin rug and a bottle of *Veuve Clicquot* '32 would do nicely," Adélaïde said playfully.

Ardan's bronzed skin, even under cover of the darkened office, turned ten shades of red.

"No reply, *mon chéri*? Pity. Well, what's it all about? I suppose the story of the Eye of Oran being a fake, and you working with Burma to track down the real Eye–that was all a charade to lure me here?"

Last month, Adélaïde Lupin had tricked Doctor Francis Ardan and the French Intelligence agency S.N.I.F., making off with a precious gem, the Eye of Oran–also known as the Silver Eye of Dagon–using Ardan's experimental Cirrus X-9 rocket pack.

Doc Ardan nodded. "Yes, the story was a plant to draw you out. This man is a representative of the French government. If you turn over the Eye to me, they are prepared to drop all charges. You'll go free, no questions asked."

"All true, Mademoiselle Lupin." The third man said, stepping forward, limping slightly. He had grey haircut military style, and wore round-rimmed glasses. "Return the Eye and the matter will be dropped."

"I suppose you're S.N.I.F.'s Aristide? Sorry if I caused you some difficulties." A slight quirk at the corner of her mouth said she wasn't overly sorry.

"I'm not Aristide, and yes, your actions caused him no little trouble. You can call me Roger Noël. This is Jens Rolf, a mystic and expert on the Eye's occult nature."

The short German nodded curtly.

Noël continued, "Now, what do you say?"

"I say… I cannot."

"Mademoiselle," Noël replied, "if you don't return the Eye, you'll be locked up with the key thrown away."

"Don't you threaten me, you little bureaucrat. If you think any jail cell can hold Lupin's daughter for long, you'd better–"

"Enough," Ardan interrupted. "Gentlemen, would you excuse us please. I'd like a moment alone with Mademoiselle Lupin."

Burma looked at Noël and Rolf, shrugged, and got up. They all stepped into the outer office.

Adélaïde looked at Ardan, red lips parted expectantly. "Well, it's about time, *mon cher* Francis, I've practically been throwing myself at you."

"Drop the act, Adélaïde. I studied with your father when I was a boy. He was a thief and a scoundrel, but when push came to shove, he would do the right thing. I think you will too."

"Don't be so sure."

"I am. Do you have the faintest idea what Doctor Natas was planning to do with the Eye, before you conned us all and stole it? I've seen a lot and most can be explained without resorting to mysticism, but in this case, even I support the French in recruiting an occult expert to properly study and contain it."

"You, the medical man?" she scoffed. "The 'science detective'?"

"I grant you, almost all of the strange adventures my associates and I have had around the world have ended with rational explanations. But a few have not. When I was a young man, during the Great War, I saw a long whitish worm crawling over the skeleton of an infant, a victim of a satanic ritualistic sacrifice. Even today, I cannot classify that worm; it is unknown to science. In 1925, I encountered an entity which slaughtered many members of an Antarctic expedition. I have no explanation. Two years later, I observed our own Doctor Natas transmute lead into gold; I have not been able to reproduce this with any scientific means. In 1929, my colleague Doctor Littlejohn also traveled to the Antarctic, and had strange experiences which he, also a rational man of science, cannot explain. Three years ago, I was involved in a case in which an herbal concoction allowed its taker to see into the future. A specific prophecy came to pass. And now, the Eye."

" 'There are more things in Heaven and Earth, Horatio…' "

"Precisely. Why won't you help?"

She shook her head. "Francis, first you must help me with a problem I've run into. If you can do that, I'll gladly abandon all claims to the gem."

The gold-flecks in Ardan's eyes seemed to swirl. "Adélaïde, I promise we'll help you with whatever trouble you're in," he said solemnly.

"All right, then."

"Good. Herr Rolf will secure the Eye while the rest of us tackle your problem. Once that's handled," he said, "I want you to return the rocket pack as well."

"Deal. But, Francis, you see, the quandary is... I no longer have the Eye."

FROM: Lieutenant Montferrand, Division Protection, Service National d'Information Fonctionnelle, Paris.
TO: SNIF.
DATE: August 21, 1946
SUBJECT: Silver Eye of Dagon

The Eye of Dagon is a large silver gem reputed to have occult properties. It is now in possession of a "Madame Elisabeth" who operates a series of brothels in Normandy and Brittany, with headquarters in Paris.

After absconding with the Eye outside Oran last month, Adélaïde Lupin (A.L.) was contacted by Madame Elisabeth. Elisabeth was holding a friend of A.L.'s, one Ilona Harczy, prisoner under the threat of forced labor in one of her bordellos. A.L. was instructed to turn the Eye over to Elisabeth as a ransom payment. To date, A.L.'s friend has not been released. Ardan and Burma's scheme to bait A.L. with a story that the stolen Eye was a fake unwittingly played into A.L.'s concerns about Madame Elisabeth's failure to release her friend. A.L. appeared in Burma's offices with startling alacrity.

It's unknown how Madame Elisabeth knew of the Eye in the first place. It's possible we have a leak, or perhaps she was in league with Doctor Natas, who also sought the Eye.

We have no prior intelligence on Madame Elisabeth, and are relying on A.L. for the following information. Elisabeth and a partner purchased the network of brothels known as the Cordon Jaune, *in January of this year. It is unclear where the money for this purchase originated, but the purchase was ap-*

parently intended as an investment. The venture went bad with the passage of the Marthe Richard Law last April, banning all such houses of ill-repute. We can guess that Elisabeth needs the Eye to mitigate her bad investment.

Madame Elisabeth's partner in this venture is called "Le Chiffre," ostensibly a paymaster for the Syndicat des Ouvriers d'Alsace, *a Communist-controlled trade union. Le Chiffre is otherwise unidentifiable, having come out of the camp at Dachau last year with a case of incurable amnesia. He is always accompanied by two bodyguards highly skilled at personal defense and close range combat. He is described as small, with coarse reddish-brown hair and a voracious sexual appetite.*

Madame Elisabeth, too, is described as insatiable, but it is unlikely she satisfies her needs with Le Chiffre; during their one face-to-face meeting, she made a pass at A.L. which was "exceptionally forceful." Although A.L. portrays Madame Elisabeth as exceedingly charming and charismatic, she declined Elisabeth's offer. Doubtless Madame Elisabeth and Le Chiffre sample their wares on a regular basis. Madame Elisabeth's proclivities may also account for her failure to keep her bargain and release Mademoiselle Harczy, who is reported to be quite beautiful.

There should be no doubt: Madame Elisabeth and Le Chiffre are a deadly combination.

Under my "Roger Noël" cover, I have assembled a team dedicated to recovering the Eye of Dagon: Doctor Francis Ardan, Nestor Burma, the mystic Jens Rolf and Adélaïde Lupin. Unfortunately, we must again rely on A.L. At least, this time, we are dealing with a known quantity, but she is still a Lupin and I will proceed with care.

As an aside, A.L. learned—to her chagrin and my amusement—that Burma is also a Lupin, if only by an accident of birth. The so-called Gentleman Thief had nothing to do with Burma's upbringing, and despite Burma's leftist views I believe he will prove a reliable companion on this venture.

*Recommendation: I suggest the establishment of a formal
division dedicated to handling unknowable matters. The skills
of those I have assembled are without peer, but they are not
properly integrated as a team and have not trained together.
We are far behind the British Diogenes Club and the American FBI's Unnamables Section in this regard.*

"What are you doing here, Burma, slumming again?"
Commissioner Faroux asked tiredly. "What brings you to the
humble office of the *Police Judiciaire*?"

Burma pulled up a chair and made himself at home. "I
want to know all you can tell me about a brothel run by a
woman called Madame Elisabeth."

"Well, well, well. Don't your shady friends keep you up-
dated on the latest houses of ill repute? What would Hélène
say? She pines for you so–"

"Not for me, you dolt. I'm on a case, obviously."

"How are you involved? There have been three murders
in the neighborhood of her establishment in the last two
months! If you've been holding out on me…"

"Three murders? I came to you for information, remember? What's the scoop? And why is Madame Elisabeth still
open for business?"

"Fine, fine. Her associate greases the right palms to keep
it open. An unexpected expense since the Marthe Richard
Law, eh?" Faroux chuckled. "Now there are three girls, all
beautiful, all found dead in that neighborhood, their throats
cut. We suspect they worked at Elisabeth's, no proof, no wit-
nesses willing to say they saw any of the victims there."

"Of course not," Burma rolled his eyes. "None of this
made the papers. You're holding out on me, Florimond. What
else?"

"All right, all right. We've clamped down on the press,
don't want to start a panic, you know. So here it is. All the
girls? Not a drop of blood to be found, anywhere. Completely
drained."

Burma whistled and exhaled. "Where's her place?"

"Not so fast, your turn now. If I can connect the murders to the *Cordon Jaune*, I can shut it down, bribes or no."

Burma puffed at his pipe. "Look, you're wasting my time and yours. Far be it from me to invoke government powers, but S.N.I.F. is involved. Cough it up, or don't. Either way's fine by me, I don't give a shit. Don't and the spooks'll be down here next. What'll it be?"

"S.N.I.F.? Jesus Christ, what're you into now? All right, she set up shop in the old Benet mansion. Place has been empty, gathering dust, since Doctor Benet kicked off back in '35. You know where it is?"

Burma nodded and got up to leave.

"Goddamn it, Burma!" Faroux shouted at his departing back. "You have 48 hours to fill me in, or I'll have you back in here for withholding evidence, S.N.I.F. or no goddamn S.N.I.F.!"

Burma gave a friendly wave.

In the parlor of the Benet mansion, the shades were tightly drawn against the afternoon Sun. Le Chiffre paced nervously back-and-forth in front of Elisabeth and took a loud snort from his Benzedrine inhaler.

"You can't continue disposing of the merchandise! This is the fourth one! We're practically insolvent as it is."

Elisabeth bestowed a serene smile upon him and stretched her feline body on the chaise. A clingy black gown set off blond curls. Wrists and plunging neckline were ringed in purple feathers, a silver-blue gem resting between her pale breasts. She looked like a Hollywood starlet.

A young, white-haired girl in a *negligé* lay curled on the floor, her head and one slender arm resting in Elisabeth's lap. The girl's eyes were open, but vacant. "Shhh. You'll wake her up." She caressed the girl's hair, but stared steadily at Le Chiffre. As always, her gaze had a tranquilizing effect.

"And why should I not use the 'merchandise,' as you so artfully call it, as I please?" She continued. "I own half of this venture."

Le Chiffre sat down and smoothed his dark suit. He put a *Caporal* in a cigarette holder and lit it.

Continuing more calmly, he said, "You cannot continue to kill these girls. Our financial situation is precarious and you're making it worse by killing off our only source of income. Not to mention the police are sure to become suspicious!"

"Ah, yes, isn't that always how it is," Elisabeth sighed, a faraway look in her eyes. "Always the peasants hound us, chase us on to the next village. Don't we have a right to peace and quiet, like everyone else?"

"Just promise me you'll stop. Eventually I may be able to sell off the *Cordon Jaune*'s assets, recoup our losses, but not if we're both in gaol, Elisabeth... Elisabeth!"

"Hmm? Oh yes, of course I promise, of course."

A discreet knock came to the parlor door, and one of Le Chiffre's bodyguards entered. The man was tall, with wide lips and slightly bulging, glassy eyes. He came over and whispered in Elisabeth's ear.

"Oh, by all means, do show her in, Denis, bring her to me!" Elisabeth clapped gleefully. At the noise, the white-haired girl awoke. "Plaster, we have a visitor. Go help Denis bring her to me."

The girl obeyed, and in a moment they escorted a tall, well-built redhead into the parlor.

Elisabeth looked at the newcomer and cocked her head in seeming puzzlement for a moment; then a smile spread across her face and she clapped her hands again in approval at Le Chiffre. "Beautiful! Splendid! What a find. All legs and curves and breasts. She'll do magnificently for us."

Speaking to the girl, Elisabeth said, "You understand our working arrangements, my dear?"

The redhead nodded.

Back at Le Chiffre: "Bravo, she's wonderful, quiet and shy as well. Herr Ziffre, you've outdone yourself. Denis, escort our newcomer–what is her name again?–yes, escort Jeannette to her room. No. 13 will do, I think. Yes, take her there

287

straightaway, let's get her settled in, and rested. She starts to-night!" She blew a kiss at the retreating figures.

Le Chiffre looked at her warily. "You promised…"

"Oh, don't be tiresome, Ziffre. We've nothing more to discuss. You may leave me now."

Le Chiffre frowned once more, then shook his head and left.

A little while after he exited, Plaster returned the parlor and came to kneel before her mistress. Elisabeth took her hand. "Did you and Denis make our newcomer… comforta-ble?"

The girl nodded eagerly. "*Oui, Madame*."

"Excellent."

Half a block down the street from the *Cordon Jaune*'s Parisian headquarters, a nondescript 1932 Citroën C6G pulled up at the corner. Roger Noël was at the wheel. Doctor Ardan sat next to him in the front, while Nestor Burma and Jens Rolf sat in the back.

Noël looked at his watch and ticked off the time. Adélaïde Lupin had gone in 20 minutes ago. Ardan didn't need the watch; his internal clock was as accurate as the atom-ic chronometer in his New York headquarters. His only re-sponse was a slight twitch of an index finger.

Burma noticed.

"Aren't you at all worried, Doctor?" Burma inquired. "Such a beautiful girl… Might she end up in a compromising position this evening?"

"Why should I worry, Monsieur Burma? She knows the risks. Besides, according to the plan, she'll be out of there long before evening falls."

"*Tu parles*. I've seen the way you look at her." He tapped the side of his head. "I'm a trained detective."

Doc turned away without responding. Was he flushed again?

"Do you mind?" the usually quiescent German asked Burma. "If I am allowed to concentrate, I may be able to sense the Eye from here and pinpoint its location."

Properly chastised, Burma settled deeper into the back seat and lit his pipe.

Adélaïde followed Denis and the white-haired girl through the corridors of the *Cordon Jaune*. She reflected smugly on her disguise's success. She had only met Elisabeth once, briefly, and had correctly predicted she would not be recognized. Ardan had objected, but Noël had wisely over-ruled him.

When these two left her alone in her quarters, she'd be free to explore and locate Ilona. Then back to the parlor to rip the Eye of Dagon from where it hung around Elisabeth's translucent neck.

The whole place had a freakish ambiance to it. Noël had briefed them all before sending her in. The mansion used to be the clinic of Doctor Felix Benet. Benet had used a new source of radiation–Radium-X–to cure blindness and other illnesses, and had been brutally murdered here. It still stank of death.

Add in the mansion's current occupants: Trollish Le Chiffre snorting his amphetamines. Languid Elisabeth… fascinating in a menacing sort of way, like a flame drawing in the moth that cannot resist. Did she have a slight Hungarian accent? And her two escorts, they were quite a pair. Denis with his bulging eyes and bluish-green, almost oily skin emanating a squalid fish smell; he was in serious need of a shower. And silent Plaster, a girl of no more than 20 with a shock of white hair. Was it the fear permeating this place that robbed her hair of color?

As they passed a large mirror hanging in the hallway, Adélaïde caught a quick glance in it and could have sworn… Had she really seen only her own and Plaster's reflections? No, she must have missed foul Denis' reflection because he was lumbering a few steps ahead of them.

No matter, she'd be in and out of here quickly. Free Ilona, snatch the jewel and disappear. It was a bit of a trek to Room 13, though, and they seemed to be headed toward the basement…

As they approached a heavy wooden door, Plaster's hand clamped over her mouth and nose with a chloroform-soaked rag. The last thing she saw was her friend, Ilona, shackled and hanging in the dank cellar.

When the Sun declined, the ladies of the *Cordon Jaune* were brought down for their evening lineup before Le Chiffre and Elisabeth. Counting the new girl–had anyone met her yet?–there were ten women currently working at this establishment. Last night, before Jeannette had come on board, so to speak, there had also been ten, but Claudette had left.

People came and went in this line of work, and the ladies weren't concerned. They might have been if Madame Elisabeth allowed them newspapers or radios–Claudette's body had been discovered nearby just that afternoon. Her corpse was completely depleted of blood, and the police, as usual, were baffled.

Le Chiffre, conversely, was concerned. Of the ten, only nine appeared at the lineup.

"Elisabeth!" he shouted, then turned back the women. "Back to your rooms, all of you! Now!"

Several of the girls, lead by the waif Cabiria, protested but complied on further threats from Le Chiffre.

After the ladies dispersed, he beckoned to his two looming bodyguards, and faced Elisabeth.

"Where is the new girl? Where is Jeannette!"

Elisabeth smiled at him lazily. "Ziffre, you really must learn to control your temper."

"Woman, you'll be the end of us all. Denis, Karl–" He snapped his fingers at the bodyguards "–take Madame Elisabeth to her room and lock her there."

Elisabeth began to giggle softly. She raised one elegant arm and pointed behind him, urging him to look.

Le Chiffre slowly turned and almost fainted. Denis and Karl's dark tailored suites were splitting at the seams. Eyes swelled in their sockets. Snouts elongated. Webs formed between fingers and toes of feet which no longer fit in discarded shoes. Oil seeped from bluish skin showing through the splits in once stylish clothing.

Thick red lips opened, showing row upon row of razor-sharp fangs. The incisors were particularly lengthy.

The jewel at Elisabeth's throat glowed momentarily with ice-blue intensity, and then softened.

"Gentlemen, Herr Ziffre is becoming a nuisance. Take him to the cellar. No, no! Don't hurt him–yet. He may still have his uses."

Karl punched Le Chiffre in the face, and the two fish-men started to drag him away, gibbering quietly to themselves.

"Oh, and gentlemen?"

The two creatures paused.

"Better stay out of sight. We wouldn't want to frighten the girls, would we, darlings? I'll call them down for this evening's lineup."

The two fish-men gesticulated in parody of a human nod, and continued to shamble away, dragging Le Chiffre and leaving a faint trail of fish-slime in their wake.

It had been too long. Adélaïde should have been out over an hour ago. Time for Plan B.

Doc Ardan and Jens Rolf had come into the *Cordon Jaune* with the evening's first round of customers. They had both noted the Eye of Dagon hanging from the Madame's neck, but the first order of business was to locate and liberate Adélaïde and Ilona. The Madame had made cooing noises over Doc, murmuring over the handsome bronze giant and making a point to caress his shoulders and biceps.

Elisabeth was undeniably mesmerizing, but Ardan could sense something vile and repellent at her core. He stoically bore the indignity of her touch, but when Elisabeth prattled on about what a lucky girl Plaster would be that night, Rolf kept things in motion, playing his part perfectly.

"Fraulein Elisabeth," the German snapped, consulting his watch, "if we could proceed, our time is limited."

"Of course, Mein Herr, forgive me. This girl's name is Manon. I presume she is acceptable?

"Quite, thank you."

Now both men were in separate rooms with the girls. Doc had broken a small glass tranquilizer under Plaster's nose and eased her into a comfortable position on the bed. As he exited, Jens Rolf silently came from the room across the hall. Through the open doorway, Doc could see the girl Manon sitting straight up in a chair, eyes open and yet vacant.

"A slight trance, she'll come out of it shortly," Rolf whispered.

Doc nodded, and scanned the corridor in both directions.

"That woman, Elisabeth," Rolf continued. "Something evil and depraved owns her soul."

Doc nodded again, and raised a hand for silence. After a moment, he pointed and the two men made their way toward a butler's staircase at the back of the house.

Nestor Burma was stationed out back of the Benet mansion at a basement window. His associate, a reformed burglar called Zavatter, worked at the lock.

"*Voila*," said the cracksman as the lock came loose. Burma paid him off, sent him on his way, and held his position.

After 30 minutes, Ardan and Rolf had still not appeared with the women and the Eye. Burma emptied out his pipe on the pavement. He sauntered casually from the back alley and down the block to the idling Citroën.

He said a few words to Noël, then retraced his steps, crouched, and went in the open window.

Adélaïde's wrists were shackled to chains hanging from the cellar ceiling. The room was featureless save for the tendrils of greenery which snaked the ground around her feet.

Adélaïde had been stripped down to undergarments and pumps. Her red wig was gone. She yelled at Ilona to wake up, but her friend was unresponsive. Adélaïde quieted when she heard the click of footsteps on the wooden stairs descending from the cellar door.

Elisabeth appeared, wearing black riding pants tucked neatly into black patent leather riding boots, and a white blouse cut low at the neckline. She held a riding crop behind her in both hands. Out for a day at the races.

"Welcome my dear, welcome!" She smiled broadly at Adélaïde, then whispered conspiratorially in her ear. "I knew it was you earlier today, as soon as you came into the parlor. I have an unusually strong sense of smell, and I could never forget your alluring scent."

"What do you want?"

"What? What do I want?" Elisabeth asked innocently. "Why my dear, shouldn't it be obvious? I want you."

Adélaïde shook her head in confusion.

"Oh, I admit, I probably should have left Paris long before now, but once I met you when you delivered the Eye– isn't it just exquisite, by the way?" She gestured at the luminescent jewel hanging between her pale breasts. "In any event, once I saw you, I knew it would be worth the risk of remaining a while longer. And I was right! Here you are, pretty as a package."

"I still don't understand. This was all a trap? For me?"

"But of course! When I met you, I could tell right away if I kept the Eye, you'd come here looking for Ilona. I'm a very good judge of character, you know."

"Why me?"

"Do I have to explain everything? Dear Adélaïde." Elisabeth pouted, puffing out her lower lip, then caressed Adélaïde's cheek with the end of the crop. Adélaïde stiffened.

"Oh, don't worry, this is just for show." She pointed at the cuts on Ilona's neck and wrists. "You see, no crop made those cuts."

Adélaïde shook her head.

"Oh, very well, I'll explain, though it doesn't matter in the end. Soon you'll be pleading to join me. So. Your friend, Doctor Natas. Remember him? Once you had escaped from Oran with the Silver Eye of Dagon, he was able to piece together what really happened. He discovered the true thief of his prize. And–surprise! He put a price out on your head and a reward for the Eye's return!" Elisabeth's smile illuminated the room.

"Word spread–I am somewhat well-connected in that area," she said modestly. "Natas' head of intelligence, Pao Tcheou, also sent out a personal dossier on you. Information on your parents, your friends, anything that might be of use. You can imagine my astonishment to find Ilona Harczy listed as one of your closest friends."

Adélaïde stared at her blankly.

"No? You are still confused?" Elisabeth sighed. "I once knew another Ilona Harczy. I was forced to kill her in Vienna, long ago. I counted it a stroke of good fortune to learn my late nemesis had a distant namesake! Out of curiosity, I sought her out, and discovered she was a chanteuse at the Calyx Bar–yes, the very place I took delivery of the Eye from you! I must say, the latter Ilona is much more beautiful than her predecessor, and once I saw her, I decided to keep her.

"Killing two birds, as the saying goes, I contacted you and arranged to exchange her for the Eye. After all, why not still collect on Natas' reward? When we met, I knew I'd have you as well. I was smitten, I confess. It's extended my Parisian stay a bit, and I probably should've moved on by now, but adding you and the lovely Mademoiselle Harczy to my stable will be well worth the risk and undue attention."

"Undue attention?" Adélaïde asked. "It's you. You've been killing those girls."

294

"Well, one needs to replenish, after all. I think I've been pacing myself quite nicely, but you're right, it is time we leave this place before the day breaks."

"I'm not going anywhere with you."

"Oh, you will," Elisabeth said softly, and kissed her cheek gently. "You'll beg to come with me."

In the upper cellar, Burma had discovered and released Le Chiffre from his cell. The small man was volubly cursing Elisabeth and Denis and Karl.

"Where is Madame Elisabeth, Monsieur? I must locate her."

"I have no idea," the other man growled, "and I don't aim to find out."

"Not so fast. You know your way around this chamber of horrors. You're going to help me find her, and the new girl–a redhead–who came here earlier today." Burma began to reach inside his trenchcoat, then stopped, slowly withdrawing his hand.

Le Chiffre had anticipated Burma, producing a gleaming Eversharp razor blade from the heel of his left shoe. "I'll flick this blade in your eyeball. Don't twitch, don't sneeze, you understand? Nod slowly if you agree."

Burma nodded, and Le Chiffre took off.

Ardan and Rolf approached the late Benet's laboratory. The scientist held up a hand, tapped his nose and raised two fingers. His sense of smell, akin to an ape's, far exceeded that of a normal human.

There were two… somethings… waiting in the laboratory.

Rolf understood Ardan's signal, and the two went in.

Nevertheless, neither was prepared for the ferocity of the attack. Sharp claws extending from rubbery webbed hands embedded in the wall inches from Ardan's head. Razor sharp teeth with exceedingly long canines snapped at his face. The scientist dove past the creature, and the creature's other set of claws raked across his chest, drawing blood. Doc jabbed a strong elbow into the creature's back.

The other fish-man backhanded Jens Rolf across the room, knocking him almost senseless. The second creature then leapt for Ardan, who rolled to the side and bounced up lightly on his feet.

The first creature freed its claws from the wall, and now both approached the scientist, backing him into a corner.

Four sets of claws came flying at Ardan.

"Never," said Adélaïde, "never will I willingly accompany you."

"You will, darling, but let us not argue. Soon you will love me."

"You're delusional. What you've said makes no sense. You decided to collect on Natas' reward, and yet you still have the gem and I'm hanging in your dungeon."

"As for you, I thought I had made myself clear. I have decided to keep you for myself. As for the Eye... I quickly discovered its special properties, and how to tap into them. One as well-traveled as I picks up quite a bit, you know. Human servitors are tedious; with the Eye I have created two completely loyal, relentless servants."

Her expression became wistful. "As the years have passed, it has become increasingly difficult to stay ahead of the forces of so-called 'justice,' moving from town to town, city to city, stopping only long enough to rejuvenate once or twice and then moving on. Now I can stop running, return home to Čachtice Castle. The Carpathians are particularly beautiful this time of year, as autumn approaches. As you'll see.

"These servants will go forth and gather the sustenance I require. All they'll need is the lake nearby the castle in which to replenish themselves. No more vagabond lifestyle. Home.

"So you see, I too have reason to keep the Eye for myself, and fully intend to do so. I am tired of running."

She went over to Ilona and began releasing her chains. "By tomorrow, we–the three of us–will be home."

Ilona slumped to the cold floor, senseless. Elisabeth left her there and returned to Adélaïde, made a swift cut above her left breast, and began to sup. As the blood flowed into Elisabeth's mouth, Adélaïde began to go into another world; it was pleasurable, but another part of her mind screamed silently in resistance.

Uncounted minutes passed, and Adélaïde came back into focus. She saw Ilona approaching Elisabeth from behind. Her approach seemed somewhat stealthy, and Adélaïde surged with hope. Elisabeth had made a tactical mistake in releasing the other girl. But she was weakened and pale… Would she be able to immobilize Elisabeth?

Ilona crept closer and closer, reaching in toward Elisabeth, who still was bent over Adélaïde, draining her life-blood. Adélaïde faded out and in once more again, and now Ilona was impossibly closer, about to grab the Madame and thrust her away from Adélaïde. Ilona took her shoulders, and Elisabeth reached back an arm, slipping it around her waist and pulling her in toward her victim.

Elisabeth kissed Ilona, covering her lips in Adélaïde's blood, then made another cut above the girl's right breast. The blood started to pour out, and she pushed Ilona's mouth down to the wound.

Ilona drank greedily of Adélaïde's blood.

The now-healthy and budding greenery which snaked around her feet seemed to be moving slightly, as if intercepting any stray falling droplets of blood.

Elisabeth returned to her victim's breast and joined Ilona in the feast.

Doc Ardan's superfirer pistols hummed busily, shooting hundreds of rounds of anesthetic "mercy bullets" at the two misshapen amphibians.

To no avail. The creatures advanced upon him. And advanced. Then stopped.

Rolf had regained his senses. He chanted words in an ancient and arcane language.

"*Ph'nglui mglw'nafh Cthulhu R'lyeh wgah-nagl fhtagn. Iä!*"

The two monsters who had been Karl and Denis strained. Their eyes swelled in their sockets but they were otherwise immobilized.

"Hurry!" the German mystic yelled at Doc. "This hex will not hold them long!"

Doc nodded once and went for the opposite corner of the laboratory, an area he had not been able to reach during the pitched battle.

Moving faster than most humans could conceive, the bronze man began to gather and piece together large pieces of old, dusty equipment.

"Faster!" Rolf yelled.

"I am," came Ardan's curt reply. Finishing the assembly, he hefted it under his massive, cabled arm. The object was black and conical, the tip coming to a rounded point of glass or some other transparent substance.

Doc reached inside his equipment vest and pulled out a small rectangular box. He wired the box to the cone, which came to life with a high pitched whine. The transparent emitter at the tip illuminated. He pulled out two pairs of goggles, put one on and tossed the other to the German.

Ardan nodded at Rolf, who released the spell and collapsed.

The two fish-men came toward them, moving faster than their deformed shapes gave them any right to.

Doc flipped a switch on the black cone, and the light of a thousand suns, powered by Radium-X, burst out from the emitter.

The beam hit Denis, then Karl, and both fish-men shrieked and burst into flames. Within moments, both had dissolved. All that remained was two piles of ashes on the floor, and a stench.

Burma came running into the room, pistol in hand, and stopped short at the sight and smell. "Mmm. Burnt rancid fish. My favorite."

Elisabeth and Ilona were still bent over Adélaïde. She became more and more pale, but paradoxically felt a strange warm sensation exploding out from the center of her body.

Mercifully, she had almost passed from consciousness when Ardan, Rolf and Burma burst into the dungeon.

"She's almost there! Don't stop!" Elisabeth ordered Ilona, and turned to face the men.

Ardan held the Radium-X projector under his left arm, a superfirer in his right hand. He sprayed Adélaïde's attackers with mercy bullets, but Elisabeth laughed it off, while Ilona continued to draw the remainder of Adélaïde's blood.

Ardan tossed the spent superfirer away and hefted the projector into position.

Simultaneously, Rolf uttered incantations–"Iä! Iä! Ph'nglui mglw'nafh Cthulhu fhtagn! Méne!"–and the Eye of Dagon exploded off of Elisabeth's graceful white neck in a detonation of blood and bluish light.

The gem bounced on the stone floor and rolled toward Ardan. Before he could seize it, the energy released from the Eye crackled and struck the Radium-X projector, frying and fusing circuits.

The projector began to heat up and blaze white hot in an uncontrolled reaction. Ardan dropped the projector before it could burn his hands. It bathed the room with sun-like light. Burma, *sans* goggles, was blinded.

Elisabeth and Ilona screamed and collapsed, writhing on the floor. "The light! The Sun!"

"The projector is going to blow. It'll take out the whole cellar, maybe more. I can't stop it!" Doc yelled at Rolf. He gestured to Burma. "Help him out of here. I'll follow you with Adélaïde and these two."

Ardan turned toward Adélaïde, but paused at Rolf's hand on his arm.

"These women," Rolf said. "I understand and respect your policy of humane rehabilitation. But these women are gone. You cannot help them."

Doc paused a moment further, then nodded and went toward Adélaïde.

Minutes later, he burst from the front of the Benet mansion. Adélaïde looked like a small child cradled in his massive arms, broken chains trailing from her wrists. He placed her gently in the back seat of the Citroën.

Roger Noël gunned the engine and floored it, Ardan mounted on the running board, as a violent explosion rocked the *Cordon Jaune* headquarters.

Just before sunrise, large boulders shifted and rolled down the piles of rubble in the debris of the Benet mansion. A large vine, now the circumference of a man's torso, pushed the rocks away. At one tip of the vine was a pod which vaguely resembled a Venus Fly Trap. The vine slithered free, and glided down the Paris streets.

Anyone who may have observed this singular phenomenon could also have heard, just at the edge of audible range, a tiny whispering voice, barely distinguishable from the slight breeze.

"*Nourrissez-moi ! Nourrissez-moi!*"

The murmurs gradually faded into the morning dawn.

FROM: Lieutenant Montferrand, Division Protection, Service National d'Information Fonctionnelle, Paris.
TO: SNIF.
DATE: August 26, 1946
SUBJECT: Silver Eye of Dagon

The Eye of Dagon has been secured and turned over to Doctor Ardan. Jens Rolf has provided Ardan with detailed and specific instructions for its safekeeping.

There was no sign of Le Chiffre anywhere in the Cordon Jaune *headquarters, nor of any of the other women employed* in his house of ill-fame. It is presumed they all escaped in the confusion prior to the explosion.

Burma's blindness was temporary, and Ardan has given him a clean bill of health. According to Ardan and Rolf, A.L. will suffer no lasting ill effects from her experience.

When the rubble was cleared from the lower cellar of the Benet mansion, Elisabeth and Ilona Harczy's bodies were recovered and taken to the morgue. However, the next day, the bodies were inexplicably gone.

Recommendation: The International Police Commission should be on the lookout for two women matching their descriptions.

Deep in the Arctic, in a solitary fortress, Doctor Francis Ardan checked on the Eye of Dagon. It was stored safely away from those who would use it for ill purposes. Likewise Doctor Benet's Radium-X projector.

He moved silently into the next chamber, a warm room decorated in the fashion of an Adirondack hunting lodge. Then, through the fortress' insulated walls, he heard the mechanical whine of rocket engines.

In a huge stone fireplace, embers from a once-crackling fire still glowed. A large bearskin rug in front of the fireplace was askew. A note was pinned on the mantle, near a half-empty bottle of *Veuve Clicquot* and one champagne flute (Ardan did not drink):

My Dearest Francis (the note began),

What a wonderful storehouse of treasures your little hideaway is! I left you the gem this time, although you know, of course, I easily could have taken it. Thank you for refueling the Cirrus X-9 for me. I know you'll be cross with me for making off with it again, but really, how else can I make certain we'll see each other once more?

Au revoir, mon sauvage.
Mon amour,

Adélaïde

He shook his head ruefully and smiled faintly. He just couldn't seem to hang on to those damn rocket packs.

But he didn't really care.

COUNTESS CARODY

Countess Nadine Carody, played by the beautiful Soledad Miranda, is the star of Vampyros Lesbos, *a 1971 German-Spanish co-production written and directed by the famous Spanish director Jesús (Jess) Franco, who borrows happily from both* Carmilla *and* Dracula. *On a remote Mediterranean island, the Countess lures unwary victims with her seductive nightclub act. In the film, she sets her sights on silky blonde Linda (Ewa Strömberg), initiating her into the realm of lesbian love beyond the grave. Later, Linda falls under the care of Dr. Seward (Dennis Price), who is intent on using Nadine to become a vampire himself.*

Artikel Unbekannt: *Blood and Fire*

To Dolores Lesta

Tonight will be the last. I know it, I feel it in my veins, my inner flame is flickering and gradually going out. The deadline is closing in, hour by hour, minute by minute. I see the grains of sand slipping one by one through my clenched fingers. I would give everything to see her again. I would sacrifice my past with no regret and my future without remorse. I would kill my mother and father and sell my soul if I could have her just one more time.

Before her, I was dead. Passing through life like a ghost. I exploited one side, took advantage of the other, and left not the slightest trace. Without ever returning to the scenes of my crimes. A shadow. How many broken hearts? How many des-

303

ecrated virginities? What does it matter? A greedy vulture, that's what I was. A cold monster taking pleasure in drinking at the intimate sources to drain them all the more.

Without knowing it, I had spent my life waiting for her. And yet, I believed I was protected. Shut into my ivory tower. Shut into my sarcophagus. Impenetrable shell and well-oiled armor. What a joke! As soon as she appeared, I felt like a nuclear sun had burned my eyes. And when I felt her sweet venom penetrate me, it was too late. Her fire had melted my ice.

I met her for the first time in the wee hours one Sunday morning. After a grisly night of orgy, I had decided to wash off all the smut sticking to my skin. The beach was deserted. I headed for the ocean in the buff and dove in. After a hard, bracing swim that quickly carried me far from shore, I felt a shiver run down my spine, but not due to the cold. I turned around straightaway and saw a dark figure standing by my clothes on the beach.

Where did it come from? The entrance to the beach was too far from where I had left my clothes for someone to get there in so little time. A little astounded, I came out of the water. After 50 yards or so, I could see more clearly and the motionless shadow turned into a very beautiful woman with long, black hair and sparkling eyes.

Not bashful by nature I approached her without trying to hide my nudity, which she scrutinized with a strange ferocity. Then she looked into my eyes briefly before opening her cloak. She was wearing nothing underneath. I barely had time to contemplate the harmony of her voluptuous curves when she stepped closer without saying a word. She started rubbing her body against mine before caressing the most sensitive part of my anatomy. Then she kneeled down before me and took me in her mouth.

I did not dream of resisting. Besides, I was thoroughly convinced that it would do no good. From this mysterious creature dressed in black emanated such a magnetism that I felt like a fly caught in a spider's web. The thought came to me that she was acting like a praying mantis, even if the actions she was guilty of had nothing in common with religion...

What she did to me, I cannot describe very clearly since the way she did it was like nothing I had ever experienced before. She accomplished it with unbelievable refinement and ardor and her subtle blend of majesty and savagery brought me very quickly to the peak. She drank me entirely. With animal voracity. As if her life depended on it...

Then I fell to my knees facing her and buried my face in her hair. At the moment I embraced her, I experienced an illumination: she was the one I had always hoped for without ever daring to admit it. She whom I had been looking for through the ether haze and opium fog. This realization struck me with such force that my head spun and my heart skipped several beats. I tried to stand up but I was too dizzy and I fainted.

When I came to, it was daytime and she had disappeared. The beach was deserted again and I was alarmed to see that my strange companion had left no footsteps in the sand. Her prints were elsewhere. My whole body was howling for her. Her mouth had branded me. And mine opened in a silent cry when I realized that I knew nothing about her. Not even her name.

I went back the following night and spent the whole of it waiting. In vain. Mortified by this failure, but with no other possibility to find her, I decided to carry on. I was right to do so because, a few days later, the young woman reappeared a little before dawn, as if she came out of nowhere, naked again under her black cloak. And we surrendered to each other without saying a single word.

This time, in spite of our violent embrace and the primitive intensity of my orgasm, I managed to keep a minimum of control over myself. I wanted the pleasure to last and, above all, I feared not to perform lest my lover vanish again. Feeling her desire for independence, I knew I was setting myself up for a frank refusal, so I simply slipped my hand into hers. The move must have caught her completely off guard her because, quite unexpectedly, she followed me.

The ensuing nights were, for me, a real honeymoon. I abandoned myself to the sweet and savory taste of her spicy kisses, to the softness of her velvety skin and to the heady, harmonious fragrance that her body exuded. I always wanted more. And she answered my expectations with a mad excess of tenderness and passion. While pulling from me the strength that she needed, she left me with the agonizing feeling of emptiness every time she went away.

For, she went away every day. Our "us" existed only at night. The waiting was excruciating and the lack that I felt was physical, as if I was deprived of some part of me. Unable to fix my attention on anything, I spent my days walking down the deserted beach with my head lowered. I paid no attention to the violent waves crashing onto the shore, nor to the foamy spray that would sometimes lash my face. Out of season and out of the world, I breathed only her.

I wandered about like a lost soul in a cold and empty hell. And this special place that I once loved so much was now like a block of frozen marble in which I had become imprisoned alive. Some of my friends tried to get me to go out, but all their attempts ended in utter failure. Only my beautiful jailor had the key…

My friends, however, did not readily see the gravity of my situation. It must be said that I felt an irresistible aversion to confiding in them. Therefore, they just suspected I was a little depressed, and they tried to "cure" me by taking my mind off it. After some resistance, I finally, half-heartedly, let them drag me out. But the cure ended up being worse than the illness.

The "special" establishments that we frequented in the past were now loathsome to me. My former escapades seemed dull and, on discovering their true face, I felt as if I was suffering from a terrible hangover. In these offered bodies, I saw nothing but *her* curves and the strong odors exuding from the piles of entwined flesh could not eclipse *her* perfume.

In the smoky darkness, the masked figures distorted, melted, dissolved, until the features of my beloved blotted out their foul forms. After a few tense evenings of rejecting the pathetic assaults of ageing libertines, I decided to put an end to the sham. This pitiful fool's bargain was deceiving no one and I could no longer pretend. Everything reminded me of her.

A man in my circle, however, was not so willing to let me go. This man, who was considered as a kind of spiritual guide to our little decadent community, called himself a "doctor," though none of us knew to what field this title applied. Endowed with charisma and extraordinary learning, the elegant man in his 50s "inspired respect," as they say. When he showed up at my house one morning, I did not long hesitate to receive him, in spite of my desire to stay alone. We sat in my salon in front of the large picture windows.

"I imagine your visit owes nothing to chance, Dr. Orlof" I asked. "What can I do for you?"

"I should be the one asking you that question, my young friend."

"I don't understand."

"Don't take me for an idiot, please. Do you think I haven't noticed your change in attitude?"

"I'm not feeling under the weather."

"Under the weather, no. But maybe under a spell?"

While I scowled without answering, my visitor continued.

"Have you ever heard of the Dark Countess?"

Before I could say anything, a weird malaise gripped me and my denial turned into a pitiful stuttering that made my guest smile ironically.

"I see," he said. "Well, can you imagine that a strange rumor has been going round lately? A beautiful, silent woman dressed in a black cloak is seducing men every night around here. There's nothing wrong in that in and of itself... if the young men in question were not being found drained of blood after being despoiled of a more intimate substance. That's why I'm wondering if you've encountered this creature whom the locals call the Dark Countess. Of course, you're still alive, but you seem to be suffering from a lethargy that's unlike you."

Dr. Orlof had barely finished speaking when a shadow appeared behind him in the window. Then the form of a supernatural beauty took shape behind the glass. Supple and slender like a vine, the young woman was wearing only a tiny, black, fringed robe that was so transparent it left nothing of her statuesque form to the imagination. She was radiant, literally. Her perfect but hard face seemed to absorb the light of the sun to better reflect it on anyone so bold as to look at her for too long. She emanated the same brute and animal seduction that I felt from my mysterious lover.

Realizing that I was not listening anymore and looking over his shoulder, my guest turned around. But there was nothing but a warm mist where the woman had been a few seconds earlier. The doctor stared me, then, with kindness, said:

"Well, I see that I'm not holding your attention. I hope you won't regret it. But you should know that I'm at your disposal. And don't forget," he added as he left, "that in 'libertinism' there is 'liberty.' If you go on like thus you'll risk losing both."

Dr. Orlof's warning bothered me the whole day but faded away as night fell, replaced by the spells of her whom I no longer hesitate to call the Dark Countess. I desired her with agonizing, obsessional ardor. The fire of love was making my blood boil. I could not sleep because my vital fluids were seething all the time, pounding my head and my guts with the reminder of her absence. Her image haunted me. I kept seeing her lick her lips greedily and giving me one last obscene look before disappearing.

This situation lasted for weeks on end until one day, crazed by the imminent want, I decided to follow her. Therefore, I left my home and dove into the stifling humidity of the seaside town beaten by the sun. Slipping from one shadowy corner to another, I managed not to lose track of my beautiful lover, who walked through the maze of cobbled alleyways without turning around.

The weird thing was that nobody seemed to notice her. However, her dark cloak clashed loudly with the light, colorful clothes sported by the vacationers. But, as if under some spell, they went about their ridiculous business unmindful, not even turning to watch the dark angel parting their crowds so gracefully. I trailed her for more than half an hour to a remote house located on the edge of a coastal path.

I thought I must have been seeing things because, even though I had lived in the area for years, and was a frequent visitor to the beaches, I had never seen this house! And even stranger was its eccentric, cubist architecture of the house, that was completely unlike the austere tendencies of this conservative region.

Seeing an older lady walking down the path I asked her if she knew who lived there. To my great surprise, she crossed herself, turned her back and uttered a name with obvious disgust, like she was spitting on the ground: "Carody."

In the meantime, my lover had reached the front door of the house. Without ringing or knocking, the door opened and I had barely enough time to hide behind a bush before being spotted. That was when I felt my blood freeze. For it was the young lady who had appeared in the dream at my window during Dr. Orlof's visit who was standing there!

This time, the only clothing she wore was a tunic as flimsy as a veil, with a leather belt around her waist. The outfit, both simple and traditional, only enhanced the ancient majesty of her bearing. Holding out her hand to her visitor, she took her inside without saying a word. The two forms faded down the hallway, swallowed by the shadows, before the door closed as if by a draft of air. No gust of wind, however, had cooled the scorching heat of the day…

I let a few minutes pass, then made a decision—I had to because I could not miss this opportunity to know more. Wavering between fear of what I was going to find and an irresistible need to confront it, I headed toward the house. After sneaking along the walls, hoping to find an open window, I ended up in the back yard and what I saw took my breath away.

A miniature jungle was growing before me. Stunned by the lushness of the place, I gazed upon the rows of palm trees, sequoias, sycamores and olive trees. I inhaled with delight the wild, heady smells emanating from this open air greenhouse. And then, I heard a woman's tinkling laughter, immediately followed by a more manly exclamation that paralyzed me. For, just this "no" was enough to recognize the voice of who was protesting.

Trying to resist somehow the queasy feeling in my stomach, I pulled away from the wall I had flattened against and started approaching the voices. Just as I had hoped a window was cracked open. I risked a peek. What I saw turned my anxiety into fear merging with disgust.

Dr. Orlof was lying down, naked, on a huge canopy bed. His hands and feet were handcuffed to the four posts. The two women kneeling on either side of the prisoner and completely naked as well were each caressing a very precise part of his body. Nauseous and fascinated at the same time, I watched the scene while biting my lip so I would not scream out. Then the creatures slowly leaned over the areas they were touching. Finally, she whom the old lady had called Carody jumped on the doctor's throat and kissed it voraciously while my lover took the man's sex into her mouth.

I could not take anymore. I almost entered the room, but dropped the idea when I realized not only how ridiculous but dangerous the situation was. Because I understood that, on this sweltering morning, *I had been spared*. The Dark Countess, for some obscure reason, had decided to make her pleasure with me last, and I had to make the most of this before she changed her mind. That was why, sick at heart, I decided to leave the place in silence.

I never saw Dr. Orlof again.

Even today, I do not know how I managed to get back home. I felt like a drunkard who had blacked out. The oppressive heat was stifling me; my head was spinning; and my heart skipping every other beat. The tourists stepped out of my way like I had the plague, the black death... Even if the sickness I was suffering had a different name, I guessed from the symptoms that the result would be the same...

Something had snapped in me. I felt like a puppet without strings. I spent the rest of that sinister day waiting for my lover to return and lie on my bed. When she came at nightfall, I could see in her eyes that she knew: *she knew that I knew*.

In any case, I felt incapable of lying to her. An irony of fate, I anticipated her punishment like a condemned man putting his head on the chopping block without asking for one last cigarette.

She preferred abandoning me to killing me. I saw in her eyes that she did not have the courage. I spent the next six months calling out for her from the depths of my prison without bars.

Tonight, she finally answered me, accompanied by the other *femme fatale*, Carody. I smelled their perfume before seeing them step out of the shadows. The hour of my deliverance was tolling. I awaited the final blow with pleasure.

She took everything from me. My heart, my body, my mind, my soul. She sucked up everything in me. I am nothing but rags and waste. But I do not blame her. She was just obeying her deep, dark nature. Her nature which she had opened up by gratifying me with the best present of all: the gift of life. My life in her hands, my life in her mouth, until I lose all my blood. My life that she is coming to take.

The circle is closed.

The two creatures have already lost their clothes. They are coming to me. Their dilated pupils stare with that bestial intensity that is now so familiar to me. Impatient and calm, I am ready for my final transfusion. They lie down next to me, lewd and cat-like. I breathe in their intoxicating scent, graze their satiny skin, feel their greedy mouths all over my body. Soon their movements become more precise, their kisses converge on my throat and on my sex, the double source of life on the verge of running dry.

My Dark Countess, you put my existence to fire and sword. And when I succumb to your final embrace, I would like to give you your present. Your heat on my cold. The unbearable certainty that I cannot take it with me. So, take it before your darkness prevails, keep this sorrowful proof close to your heart and do not forget, when your terrible thirst awakens, that I burned for you. To death.

(English adaptation by Michael Shreve)

THE VAMPIRES OF MARS

The Vampires of Mars were introduced in Gustave Le Rouge's
Le Prisonnier de la Planète Mars *(1908)[9], a book often hailed*
as a classic of early French science fiction, a significant pre-
cursor of the "planetary romance" of Edgar Rice Burroughs
*(*A Princess of Mars *first appeared in serialized version in*
1912), which also anticipates the "cosmic horrors" that H. P.
Lovecraft and Clark Ashton Smith would unleash upon their
readers in the 1930s. Le Rouge's account of engineer Robert
Darvel's Martian odyssey bears a closer resemblance to
Lovecraft's "At The Mountains of Madness" than it does to A
Princess of Mars *because it follows the Vernian precedent of*
being a wonderstruck Robinsonade rather than a pure ac-
tion/adventure story. Indeed, the narrative swings so frequent-
ly between the moods of cosmic horror and interplanetary fan-
tasy that the characters continually metamorphose from help-
less bundles of gibbering terror into swashbuckling he-men,
and vice versa. This story by Matthew Dennion brings togeth-
er Edwin Arnold's hero Gullivar Jones from his 1905 novel Lt.
Gullivar Jones: His Vacation *and Le Rouge's fundamentally*
unknowable Vampires of Mars...

Matthew Dennion: *Predators and Prey*

The Erloor started to stir as the last rays of sunlight began to fade from the opening to their massive cavern. A cool
wind blew through the cave, heralding the onset of dusk. The

---

[9] Available from Black Cot Press as *The Vampires of Mars*,
ISBN 978-1-934543-30-6.

breeze circulated the odor of the remains from the slain elderly on the bottom of the cavern into the nostrils of the slowly awaking members of the rookery. Long, yellow wings ending in imposing claws began to extend from the Erloor who hung to the stalactites which comprised the ceiling of the cavern. The alpha male was the first to open his eyes. He unleashed an ear-piercing shriek and the rest of the rookery responded in kind. The communal screech was more than a simple call to wake the Erloor who were still sleeping. It was the first step in beginning the night's hunt. The call would travel out of the cave and over the surrounding forest. The sound waves would connect with solid targets and then bounce back to the Erloor, alerting them to every potential meal within 50 kilometers of the cave.

A moment after the screech was unleashed, the first wave of information returned to the Erloor. In unison, they all began to exchange looks of mixed confusion and excitement. The call had found something new not far from the cave. From the echo, the Erloor could tell that the creatures were similar in structure to the small humanoid mammals they often fed off, but much larger.

Led by the alpha male, one by one, the Erloor dropped from their stalactites and spread their wings, allowing the wind in the cavern to carry them out of the cave and into the night sky. They exited their lair, and the twin moons of Mars silhouetted hundreds of them while they glided through the darkness.

As they approached their prey, the Erloor began to send out ultrasonic sounds which only their sensitive ears could hear. These where much more intricate then the call which gave them the overview of the landscape. Its echo informed them that there were seven creatures in the group they were targeting. The Erloor could further decipher that six of their targets were massive creatures that moved freely about their camp. The seventh figure was much smaller and yet, still larg- er than the humanoids they typically preyed on. This smaller creature also seemed to be confined almost as if it were entrapped in a net. The Erloor began to salivate as they closed in on their prey. One thought dominated their bestial minds: larger bodies meant more blood for them to feed on!

When they were within two kilometers of their prey, the alpha male led the flock high into the sky and adjusted their course so that the moons would no longer cast their silhouette. Centuries of hunting had perfected the Erloors' techniques. For a group of large and potentially dangerous targets, a method was required which would allow the Erloor to utilize the element of surprise while, at the same time, causing as much fear and confusion in their prey as possible.

The Erloor circled above the camp at a high altitude, preventing any land-bound creature from seeing them. Saliva continued to drip from their fangs while they waited for the opportunity to attack. They began to fly in a tighter circle when they saw a long, dark, and low-hanging cloud slowly drift toward them. When it was beneath them and over the camp, the Erloor began a sharp dive into the floating condensation.

The Erloors' attack was both precise and brutal. The massed vampires flew out of the bottom of the cloud and then dove directly into the center of the camp. While they were diving, they were also screeching loudly at a frequency which their prey could hear. The effect of their approach was exactly as they had desired: the large hairy humanoids screamed in fear and began to scatter in all directions.

Most of the Erloor spilt into small groups following the large humanoids as they ran away from the camp. The Erloor quickly fell into the pattern they used to attack larger prey. As their targets scattered, the group which followed each individual would attack in alternating groups of two. The lead attacker would strike at the prey's head and shoulders, causing the large creature to flail, its arms wildly above its head. With the prey's powerful arms distracted, the second attacker would fly low and use its claws to cut deep into the victim's legs, slicing through muscles, tendons, and ligaments. Before the prey realized what was happening to him, his legs became useless and collapsed beneath him. When it fell to the ground, the gathered Erloor would land on top of it and sink their fangs into its body. Within seconds, the entire body of the fallen victim was exsanguinated, leaving nothing but a dry husk. The entire attack lasted only three minutes before all of the large, hairy humanoids had been drained of their blood.

Two of the Erloor landed atop the structure that held the seventh and smaller prey. It was unknown to Erloor. It looked like one of the nets that the elderly wove to entrap certain prey, but unlike them, the bonds were solid. The two Erloor probed the structure as the cloud above them drifted from under one of the moons and allowed the woman inside to behold her attackers. When the moonlight illuminated the Erloor, her eyes widened and she began to scream in horror at the sight of them.

Princess Heru looked through the bars of her cage and beheld a living nightmare. The creatures were as tall as a man, with thin bodies that were covered by a pale yellow skin. Long, thin, with winged arms that extended from their torsos and ended in claw-like hands. Their bodies were supported by thin legs that ended in claws identical to their hands. Their heads were dominated by massive jaws and long, protruding fangs. The beasts' haunting eyes were condensed into two tiny red orbs. Their noses were turned up and their ears were long and pointed. Heru had heard legends of the blood-sucking Erloor, but what she had been told as a child did not prepare her for encountering these horrors in person.

Heru placed her face in her hands and began to cry. Several days ago, she had met the love of her life. His name was Gullivar Jones and he claimed to be from Earth. She had no sooner met him than the brutish Tither people had abducted her. Gullivar had followed them and managed to rescue her. His efforts, however, were in vain. The Tither people followed them back to her city, that of the Hither people, and ransacked it. Heru and Gullivar were preparing to make a last stand when the mystical carpet that had brought the Earthman to Mars

316

suddenly wrapped around him and whisked him away. Heru was then, again, captured by the Tither people. They placed her in a wooden cage and set off to return to their own country. However, the foolish brutes lost their way and wandered into the land of Erloor. While Heru detested the Tither people, she feared the Erloor. The Tither people would have made her a slave, but at least she would have been alive. The Erloor would offer only an agonizing death as they drained the blood from her body.

In her despair, Heru had let her left foot slide to the bars at the side of the cage. One of the Erloor took the opportunity to slice at it with his claw. Heru screamed in pain as the Erloor squatted down and began to lap up the blood which had leaked out of the cage. After one mouthful, the Erloor threw his head back in ecstasy. The blood of this new prey was far, far sweeter than any he had tasted before. In reaction to their comrade's call, the gathered Erloor descended on the cage and, in a feeding frenzy, attempted to lap up the blood from their new prey. The few that had managed to taste the blood of the princess called out in delight as well. They, too, found her blood intoxicating.

Heru quickly slid to the center of her cage and pulled her arms and legs in as close to her body as she could. Her ears were assaulted by horrifying screeches and her body was battered by the wind kicked up as a dozen Erloor flew around her cage biting and scratching at it in an attempt to pry it open.

Eventually, the Erloor found that they could not penetrate the cell constructed by the powerful hands of the Tither people. The alpha male landed atop of it and vocalized three short bursts, which signaled to the others that he required their attention. The flock quickly calmed down and directed their attention to him. The alpha male looked over them and communicated his thoughts:

The new prey would be taken back to the cave and placed atop a high perch. From there, the blood seeping from her leg would slowly drip out, allowing all in the cave to drink it. As the new prey tired, she would eventually relax her muscles and stretch out her arms and legs. Her outstretched body would then allow them to make fresh cuts and increase the blood flow. In this fashion, the new prey would be kept alive as long as possible and provide them with the delicacy of her blood for months on end.

The alpha male gestured toward another large Erloor to join him atop of the cage. They began to flap their wings in unison and slowly the cage was lifted into the air. The remaining Erloor took to the sky as well. Several of them landed on the drained husks of the Tither Peoples' bodies. They lifted them into the air and, as one, the flock returned to the cave.

They reached their destination shortly before sunrise. The alpha male and his companion placed the cage on the floor. From inside, Heru watched as the alpha male turned to one of the massive, mole-like Roomboo standing on the cave floor. The alpha male made a series of grunts at the Roomboo. The blind creature made no reply, but simply turned toward the cave wall and began tunneling into it. Moments later, the Roombo's head emerged from the cave wall several meters above. The Roomboo continued to tear out large chunks of the cave wall creating a ledge. When he had finished, he slid down the cave wall back to floor. The Roomboo waited for a moment, and then was rewarded for completing his task when an Erloor tossed one of the dried husks of the Tither people at his feet. The Roomboo bellowed loudly and then began to devour his grisly meal.

The tales Heru had been told as a child suggested that the Erloor kept the Roomboo as slaves, but she now saw the true nature of their symbiotic relationship. The Roomboo burrowed out the tunnels which the Erloor required, and they, in turn, fed them the remains of their victims. Heru's observations of the beasts were interrupted as the alpha male and his companion began flapping their wings and lifted her cage off of the ground. They flew it to the newly-created ledge and placed it there. Their task completed, the Erloor flew to the stalactite at the top of the cavern and wrapped their hellish wings around their bodies.

As the majority of the Erloor prepared to sleep while the sun completed its journey across the sky, the alpha male turned to one of his flock and uttered several grunts. The Erloor whom the alpha male had addressed released his grip on the cavern ceiling and flew down next to Heru's cage. If the prey relaxed her grip, even slightly, he was to open new wounds, thus increasing the flow of her precious blood.

Hours passed and the sun was again beginning to rise as the designated Erloor continued to watch his captive prey. Every once in while, he indulged himself by licking up the delicious blood that leaked out of her cage. He could hear her heart pumping the fluid through her body and he could see her limbs shaking as she struggled to keep her muscles tensed.

The Erloor prepared himself to strike when, suddenly, another scent caught his attention. It was like that of the prey, yet slightly different. The beast sent out an ultrasonic call to identify the invader. When the echo returned, it showed a creature similar in size and build to the prey. The Erloor was both excited and bewildered. The thought of additional blood like that of the prey was thrilling, but he could not comprehend why another prey would willingly enter the cavern and face certain death.

The Erloor's primitive mind quickly pushed its curiosity aside and focused on food. He flew down to meet the new prey. When it came into view, he could make out that it was indeed similar to the prey in the cage, expect that this one was male and covered itself in strange, blue garments. The Erloor landed in front of it and spread his wings to attack him. Suddenly, the prey lifted his arm, revealing a long claw that reflected light like the moon itself.

The Erloor stared at the "claw" until they prey brought it swiping down and sliced off his right wing. The Erloor screeched in pain, awakening his brothers and sisters. His screech ended when the prey used his "claw" to decapitate him.

The rest of the Erloor, which were waking up from their long sleep, looked down to see a new prey similar to the female in the cage. The alpha male hissed in anger when he realized that the new male prey was tearing her cage apart.

They heard the female cry out: "Gullivar! My love!"

The male wrapped his arm around the female and leapt from the ledge toward the entrance of the cavern. Seeing their prize escaping, the alpha male screeched. His call directed the others to fly after the escaping prey. The prey had jumped out of the cave and were running towards an oddly-colored piece of land. Deterred by the setting sun, the Erloor stopped at the cave entrance and watched in surprise as the oddly-colored piece of land lifted off of the ground and began to fly away with the prey on top of it.

The alpha male made his way to the front of the group and flew out into the dreaded sunset. The remaining daylight burnt his pale skin and sensitive eyes, but the pain was worth the effort if he was able to retrieve the precious blood of the new prey and her companion. As the Erloor flew toward the setting sun, the rest of the flock followed him. They kept their eyes closed and used sonar to track the prey. When the echo returned, they could sense that the prey was flying toward a solid mass. Knowing how high they were, the Erloor guessed that the prey must be flying toward a mountain. They increased their speed as the prey came closer to the land mass.

The Erloor could not understand what occurred as the prey somehow managed to continue flying *through* the land mass. Driven by his voracious desire, the alpha male led the flock into the land mass. He could feel the land mass sliding along the sides of the body. In addition to feeling it on his body, he also noticed that his skin had ceased burning.

Sensing that that the cursed sun had finally set, the alpha male opened his eyes. When he saw the thick, green terrain floating in the air around him, he screeched in terror, urging his flock to turn around and fly out of the land mass.

Suddenly, he heard a chilling laughter and he felt powerful tentacles wrap around his body and crush his wings. He watched in despair as numerous other members of his flock were trapped in the same fashion. He felt thousands of tiny punctures forming on his body and then he felt the excruciating sensation of having his own blood drained through those tiny punctures.

He screeched in agony as he died, and dozens of his flock repeated his call as they suffered the same fate.

Gulliver and Heru were flying away from the carnage on the Earthman's magical carpet when Heru wrapped her arms around her lover.

"Gulliver, thank Isis you came for me! How did you find me and what happened to the Erloor pursuing us?"

Gulliver quickly kissed his princess.

"When the Thither people attacked your city," he replied, "I suddenly found myself wrapped up in this carpet which returned me to Earth. I was consumed by the thought of the Thither people capturing you once more. It took me nearly an entire day, but I finally was able to master how to use of the carpet. I armed myself with my saber and pistol, as well as gun powder and ammunition. I then directed the carpet to fly back to Mars and to your city. I tracked the group that captured you and found the spot where the Erloor attack occurred.

"I was able to determine from the blood trail left by your injury that you were still alive. I followed that trail back to the Erloors' cave. I had learned from our encounter with the Thither people that to simply rush in and rescue you would have been a fool's errand. Had I simply stormed in and took you from their grasp, the Erloor may have followed us back and attacked not only us, but your people as well. So I used to the carpet to fly around the cave, looking for a way to trap the Erloor in their mountain. When I found the flying jungle, I thought that there might be something in there I could use. I had no sooner entered it than I felt something like the tentacles of an octopus wrapping around me. I passed out and awoke to find myself inside a massive glass tower, trapped in a glass room with only a bowl of blood in it. My foe had neglected to take my saber from me and I used it to smash through my cage. Obsessed with the thought of saving you, I ran through the tower, smashing everything I came across searching for my carpet to carry me away. As I smashed through the tower, the only sound that I could hear was deep laughter at my efforts. Finally, I found my carpet in a room with an opal helmet. For some reason, I felt compelled to put it on. Then, I was finally able to see them..."

Gulliver stopped talking and took several deep breaths to compose himself. Heru pressed her cheek against hisand asked:

"What my love? What did you see?"

"Vampires," Gulliver whispered, " but these creatures were unlike any from the stories I was told on Earth. These are invisible beings, whose bodies are comprised only of a massive, grotesque face with wings attached to the sides and tentacles undulating underneath it. In addition to allowing me to see them, the helmet translated their laughter into a language that I could understand. I told them my story, which intrigued them. They informed me that the creatures which had captured you were known as the Erloor, and that their blood was one of the vampires' most prized sources of food.

"However, since the Erloor were nocturnal and the vampires slept at night, it left them only a small window at dusk and dawn to hunt the Erloor. The vampires offered to release me if I agreed to participate in a course of action that would be mutually beneficial to both of us. They had devised a plan for me to rescue you as the sun was setting so that, despite being disoriented, the Erloor would follow us. Once they were chasing us, I was to lead them into the vampires' hunting ground, that floating jungle. The vampires would then feed off of the Erloor, thus satiating their hunger and, at the same, eliminating the threat of the Erloor following us to your city."

Heru looked back at the carnage. She saw the Erloor being drained to lifeless husks devoid of blood just as they had drained the Thither people the previous night.

"Then I owe the vampires my thanks and my friendship for saving me and our city from the Erloor," she said.

Gulliver pulled Heru close to him.

"Give the vampires your thanks, but do not offer them your friendship. You cannot see them, but believe me when I tell you that they are creatures far more terrifying than the Erloor. I simply thank the Lord that they seem to prefer the taste of Erloor blood to that of the Hither people. I shudder to think what would happen if they decided to prey on your people. If they decided to attack the Hither people, I am not sure that there is much we could do to stop them."

Gulliver sat down on the flying carpet and looked into the rising sun.

"I wonder," he continued, "if I have truly have learned anything from our encounter with the Thither people? I have eliminated the threat of the Erloor, but have I brought your city to the attention of a much greater threat..."

Heru sat down next to Gulliver and slid her hand into his. They interlocked fingers and flew toward the rising sun as their ears were filled with the anguished cries of the Erloor and the horrible laughter of the Vampires of Mars.

Credits

Hope for Forgiveness

Starring:
Lenore
The Scarlet Pimpernel
Captain Kronos

Created by:
Gottfried August Burger
Baroness Emma Orczy
Brian Clemens

The Confession of Mary, Queen of Scots, Regarding Lord Ruthven

Starring:
Lord Ruthven
Many, Queen of Scots

Created by:
John William Polidori
Historical

Entretien *with a Vampire*

Starring:
Lord Ruthven
Alexandre Dumas, *père*
Alexandre Dumas, *fils*
Marie Dorval
Victor Hugo
Charles Nodier
Rocambole
Baccarat
Sir Williams

Created by:
John William Polidori
Historical
Historical
Historical
Historical
Historical
P.-A. Ponson du Terrail
P.-A. Ponson du Terrail
P.-A. Ponson du Terrail

Schrodinger's Blood

Starring:
Alinska

Created by:
Etienne-Léon de Lamothe-Langon

| Edward Delmont | based on de Lamothe-Langon |
| Sâr Dubnotal | *Anonymous* |

Vampire Renaissance

Starring:	**Created by:**
Addhema	Paul Féval
Marcian Gregoryi	Paul Féval
Janos Szandor	Paul Féval
Dracula	Bram Stoker
Co-Starring:	
Armand Tesla	Griffin Jay, Kurt Neuman
	& Randall Faye
Count Yorga	Bob Kelljan
Great Old Ones	H.P.Lovecraft
Slidith the Drac (Draco)	Lin Carter,
	Peter Tremayne,
	Sylvie Miller
	& Philippe Ward
Yiggurath (Yig)	H.P. Lovecraft,
	Zealia Bishop
	& Robert Bloch
Tiamit of Arabu	Robert E. Howard
Adana	Abraham Merritt
Set (Great Serpent)	Robert E. Howard
Serpent Men	Robert E. Howard
	& Clark Ashton Smith
Werewolf Folk	Robert E. Howard
Akaana	Robert E. Howard
Red Brotherhood	Lin Carter
Dragon Kings	Lin Carter
Rammon	Robert E. Howard
Akivasha	Robert E. Howard
Simon the Mage (Simon of Gitta)	Richard L. Tierney
Gilles Grenier	Clark Ashton Smith
Matthias Corvinus	*Historical*
Pontius Pilate	*Historical*

The Three Lives of Maddalena

Starring:	Created by:
Maddalena Ernestine (The Bride)	William Hurlbut & John Balderston & James Whale
Carmilla Karnstein	Sheridan Le Fanu
Dr. Victor Frankenstein	Mary Shelley
Elizabeth	Mary Shelley
Dr. Septimus Pretorius	William Hurlbut & John Balderston & James Whale

The Moon Hag

Starring:	Created by:
Carmilla Karnstein	Sheridan Le Fanu
Madame Strenkin	Sheridan Le Fanu
Prof. Quercus	Sheridan Le Fanu
The Moon Hag	Sheridan Le Fanu
Houe of Dolingen	Bram Stoker

To Die For...

Starring:	Created by:
Carmilla Karnstein	Sheridan Le Fanu
Laura	Sheridan Le Fanu

Quest of the Vourdalaki

Starring:	Created by:
Yvgeni	Matthew Baugh
Hella	Mikhail Bulgakov
Gorcha	based on Alexei Tolstoy
Ayub	Harold Lamb
Boris Liatoukine	Marie Nizet
Taras Bulba	Nicolai Gogol

Doroscha	Nicolai Gogol
Quentin Moretus Cassave	Jean Ray
The Magister (aka Woland)	Mikhail Bulgakov
Khlit	Harold Lamb
Menelitza	Harold Lamb
The Koshovoi Ataman	Harold Lamb
Ivan Sabalinka	Robert E. Howard
Zaroff	Richard Connell
Ivanushka	Richard Connell
Vseslav	*Historical*
Chernobog	*Mythological*

City of the Nosferatu

Starring:	**Created by:**
Boris Liatoukine	Marie Nizet
Count Dracula	Bram Stoker
Commander Sponsz	based on Hergé
Graf Von Orlok	Henrik Galeen & F.W. Murnau
Count Szandor	Paul Féval
Baron Iskariot	Paul Féval
Baroness Phryne	Paul Féval
Otto Goetzi	Paul Féval
Polly Bird	Paul Féval
Professor Van Helsing	Bram Stoker
Jure Grando	Historical/Mythical
Ann Radcliffe	Paul Féval
	based on the historical character
Selene/Sepulchre	Paul Féval

All Predators Great and Small

Starring:	**Created by:**
Claude Gabriel Dupont-Verdier (a.k.a. Satanas)	Louis Feuillade
Aguilar	Giuseppe Magione & Warren Garfield

Siegfried von Frankenhausen	Miguel Morayta
Eugenia von Frankenhausen (a.k.a. Szandra, Countess Dracula, Countess Alucard)	Miguel Morayta
Hildegarde	Miguel Morayta
José Alejandro Balsamo	Miguel Morayta
Ricardo Peisser	Miguel Morayta
Anna Peisser	Miguel Morayta
Captain Thompson	William Hope Hodgson
Dracula	Bram Stoker
Urania Caber	Philip José Farmer
Josephine Balsamo	Maurice Leblanc
Jillian Blake	Philip José Farmer
Madame Delhomme	Emile Zola
Joseph Bridau	Honoré de Balzac
Baron Kralitz	Henry Kuttner
The Durwards	Brian Clemens
Count Szandor	Paul Féval
Sharita	Gardner Fox
Henri de Belcamp (a.k.a. Serge Dolgolruki)	Paul Féval & Maurice Leblanc
Sara Balsamo (a.k.a. Madame Sara)	L.T. Meade & Robert Eustace
Gorcha the Vourdalak	Alexis Tolstoy
Felina de Valgeneuse	Frédéric Soulié & AlexAndré Dumas
The Black Coats	Paul Féval
Léonard	Maurice Leblanc
Madame Koluchy	L.T. Meade & Robert Eustace
Larry Parker	Sir Arthur Conan Doyle
Jacob Dix	Fergus Hume
Abraham van Helsing	Bram Stoker
Irma Vep	Louis Feuillade
Introducing:	
Sabine Balsamo (a.k.a. Dr. Absalom)	Rick Lai

And:

Akivasha's Tear	Yutaka Kaneko
	& Robert E. Howard
Yiggurath	H.P. Lovecraft
	& Robert Bloch
Slidith (Draco)	Lin Carter, Peter Tremayne
	& Robert E. Howard
The Great Old Ones	H.P. Lovecraft
The Elder Sign	August Derleth
Charles Loridan's *L'Essence du Dragon*	Rick Lai
Ludvig Prinn's *Les Mystères du Ver*	Robert Bloch

The Adventures of the Beneficent Vampire

Starring:	**Created by:**
Sherlock Holmes	Arthur Conan Doyle
Dr. John H. Watson	Arthur Conan Doyle
Mrs. Hudson	Arthur Conan Doyle
Father Brown	G.K. Chesterton
Lord Ruthven	John William Polidori
Dracula	Bram Stoker

The Blood of Frankenstein

Starring:	**Created by:**
Gouroull	Jean-Claude Carrière
	based on Mary Shelley
Herbert West	H.P. Lovecraft
Seven Golden Vampires	Don Houghton
Kah/Dracula	Don Houghton
	based on Bram Stoker
Chien Fu	Ng See-yuen
Muscular Lo	Chang Cheh
Fang Keng	Chang Cheh
The Buddhist Monk	Lau Kar-Leung

Golden Swallow	King Hu
Baron de Musard	based on Philip José Farmer
Karnstein	Sheridan Le Fanu
Sifu Lee aka Bruce Lee	*Historical*

The Ultimate Prize

Starring:	**Created by:**
Judex	Arthur Bernède
	& Louis Feuillade
Prosper Cocantin	Arthur Bernède
	& Louis Feuillade
Michel Cocantin (Licorice Kid)	Arthur Bernède
	& Louis Feuillade
Gabrielle Deslys	*Historical*
Dracula	Bram Stoker
Jules Maigret	Georges Simenon

Requiem for a Regime

Starring:	**Created by:**
Léo Saint-Clair the Nyctalope	Jean de la Hire
Professor Clairembart	Henri Vernes
Bob Morane	Henri Vernes
Heinrich Müller	*Historical*
Dracula	Bram Stoker
Harker	based on Bram Stoker

The Girl from Odessa

Starring:	**Created by:**
Léo Saint-Clair the Nyctalope	Jean de la Hire
Harry Paget Flashman II	based on George
	MacDonald Fraser
Sgt. Ballantine	based on Henri Vernes
Koschei	*Russian folklore*

Countess Anastasiya Belinskya   based on Kazuo Ishiguro
Gregor   David McDonald

A Game of Death

Starring: **Created by:**
Count Orlok   F.W. Murnau & Henrik Galeen

The Lesser of Two Evils

Starring: **Created by:**
It   David McDonald
Goetzi   Paul Féval
Eckhart   Eric Kripke & Ben Edlund
Selene   Paul Féval

Les Lèvres Rouges

Starring: **Created by:**
Ilona Harczy   Pierre Drouot, Jean Ferry,
                                  Manfred R. Köhler
                                   & Harry Kümel
Countess Elisabeth Bathory   Pierre Drouot, Jean Ferry,
                                  Manfred R. Köhler
                                   & Harry Kümel
Nestor Burma   Léo Malet
Doc Ardan   Guy d'Armen
                                         Lester Dent
Lt. Montferrand (a.k.a. Roger   Vladimir Volkoff
Noël)
Jens Rolf   Anonymous
S.N.I.F.   Vladimir Volkoff
Florimond Faroux   Léo Malet
Le Chiffre   Ian Fleming
Plaster   Will Eisner
Cabiria   Federico Fellini,

	Ennio Flaiano & Tullio Pinelli
Manon Lescaut	Henri-Georges Clouzot
	& Jean Ferry
	based on Abbé Prévost
Zavatter	Léo Malet
The Fish-men	H. P. Lovecraft
Audrey (a.k.a. The Vine)	Charles B. Griffith
Adélaïde Lupin (a.k.a. Monique d'Andrésy)	Win Scott Eckert
The Silver Eye of Dagon	Roy Thomas
	based on Robert E. Howard
	& H.P. Lovecraft
Le *Cordon Jaune*	Ian Fleming
Radium-X	John Colton,
	Howard Higgin
	& Douglas Hodges

Blood and Fire

Starring: **Created by:**
Countess Nadine Carody   Jaime Chávarri, Anne Settimó
                                                    & Jess Franco
Dr. Orlof   Jess Franco

Predators and Prey

Starring:	**Created by:**
Vampires of Mars	Gustave le Rouge
Erloor	Gustave le Rouge
Romm-Bo	Gustave le Rouge
Gullivar Jones	Edwin Arnold
Princess Heru	Edwin Arnold
Thither People	Edwin Arnold

The Authors

Matthew BAUGH lives and works in Albuquerque, NM. He is the pastor of a small church and an editor for Permuted Press. He is also an author and a regular contributor to *Tales of the Shadowmen*. His first novel, *The Vampire Count of Monte-Cristo*, a mash-up of the classic story of adventure and revenge with vampires, ghosts and Faustian bargains, is now available. Matthew is also the co-author, with Win Scott Eckert, of *A Girl and Her Cat*, which continues the adventures of classic TV heroes, Honey West and T.H.E. Cat. He is currently editing Volume 2 of *The Lone Ranger Chronicles*.

Nathan CABANISS is based out of Atlanta, GA, where he lives a life consisting primarily of danger, intrigue and Netflix. His stories have appeared in *Tales of the Shadowmen*, *Voluted Tales* and *Cranial Leakage: Tales from the Grinning Skull*, and he can be found online at his website, *Girls, Guns & Cigarettes*, where Nicholas Roeg films and the finest in Italian exploitation trash are held in equally high regard. He is the creator of *Beyond Order & Chaos*, an online, interactive superhero novel still forthcoming.

Matthew DENNION lives in South Jersey with his beautiful wife and daughters. He currently works as a teacher of students with autism at a Special Services School. Matt has been a huge fan of Edgar Rice Burroughs ever since he first picked up *A Princess of Mars*; he is also a big follower of Sherlock Holmes, Doc Savage, Spider-man, Batman and James Bond. In addition to being a regular contributor to *Tales of the Shadowmen*, he also writes stories involving giant monsters for *G-fan* magazine.

Win Scott ECKERT holds a B.A. in Anthropology and a Juris Doctorate. He is the editor of and contributor to *Myths for the Modern Age: Philip José Farmer's Wold Newton Universe*, a 2007 Locus Award Finalist for Best Non-Fiction book. Win's latest books are the encyclopedic two-volume *Crossovers: A Secret Chronology of the World*, and the Wold Newton novel *The Evil in Pemberley House*, about Patricia Wildman, the daughter of a certain bronze-skinned pulp hero (co-authored with Philip José Farmer). He is a regular contributor to *Tales of the Shadowmen*.

Brian GALLAGHER has a BA in Politics and Society and lives in London. He works in the media and for many years has written on the politics, economics and many other aspects of Croatia and has been quoted in Croatian and international media. In relation to that he has written extensively on Croatian-related cases at the International Criminal Tribunal for the Former Yugoslavia. He has always been interested in science fiction, classic horror, comics and is proud to be a lifelong *Doctor Who* fan. He is a regular contributor to *Tales of the Shadowmen*.

Martin GATELY is most recently the author of S*amdroo and the Grassman* in *The Worlds of Philip Jose Farmer 4 - Voyages to Strange Days* and of the comics novella *Sherwood Jungle* in the *Phantom: Generations* series. He is a regular contributor to the UK's journal of strange phenomena *Fortean Times*, for which he also created the *Cryptid Kid Investigates* comic strip. His writing career began back in the 1980s when he wrote for D C Thomson's legendary *Starblazer* comicbook. He lives in a decaying mansion in Nottingham that has a view of a former insane asylum. He is a regular contributor to *Tales of the Shadowmen*.

Rick LAI is an authority on pulp fiction and the Wold Newton Universe concepts of Philip José Farmer. His speculative articles have been collected in *Rick Lai's Secret Histories*: *Daring*

Adventurers, Rick Lai's Secret Histories: *Criminal Master-minds, Chronology of Shadows: A Timeline of The Shadow's Exploits* and *The Revised Complete Chronology of Bronze.* Rick's fiction has been collected in *Shadows of the Opera, Shadows of the Opera: Retribution in Blood* and *Sisters of the Shadows: The Cagliostro Curse* (the last two titles are available from Black Coat Press). He has also translated Arthur Bernède's *Judex* and *The Return of Judex* into English for Black Coat Press. Rick resides in Bethpage, New York, with his wife and children. He is a regular contributor to *Tales of the Shadowmen.*

Jean-Marc & Randy LOFFICIER, the editors of *Tales of the Shadowmen* as well as this anthology of vampire fiction, have collaborated on five screenplays, a dozen books and numerous translations, including *Arsène Lupin, Doc Ardan, Doctor Omega, The Phantom of the Opera* and *Rouletabille.* Their latest novels are *Edgar Allan Poe on Mars, The Katrina Protocol* and *Return of the Nyctalope.* They have written a number of animation teleplays, including episodes of *Duck Tales* and *The Real Ghostbusters*, and, in comics, such popular heroes as *Superman* and *Doctor Strange.* They created the Mayan detective series *Tongue*Lash.* Randy is a member of the Writers Guild of America, West and Mystery Writers of America.

David McDONALD is a professional geek from Melbourne, Australia, who works for an international welfare organisation. When not on a computer or reading a book, he divides his time between helping run a local cricket club and working on his upcoming novel. He is a member of the Melbourne-based writers group, SuperNOVA, and the Australian Horror Writers Association. He is a regular contributor to *Tales of the Shadowmen.*

Frank J. MORLOCK is the author of numerous original plays as well as an accomplished translator who has adapted a great number of stories and plays by many classic French writers such as AlexAndré Dumas (Père et Fils), Honoré de Balzac, Francis Diderot, Victor Hugo, Alfred Jarry, Alain-René LeSage, Moliere, Charles Nodier, Philippe Quinault, George Sand, Jules Verne, Voltaire, Emile Zola, etc. Frank J. Morlock has also written articles on Napoleon for the *Napoleonic Journal*.

Christofer NIGRO is a writer of both fiction and non-fiction with a strong interest in pulps, comic books and fantastic cinema, and a regular contributor to *Tales of the Shadowmen*. He may be known to some by his extensive writings in cyberspace, including his websites *The Godzilla Saga* and *The Warrenverse*, as he is an authority on the subject of *dai kaiju eiga* (the sub-genre of cinema specializing in giant monsters), and the characters featured in the fondly remembered comic magazines published by Warren. He has recently revived and expanded Chuck Loridans' classic site MONSTAAH, and has since been published in the anthologies *Aliens Among Us* and *Carnage: After the Fall*. He is presently at work on a novel, and works as a website administrator and freelance editor.

Catherine ROBERT lives in Bastogne, Belgium, with her children. She is a writer of fantasy and horror, two genres which she's enjoyed reading since her teens. When she does not let her dark thoughts guide her pen, she likes the words of other writers whose books she sells them as an itinerant bookseller. One of her recent stories, *Sin of the flesh*, was selected to be published in the prestigous French anthology *Ténèbres* in 2015.

Dola ROSSELET was born in the French Alps. She lived there for twenty years before her work as an aroma thereapist took her to Berlin. She loves the works of Edgar Allan Poe and Guy de Maupassant, two authors who opened her mind to visions of other worlds. After reading more stories than she can remember, she decided to try her hand at writing. This is her first publication; another of her stories will soon be published in a French anthology.

Frank SCHILDINER has been a pulp fan since a friend gave him a gift of Phillip Jose Farmer's *Tarzan Alive*. Since that time he has published articles on *Hellboy*, the Frankenstein films, *Dark Shadows* and the television show's links to the H.P. Lovecraft universe. He has had stories published in *Secret Agent X, Ravenwood, Stepson of Mystery, The Black Bat Mystery, The New Adventures of Thunder Jim, The New Adventures of Richard Knight* and *The Justice Files*. He is a Senior Probation Officer in New Jersey and a martial arts instructor at Amorosi's Mixed Martial Arts. Frank resides in New Jersey with his wife Gail who is his top supporter. He is a regular contributor to *Tales of the Shadowmen*.

Michel STEPHAN was born and lives in Brittany with his wife and two children. He has been a fan of science fiction, fantasy and horror since age 10. He loves Universal monster movies (especially the *Frankenstein* series), sci-fi serials and collects Aurora model kits. He has recently written a new *Madame Atomos* novel for Black Coat Press's French imprint, Rivière Blanche, and is a regular contributor to *Tales of the Shadowmen*.

Artikel UNBEKANNT (not his real name!) lives in western France and is the author of several short stories published by Black Coat Press' sister imprint, Rivière Blanche, as well as a horror novel, *Bloodfist*, released in 2013.

FRENCH HORROR COLLECTION

Cyprien Bérard. *The Vampire Lord Ruthwen*
Aloysius Bertrand. *Gaspard de la Nuit*
André Caroff. *The Terror of Madame Atomos; Miss Atomos; The Return of Madame Atomos; The Mistake of Madame Atomos; The Monsters of Madame Atomos; The Revenge of Madame Atomos; The Resurrection of Madame Atomos; The Mark of Madame Atomos; The Spheres of Madame Atomos; The Wrath of Madame Atomos* (w/M. & Sylvie Stéphan)
Jules Claretie. *Obsession*
Harry Dickson. *The Heir of Dracula; Harry Dickson vs. The Spider*
Jules Dornay. *Lord Ruthven Begins*
Sâr Dubnotal *vs. Jack the Ripper*
Alexandre Dumas. *The Return of Lord Ruthven*
Renée Dunan. *Baal*
Paul Féval. *Anne of the Isles; Knightshade; Revenants; Vampire City; The Vampire Countess; The Wandering Jew's Daughter*
Paul Féval, *fils. Felifax, the Tiger-Man*
Léon Gozlan. *The Vampire of the Val-de-Grâce*
Paul Lacroix. *Danse Macabre*
Etienne-Léon de Lamothe-Langon. *The Virgin Vampire*
Marie Nizet. *Captain Vampire*
C. Nodier, A. Beraud & Toussaint-Merle, V. Hugo, P. Foucher & P. Meurice. *Frankenstein & The Hunchback of Notre-Dame*
J. Polidori, C. Nodier, E. Scribe. *Lord Ruthven the Vampire*
P.-A. Ponson du Terrail. *The Vampire and the Devil's Son; The Immortal Woman*
Jean Richepin. *The Crazy Corner*
Angelo de Sorr. *The Vampires of London*
Kurt Steiner. *Ortog*
Villiers de l'Isle-Adam. *The Scaffold; The Vampire Soul*
Philippe Ward. *Artahe; The Song of Montségur* (w/ Sylvie Miller)

www.ingramcontent.com/pod-product-compliance
Lightning Source LLC
Chambersburg PA
CBHW022209010726
47493CB00002B/479